OUTSTAN... ...
MICHAEL ...

W9-BGU-581

THE TEN THOUSAND

"The descriptive language throughout is heroic, at times echoing the *Iliad*. Ford brings an interesting, fictively personal outlook to one of the classics. Inspired and highly informed, *The Ten Thousand* may lead many readers back to the original [*Anabasis* by Xenophon]."

—*Kirkus Reviews*

"The Greek mercenaries of the time of Socrates lost a war to the Persians but gained immortality. Thrilling, eloquent, illuminated by scholarship comes this retelling of the epic running battle of *The Ten Thousand* from Babylon to the sea."

—James Brady, author of
the bestselling *The Marines of Autumn*

"There is no more gripping story of desperate courage than the march of *The Ten Thousand*. Yet few Americans know anything about their astonishing trek out of Asia some 2,400 years ago. Michael Curtis Ford's moving account of the fighting and dying of these heroic Greek mercenaries is not only historically sound, but very human, in making Xenophon's tale come alive in a way that no ancient historian or classicist has yet accomplished."
—Professor Victor Hanson, author of *Carnage and Culture*

"Michael Ford is at his best when he is describing or philosophizing. At times, as in his description of a trip to the oracle at Delphi, this can be genuinely thought-provoking . . . Pressfield's fans will . . . be delighted to discover this new author."

—The Historical Novel Society

MORE...

St. Martin's Paperbacks Titles
by Michael Curtis Ford

The Ten Thousand: A Novel of Ancient Greece
Gods and Legions: A Novel of the Roman Empire
The Last King: Rome's Greatest Enemy
The Sword of Attila: A Novel of the Last Years of Rome

GODS AND LEGIONS

A NOVEL OF THE ROMAN EMPIRE

MICHAEL CURTIS FORD

St. Martin's Paperbacks

GODS AND LEGIONS

Copyright © 2002 by Michael Curtis Ford.
Excerpt from *The Last King* copyright © 2005 by Michael Curtis Ford.

Map by Jackie Aher

ISBN: 0-312-98940-7
EAN: 978-0-312-98940-8

Printed in the United States of America

St. Martin's Press hardcover edition / November 2002
St. Martin's Paperbacks edition / September 2003

St. Martin's Paperbacks are published by St. Martin's Press, 175 Fifth Avenue, New York, NY 10010.

10 9 8 7 6 5 4 3

For Eamon, Isabel, and Marie

HISTORICAL NOTE

Of all the great figures of antiquity, few are so compelling yet enigmatic, few so admired yet vilified, as Flavius Claudius Julianus Augustus, the man known to history as Julian the Apostate. A Roman emperor who never set foot in Rome and spoke Latin only with difficulty, a brilliant and ruthless general who never picked up a sword until well into his adulthood, the richest and most powerful man in the world, yet a celibate who ate only vegetables and slept on the floor—he was a man of profound convictions and contrasts, and one whose beliefs were deeply disturbing to friend and enemy alike. In almost any other period of the Roman Empire his crusades and eccentricities might have been tolerated, perhaps even expected of an emperor; but this was no ordinary time.

The fourth century A.D. was one of the most wrenching periods in European history. After a series of weak leaders, barbarian invasions, and brutal religious persecutions, Rome suddenly produced an emperor—Julian's uncle, Constantine—who, astonishingly, became a Christian. Until that time Christianity had been a sect primarily of slaves and the poor, alternately derided and ignored, yet now it became the state religion. Ancient pagan temples were restored as churches, many men and women of the upper classes converted to the religion of their Emperor, and a new culture began to take root, but an empire as vast as

Rome's could not change in a day. The Germans and Goths continued to wreak havoc in the West, the Persians in the East, and the Roman army, especially its powerful Eastern legions, remained largely pagan, faithful to such deities as the bloody and wrathful bull-god Mithras.

It was within this context of upheaval, religious fervor, and terrible wars for Rome's borders, indeed for its very soul, that Julian came to power, by some accounts reluctantly, by others through his own cunning. It was a time when the Empire stood poised on a balance—a determined, sustained push by a strong leader could take it in either of two directions. Julian was such a leader, a man of action and resolve, the shrewdest and most strong-willed emperor since Constantine or perhaps long before, a man with an agenda to fulfill.

And in the world of ancient Rome, there were precious few checks and balances to hinder a powerful ruler—where walked the Emperor, there followed the world.

Those whom the gods would destroy
They first drive mad.

—EURIPIDES

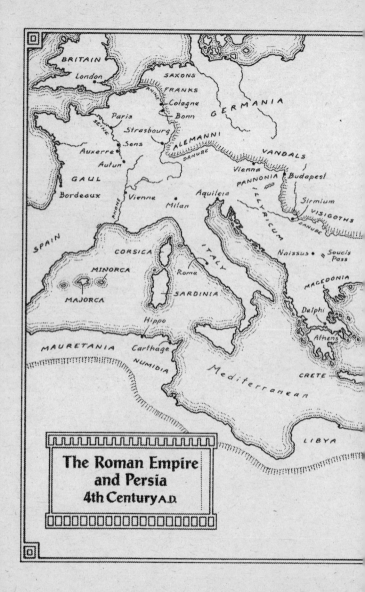

The Roman Empire
and Persia
4th Century A.D.

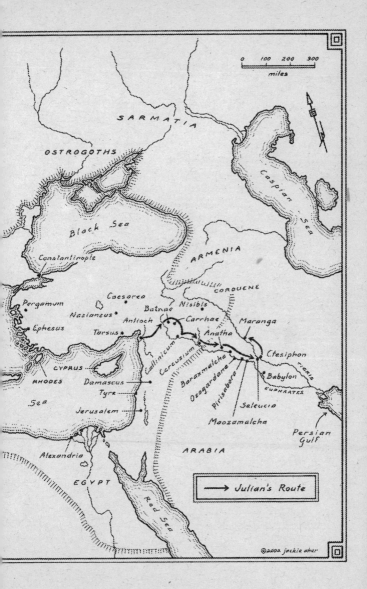

GODS AND LEGIONS

A NOVEL OF THE ROMAN EMPIRE

From Gregory of Nazianzus, a devoted servant of the Church,

To the Holy Pontiff, Pope Siricius, beloved of God and condemner of heretics, defender of the True Faith and heir to the throne of the blessed Saint Peter in Rome:

Grace and mercy be upon you.

As you are aware, my late brother Caesarius, a physician of skill and renown in the court of the late Emperor Constantius, had, as a young man, transferred his professional services to the Emperor's rival and eventual successor, the damnable pagan and apostate Julian. This he did not out of sympathy for Julian's unholy cause (for Caesarius was unwavering in his Christian belief), but out of aspiration for professional advancement, and a desire to convert the pagan from his efforts to suppress the faith; I leave it to you, Your Eminence, to consider the evidence of his motives.

I bring to your attention a journal my brother kept at the end of his life, employing it as a confessional of sorts, concealing it out of fear should its words fall into indiscreet or unfaithful hands. This journal treats of many aspects of his dealings with the rogue Julian, about which Your Worship may not be aware. Such document I enclose herewith, entreating only that you guard it as carefully as its contents merit.

Whether my brother's soul be punished or rewarded for his actions I leave to God to pronounce. It is He, and He alone, who was privy to the hidden thoughts and motives of my sibling, a man who was dear to me in life yet who, since my discovery of this document, has been a source of unending consternation to me. I commend it into your hands that I may be free of its burden, whether of sin or saintliness, as described herein and as judged by the Everlasting God.

I remain,

Ever yours in Christ,
Gregory of Nazianzus, Bishop of Constantinople

BOOK ONE

GENESIS

Beware that thou not be made a Caesar, that thou not be dyed with such dye . . .

—MARCUS AURELIUS

I

I write of warfare and of a man, and of a man at war, though he was not always such a man. For the world made him one, fashioned him thus from weak and unpromising materials, like a sublime sculpture made of humble river clay—and then the world recoiled at what it had made, though it would be many years before it would know to do so. A man's destiny is forged by events, surely, for we cannot help bearing the crowns and the scars that random fate has bequeathed to us in our lives. But more than events, it is a man's own free will that shapes him—that reflection and echo within him of the very God who created him. Free will, like God, can rise above any circumstances or obstacles one may face; like God it can make the humble great, make a weak boy into a strong man, make a timorous student into the Emperor of the world. And like God's own rival, Lucifer, it can cause him to flail his fists fruitlessly against the breast of his very Creator, if by his free will he so chooses.

On a moonless night a thousand miles from home, an exhausted army slept in a desolate wasteland of dust and black ashes. None of the myriad sounds a resting army makes—the snuffling of horses, the moans of the wounded, the shouts from the guards calling the watch—none of these had disturbed my dreams, so accustomed to them was I that I found them almost comforting. Something, however, per-

haps some soft breath of air suddenly entering the tent, had
summoned me, though I remained motionless, slumped in
the hard, high-backed camp chair where I had slipped into
a restless doze. Only my eyes stirred beneath half-hooded
lids as I peered past the flickering light of the tiny oil lamp.

She was a goddess, otherworldly in her beauty, her skin
and hair shimmering with a dim aura as she passed through
the silent awnings, winding her way smoothly and effortlessly through the assorted maps and volumes scattered
about the floor. Like a spirit, she scarcely moved her feet,
not deigning even to glance down to discern their placement, her luminous eyes ignoring me and the others resting
fitfully in their corners, her gaze fixed only on him; and I
saw that Julian, too, was awake and alert, sitting up in his
cot, his body tense and motionless, staring back at her un-
blinkingly and without fear.

In her profile, in the welling of her eyes, there was a
depth of sadness impossible to describe, an ineffable sorrow
that illumined her beauty like moonlight on the white limestone facade of a temple. The gown floated featherlike
around her, swirling at her feet, though the heavy desert air
offered not a breath of wind to relieve us of the stifling
heat. The veil over her head and face, fastened in the manner of one in mourning, was gossamer, transparent as a
spider's web, enhancing, rather than obscuring, the smoothness of her neck and face. Her braids, wound in the ancient
style beneath the veil, were scented with the biting fra-
grance of the myrrh that had been suffused into the dressing. I sat stone still, my nails cutting into the palms of my
hands, as she approached, soft as a psalm, silent as a prayer.

Stopping just short of the foot of his bed, she stood
motionless for a long moment. A glistening tear coursed
slowly down her cheek, disappearing into the darkness at
her feet as it dropped. Julian looked on in wonder as she
held her arms out toward him, cradling in them a burden,
what I at first took to be an infant, but what I later realized
was not a living being. She showed it to him and his face
clouded—in disappointment? fear?—and as she turned

away her gaze lingered on him for a brief moment longer, as if she were reluctant to leave.

Passing back across the floor with a measured cadence, her head bowed in sorrow, she paused before slipping out the door, and to my astonishment she then turned slowly and deliberately toward me, lifting the veil from her face with one hand and raising her downcast eyes. As she focused directly on me, her serene, sorrowful expression twisted suddenly into a snarl of such utter malevolence and loathing that I gasped and leaped up, toppling the chair on which I had been sitting with a loud clatter. The veiled woman then vanished through the tent hangings, as silently as she had appeared.

Dawn came impossibly early, bringing on a sickly light for ill mankind, a pallid harbinger of toil and distress. A pale yellowish desert fog had sprung up, as it often did on those early summer mornings, a moistness not refreshing like the cool mists of Gaul I had so loved, but rather stinking and malignant, clammy in the heat that was already starting to build though the sun had scarcely risen. The dampness lent an oily stickiness to the skin, which combined with the smoke from the smoldering fires and the grit in the air to coat one's face with an irritating film. Gnats and flies swarmed everywhere, seeking moisture at the corners of one's eyes and lips, driving the pack animals mad with their incessant buzzing and stinging, and gathering in lethal clouds on the bare asses of the men squatting in the fetid latrines, cursing the leisurely pace of their bowels. The troops broke camp in a resentful silence, and before the sun was half exposed above the horizon the cavalry scouts had thundered off beyond the army's flanks in a blinding cloud of heavy dust. The vanguard cohorts and the rest of the legions were not far behind, shouldering their packs and marching forward at a brisk pace, the men still gagging down their dry breakfast of rock biscuit.

As we marched, the Persians, who had learned from

their previous defeats at the hands of Julian's troops to avoid pitched battles, adopted a strategy of piecemeal harassment, dogging our steps at every turn without ever committing to a full-scale assault. From various vantage points we could see King Sapor's army, divided into two parts, each half marching a route parallel to our own on the high hills on either side of us. Outlined against the hazy, whitish-blue sky were the ranks of thousands upon thousands of his heavy infantry, fierce warriors from Media with their fish-scale armor reflecting blindingly in the sunlight, passing in and out of the swirling dust raised by the huge forces of Persian cavalry trotting in close formation before them.

On the left ridge marched the swaying corps of Indian elephants, wrinkled gray monsters of enormous height, their dreadful bulk dwarfing the lines of soldiers marching before and behind. The beasts plodded heavily, bearing large platforms on their backs, "towers" of wood-framed leather walls, each containing four archers and spearmen. The animals were painted in horrifying colors, circles and spirals around their eyes, flapping ears blood-red and rimmed with black. Plates of gleaming bronze fitted closely across their foreheads were adorned with stiff, plumed crests dyed a bloody crimson. A large lance, like a third tusk, had been fitted by stout leather straps to each monster's chest, and leather bands, studded with glistening spikes, encircled their legs. They bore gleaming armor and bangles on their heads and shoulders, and blinders on their eyes, forcing them to look relentlessly forward, to prevent them from being distracted by activities to the side. The animals were led by a huge bull, his yellowish eight-foot tusks tipped with lustrous bronze spear points. The wind shifted in our direction, wafting toward us the beasts' rank odor, rendered even more foul by the rancid tallow the Persians had smeared on their hides to prevent cracking and chafing in the dry desert heat. Our horses visibly shuddered and shied.

I cantered up to the Emperor where he rode hollow-eyed and stoop-shouldered, lost in silent thought.

"Julian," I said. "Our men haven't fought against elephants. The Gauls have never even seen them before, except from a distance."

He roused himself as if with a great effort, and glanced warily up the ridge where the lumbering column seemed to hover over us, their long shadows reaching almost to our own line of march. He then looked back at me, a faint smile showing through his wiry, dust-laden beard.

"Caesarius—always worrying, always planning, eh? If only my generals were as concerned about my welfare as is my physician. How long have we been friends now—eight years, ten? With your help I conquered Gaul and Germany, with you beside me I was raised to Emperor! We have sacked every Persian fortress on the Euphrates, and have defeated King Sapor's garrison under the very walls of his palace. The men are at their prime, Caesarius, they are like hounds, baying for Persian blood! Sacrifices to the gods were made this morning, three oxen. The omens were favorable this time, the livers healthy—the gods are with us now! Caesarius, I saw the livers, this time the gods are with us. . . ."

He was rambling again, and I moved quickly to calm him, not as a subject to his Emperor but as a friend to a friend, as a physician to his patient—as a concerned soldier to his mad general.

"Eight years we have been together, Julian," I said, "ever since we met in Athens. God has been good to us. Nevertheless . . . the elephants."

Julian stared at me, his eyes focusing with difficulty, his lips moving as if he were about to say something. I continued before he could interrupt.

"The men are nervous and the horses skittish. The army has no experience with such beasts. We need a plan."

He glanced again up to the ridge. "No experience," he muttered, then lifted his head sharply. "But they are only animals! I have read of them, Caesarius." He paused for a moment, recollecting the lessons in military strategy and tactics he had absorbed years before, under Sallustius' tutelage. "The Persians used elephants against Roman troops at Nisibis thirteen years ago. They killed many of our men, but then they began running amok among their own, devastating the Persian lines. Look—you see the drivers? King Sapor has learned his lesson well."

I peered up through the haze. Each elephant in the column was guided by a slightly built, armored driver perched precariously on the back of the beast's head. I nodded.

"Indians," Julian continued. "They know best how to control them. Each one ties a long, stout spike to his left wrist. If the elephant loses control the driver thrusts it into the animal's neck at the base of the skull, severing the vertebrae and killing the animal. They carry wooden mallets to pound the spikes in deeper."

"But that would topple all the men in the tower as well. Falling from such a height . . ."

Julian shrugged. "Just so. They are crushed or killed. Better them, the king reasons, than a whole line of his own troops in the middle of a battle."

"So how do we fight them?"

He rode in thoughtful silence for a moment before turning again to me.

"Pigs."

"Pigs, Julian?"

"They say that elephants are terrified of squealing pigs. You smear them with fat and set them on fire, and then send them to run squealing amongst the elephants' legs."

I paused to consider this extraordinary suggestion— whether it was based on fact or the product of madness.

"We don't have any more pigs," I said cautiously, and not without some relief.

Julian sighed. "Then we'll just have to hope Sapor keeps to his truce."

Five hours we marched that morning through the desolate valley known locally as Maranga, in full armor and battle formation, along a trackless route visible only to our Arab scouts. The earth had been scorched by Sapor's advance guard to prevent us from obtaining grain or game, and the landscape was nightmarish—lacking in all color but shades of gray, ashy dust that settled on every object, softening the stark blackness of the charred stumps and brush that still smoldered here and there along our path. A haze rose up from every man as he marched, every step producing a burst of fine, black ash that settled between the toes and mingled with the sweat flowing in rivulets down his face and neck. The men were parched and flagging under the relentless heat and the tension of constantly monitoring the king's armies on the ridges above us, who in their cooler and lighter gear and their acclimation to the heat appeared distressingly fresh and energetic. Our flanks were strongly guarded by the cavalry and heavy infantry, but the roughness of the terrain had rendered our formation somewhat ragged, and the line of march had now stretched to beyond three miles from van to rear.

Suddenly, we heard a commotion far behind us, the faint blare of trumpets and the high-pitched, womanlike screams of wounded horses. Julian, riding beside Sallustius and several other advisers just ahead of me in the vanguard, galloped out of the line of march and wheeled his horse, peering to the rear through the haze.

Shouts passed up along the line by heralds brought the news to our ears within seconds.

"Persian attack on the rear! Cavalry and light-armed infantry!"

Julian had expected more warning from the normally heavy-handed Persians. Contrary to his own orders, he had earlier removed his armor against the heat, and he paused now only to pull down his helmet, which hung from his shoulders, and to seize a shield from a cavalry officer standing nearby. He set heels to flanks and sprinted back along the line of march in the direction of the tumult, shouting as he did so for the rest of the army to continue its march forward but to remain alert.

I broke rank and raced along with his guards and generals, weaving half blinded through the thick dust they raised, and within moments we approached the rear. Judging from the terrifying clamor and roiling cloud of dust

ahead of us, full-scale battle had already been joined. We
were surrounded by surging masses of grim-faced men,
their skin black and shiny as they raced to the rear in confusion to assist their comrades. Julian craned his neck, peering through the dust in search of an officer who could tell
him what was happening, when we were suddenly startled
by another trumpet blast, this time from behind us, toward
the column's front.

"What in Hades . . . ?" Julian muttered, as Sallustius
wheeled and galloped back toward where we had just ridden. He was met by the officer who had lent his shield.
Sallustius conferred with him briefly, then raced his mount
back to Julian, who was still struggling to force his way
through the throng of men to the rear.

"My lord!" Sallustius called out. "Sapor is attacking the
front as well!"

Julian stopped short and wheeled his own horse, his
grimy face twisted in rage.

"By the gods!" he shouted. "Sallustius, you lead, return
to the front! We are still under a truce with the Persians—
Sapor will pay for his treachery!"

Leaping forward, he raced back up the track, against the
tide of running men who at Sallustius' frantic shouts hastened to step aside to avoid the sharp hooves of the Emperor's horse.

We cleared the rear guard, crossing the gap that had
opened between the army's two ends and joining the weary
units of troops trotting resignedly to the front. Just then,
we were startled by yet more trumpeting, this time maddened and frantic, from what sounded like dozens of instruments, not behind us or ahead, but directly to the side.
An enormous cloud of dust surged down the high ridge
from the Persian troops on our left flank. Straining to see
through the dense haze I could make out the gleam of glittering armor and weapons, the helmets and spear tips seeming to advance at an impossible height relative to the
ground. The horrifying trumpeting continued, pressing ever
louder, and the troops beside us froze in awe and horror at

the sight—a brigade of the King's armored war elephants, bearing down on us at a speed unmatched by any beast or machine on earth.

At the dreadful sound of the trumpeting elephants, the Roman horses reared, rolling their eyes in terror, and even Julian's well-trained mount almost threw him in the dust. The elephants' awful appearance, their gaping jaws and horrendous smell, struck fear in man and animal, and as the line of beasts approached, the earth physically trembled under the terrible weight of their stumplike feet. They thundered straight toward the center of our panicking column as the drivers perched precariously on the base of the beasts' necks, peering down at us with evil grins, their white teeth gleaming through the blackness of their faces.

The beasts plowed into our line, enraged at the screams of our terrified troops. The men scattered, fleeing for their lives, while the elephants reared in their midst, bellowing and trumpeting, stomping again and again on the bodies of those they had trampled until they were nothing more than dark smears in the sooty earth. Roman limbs and torsos hung limp and dripping from the tusks, emboldening the animals further in their blood rage. The archers in the towers above rained arrows down upon our men, felling them where they stood to create lines of writhing wounded whom the elephants hastened to stamp upon and crush, or to scoop up in their tusks and tear apart with their jaws. When our Gauls finally managed to scramble out of range of the flashing ivory, the elephant drivers deftly maneuvered their beasts away from the scene of slaughter and formed up in a rank to prepare for another charge at our massed and terrified troops. Behind them, marching implacably down the ridge in tight formation, came an enormous body of Persian infantry, raising their ululating battle cry, preparing to rush in and finish off the destruction begun by the elephants as soon as the terrible beasts had completed their work.

As the elephants withdrew and began re-forming, Julian plunged into the thick of his troops, his energy restored,

eyes glinting with an almost terrifying intensity behind the
visor of his battle helmet. The man was everywhere, wheeling and careening his horse like one possessed, shouting
encouragement, arranging his troops into a tight battle formation, bellowing instructions for defeating the monsters
when they next attacked. The Gauls stared, but swallowed
their fear and their impulse to flee into the desert, obeying
him with the military precision he had instilled in them over
years of campaigning. Shields were raised, bronze-tipped
pikes lowered into position, and as the thick black dust
settled on our heads we turned to face the elephants' renewed onslaught.

It came immediately. Led by the huge bull, its red mouth
gaping and lips flapping, the beasts charged again into our
column, twenty or more of them, shoulder to shoulder in
ranks of four. One carried a Roman soldier, impaled
through the belly on the beast's chest spike during the previous charge, the man's legs and head flailing helplessly
with the animal's swaying strides, his lifeless eyes staring
forward at his comrades like a bloodied figurehead on the
prow of a ship. Onward they charged, trumpeting, the
ground trembling, and as they approached, the men fell
silent and tensed.

"Stay your weapons!" shouted Julian, his lips twisted
into a kind of mad grin or a grimace, eyeing the onrushing
brutes, blinders forcing their stare straight into the thick of
the Roman legion. "Stay!" he repeated, his voice rising, and
the terrible, rancid stench of the animals filled our nostrils,
mixing with the reek of the blood and excrement covering
our feet and the ground around us, "Stay! . . . Until I say . . .

"NOW!"

As the elephants thundered furiously into our midst, the
ranks of men suddenly parted in the middle like a split sheet
of parchment, the two halves of the cohorts leaping frantically to the sides, leaving nothing but empty ground in
the middle as the enraged elephants raced through the passage left between the men and skidded to a confused stop.

Instantly our troops let out a roar, drowning out the

trumpeting of the angry beasts, which wrenched their heads in bewilderment from side to side as they sought to peer around their blinders and make out the source of the sound.

"Pikes!" screamed Julian, though his order was super-fluous, overwhelmed by the bellowing of the furious troops. A hundred, five hundred heavy-shanked spears flew through the air simultaneously at point-blank range, pene-trating the elephants' thick hides with a slicing sound, bury-ing themselves deep in flanks and ribs. The beasts reared, thrashing front legs and trunks in fear and agony, as the archers in the towers on top ceased to fire and struggled to hold on to their ominously rocking platforms.

Emboldened at their success, the men rushed in closer to the enraged animals, encircling each elephant on all sides, cutting off the beasts' contact with one another. Sol-diers who had kept or recovered their pikes dove in toward the elephants' stamping and circling feet from behind, pok-ing and slashing at the backs of their legs and arses, further maddening the animals, which shook and stamped in a des-perate effort to dissuade their tormentors. The tower on the enraged bull tilted precariously off its back, leaning almost horizontally to the side as the Persians inside clung to the support posts with their hands, and then the girth strap broke, sending the entire contraption tumbling to the ground, where it crumpled into a confused jumble of leather, lumber, and broken limbs. Twenty Gauls surged forward to finish off the hapless archers, but scrambled back as the bull did the job for them, wreaking revenge for the years of training and torment his masters had put him through as he leaped upon the broken structure and stomped and slashed at the screaming survivors until they were si-lent.

A cheer rose from the Roman troops as the first of the beasts dropped bawling and trumpeting to the ground, the tendons at the back of its knees severed. The drivers had lost control of their terrified mounts now, and all around were thrusting their great iron spikes into the necks of the doomed beasts. One by one the monsters dropped, to the shrill shouts of triumph of the Gauls, who now swarmed over them even before they fell. One ill-trained driver thrust frantically again and again into the leathery hide of his animal's neck, each time pounding the spike in deeply with his mallet in an unsuccessful effort to find the fatal spot. Another elephant slammed into it with a terrible scream, and then a third, creating a wall, a writhing mountain of bloody flesh, legs kicking and trunks flailing. The Romans flung spears and shot arrows into the heaving mound, and one of the animals, thrashing blindly about with its trunk, seized a dead driver from off the neck of another and placing the man's torso between its great rubbery lips, proceeded to tear off his limbs one by one in its own terrible death throes.

Seeing that the elephant charge had been repelled, the body of Persian infantry, who had now approached to the very edge of our lines, stopped suddenly in a confused jumble, their officers unsure whether to follow through with the attack or retreat to safety on the ridge top. Julian did not hesitate. Turning the attention of his troops away from the dying elephants to the greater danger they faced from the Persians at their backs, he quickly organized a charge. The Roman troops howled for revenge for their downed comrades, their shields and weapons smeared with elephant and Persian blood. They leaped at the enemy, slashing and hacking, blood spraying the filthy dust which was now scattered with severed limbs, and no longer were there distinct lines of battle, for the two sides had become thoroughly confused with each other, the one seeking only to preserve their lives, the other seeking the enemy's complete annihilation. A black cloud rose into the thick and sweltering air, obliterating any view of the heights above, obscuring the direction of retreat, preventing the Persians from identifying the route to safety except by the feel of their feet as they sought to run uphill toward the ridge top.

Sallustius had long since been diverted to another part of the field, and even Julian's crack escort of Gallic guards had been scattered. They raced frantically through the dust, seeking sight of their Emperor, shouting to him to break free of the dangerous surge of Persians around him. Only I had somehow managed to stay close at hand, and even while wheeling my horse through the swirling dust, slashing at the mass of enemy rushing in from all sides, my eyes never left him.

Julian ignored caution, charging heedlessly into the midst of the battle, urging his men on. Terrified Persians surged around him and his horse, seemingly unaware that the sovereign of the Roman Empire was rearing and hacking with his sword in their very midst. A huge Mede, overcoming his comrades' panic, leaped at the Emperor's horse, wrapping his arms around the animal's neck in an effort to drag him and his rider down into the dust. Julian plunged his long blade up to the hilt just under the man's collarbone, and then drew it backward, streaming death, half the broken sword remaining still in the man's lung. The Mede stared for a moment in surprise, and then belching crimson, dropped from the struggling horse's neck to the ground beneath its sharp hooves.

He was replaced a moment later by another snarling attacker, who leaped from the fray to seize the Emperor's leg while hacking at his shield with a sword, seeking a gap through which to drive the blade home. Julian smashed again and again at the Persian's face with the hilt of his own broken sword until, with skull bones shattered to the brains, the man released his grip and dropped to the black mire beneath. Julian lifted his broken sword in triumph, bellowing incoherently, and his horse wheeled over the Persian's body, stamping and mutilating the man's torso with its sharpened hooves. Never had I seen the Emperor so taken with violence, so maddened with killing. So absorbed was he, so engrossed in this wanton display of brutality, that he had lost all sense of the battle and danger surrounding him.

Suddenly, I saw a hand raised from among the mob, a finger pointing at Julian as he cut and slashed his way through the enemy, and a moment later a thin, reedy spear, a javelin used for throwing at the enemy from the middle distance, emerged from among the sea of bronze helmets, aimed carefully and flung directly toward the Emperor. I lunged on my horse, urging it forward and nearly trampling the soldiers in front of me, all the while watching the missile. It coursed through the air for the short distance, its tail wobbling slightly at first until it found its momentum and truth of aim, and then sheared into Julian's side, unprotected by the breastplate he had neglected to don before racing to oversee the battle. Like a bird shot from the sky by a boy's arrow, he toppled from the horse out of my sight, disappearing beneath the feet of the fleeing Persians and Roman pursuers, his horse continuing on its way, riderless, as if unaware of its loss. I leaped off my own mount and pushed frantically through the milling throng to where I had seen him fall. Mercifully, after a moment's search on the ground, I found him.

To my astonishment, he had not been trampled by the panicked hooves around him, nor even injured by the fall itself. Writhing in the dust, however, he clutched at the spear. Its point had scarcely penetrated his body, as it had become firmly embedded in his bottom-most rib. As I knelt beside him, the commotion around us quickly subsided and the Persians' retreat turned into a general rout. The Roman troops had now raced past us and were pursuing the enemy up the ridge, hacking at the Persians' backs and legs just as they had the elephants'.

Three guards thundered up on their horses, their faces ashen even through the grime, staring down at the groaning and writhing Emperor on the ground.

"Physician! How is he hurt?"

I pried Julian's hands off the spearhead. The light weapon, thrown from close in, had struck him a glancing blow that had pierced so shallowly that the sharp cutting edges and double barbs of the head were still outside his body. Had the hooklike barbs penetrated, it would have been terrible work to remove the spearhead without tearing the flesh and vital organs; yet even so, they had made deep slashes in the Emperor's fingers and palms where he had grasped the head in an effort to pull it out of his rib. The shaft, too, had broken off at the iron socket upon impact, as it was designed, to prevent the enemy from picking it up and launching it back.

"I will attend to him," I said, in a voice that was far calmer than I felt. "Don't hover over me with your horses— you'll trample us if they take fright. Form up in a line toward the ridge and prevent any Persian strays from returning and overrunning us. We'll carry him to camp in a moment."

The guards nodded, relieved to receive concrete orders, and wheeling their mounts they galloped several hundred feet toward the ridge, shouting for their fellows to join them in forming a barricade. They sat their skittish horses in the slowly subsiding dust cloud, watching the battle move away from them and listening to the cheers of the Roman victors, who continued to slash at the backs of the retreating enemy.

I bent back down to Julian, who by this time had fallen into a swoon from the pain. Quickly I removed his helmet, the metal of which was almost too hot to touch, and a trickle of sweat poured out the basin. I then turned to the spearhead embedded in his rib. Muttering silent thanks that he was unconscious, and resting my left hand carefully on his rib cage, I grasped the shaft with my right and gave a hard, quick jerk.

Despite my effort to pull straight back, the surprising weight of the long iron tip and socket created some torque, and I heard an audible snap from the already weakened rib as the weapon popped out. Julian twitched, his right arm flailing blindly and his mouth contorting into a grimace, even in his swoon. The piercing bled freely, though no more than would be expected from such a wound, and the blood showed a bright, clear red, a good sign.

I held the point of the spearhead up before my face, viewing its symmetrical, deadly outline against the pale sky. For a long moment I stared at the tip, at its beautifully cast smoothness and blackness, the carefully balanced barbs, the razor sharpness of its point and edge undulled by its recent impact with hard bone, its effectiveness unimpeded, its deadly potential yet unfulfilled. . . .

I glanced down at my unconscious patient, face streaked with sweat and dust, expression contorted with pain, and I hesitated. Great evil was afoot in the world. Vows had been taken, oaths had been sworn, and these could not be discarded lightly. It is not often that a common man, a humble physician, has a chance to affect the very course of history, and I prayed to God for courage to be worthy of the opportunity. I glanced up at the guards, making sure they had secured the area and were remaining on vigilant watch against any possible recurrence of the Persian attack.

I then bent to complete my work.

II

But I have moved far ahead of myself, Brother, for truly this is the very end of my story, not the beginning, and I shall have to return to it again in due course. My only excuse is that it was this momentous event that first prompted me to consider recording my thoughts on the matter. The chronological beginning is the only proper place for a narrative to start, for thus commence even the Scriptures themselves—*In principio* ... —and though far be it from me to compare this hurried journal to our sacred texts, certainly one is not ill-advised to seek to emulate them. Let us therefore start this effort again, not at the conclusion of our story this time, but at its foundations, its very roots— in the beginning.

It was in Athens that our paths first crossed, as well you know, for you were there too, having been sent by Father to pursue your philosophical studies at the Academy. I, by a happy coincidence of timing, had at the same time been referred to the city's learned physicians by the Emperor Constantius, Julian's elder cousin, in recognition of my studies at Alexandria and my promising future as the Emperor's court physician.

We roomed together, you and I, in modest yet adequate lodgings hard by the malodorous fish market, though there were few moments that we actually spent with each other. You were engrossed in your learned discussions, sitting on the roof of our apartment disputing obscure points of theology till dawn, fasting every other week. I, on the other hand, was immersed in the physicality and sordidness of medicine, trolling the streets for subjects of study or up to my elbows in the putrid abdominal contents of a recent plague victim in the autopsy hall. I had no time or inclination for the ephemeral, spiritual realm you inhabited, while you, on the other hand, had no desire to delve into the filth and the ecstasy of my worldly existence.

We met Julian at the same time, through the same small circle of mutual acquaintances. He and his guardian Mardonius rented rooms not two streets away from ours, and he often frequented the same taverns, eating houses, and public baths as did we. From almost the very moment Julian and I clasped each other's shoulders in greeting, we recognized a link, a connection that extended beyond the normal levels of shifting friendships and alliances. We saw in each other an honesty and sincerity, a desire for truth and knowledge, a disdain for frivolity; in short, a purity, if you will, unlike that prevailing among our general circle of acquaintances. It seems strange now for me to look back on those days, but I can scarcely remember a time when I did not know Julian, though I was well into my adulthood when I first met him.

Like you, Brother, he was a philosopher, pursuing many of your own intellectual paths, while at the same time he was a sensualist like me, seeking knowledge of astronomy and the healing arts. But here the differences between you and me, Brother, become truly apparent, beginning with our own, individual impressions of him, for when you and I spoke about him in later years I found that we could not even agree on his physical appearance. Whereas I saw a not uncomely man of medium height, with intelligent eyes and a straight, aristocratic nose, you saw a gaze that was wild and wandering, and nostrils that breathed hate and scorn. Where other men saw a perfect runner's build and a regal bearing to his head and shoulders, you foresaw that nothing good could come of a man with such a weaving head and shifty feet. Where I saw a well-trimmed and fashionable beard, neat hair, and a fleshy, sensuous mouth, you saw pride and contempt in the lineaments of his face, senseless, disordered thinking, opinions formed with no basis in reason or morality. "What a monster," you wrote, "the Roman Empire is nourishing within itself." It is perhaps wrong of me to complain, for your premonitions as to Julian's fate have certainly been more accurate than my own. Even the rabble at Antioch years later, who laughed as he strode through their streets, referring to him as a Cecrops, one of Zeus's mythical apes, because of his simian beard and broad shoulders, have more reason than I to boast of the truthfulness of their impression. Yet at that time, he was more to be pitied than feared, more to be admired for his intellect than derided for his stubborn dogmatism, and his was a friendship that I valued, as I still cherish its memory.

His family—father, uncles, even his brother Gallus— had been murdered by his cousin, the Emperor Constantius, as soon as they came of age or rose to sufficient rank as to be perceived a threat by the paranoid emperor. Only Julian survived, due to the Emperor's view of him as a harmless moron interested only in philosophy and books, and perhaps also to the protectiveness of his early guardians, the saintly Marcus of Arethusa and his brother ascetics. These good men raised the poor boy in a devout Christian setting within the silent cloisters of their monastery, imbuing him with the spirit of such stirring models as the holy Nicholas of Myra, the patron saint of children, who even as an infant was known to be so pious as to observe Church fasts by refusing to suck the breasts of his mother, to her great awe and even greater discomfort, and the child martyr Saint Lucia, who died during the persecutions of the Emperor Diocletian, in horrible depiction of which she is portrayed in her icons as smiling beatifically, with her lovely eyes sitting beside her in a bowl.

A more naive traveler to Athens than Julian you never did see. He had been so sheltered by the overwhelming protectiveness of his tutors that his ignorance upon arriving in the worldly city was almost comical. Until his arrival in Athens, the Scriptures and Homer had been his entire life, and indeed his lack of worldliness may go far toward explaining why he was perhaps the only intelligent man in all of Athens not deeply disappointed by the city's faded glories. Rather, he praised his good fortune, as though some great feast were being celebrated, quoting his precious *Iliad* in having gained "gold for bronze, the value of a hundred oxen for the price of nine."

Nevertheless, for one so abstemious as Julian in his sensual pleasures, he was remarkably open-minded in his spiritual ones. Before I made his acquaintance, he had even spent several months studying in Pergamum and Ephesus, ancient centers of pagan learning and dark magic, where he had developed a taste for the rather exotic side of human spirituality. He was forced, however, to remain discreet in this regard, out of deference to his role as the closest living male relative of Constantius, the Defender of Christianity, who was of mixed mind about the wisdom of allowing any pagan sects to practice their ancient rites at all. The Emperor, a devout Christian, had in the past meted out harsh treatment to officials who had displayed too personal an interest in the gods of their ancestors, and he would not have taken kindly to even the slightest whisper of Julian's interest in these affairs.

Despite the Emperor's dictates, however, the common people continued to follow age-old custom. That autumn, as had been the case for a thousand autumns past, the squares and streets of the Eleusis temple sanctuary, eleven miles from Athens, thronged with masses of worshipers celebrating the Greater Mysteries, reenacting the myth of the two goddesses Demeter and Kore. This was perhaps the one occasion during the year when the ancient cults even came close to regaining their glories of old. For the rest of the year, a priest's dedication to the service of the pagan gods was an exercise in misery and hunger, of begging alms and fruitlessly urging passersby to return to the old religions.

But the ceremony of the Greater Mysteries was different. A number of preliminary rites were performed openly in the streets: the public procession of initiates to the sanctuary of Eleusis, their purification in the bay of Phalerum, and other secondary rites. Julian, of course, could only observe these public celebrations of the Eleusinian mysteries from afar, as a bystander. Yet his scholarly interest in the event did not allow him to completely avoid participation "for research purposes," as he said, although not, I suspected at the time, without some youthful rebellion at the constrictions of the Emperor. He secretly sought out the chief minister of the rite, the hierophant, convincing the old man of his sincerity in wishing to be introduced to the community of Eleusinian worshipers, and gaining permission to actually participate in several of the secret culminating rituals. The ceremony he attended lasted three days, taking place in the interior of the sanctuary. When he described it to me after the fact, I was astonished.

"Julian—you're a Christian!" I exclaimed. "Why do you participate in these pagan practices?" The whole notion was distasteful to me in the extreme.

He shrugged, though not without a hint of defiance, as if it were merely an excess of uncut wine in which he had indulged. "I am a scholar, not a religious partisan. I seek to understand. Surely you can't deny me that."

"But not only do you risk your head, if Constantius were to even discover it, but you risk corrupting your faith."

"Nonsense," he retorted. From the way he began to flush and get worked up, I felt I had clearly struck a nerve.

"I study paganism as well as Christianity because I'm interested in both," he continued. "Even Seneca said one should make a practice of visiting the enemy's camp—by way of reconnaissance, of course, not as a deserter. Worship of the ancient gods is the history of our culture—Caesarius, it *is* our culture! Out of it all our triumphs have flowed—our literature, drama, art. A thousand years, two thousand, perhaps, of glory! Christianity is our present. It is practically new, and has had no cultural effect. Look at the proportions—there is nothing there for a scholar to study, even a Christian one!"

"You could study the Scriptures, for a start," I remonstrated, but he scarcely heard.

"The Scriptures. Caesarius, I have studied the Scriptures since I was eight years old. But I'm not a priest. My vocation is to be a scholar, a philosopher. You tell me—where should I best dedicate my time in order to be a knowledgeable, cultured man? On two millennia of glory, albeit pagan glory? Or on one generation of Christianity since my uncle Constantine legalized it? One generation alone—a generation that saw every male member of my family killed by Christians."

I protested at the conclusion he was implying. "You can't blame Christianity for the murders of your father and brothers," I challenged. "That was not the triumph of Christianity, but its absence."

Here I saw Julian's expression soften, and he unaccountably began chuckling. I realized, with some embarrassment, that my own face and words betrayed at least the same level of earnestness as I had wondered at in him only a few moments before. To him, however, my sober words were humorous. This only exasperated me further.

"Don't play the Sophist with me, Julian," I continued. "If you're arguing merely for argument's sake, I will have none of it. If you wish to sharpen your rhetorical skills, pick a topic other than religion—or go to my brother Gregory. Case closed."

In an effort to distract him from such distasteful studies, and to focus him on the more worldly miracles of the One True God, I once invited him to attend one of my clandestine autopsies, which he accepted with eager relish, somewhat to my surprise. Our research subjects were normally collected on a rather irregular basis, whenever I or my fellow students were fortunate to hear of the death of an indigent somewhere in the city. Only rarely were we able to acquire a cadaver in appropriate condition for research, for our quest at all times involved a race against not only the city's other medical schools, of which there were a considerable number, but against the Church. You and I have discussed this before, Brother, how the Christian presbyters are scandalized at what they view as the medical schools' desecration of the dead. As for myself, I feel that there could not possibly be anything more holy than to advance man's medical knowledge and reason, which must serve as the basis for true and lasting faith, in order to better serve the living. Julian was shocked and then delighted at the whiff of illicitness about the whole affair.

On this occasion, fortunately, I was able to spare him the mad dash through the city upon hearing of an indigent death, and the clandestine walk back, skulking through alleys carrying the cadaver as best we could wrapped in rags and sheets, to avoid contact with sharp-eyed priests and other observers not favorable to the cause of science. Athens had at this time just emerged from the grip of a cholera epidemic, and for the first and only time of which I was aware, the small cellar of my medical school was well stocked with appropriate subjects for examination. Six or seven, in fact, had been acquired over the past several days alone, laid in hastily assembled pine boxes. In a somewhat careless effort at preservation, we strove to maintain a constant temperature in the boxes by packing the bodies tightly with wood shavings and sawdust swept up from the floor of the joinery next door, in exchange for which the carpenter jokingly made us promise *not* to collect his body should we ever come across it in the streets.

As Julian and I, along with several others, arrived at the door of the school that night at the agreed-upon time, I swore him to secrecy, and briefly described for him the procedure he was about to witness, so that he would not be needlessly shocked and repelled. Our assignment this evening was to verify the observation made three centuries ago by the physician Apion, that the human body contains a delicate nerve that starts from the left ring finger and travels to the heart. It is for this reason, he claimed, that it is most appropriate to favor that finger above all others when wearing a wedding ring, in view of the close relationship between it and the principal organ.

One or two of my colleagues, however, expressed hesitation at allowing an outsider such as Julian to view our work. Pharon, a tall, thin young pagan from Alexandria who claimed proud descent from a long line of Egyptian priests and who therefore was most skilled in the preservation of the dead, was particularly vocal in his objections. I explained who our guest was.

"Pharon—he's not just a friend; he's the cousin of the Emperor. If he understands and approves of our work, he could be of assistance to us in the future."

The Egyptian peered down his long, aristocratic nose at Julian, blinking at him skeptically. "I don't care if he's the sun god Ra. It's not right for him to view the procedure."

I was annoyed at Pharon's blatant disrespect, but when I glanced over at Julian he did not seem dismayed in the slightest. After several moments of hurried negotiations and argument in the middle of the street, the Egyptian finally shrugged grudgingly. "Very well," he said, "but, Caesarius—our safety is on your head."

I assured him I took full responsibility, and then unlocked the door.

We entered and felt our way down the stairs in darkness, assisted only slightly by the diffused light of the half-moon shining weakly through a high, narrow window. A lantern would not be lit until the very last moment, to avoid detection from curious passersby, and then would be snuffed as soon as the hasty procedure had been completed.

By the unwritten rules of our group, at those times when we were blessed with more than one cadaver for study, students were required to first use the older one, by which I mean the one that had been stored the longest in the cellar, to prevent its going to waste. I was dismayed to be reminded by one of my students that this meant that, despite our recent fruitful harvest from the city streets, we were obliged to perform our examinations on a fellow who had died a good eight days earlier. Although the cellar was cool, and he had been carefully packed in sawdust, nevertheless I did not relish the anticipation of the cadaver's odor and physical condition, and I warned Julian of what was to come.

Drawing the sealed box out from its shelf and carefully laying it on the examining table in the dim light, a strong stench of decay seeped through some crack in the planks. I forged on, nevertheless, though when I encountered difficulty prying the nails out of the lid, I called for Julian to uncover the ember we had brought sealed inside a small ceramic jar, and to light up a tallow for light. There was a pause as he fumbled to open the container in the dark, and then Pharon shouted, "Stop!" in a panic, nearly causing the rest of us to jump out of our skins. After fearful shushing all around as we listened carefully for footsteps outside our door, I turned to Pharon in annoyance.

"What the hell was that for?"

"Don't light the candle," he said. "Open the box and let the gas dissipate first."

"Gas?" Julian asked nervously. "Caesarius, I thought you said he was dead."

"Gas from the wood shavings, you dolt," rejoined Pharon with a hiss. "Organic material creates gas as it decays. Even ignorant Alemanni peasants know that—that's why they store grain in vented barns. You'll smell the gas when you open the box. The body stored with it also produces humors from the same process. The combination of the two could be dangerous."

I scoffed at this. "That's absurd! Julian, light the candle."

"Wait!" Pharon hissed again, this time with increasing urgency. His large eyes shone brightly, in eerie contrast with the darkness of his skin and the shadows of the room. "I once thought as you did, Caesarius, until last year, when I opened a casket the same way, and held a candle close to view the body. There was a burst of flame and a noise like a loud puff of wind, and it blew the candle out completely. I was blinded for a moment, and when I was able

to relight the candle and look in the box again, I found that
the flash had singed all the hair off the man's body. At least
it made it easier to dissect him. Unfortunately, it did the
same to my face. For three weeks I was mistaken for a
Syrian eunuch. Believe me, it's better to let the gas dissipate."

I could hear stifled snickers breaking out from around
the table and I stood stiffly, wondering whether to let this
outrageous tale pass unremarked. By this time, unfortunately, Julian had had enough. His eyes wide and gleaming
in the dim light, he begged my pardon and pleaded to be
released back to the street. I consented, and he slipped out
quietly the way he had come, stifling his nausea at the overpowering smell. Although that occasion gave rise to great
merriment among my colleagues for many weeks afterward,
it was also, I believe, the source of the great esteem, and
possibly fear, that Julian held of the physician's skills and
knowledge.

Would that you held me in the same respect as did he,
Brother.

III

Julian stayed in Athens less than a year. When in midsummer he was unexpectedly summoned by the Emperor to attend him at his residence at Milan, the command was anything but welcome. The day Julian received it, he wandered out of his apartments in a daze. It was only with great difficulty that I was able to find him hours later, lying prostrate in the semi-darkness in the Parthenon before the enormous statue of Athena, mumbling unintelligibly.

"Caesarius," he said hoarsely, sitting up with a start and looking around when I touched his shoulder. "What are you doing here?"

I looked into his face for signs of illness, but seeing none I relaxed.

"Gregory said you wandered out of the house looking like a poleaxed ox. I've been looking all over for you, friend—but this was the last place I'd have thought to find you." I looked suspiciously up at Athena, then smiled and thumped his shoulder cheerfully. "Julian, it's Milan! The imperial court! If Constantius truly had evil designs he wouldn't be recalling you. What can be so bad as all that?"

Julian's face reddened in anger. "He's a madman! He killed my father and brother—and yet he asks me to *attend* him in Milan? I will not be . . . *toyed* with, Caesarius, like a mouse! Why doesn't he simply send his assassins here and do the job cleanly? Coward and madman!"

I rolled my eyes at the melodramatics, but in truth Julian had good reason to be livid, knowing that it was just such a summons that had led to the torture and execution of his brother Gallus several years before. No doubt he also suspected that his indiscreet investigations into the worship of the ancients had finally been brought to the Emperor's ears. I placed my hand under his arm and lifted him to his feet, concerned that he not compound his troubles by being seen lying prostrate before an image of a pagan god. He stood looking about himself fiercely, planting his feet stubbornly as if determined to stay and give the assassins no occasion to find him in the street, to deny them at least that satisfaction.

"Julian," I whispered harshly, "you'll call attention to yourself by lingering before Athena. You've suffered enough for one day, and no doubt the gods have had enough of your pestering, too. Come, I'll take you home. A cup of wine will cheer us both."

He stood motionless on the great marble-tiled floor before the statue, gazing up at the polished golden visage, before finally dropping his eyes to me, and with a great sweep of his arm, he indicated the vast, semi-dark colonnaded sanctuary around him.

"I wanted only a beautiful spot," he said hoarsely, "a monumental spot, the most evocative spot in all Athens, one that I could take with me in my memory to Milan, in case . . . in case . . ."

He faltered, and I didn't press him further. I clapped my hand on his shoulder and gestured toward the door. He squared himself and with great dignity strolled out of the temple and down the steep streets to his lodgings, where he packed his bags swiftly and in silence.

Since by that time I had practically completed my own studies, and was due back at the Emperor's court to render account of my new training and skills, I offered to accompany him on his journey. For the sake of comfort, we elected to go by sea for the first leg of our trip, and passed many hours of the voyage recounting our experiences to each other, as we were almost precisely the same age, but had lived such contrasting lives to that point. On one occasion I was startled with his line of questioning.

"Tell me about Constantius," he said.

"What about him?" I asked cautiously. "His actions as Emperor are common knowledge. Besides, you saw him just last year, before he sent you to Athens."

Julian shook his head somberly. "Not true. I was at his court, but only briefly, and not once did he meet with me. I spent my entire time there defending myself against the jealous gossip of his eunuchs, who said I was disobedient and was planning to conspire against him. I suspect he simply tired of my requests for an audience and wished to be rid of me, so he allowed me to leave to study in Athens."

I was amazed at this. "So you've never seen your own cousin, the Emperor?"

"Not since I was a boy. When I was small, he seemed like a god to me. Later, I was told what he had done to my family. . . ." He seemed suddenly wary of voicing his thoughts, and glanced over his shoulder cautiously. "You're his physician, Caesarius. You examine him monthly, and his wife, Eusebia. Surely you know more of his strengths and ailments, both physical and psychological, than any man alive."

"I would hardly presume to conjecture about his psychology," I said cautiously, "nor about the Empress. She does not actually permit a physical examination, but merely asks questions about her bodily functions as she examines herself behind a thick curtain."

"Very well, limit yourself to appearances, then—what does he look like? His image is all blurred in my mind."

At this I hesitated, Brother, for to give a diplomatic description of Constantius to one who is a near relative is not an easy task. You never met him yourself, for if you had, you would have understood my difficulty. Perhaps the best way to explain his appearance would be to digress briefly, by recalling the time when both you and I were boys, and accompanied Father and Mother on a pilgrimage to Rome to meet the Holy Pontiff Sylvester, who would confirm our father's investiture as bishop. Do you recall that enormous statue of the Emperor Domitian that had been erected two centuries before, on the street leading up to the Capitol, on the right-hand side as you approach from the Forum? Domitian's monstrous behavior had left the Romans with such a bad taste that after his murder, the Senate ordered his entire body carved up into tiny pieces; yet even this did not exhaust their indignation toward him. They decreed a *damnatio memoriae,* an order that not even the Emperor's name should remain on any monument, nor should any portrait or statue of him survive. On every inscription everywhere in Rome, and indeed throughout the entire Empire, his name was chiseled out, leaving the remainder of the text intact. Nowhere in the world is there a single likeness of him except that one bronze statue, which survived because of a macabre twist.

The Emperor's wife, Domitia, was a woman of good birth, and highly respected, or at least feared. Some say she had never herself done the least wrong to any man alive, nor consented to any of her husband's wickedness, while others suspect that she had a guiding hand in her husband's murder, in which case she committed the most mortal of sins, though for a higher cause, may the soil rest lightly on her grave. In any event, the Senate esteemed her highly, and after Domitian's death invited her to request anything she liked. She asked for but one thing: that she might take and bury her husband's body, and erect a bronze replica of him. The Senate agreed, and the widow devised a plan. She collected the bits and pieces of her husband's flesh, painstakingly reassembled them into a semblance of the original, and then stitched and strapped and braced the whole grotesque contraption together. This she showed to the sculptors, and asked them to make a bronze statue portraying him exactly as he was at that time.

Hence, Brother, the odd appearance of that statue, visible even beneath the years of grime and corrosion that had accumulated when we viewed it as boys: the misshapen, lopsided face, the eyes aimed in slightly different directions, one arm and one leg apparently longer than their respective peers, which I attributed to the devoted widow's not having had proper anatomical training and perhaps inadvertently fitting several crucial parts in error. Hence too my difficulty in describing to Julian his older cousin's appearance, for Constantius had always given me much the same impression, of body parts reassembled in haste from whatever might be available: the enormous corpulence of his girth; the tiny head delicately positioned atop the shoulders with no apparent neck, like a pea on a pumpkin; the equally fat thighs narrowing down unaccountably below the knee to white, chickenlike shanks and almost dainty feet; the small, piggish eyes that missed nothing, and in fact were constantly darting restlessly this way and that, the mark of an extraordinarily intelligent and inquiring mind; and the soft, sensitive hands that belied the tremendous strength of his upper arms and chest. As a physician, I had never failed to be astonished at this study of contrasts when I performed his monthly physical examinations.

Yet how to describe this to Julian? I resolved to be honest in my description, yet not as brutally so as I just was with you.

"Your cousin is far from being in the prime of his life anymore," I answered. "Remember, he's past forty, he's no longer young. He's obese and sweats and grunts like a boar even when merely walking or rising from his seat. He's desperate for an heir, which Eusebia has been unable to produce, though she herself is in the prime of her life, barely older than you and me, and a stunning beauty."

"Perhaps the Empress is barren?" Julian asked sympathetically, though with curiosity.

"Perhaps—but I think the problem lies with Constantius himself. I tell you this because I trust your confidentiality, and because if you were to order me to, I would have to tell you anyway. The Emperor has one undescended testicle, and the other is swollen to the size of a Numidian orange, a goiter, perhaps, or a cancer, a state of affairs about which he is quite defensive. He openly blames Eusebia for her failure to conceive, and the Empress is increasingly distraught, yet to me it's quite clear that conception is simply not a possibility."

After a week of uneventful sailing, we arrived at the old Augustan seaport of Fano, the point where the Via Aemilia from Milan meets the coast. We were met by a small though luxurious sedan with six Thracian bearers led by a sullen centurion. The prospect of traveling two hundred miles overland to Milan alone in this claustrophobic contraption, possibly to his death, was too much for Julian to stomach. He dismissed the centurion, to the latter's chagrin, and elected instead to ride, with me as his comrade. He purchased horses from a dealer the very day of our arrival off the boat, and we set out at once. The centurion insisted on following behind us with the sedan-bearers, true to his orders from Constantius to convey Julian safely to the city, so we at least took advantage of the situation by stowing all our own baggage in the passenger compartment, which allowed us to travel quite unencumbered and make numerous side trips through the Apennines and across the Po valley, finally arriving in Milan, in September, several weeks after he had actually been expected.

Apparently peeved at this delay, Constantius declined to meet him when he arrived at the palace, sending word only that his younger cousin was to take for his lodgings an ancient villa the Emperor owned in the countryside eight miles outside Milan. Julian was not even permitted the time to take a cool drink before the centurion was ordered to turn around and lead him back out of the city. We arrived just before nightfall, and in the waning light the old mansion was not without its charm. Though it had been uninhabited for years, the extensive gardens and orchards within its winding stone walls had been carefully maintained, and afforded numerous nooks and shady benches for quiet reading and study. The house itself, though silent and musty from years of abandonment, was in good repair. The only cloud on this small horizon was the uncertainty of knowing how long Julian would be required to remain here before being allowed to return to his studies, or otherwise disposed of by the Emperor.

Julian and I wandered through the vast, echoing halls and atriums, as he alternately gaped at the luxurious surroundings and scoffed at the wastefulness. Finally, he planted himself in a small office, an anteroom off the well-stocked library.

"I will take this room," he said simply.

"Very well, sir," said the steward. "For your study, I presume?"

"For my lodgings," Julian replied. The steward raised one eyebrow suspiciously. "My cot against the wall, please, the table and chair in the middle, a chamber pot behind that screen in the corner. The library is just through that set of doors. Lease out the rest of the villa, or burn it for all I care. You will not see me in any other room. What better place to spend one's last days than in a library?"

The steward went out, shaking his head in wonder.

That first morning, as Dawn illumined the earth with Phoebus' torch and scattered the dampness and night-gloom— Ah, Gregory, even at this distance, at this late date, I can see you cringe as I write these words.

" 'The sun rose on another day,' " you told me when I was but a boy, as you corrected my composition exercises. "Just write: 'The sun rose on another day.' Why must you forever confound your words with false embellishments of a simple fact of nature? It's a sunrise! 'Phoebus' torch,' indeed."

I painstakingly scratched out the offending phrase and with adolescent rebelliousness began again: "When early Dawn, leaving Tithonus' saffron bed, sprinkled the earth with new light, the sun poured down, and all the world was made clear. . . ."

You scolded me again after viewing my work. "I told

you to write, 'The sun rose on another day.' Why do you defy me with this overwrought trash?"

"Because it's beautiful," I replied petulantly. "It's descriptive. It recalls Homer, and Virgil."

"Homer and Virgil. Any sensible Christian would simply write, 'The sun rose on another day,' and be done with this pagan nonsense."

"But why?" I persisted. "Just because we are Christian, must we forgo beauty?"

You sighed patiently. "Of course not, Caesarius. By simplifying, by getting to first principles, you do not forgo beauty, but enhance it. Beauty is truth, and by writing, truth you bring beauty to the fore. You emphasize God's Creation in its purest form."

I must have looked saddened, gazing at the bescribbled manuscript over which I had labored for so many hours, for you softened your voice and put your arm across my shoulder.

"In the end," you continued, "the simplest form of writing is the happiest form—for you acknowledge that nothing is greater than God's work, no mere words can improve on the ultimate beauty of the world. A man cannot possibly express more joy in creation, more optimism in the perfection of the Kingdom to come, than by simply writing, 'The sun rose on another day.' "

In principle, Brother, I agreed—yet still, then and perhaps even now, my desire to express myself in purity and simplicity was sometimes outweighed by a perverse pleasure in annoying you.

That first morning, as Dawn illumined the earth with Phoebus' torch and scattered the dampness and night-gloom, Julian was startled nearly out of his wits by a crowd of servants thrown into action by the clangorous ringing of a gong. They flung themselves into his room bearing quantities of buckets, dust cloths, ladders and stools for reaching the ceilings, long poles bearing dripping sponges, feather dusters and brooms. He timorously inquired whether the villa was undergoing some type of renovation, but when the steward proudly informed him that this was the daily cleaning routine that had been devised to ensure the sanitation of Julian's lodgings, the appalled youth quickly dismissed the entire army of servants and told them not to return to his rooms unless he specifically called for them— which he did not intend to do, ever. He spent all his days locked in his room, emerging only briefly to attend daily prayers in the villa's chapel, chanted by the broken-down old presbyter who came attached to the property, as much a part of the furnishings as the garden statuary or the chamber pot in the bedroom. He was accompanied only by the house's vast quantity of books, and saw only me and the veiled servant girl whom Eusebia had assigned to his service, who cooked a simple and often vile fare, though Julian rarely took any notice of its quality, and who entered his room several times a week to make sense and hygiene of his notorious untidiness.

One sweltering day found the girl rustling about behind him as he ignored her soft humming, absorbed completely in his studies and absentmindedly swatting at a fly that buzzed lazily around his head. Suddenly, as he afterwards related to me, the girl spoke to him softly, which was unprecedented and not entirely welcome in that it broke his concentration on a particularly knotty philosophical problem he had been working through.

"Master? Begging your pardon, sir, for disturbing you . . ."

There was silence for a long moment before he mumbled, "Hmmm? What is it?" without turning around.

"Should I place your Plotinus scrolls alphabetically next to Plato, or do you prefer me to file them separately among those of the theurgists?"

"Plotinus isn't a theurgist," Julian muttered distractedly, and then lapsed into another long silence, punctuated by an irritated swat to the back of his neck. Suddenly, he spun around in his chair, his eyes wide. "You're not my regular cleaning girl!"

Her eyes lowered demurely behind the veil. "Begging your pardon, sir. Lucilla is sick. I'm taking her place."

"But you can read Greek?"

"Of course!" she exclaimed. Then a nervous giggle. "I mean, only a little. Just enough to read the titles."

"But you know Plotinus and the theurgists!"

"No, sir," she said softly, "that is, not well. I must have overheard the palace scholars discussing them."

The next day, silent and illiterate Lucilla had returned, back to her old habits of hopelessly misarranging all his work.

As the weeks passed, Julian spent his time in a mixture of fury and relief, waiting for Constantius to see him and inform him of his plans for the future. At first Julian had written daily, seeking an audience and receiving only form apologies from the Emperor's ministers and eunuchs, who curtly informed him of his busy schedule, or of his feeling indisposed, or of an unexpected emergency that had taken him out of town. Julian soon cut his entreaties down to a weekly basis, and then stopped corresponding with the palace altogether. The Empress Eusebia, however, perhaps out of remorse at her husband's rudeness, did take the occasion to send her young cousin-in-law an enormous quantity of texts, including many that were recently transcribed, by all the most fashionable modern philosophers, rhetoricians, and historians, many of whom were still living. She also sent him frequent missives expressing her goodwill toward him, reassuring him about the delay, and telling him to abide patiently, that all would be well.

Upon the arrival of the welcome gift of scrolls and codices, Julian wrote a letter to her expressing his gratitude, and requesting an audience with her, if not with her husband. This he handed to the eunuch who had been the most frequent conveyor of the Empress's letters, and who upon receiving it handled it gingerly between two fingers, with as much distaste as if it had been spat upon by a leper. He set it quickly upon a marble hallway table while he pretended to tighten his sandal strap, and there it was left for Julian to rediscover, many days later, after much wondering and bewilderment at the Empress's stony failure to respond to his request. It was not until I myself informed him that it would have been a grave violation of palace protocol for him to have corresponded with the Empress at all before obtaining leave from the Emperor, that he understood the eunuch's sensitivity to receiving such a document. For this very reason, an audience with Eusebia was completely out of the question for the time being; indeed, outsiders, even relatives, were rarely allowed in the gynaeceum, the women's quarters, a fact that I had forgotten, or never actually assimilated, given my own unimpeded access to the royal family by virtue of my capacity as official physician.

IV

At this point, Brother, I must recount for you an extraordinary incident which, although not involving Julian directly, goes far in explaining many of the later events that affected both him and me so significantly.

I had been attending Constantius with the rest of his courtiers at one of his interminable strategizing sessions at the palace. Such meetings involved the Emperor's summoning several of his chief advisers simultaneously to the vast throne room on the ground floor of the palace in Milan, whom he would proceed to line up in a loose row, with their various subadvisers and lackeys behind them. He would then stalk up and down the line, followed by his own tripping, mincing crowd of eunuchs and sycophants, grilling and haranguing each adviser until by dint of pure luck and guesswork they were all forced to come to the same conclusion—the one at which Constantius had already arrived before he had summoned them in the first place. From the graveled patio I heard faint shouting and the galloping hoofbeats of a single horse, and bored and disgusted with Constantius' farcical planning exercises, I wandered over to an open window and peered outside.

An exhausted, dusty courier had been practically yanked off his horse at the palace gates and was being led straightaway up the massive colonnaded balustrade and through the iron doors. He had not even been given the customary goblet of wine to cool his parched throat, and the splash of cold water over his face and neck to calm his labored breathing. He glanced longingly at the bubbling fountains and pools he passed in the courtyard, and he marched limping in pain, his riding togs filthy, the battered leathern pouch slung carelessly over his neck and shoulder by one precariously threadbare strap. The sweat from his lank, uncut hair dripped steadily into the weeks-old growth of beard and thence to the polished marble floor of the steps, leaving a treacherous, slippery trail in his wake.

I turned back away from the window. The Emperor, whose face in fact was a close image of Julian's, though much doughier and with more of an expression of suspicion or cunning about the eyes, was pacing angrily up and down before a small knot of whispering courtiers. The jiggling rolls of flab at his lower back struggled to keep up with their firmer, more disciplined brethren at his belly, as if in a contest of extraneous tissue, the entire sordid battle visible beneath the fine, rapidly dampening linen fabric of his tight ceremonial toga. I shook my head in disgust at this line of thinking, one that could only have been possible to a bored and underworked imperial physician, until I was interrupted by the messenger's arrival. The Emperor had been in an agony to hear the news personally ever since the first cryptic indications of the disaster had been received in Milan four days before, over the series of coded signal flares erected on mountains and watchtowers the length and breadth of the Empire.

When the man burst into the room flanked by two beefy guards, Constantius waddled up to him with a speed and energy astonishing for one of his ponderous girth.

"Out with it, man—is it true? What of Cologne!"

The courier stopped short, barely into the doorway, and took a moment to get his bearings as he found himself unexpectedly gazing straight into the angry eyes of the Emperor.

"I don't know what you have been told, Your Highness," he said simply. "I know only that five days ago Cologne fell to the barbarians. All are dead, and it is only by the grace of God that I myself was able to escape and reach Milan by the post road relays. Chonodomarius is a devil." The man swayed and blanched a sickly pale, and I feared he might collapse at the Emperor's feet in his exhaustion.

Constantius glared at the man in a rage, almost as if he would strike him, and the messenger shrank back slightly, his mouth working as if he were about to tell something more—but what more could he say? Finally the Emperor muttered at him, "Tell no one of this," whirled, and stalked back to the throne set in the middle of the room, where courtiers and aides had gone silent as they watched the proceeding. His face reddening in deep anger, he immediately began issuing orders to his generals and advisers. Eunuchs scurried in all directions, and I rose and sidled along the walls to the bewildered courier, who now stood abandoned and silent, looking ill, and seemingly wishing to shrink into the very cracks of the stonework.

"Come, soldier," I said, touching his elbow gently.

He started, then looked at me with unutterable relief at hearing his first friendly words in possibly months.

I led him down a back passage to my rooms, where he collapsed on my couch, and I offered him some cold meat and stale bread left over from my breakfast that morning. He wolfed it down gratefully, though wincing at a stomach pain, which he attributed to cramps from this being the first meal he had eaten in three days. He also said it was the first food lacking in maggots that he had eaten in a month. Brother, what kind of a physician am I that I accept a patient's own diagnosis unquestioningly? I was ashamed at my employer's rudeness in not having attended to the poor soldier upon his earliest arrival, and embarrassed at my own lack of provisions to offer, for the only other nourishment I had in my store was a bruised apple, which he also gulped down in three or four bites, core and all. I rang for a slave and demanded more food and some uncut wine. While we awaited the servant's return I asked the messenger to relate his story.

"For months," he said, "the Cologne garrison has been under siege by the Alemanni. Their king is Chonodomarius; we call him 'the Beast.' He's leading them personally. Our garrison commander, Lucius Vitellius, sent runners asking the Emperor and the legions of Gaul to send reinforcements, but got no answer. We figured the messengers had been captured."

I said nothing at this, but I knew the messages to Constantius had indeed arrived. The Emperor, dismissing the situation in far-off Germany as inconsequential compared with his more urgent concerns in the Empire's tinderbox Eastern regions, refused to transfer troops to the suffering garrison, believing that his commanders in Gaul and Britain would find the wherewithal to lift the siege.

"We finally broke, five days ago. The men were starving, sir, and the barbarians had poisoned the city's water supply. I think we might've been able to hold out a few more days, but we broke when the Beast started raining heads down on us."

"Soldier," I said, "I've never been to war, but I've heard that this is often a tactic of the besiegers—to place the heads or even the bodies of their captured enemies onto the engines and launch them into the fortifications to demoralize the defenders. Surely you expected something of the sort."

"Indeed we did, sir, but nothing like this. You see, sir, they weren't even Roman heads. It was worse. They were Germans. You could tell by their long blond mustaches."

I looked at him in puzzlement. "German heads? Why would Chonodomarius rain German heads on you?"

"We asked the same question, sir, of course. Then it dawned on us when we looked out at the hills. Sir, the hills were swarming with Germans, on every side. Just arrived. Every tribe from the Pannonians to the Frisians had sent their men in reinforcement, thousands, tens of thousands. They were cutting down every tree to the horizon, making hundreds of catapults, battering rams, siege towers—you name it, sir, they'd learned their lessons well from us. But the Beast didn't have Roman heads to shoot at us. Hell, he hadn't caught enough of us outside the gates, I suppose. So he used his own Germans. Lord, he had enough to spare, he just had his guards seize a couple hundred prison drunkards, lopped off their heads, and sent them on over. When we saw that we knew we were through."

I sat in stunned silence.

"And that's not the worst of it, sir," the man continued after a short pause to catch his breath. "The worst was when Chonodomarius himself rode up to the gates of the city, bellowing at Vitellius to come out and parley. Sir, you've never seen a man like the Beast."

The messenger shuddered, and I begged him to continue.

"He's a giant, sir—stands seven feet if he's an inch, and with muscles like an ox. He wears a blood-red plume from some huge evil bird affixed in his helmet, and no clothes but a loincloth—just paints his body with red and blue streaks, the worst sort of barbarian you can imagine. He rides up like that practically naked, hair and mustaches flowing in the wind, on his enormous white horse, itself painted with flames like the devil's own steed, foaming and rearing, its eyes rolling around in its head, and he waves his weapon in the air, not a spear like any normal barbarian would carry, but a *harpoon*—sir, I haven't seen the likes of that thing since those whalers from Hibernia. I swear, no normal man could even *lift* it, but the Beast is waving that piece of iron around in the air like it was a twig, and bellowing for the garrison commander to come out of the gates and surrender.

"Well, sir, I hand it to old Vitellius, he doesn't flinch from anything, not even this barbarian. He calls two cohort commanders to come with him, and they're trembling like virgins on their wedding night, I tell you, but Vitellius, he's cool as a Spanish melon. Out they go, the three of them, in full polished dress armor, the horses all brushed and freshened to make it look like we've all been having a wonderful comfortable old time for the past three months in that death trap. They walk their horses up to that fire-breathing barbarian while thirty thousand Germans behind him fall silent and all of us are standing there on the ramparts watching the proceedings."

I was breathless. "What happened to Vitellius?"

The man shuddered. "It was horrible, sir. Chonodomarius didn't even wait to allow him to surrender. He just gave the nod, and his men surrounded our commanders and dragged them right off the horses. Kept them in the same sitting position as when they were riding, but turned them around to face us, up on the walls. Before you could blink an eyeball, the Germans had set all three of them down on long stakes they had pounded into the dirt. Right up their arses, sir, you're a physician, you know what that'll do to your insides. Points came out their necks, spewing filthy blood all over the place. God Almighty, it was dreadful. The two cohort commanders died on the spot, or maybe passed out and saved themselves some pain before they did die, but old Vitellius wasn't ready to go. He jerked and twitched on his stake like a fish on a spit for a good long while, and the Beast stood there bellowing out a laugh to raise the dead. He finally got tired of Vitellius' moaning and walked over himself, grabbed the man's head with his two hands, gave it a good twist, and ripped it off his shoulders by the roots like you do to a chicken when you don't have an ax to finish the deed more cleanly. I nearly puked when I saw that, and we all knew the game was over. Chonodomarius lifted that head, with the neck bones and skin flaps still hanging out the bottom, and heaved it at the gate. Splattered like a rotten egg, and then all those barbarians set up an awful roar and charged it in a mass. Broke the gates down by their sheer weight, they didn't even wait for the battering rams. Must have killed a couple hundred of their own men by trampling.

"I didn't wait, I tell you. I dove into some old sapper tunnels we had found a few days earlier, and stayed there till night, till I got lost and crawled out just outside the walls, where there was still a mob of barbarians milling around, drunk as mule drivers. They must have thought I was one of them on account of the beard, and figured I had just stolen my armor as plunder, so they took no notice of me. I found poor old Vitellius' horse still tied to his master's stake, hopped on, and rode as casually as I could out to the post road. The barbarians hadn't even placed guards, I wasn't challenged once. And then I hightailed it here, stealing horses as I went. I believe I'm the only survivor."

I stared at the man, appalled at the horrifying story and deadpan delivery. Was this what we were up against in Gaul? Just then there was a light knock at the door, and the sour-faced slave minced in, bearing a tray heaped with more cold meat, a large platter of chilled grapes and sliced peaches, and decanters of wine and cold water. I upbraided the surly brute for taking so long, and then cleared room on my low table, which I normally use as a resting place for half-read books, scrolls, and medical reports.

The slave took twice as long as he should have arranging the food and carrying out the tray, and when he finally left I latched the door behind him for privacy and turned back to my filthy and starving guest.

He sat motionless, his eyes wide as they took in the platter of artfully arranged food, and a look of calm resignation on his face. A small pool of blood, however, which I had not noticed during his tale, had formed on the floor beneath his couch.

I rushed forward to help him, almost slipping in the trail of sweat drippings he had made when entering the room, and ripped open his tunic from neck to belly. His ribs were wrapped tightly in filthy linen, stuffed to bursting with blood-soaked dittany leaves. I seized a penknife from a nearby writing desk and cut into the crude wrappings, my task made more difficult by the foul smell that wafted out. The fabric had adhered to the skin as securely as glue, from the combined effect of the dried blood, sweat, and the juices of the crushed plant. Beneath the navel and somewhat to the side, the broken shaft of an arrow protruded just beyond skin level, the puncture wound around it swollen and an angry purple, oozing pus in an advanced stage of infection.

The arrowhead itself was lodged deep in the liver. I looked up at his face questioningly, demanding to know why he had not told me earlier that he was wounded, my mind racing to decide what measures could be taken to extract the arrow as quickly as possible.

It was too late, Brother. The man was dead.

V

I had no time to dwell on such matters, however, for the fall of Cologne had thrown Constantius into a flurry of activity. Because he had ordered the soldier's news to be kept secret as long as possible, however, the court staff could only wonder at the unusual shifts in troop deployments the Emperor ordered, the sudden cancellation of social events at the palace, and the constant comings and goings of tight-lipped senior military and diplomatic officials. For several days it was all I could do to keep up with Constantius as he waddled swiftly through the corridors from conference to advisory session to negotiations with foreign emissaries. During that period I had no time to see Julian, nor even to apprise him of the general situation at the palace, though in the past I had visited him at the villa several times a week. No doubt these new distractions would even further delay the Emperor's decision as to my unfortunate friend's fate.

Strangely enough, I needn't have concerned myself on this account: at the very height of the palace uproar, Julian's presence was suddenly recollected, and a peremptory summons was issued to him for an audience with Constantius in little more than an hour. On horseback, I accompanied the litter-bearers out to the villa to retrieve him, and watched as he prepared himself with resignation, for he was still completely in the dark as to what was to become of him. I myself had overheard fragmented discussions of his fate over the past several days from among the courtiers and eunuchs, hints of argument and dissent, of urgings for him to be eliminated as a possible threat to the throne, countered by equally persuasive arguments that the Emperor was in need of delegating his duties, so as to focus more of his own attention on the Empire's crumbling eastern borders. None of this, however, did I recount to Julian—he had no doubt already heard it all before, through his previous dealings with the palace eunuchs.

The trip into the city was the first Julian had taken since his arrival many weeks before, and he peered out the curtains of the litter in astonishment at the numbers of people thronging the streets. The occasion might have equally been a market day, or a public execution at the gallows platform in the palace courtyard. In response to Julian's shouted questions directed at the bearers, he received only a stony silence.

Arriving at the back gates of the palace to avoid the crowds gathering ominously at the front, he was met by a silent, scowling group of eunuchs, who inspected him there on the street. Even from where I stood at the edges of the group, quietly observing the scene, I could sense his agitation and contempt as he looked about him, trying to peer through the crowd of smooth and haughty courtiers surrounding him. They led him into the palace, where he was hastily stripped and rebathed, his hair dressed and oiled in the dandified manner he had despised ever since his school days. He was given a fresh and exceedingly elegant tunic and toga to replace the clean though threadbare student's clothes that had served him well since his trip to Athens months earlier. All his questions, put both politely and rudely, in both Latin and Greek, were met with studied silence, as if the attendants had been expressly forbidden to speak with him or, more likely, disdained to do so even if permitted.

At length he was led into the reception hall, where by this time the entire inner court had gathered in anticipation of the great event Constantius was about to stage. As always, I remained close to the Emperor in the event he should feel the need for one of the many syrups and tinctures I kept for his constant stream of maladies, both real and imagined. Though I tried to catch Julian's eye, to reassure him with a wink or a smile, his gaze as he approached was fixed steadily on the Emperor.

Constantius stood near a small fountain burbling into an exquisite mosaic rendering of the sea god Triton astride the backs of two dolphins. The eunuchs led Julian through the scattered groups of advisers and courtiers, who parted for him in goggle-eyed silence, their eyes ranging back and forth between the slim, hunch-shouldered young man, and the pacing, restless sovereign, the supreme ruler of the Roman Empire, the Augustus. As Julian approached, the room fell silent, with the single exception of the Emperor himself, who continued the low monologue he was giving to a slow-witted general named Barbatio, a lackey who had been instrumental in the treacherous seizure and murder of Gallus several years before. Constantius was facing away, and seemed to be in no hurry to finish the conversation and attend to his young cousin, and Julian shifted on his feet, staring fixedly at the back of the Emperor's head, fidgeting and tugging at the unfamiliar clothing. Barbatio glanced at him condescendingly, eyes filled with frank appraisal and malice, while the eunuchs exchanged superior smirks with each other and stood up all the straighter and more elegantly to emphasize the contrast between their own courtly and confident demeanor and that of the wretched student they had dragged unwillingly into the Emperor's presence.

Constantius finally finished his conversation and turned around, feigning surprise. Despite the Emperor's weeks of cold treatment, he greeted his cousin warmly, fatherlike, in fact, quite as if he had just arrived in the city with his feet still dusty from the road, rather than cooling his heels in the abandoned, echoing villa in the suburbs. Julian was astonished; the sight of Barbatio could not but make him wonder whether the Emperor had welcomed his brother

Gallus the same way when he had been invested with the purple, before being led to his death a short time afterward. Julian's own reaction to the Emperor's greeting was stiff and formal. It was a studied effort to disguise the utter repugnance he felt toward this man, this killer of his family, while simultaneously avoiding an overly warm approach, which all present would have recognized as dissimulation and hypocrisy of the worst kind. His feelings toward the Emperor, though they had never met as adults, nor had either of them ever spoken of the matter, could hardly have been less secret, nor could the fact that the younger man was utterly beholden to the older for his very survival at this point. Protocol and simple human decency, however, prevented this from being openly acknowledged by either.

"My boy," Constantius said, "you look splendid. I'm pleased to see that my people seem to be treating you well at your new lodgings."

Julian muttered his thanks, made brief mention of the hospitality he had been shown since arriving in Milan, and then fell silent. The Emperor stared at him expectantly, and with some irritation perhaps, as if waiting for further utterings to drop from his mouth. With a sigh, he turned to his chamberlain, who was hovering at the Emperor's elbow, wringing his hands in impatience.

"My lord," said the eunuch, "the platform has been prepared and the crowds assembled. I am afraid they are becoming impatient."

"Very well. Come, Julian. I would prefer to keep your obvious discomfort to a minimum, and to finish this distasteful duty as quickly as possible."

The young man blanched, though without losing his composure, and glanced quickly over at me. I could be of no help on this score, and after a moment averted my gaze. Resignedly, he straightened his shoulders and followed the Emperor's quick, waddling pace out the wide double doors and onto the broad wooden platform that had been assembled for the occasion over the stairs and balustrade that coursed up to the entrance. I remained with a small knot of advisers immediately behind them, in the shadows inside, just out of sight of the crowd.

Julian stepped into the harsh sunlight blinking in bewilderment, and a deafening roar rose up as the throats of thousands of men and women opened at the sight. For a hundred ranks away from the platform stood the Emperor's Praetorian guards and home legions, in perfect formation and attention, their spears in unerring vertical alignment over the thousands of brightly polished battle helmets and crimson horsehair crests, multicolored silken pennants fluttering lightly in the cool breeze. Beyond the ranks of soldiers stood the more motley crowds Julian had passed on his way into the city—townsmen and merchants who had been given the day off from their labors and summoned to the palace grounds with their families. In the distance, children and wives sat on the men's shoulders for a better view, while clusters of young, single laborers stood here and there shouting their encouragement to their fellows on opposite sides of the courtyard, waving skin wine bags and gourds, and flirting with gaggles of cackling prostitutes nearby.

Julian stood transfixed at this view of perhaps the largest crowd he had seen in his life. His reverie was broken by the booming voice of the Emperor, who stood beside him. Even with Constantius' powerful vocal range, however, and the excellence of the plaza's acoustics, the size of the crowd required that heralds be posted along the edges to pick up the gist of the Emperor's words and relay them in their own bellowing shouts to the crowds in the back of the space and beyond to the nearby streets of the city, where the multitudes were continuing to arrive to witness the extraordinary event.

"Soldiers and citizens!" the Emperor shouted. "I come before you to plead your impartial judgment for the step I am about to take." The crowd fell silent as his words echoed along the sides of the stone buildings ringing the plaza, and were taken up and reechoed by the relays of heralds.

"As you are aware, the barbarians, as if to appease their unhallowed gods with an offering of Roman blood, have disturbed the peace of our western frontier, and are raging through Gaul. In so doing, they are relying on the fact that harsh necessity requires that my attention be devoted to events at the other end of the Empire. If this mischief is countered while there is still time, by measures that have your united support, the criminal insolence of these animals will subside, and the Empire's frontiers will remain sacrosanct. It is for you to strengthen my hope for the future, and to approve my decision."

He paused a moment to allow the heralds time to relay his words. The soldiers in the front ranks stared up with wide eyes beneath their bronze visors, at the Emperor and his young cousin, who slouched beside him.

"You see before you: our Julian!" he resumed with a bellow. "My cousin! As dear to me for his personal qualities as for his kinship, a man of exceeding intelligence! It is Julian whom I propose to elevate to the rank of Caesar, to serve directly under me in my capacity as Augustus, a proposal which must be ratified by you, should you deign to grant your approval."

Constantius again paused for a moment, to allow the expected applause and shouts of acclamation to rise from the crowd. What we heard instead was puzzled muttering among the troops, broken only by the receding calls of the heralds in the distance. Julian seemed to shrink even further into himself with embarrassment. Constantius, determined to wring an acclamation out of the crowd if he had to stand there all night, had just taken a breath to begin his harangue again, when a single centurion rose and shouted enthusiastically that it was the will of God. *"Ave, Julianus Caesar!"* he cried. The man had obviously been planted in advance.

Nevertheless, the men in that centurion's company joined in their leader's example. *"Ave, Julianus Caesar!"* cried sixty or seventy other desultory voices, a shout that was immediately taken up by several other companies scattered around the plaza and by the heralds on the perimeter, themselves doing their level best to stir the crowd's excitement. Slowly, almost reluctantly, the volume of cheers mounted, filling the plaza and spreading to the mob thronging the streets beyond.

Constantius' round, sweating face broke into a broad smile. As he turned to Julian, his mouth remained fixed in its grin, though his eyes narrowed. Glancing briefly to a point behind his cousin, he gave a slight nod. Immediately an enormous eunuch, a Sicilian giant who normally performed menial tasks around the palace, stepped forward, dressed in the elaborate furs and plaid cloth breeches of a Gallic chieftain, his face painted with horrifying blue stripes, a gaudy hairpiece with long russet braids draping down his back, silver serpent-shaped bangles clamped around his massive biceps. The crowd fell into awestruck silence as the man walked ponderously to Julian's side, carrying a large bundle, which he shook out with a deliberate, dramatic flourish. He draped the heavy purple embroidered cloak over the new Caesar's shoulders and fell prostrate at the young man's feet in a position of abject fear.

As Julian stood staring in a combination of wonder and mortification at the huge trembling man, another roar went up from the crowd, this time accompanied by the deafening rattle of shields as the troops clashed them against their knees with a fearsome din. It was only later, after my careful explanation to him, that he understood that this was an indication of the troops' complete approval, and was, in fact, much to be preferred to their striking their shields with their spears, a sign of rage and grief.

"Beloved cousin!" Constantius shouted above the roar. "You have thus attained, while still young, the distinction for which you were destined by your ancestry. Be therefore my partner in toil, my colleague in danger! Assume for yourself the government of Gaul! Relieve its suffering people by generous treatment! Meet the enemy in battle, and raise high the standards of your legions! Command these men, whose valor matches your own! We will wage war simultaneously; we will aid one another with constant and mutual affection; and God willing, we will govern together, collaborators in righteousness and humility, over a world finally at peace."

The men cheered wildly, and the Emperor raised Julian's hand in his own, high over their heads, acknowledging the vast and rather incompetently choreographed demonstration of approval. When the applause continued even after many moments, Constantius led him to a sedan chair that had been positioned at the side of the platform, and which was borne by eight slaves, all of them costumed identically as fierce Gallic warriors. After the Emperor and his new Caesar had clambered onto the broad, carved, and curtained bench, the slaves carefully lifted their poles and lumbered, rocking, around the circuit of the massive plaza to the general acclaim of the thronging crowd. They were led by a squad of fifty hard-muscled Praetorians who cleared a path through the mob, sometimes with the flats of their swords. Julian stared out into the middle distance, his expression impossible to read. The slaves finally conveyed the two men back to the foot of the platform, where they stepped out and with a concluding wave, walked arm in arm back through the double doors into the reception hall.

Once inside, Julian threw off the stifling purple cloak and stuffed it into the arms of the nearest slave, as Constantius watched coldly, though with an amused gleam in his eye.

"You might have warned me," Julian muttered accusingly, certain now of his physical safety for at least the time being, and unconcerned with any offense he might give to the Emperor. "I have been weeks in Milan, begging you for an answer, any answer, as to why you might have brought me here. And this is how you tell me?"

Constantius snorted. "A life of command is full of surprises, young Julian. To this you must become accustomed." He paused, and then glanced at his young cousin with a wry smile. "Actually, I confess I may be as astonished as you. As late as yesterday, I was still undecided as to whether to erect a gallows or an investiture platform.

You should be down on your knees thanking God. You have a very persuasive patroness in the palace."

Julian stared, bewildered. "Persuasive?" he said. "This is a reward? You pluck a poor student from his studies, make him commander of six legions, and order him to defend Gaul? This is merely a slower form of execution than the one you had planned! 'Shrouded in death's dark purple by almighty fate . . .' "

Constantius chuckled. "Very perceptive of you—and clever use of Homer, though somewhat melodramatic, I would say. But please—don't flatter yourself that you will actually have any role in commanding these men. You would merely be in the way. The western legions will remain under the control of Ursicinus and Marcellus. Barbatio will assist in several capacities, as he has in the past. With you as Caesar, the Empress Eusebia is content, though only God knows why. With Marcellus in command, my generals are content. And you, my boy, will enjoy the ride and keep your nose out of the way."

Barbatio, standing behind the Emperor, stared coldly over his patron's shoulder at the younger man, his face betraying the hatred he felt for this latest young cousin of Constantius to have been vested with the purple, for no reason other than a tenuous blood relationship. Julian avoided his glare, focusing instead on the Emperor, amazed at his words.

"You mean to say I have no duties?" he inquired, astonished.

The Emperor chuckled. "Only one. Since you so rudely insist upon being forewarned about plans that affect your little life, I will do so now. You have met my sister Helena, your cousin? No, of course not. You will soon enough. In two days' time you will be marrying her." And nodding to his courtiers he strode away from the astonished Julian, resuming his earlier conversation with Barbatio as if all the events of that morning had been of no more consequence than a review of his troops.

VI

The next day, upon entering the gynaeceum escorted by me, the trusted family physician, harmless as an elderly eunuch and familiar as a lapdog, Julian marched directly to the couch on which the veiled empress was casually reclining, talking quietly with several of her ladies nearby, and knelt down on one knee. She glanced at him quickly, nodded to me politely where I knelt next to him, and then returned to finish the quiet conversation she was having. During this interval I took the opportunity to peer discreetly from beneath my brows in frank appraisal of the Empress. Though I am a professional, I am still a man, and though a Christian, I have not forsaken the appreciation of beauty.

She was a woman of exquisite taste, and with all the wealth of Rome and the goods of the world at her disposal, she had not stinted on her appearance. Indeed, I often marveled at the fact that rather than the fine linens and wools worn by most ladies of the court during the cool fall season, she still preferred the soft, clinging cotton shipped from India, and the lovely antique silks that had been carried painstakingly by caravan from China a century before, when the Parthian peace had still held. In these two materials she had draped herself voluminously yet delicately for this meeting, in the fashion of the day. The long, blindingly white cotton upper tunic fitted her body closely. A gauzy, almost transparent silken veil was thrown casually over her head and face, streaming over her shoulders and reaching down to her feet. The fabric hid and yet revealed in its folds the contours of her face, the whiteness of her teeth and eyes, and the long, olive smoothness of her slender upper arms. Around the hem of her tunic a purple braid embroidered in gold had been painstakingly stitched, a sign of her exalted status. This was matched by a similar braid fastened tightly around her slender waist, setting off the rounded fullness of her breasts and hips. Her jewelry was simple yet costly: a golden diadem in her hair, set with a single pearl; matching pearls in tiny rings on her ears; and a simple pendant on her breast. I was always pleasantly surprised to see that she had not succumbed to the current fashion of multiple bracelets, rings, and ankle circlets, for like the Greek sculptors, I detest such trappings as interruptions in the otherwise smooth, harmonious flow of the female form—from rounded shoulder to gently curved fingertip, from soft, white thigh to arched toe, an unbroken, gently undulating line that achieves perfection in its continuity and for which even the most intricately wrought Spanish silver clasp is an unendurable violation of purity.

I glanced sidelong at Julian and saw that he, too, was surreptitiously peering up at the Empress under raised brows. I returned my glance forward, and as my eyes traveled stealthily up her body to her face, I was surprised to find that even as she was talking with her maidservant, she was looking at Julian, appraising him quite as frankly as he was her; indeed, I noticed with some amusement, she was actually watching him watch her, and moreover seemed quite unabashed, even fascinated at what she saw. I raised my head as her conversation came to a close, and noted with disappointment her silent gesture with one finger of her right hand, indicating to her companions, and to me, to leave her alone with Julian.

The door clicked softly shut behind me, but Julian afterwards recounted the extraordinary conversation he had had with the Empress.

"I have long wished to meet you, my lady," he began,

"and express to you my gratitude for the books and kind words you delivered to me during my wait."

There was tinkling laughter behind the veil, which he found oddly familiar.

"I'm so glad you were able to enjoy them," she said in her warm and unprepossessing voice. "Was Plotinus properly filed, then?"

Julian looked up, startled.

"You . . . you're the cleaning girl that replaced Lucilla. . . . I mean . . . begging your pardon, Your Highness, but . . ."

Eusebia looked down at him in amusement and carefully drew back the veil, folding it across the top of her head. "You didn't know it was me, then? Oh, I am indeed delighted!"

He was stunned. "But, Your Highness, why? After all my pleading for an audience, why did you not reveal yourself to me?"

"What, you are asking me now why I did not visit you alone in your rooms, without the Emperor's consent?" She laughed teasingly. "My poor bewildered cousin-in-law. I am as fond of my head's position on my own two shoulders as I'm sure you are of yours."

She continued to laugh, then sat up on the couch.

"Though you didn't think I would propose you for the rank of Caesar without first obtaining a proper glimpse of you myself?" she asked slyly. "A woman may marry her husband sight unseen, as I did, but she does not make such a blind choice twice in her life. After all, when you arrived at Milan, your career, indeed your life, Julian, could have taken either of two different paths. To the extent that I could have an impact on the Emperor by . . . assisting him in his decision, I wished to have every possible fact at my disposal."

At this he remained silent, at a loss for words. He was overwhelmed by her beauty, as he had not been by that of any woman before, for never in his short, sheltered life had he been in the presence of a female quite so lovely, and so powerful. The combination was intoxicating, suffocating, even, and he felt the room become suddenly very hot, the air stifling. He kept his eyes fixed upon the ground for a long moment, while she looked on in bemused detachment. Finally standing up, she walked slowly toward him, and placing her hand lightly under his chin lifted his face to meet her eyes, and with a smile gestured to him to rise.

He was surprised, when he did so, at her stature, for though he was only of medium height for a man, she was of extraordinary height for a woman, standing fully as tall as him, while wearing only her thin palace slippers. She seemed to have no compunction about compressing the aloof distance she usually maintained with her staff, and stood facing him barely a foot away, her shoulders back and spine straight, almost in a military stance, but with the laughing gleam in her eye and the smooth lines of her cheek effacing any thoughts of the harshness of command. Most disconcerting of all to Julian, as he recounted it to me afterwards, was the soft contours of her breasts, mere inches from his chest, their swelling outline visible beneath the quilted silken robe draped over her body. Unlike a physician, Julian had had little contact or experience with the female form, and her extraordinary beauty was something to which I was so accustomed that I had not even bothered to describe it to Julian beforehand. As she stood facing him, he forced himself with a supreme effort not to step back or look down, either of which might have been interpreted by the Empress as an insult or an indication of fear on his part. Rather, he stood straight and immobile, facing her, his eyes focused on a point beyond the top of her head. A trickle of sweat ran down his side under his left arm, soaking into the belt of his tunic, making him long to scratch his ribs.

She examined his face carefully. "Certain things you have already received from us," she said, using the royal plural, "and if God wills it, you will receive others. This is provided that you prove to be faithful and honest toward us."

"You know I am grateful for all you have done, my

Empress. I would be honored to be of service in any way
I am able."

Eusebia again examined his face, though this time her
eyes were not smiling as before.

"I assume you have been told by our physician Caesarius
about the Emperor's . . . condition?"

Julian blushed, and gracefully lied. "I would not presume to discuss such intimate matters with one outside the
family, my lady. . . ."

She tossed her head impatiently. "Nonsense. He is a fine
physician, and completely trusted by all within the royal
family. Besides, the entire palace knows, and is aware of
the awkward position in which it has placed us both—us
all. Julian—I have been watching you for many months,
since long before you arrived in Milan, and I gratefully
accept your offer of assistance."

"I don't understand, my lady. . . ."

At this, with a slight flick of her thumb and forefinger,
she opened the clasp at the top of her robe and the two
sides of the rich fabric fell away, revealing the creamy
white skin of her breasts and her taut, dusky nipples. Beyond that he dared not glance, though he confessed to me
that his mind and his feverish imagination raced. He
quickly diverted his eyes to her face, though he found no
comfort there, either, in the penetrating stare she had locked
on him. Eusebia swayed slightly, and although she did not
move her feet she seemed to imperceptibly lean forward
toward him. Though still several inches away, he could
almost feel the heat of her breasts penetrating through his
own padded linen tunic, and just as imperceptibly, he
leaned backward the same distance.

"Julian," she said, her voice husky and her eyes pleading, "I am not making my choice blindly. . . ."

His eyes opened wide and his thoughts tumbled over one
another, as did mine when I first heard this story from his
lips. Never, with the possible exception of when he had
first received the Emperor's summons to Milan, had he felt
himself to be in such danger, or in such temptation. He

screwed his eyes shut for a moment and tried to think. Acceptance of the Empress's ultimate gift, or rejection— by which path did he stand to gain or lose more? He needed time, he had to buy time. In anguish, he resorted to the arguments of human biology, which, in fact, I myself had taught him only the previous day in preparation for his impending marriage to Helena.

"Your Highness—this is exceedingly dangerous. What if you should find yourself with child?"

"My cycle is quite regular and has been accurately timed. Now is the perfect opportunity."

"To avoid pregnancy?"

She stared at him evenly. "On the contrary, Julian—to ensure it."

He stared back. All things now became clear. The Emperor was without an heir, and blaming Eusebia for his own poor performance and physical limitations. Eusebia's position as Mother of the Empire was consequently threatened. An heir must be produced—but from where? Only a family member could produce one with the necessary physical similarities, only a devout Christian and an ascetic could be trusted to provide the service confidentially, only a newly appointed Caesar would have the political stature to ensure the offspring's survival should questions arise about its paternity, only a man soon to become a member of the imperial household could gain the requisite access to the gynaeceum to do the deed; most important, only one man was suitably moronic and lacking in ambition as to be sufficiently trusted by the Emperor at this crucial juncture. All the pieces fell into place in a flash, and Julian could suddenly see the role he had been chosen to play. All of it fit perfectly, except when it came to his own conscience.

He continued to stall. "Your Highness, I am deeply flattered—"

She rolled her eyes in exasperation.

"It is not a matter of flattery, I assure you," she interrupted. "Though you are a reasonably attractive man, my dear cousin-in-law, the palace is full of such men. Even the eunuchs could satisfy, if it were merely a matter of a woman's satisfaction. No, Julian, it is a matter of necessity, for both me and the Empire."

"But you are my cousin's wife. I am to be married tomorrow to Helena. That would make it a double betrayal on my part, not to mention the injustice I would be doing to you."

She stared at him in amazement, and then her face took on the hard lines of a sneer. "So plump little Helena is Penelope to your Odysseus?" she retorted. "While I, the wicked Calypso, am so besotted with your beauty that I must use my superior powers to trap you and keep you for my own? Go back and read your Homer, my scholar. Even Odysseus was wise enough to realize that when the goddess crooks a finger, you don't plead a headache."

With that she jerked her robe shut, spun with a flourish, and marched wordlessly out of the room, leaving Julian to make his way out alone to the anteroom, where I found him red-faced in frustration and humiliation, his mind in turmoil and his lower tunic disturbingly askew.

VII

He did not see Eusebia privately again, for the palace was sufficiently large that they could easily avoid each other while making plans for the departure to Gaul and his marriage to Helena. At the sumptuous wedding, with the Basilica illumined by the light of ten thousand candles, glinting ten thousand times more in the polished glaze of the windows and the gold of the chalices and monstrances, he glanced up at the Empress while intoning the Creed. He saw what he thought was a flash of dark eyes behind the thin veil she always wore in public, and even in the act of getting married, he confessed, he flattered himself with the thought that he was one of the very few men in the Basilica, indeed in all of the Empire, who had actually seen the Empress's face, and more.

Plump, homely Helena was as presentable as she ever would be, in the wedding raiment dictated by ancient custom: the unhemmed tunic secured around her ample waist by a girdle of wool with a double knot, covered by a fine saffron-colored cloak, matching sandals, and a thin metal collar worn tightly about her neck. Over her delicate coiffure she wore a *flammeum,* a veil of flaming orange, to modestly shield the upper half of her face. The veil was secured to her head by a simple wreath of myrtle and orange blossoms taken from the palace hothouses, and she carried a single, pure white candle in her hands. She looked for all the world like a rather heavier version of the vestal virgins. The normal unruliness of her thick, black hair had been tamed into six complexly braided plaits as is customary for a bride. They had been fastened with the traditional iron spearhead whose point had been bent, which was said by her mother to have been the tip of a lance taken long ago from the dead body of a gladiator, when such weapons were held to have some mysterious powers of their own. Her face was almost the precise image of her brother's, though lacking the spark of malevolent intelligence.

After he had intoned the solemn oath and had received her corresponding response—*Ubi tu Julianus, ego Helena*—the mercifully short ceremony was deemed complete, and he lifted the veil of his new bride. At first, he said, when looking into her eyes, he felt simultaneously charity for her and pity for himself, as if he had made a great sacrifice for the sake of duty, though what precisely that sacrifice might have been, he could not tell me then. His greatest concern, upon leaving the Basilica and striding with Helena to the designated bridal chambers, was how he was expected to lift her over the threshold.

The days following the wedding were spent in a whirlwind of preparations for Julian's departure to Gaul. This process was, if anything, as frustrating and maddening to the newly minted Caesar as had been the weeks of waiting in the villa for Constantius' summons. The Emperor was even more imperious toward his young cousin than he had been before, though he mostly managed to ignore him completely. On occasions when they were compelled to be seen together, for official ceremonies and the like, the Emperor forced a false fatherly attitude that Julian and the rest of us watching had to grit our teeth to endure. The eunuchs followed suit; as they passed by the young Caesar, they walked almost *through* him, as if he were no more than a shade, or at best a mendicant who had mistakenly wandered into the palace and was to be politely ignored until he found his way back out again. Nor was the Empress Eusebia of any assistance, as she had been before Julian's investiture;

his abrupt rejection of her favors had seen to that. He wandered the corridors in a daze, in a splendid yet severe captivity, seeking me out when he could, though the frequent importunings of the Emperor and Empress ensured that I had little time to spare for consoling him.

Two events cheered him considerably, however. One was the arrival in Milan of his personal physician, a jolly but wheezing satyr named Oribasius who had attended to the health and diet of Julian and his brother until their adult years. When the boys had moved on with their studies and careers, Oribasius had pleaded that his asthma was worsening and stepped into an early retirement, which he spent compiling an enormous, and largely plagiarized, medical encyclopedia. Constantius had insisted that a man of the rank of Caesar not travel on such an arduous journey unaccompanied by a personal physician, and, at Julian's look of incomprehension, had taken it upon himself to send a squad of guards to Oribasius' home on the outskirts of Constantinople, and drag him bodily, if need be, to Milan. Force, as it transpired, was unnecessary, for Oribasius had been bored out of his wits in his research, and welcomed the relief from his daily routine of dictating and filing. Though Julian was overjoyed at Oribasius' arrival, I myself was less than pleased at the physician's condition, for he was a specimen singularly ill-suited for harsh service in Gaul—he was as flabby as Constantius, though approximately the same age, and bore a severe limp in *both* legs, if that is possible, suffering simultaneously from arthritis and gout. I feared the physician was to be more of a patient than a healer on such a strenuous trek.

The Caesar's other source of cheer, to the great surprise of all, was his new wife. During his days of wandering the halls before the departure for Gaul, and indeed later on the trip itself, Julian took his newfound responsibilities as husband and lover quite seriously for someone who, to my knowledge, had never in his life been with a woman; and he made considerable effort to gain familiarity with the mind of his new bride. Helena was four years older than he, and an odder match you have never seen, particularly one for a Caesar. Though outweighing him by some twenty stone, despite her shorter-than-average height, her temper was as sweet as her brother's was foul. She was still a virgin despite her years, and to my knowledge had never even had suitors. Constantius' viciousness and fickleness had dissuaded them, even those who might otherwise have overcome their natural aversion to her homeliness in exchange for a chance at becoming Caesar and ultimately Emperor. Julian, however, had unwittingly stumbled onto the entire package, but was determined to take his vows seriously, and to make the best of the bewildering situation.

As for the preparations for departure: haste was imperative, since by now public reports of the disaster in Germany were beginning to trickle in, and it would be impossible to keep news of the situation confidential much longer. Julian, Constantius reasoned, had to be put on the road and be well on his way to his destination before he had an opportunity to hear confirmation of the ugly rumors or portents, and decide to escape altogether on the next mule train to the coast. The Emperor himself, in fact, had resolved to accompany the party several days out of Milan, to ensure the stiffness of his new second-in-command's backbone.

When the time finally arrived for the departure for Gaul, a blustery day in November, the young Caesar climbed into his sedan chair for the ceremonial ride out of the city next to the matching chair of his new bride, who had resolved to accompany her husband. Her bearers, however, labored hard under the weight of their burden, and each uttered a prayer to the aforementioned virgin Saint Lucia, who, when seized by Diocletian's agents to be taken away for martyr-dom, was rendered immovable by her great weight. Constantius and his enormous retinue, including myself, were accompanied by a detachment of what the Emperor referred to as top-tier, handpicked, crack soldiers to serve as the new Caesar's guard. To my way of thinking, Brother, they were the most poorly trained, underfed lot of conscripts I have ever had the displeasure of marching with. Julian himself observed that the only thing these soldiers seemed to know how to do was pray, which strangely, and somewhat unnervingly, they did incessantly, at all hours of the day and night, both singly and in groups, and perhaps it was this that later allowed us to successfully cross the Alps in the middle of December without losing a single man. If the efficacy of their praying can indeed be proven, and I'm sure, Brother, that you would be loath for me to even consider otherwise, then they were possibly the most effective detachment of soldiers the Emperor could have assigned us.

It was not until the party arrived at the designated point of separation, a place lying between Laumello and Pavia marked by two columns, that Julian was informed of the fall of Cologne. I was in the tent in attendance upon Constantius at the time, treating one of his endless series of ailments and goiters, and when the news of Cologne was imparted Julian stared in wide-eyed astonishment, and then swore at his cousin so brashly and spontaneously that Helena, who was also present in the Emperor's tent at the time, burst into tears. Constantius was not in the least put out, however, and did not even lose the smirk he had been wearing almost every moment since Julian's investiture.

"So, little cousin," he said, "is this the eloquence they teach you at the vaunted Academy at Athens? All the better that we remove you and put you among the foot soldiers where you belong."

Julian glared. "You brought me to this, Constantius—you set me up for failure. Why you didn't simply make a clean break of me, I can't imagine."

"Ah, Julian—because you're family! And you may be the only man in the entire Empire who would possibly complain at all you've been given. Now listen, ingrate: you are now traveling beyond my control. No more of your conferences with magicians, no more of your research into the nature of the pagan gods. Believe it or not, I know of your frolic with the Eleusinians in Athens. From this point on, you represent me, and the One Church. No one and nothing else. Forget that at your own peril, boy."

I suddenly realized the significance of the benighted ascetics that Constantius had dressed in soldiers' togs and sent as protection. Julian spun in a fury, strode to the waiting sedan chair, and climbed in, angrily snapping shut the curtains.

Completely on the spur of the moment, out of fear for the young Caesar's safety on his journey, I approached the Emperor a moment later, just as his own sedan chair was about to be lifted to be carried back to Milan.

"My lord," I began, "as you know, the Caesar has been like a brother to me since our initial acquaintance in Athens. Please—allow me to accompany him the rest of the journey to his headquarters in Gaul. There are many other fine physicians in Milan who will be able to attend you in the interim—but as for your cousin, there is only Oribasius, who despite his wisdom is quite beyond his capacity when it comes to caring for the Caesar on such a journey."

The Emperor looked down at me haughtily, glad to be done with Julian and impatient to return to the more pressing business of his eastern front. He seemed positively irritated at my request, not so much at losing me as at being reminded of a problem he thought he had finally eliminated several moments before.

"Yes, yes . . ." he said, waving me off absentmindedly as he scanned a dispatch one of his generals had handed him. "Just return, will you, after his arrival at Vienne?"

He gave no thought, I noticed, as to precisely how I was to return back through the mountains in the dead of winter. The Empress, upon hearing my request, looked at me in alarm, and opened her mouth as if to say something to the Emperor about the inadvisability of my leaving them. Constantius, however, was already deep in a conversation about the eastern question and could not be distracted. I turned before the Empress could say anything to detain me, raced back to the tent and to my waiting luggage, threw it upon the horse, and galloped after Julian's train, which had just departed.

I rode up immediately to his chair and announced somewhat breathlessly that he would have an additional man for company, if he would agree to take me on. His face was still flushed in anger, but turning his head he looked at me with some surprise. It took a moment for my words to sink in, but when they did his expression immediately softened, and he stretched his hand out the litter with a broad grin and slapped my forearm in delight.

"What, you're traveling with me, then? And all the way to Gaul? I saw you riding behind us just now, but I assumed you were simply being a friend and walking me out into the street, rather than merely to the threshold."

I grinned back. "A truer friend than you expected," I said. "I've requested leave from Constantius. A sabbatical, if you will. Just until I see you safely installed in one of those secure little log huts the commanders dwell in on campaign."

Helena beamed at the news of my accompanying them, for I had been her physician at the court as well as her brother's, and she was as much a hypochondriac as he. Julian, however, simply continued to stare at me with wide eyes, his face pale as the enormity of his situation slowly sunk in.

"Caesarius," he confided, "I truly had high expectations for this journey, indeed for this entire new phase of my life. The fall of Cologne, however, is a terrible portent, don't you agree?"

I stalled for an answer, unsure whether to inform him that I had already known of the disaster for some time. "It's nothing, I'm sure, that a firm hand against the barbarians cannot resolve before the next year is out."

He thought for a moment in silence. "No doubt you're right. In any case, it doesn't matter. Caesarius, I've had plenty of time to myself over the last few days to consider what sort of Caesar I'm to be—or rather, what I will *not* be. I will not be a figurehead. I will *not* be the Emperor's puppet! It's beneath the dignity of a philosopher and a scholar to simply roll over and grovel to a man who outranks him not in intellect but merely in age and propensity to murder."

He must have noticed my horrified expression at these traitorous words, for his face immediately softened and he reached over again to tap my forearm.

"I'm sorry, friend, to burden you with my resentments," he continued. "But I'm delighted you'll be riding with us on this journey. I'm afraid I can't offer you more than a position as assistant physician, since lame Oribasius has been given the principal duty. Still, I welcome your company, because I don't see much opportunity for conversation among this lot of hermits. I fear, however . . ."

"What, Julian?" I asked. "You're the Caesar, the second most powerful man in the Empire. What is there to fear?"

"I'm Caesar in name only," he replied. "I fear that my promotion has gained me nothing but the prospect of death under more trying circumstances than otherwise."

"Surely you're not that pessimistic?"

He smiled. "No, to tell the truth, I am not, particularly since I resolved to take some control of this wretched situation. And now that I know you'll be staying with us, friend, I am considerably cheered."

"I'm happy to hear that."

He smiled wryly. "At least now I won't be dying alone."

BOOK TWO

GAUL

*The gods are hard to deal with when
seen in all their glory.*

—HOMER

I

Gallia est omnis divisa in partes tres. So begins the famous treatise by the prince of military chroniclers, the deified Julius, on his conquest of Gaul, which I undertook to reread on our journey with an interest and imperative that had been entirely lacking during my schoolboy studies of the text, when I had been forced to focus more on the rigor and elegance of the general's Latin prose than on the concerns of his military strategy.

All Gaul is divided into three parts. Now, since as Virgil said, "A greater theme appears before me, and I take up a grander task," this seems the time to step back for a moment, to briefly examine the region to which fate had brought us. Much has changed since Julius Caesar and his legions swept through the hinterlands of Gaul four hundred years ago, bringing fire and devastation to hundreds of barbarian villages and towns, killing and enslaving a million men, entirely effacing from history and existence countless tribes and their distinguishing characteristics. The three original tribal divisions, the Belgae, the Aquitani, and the Celts, have largely been eliminated for all but administrative purposes and the occasional inter-legion athletic rivalry. Scarcely any traces remain of the once proud nations whose names struck fear into the first Roman settlers in the region: the Treviri, who were nearest the river Rhine; the Remi and other Belgians; the Santoni and the painted Veneti; the mysterious Morini and Menapii, who dwelt in the vast, misty ranges of the Black Forest and swamps; the strong-limbed Pleumoxii and the Parisii of Lutecia; the Aulerci Brannovices and their sister nations, the Aulerci Eburovices and the Aulerci Cenomani; the Lemovice and the other tribes whose territories adjoined the ocean; the warlike Bellovaci, the naked Atrebates, and all those in the states on the remote Celtic peninsula, who in their dialect were called the Armoricae; all are gone.

In their place, the broad empty plains, dark forests, and savage seacoasts of Gaul have been tamed, molded, and shaped, and brought wholly within the cultural and economic confines of the Roman Empire. No longer are the tall and fair-skinned men, whose savage glares and fierce natures once used to frighten outsiders, a source of wonder. The Gallic women of old, terrifying warrioresses who with swollen necks and gnashing teeth were known to swing their great white arms and deliver rains of deadly punches and kicks on their enemies and husbands alike, have softened and cultured over time into witty and intelligent maidens whose presence would successfully adorn the palace of even a Roman emperor. Where once rude wooden palisades protected thatch-roofed huts from invasions by wolves, bears, and nomadic tribes, powerful and wealthy Roman cities now flourish, from Marseilles on the Mediterranean coast to Paris in the north. Gauls have become Roman citizens and have served in the highest spheres of the Empire's administration and military. The Gallic legions are known and feared across the world for their magnificent stature, fierce bravery, and utter fealty to the Emperor. Sophisticated libraries, monuments, and churches now dot the landscape. The great Christian theologian Irenaeus, adversary of the Gnostics, hailed from the city of Lyons; and even the tiniest villages, from the remote mountain aerie of Venasque in the south, to Bourc'h Baz on the vast salt and salicorn marshes of the Celtic peninsula to the far northwest, are protected by the thick stone walls and auxiliary garrisons that are a veritable extension of the might of Rome itself.

Gaul has become Roman; indeed, it has become Rome. And the Germanic invasion of Gaul was therefore a strike at the heart of Rome itself.

II

The day after departing from the Emperor's camp, Julian remained closeted in his litter, brooding.

I spurred my horse up through the straggling ascetics as they struggled to keep up with the indefatigable sedan-bearers. The exhausted, unfit recruits stared longingly at my horse, and then continued with their uneven strides. They were laughable for men playing the part of Roman soldiers, though they themselves saw nothing humorous in their situation; nor did I, considering the fact that within two weeks' time we would be passing through territory that had recently been subject to bloody raids from roving bands of Alemanni warriors. *Almighty God*, I prayed: *Thank you for the spiritual support you have provided us in the person of these monks; a few good archers, however, would have been even more welcome.*

Trotting up to Julian's litter, I greeted him warmly, and he absentmindedly drew back the curtain. Helena, riding in a separate litter behind, remained veiled. A group of hermit soldiers behind us broke into an ill-tuned but enthusiastic hymn, to raise their spirits.

"Caesar . . ." I began, but he waved me off wearily.

"Don't mock me, Caesarius. I've always been simply Julian to you, and just because I've been invested with a sham title doesn't make me royalty. My own name will do perfectly well."

He smiled wanly, closing his eyes for a moment as if in great weariness.

"I didn't sleep well last night," he said, after a pause. "The pressures of command, I imagine, if you can call them that. How ironic. Following the path of my predecessor, Julius Caesar, to recapture what he had so brutally and magnificently seized four hundred years ago. Is it man's destiny to constantly repeat his mistakes, to gain Rome and then lose it?"

"That is not his destiny, but it is his will. May I speak with you frankly?"

"I would have it no other way."

"You are on your own now, all the way to Vienne. That is dangerous. You are your own master, for the first time in months, perhaps in your entire life. That is a boon. You have three hundred sixty singing monks, who at this point are more a source of amusement than protection. That is potentially . . . well . . . whatever we make it to be. You also have an ample supply train, though precisely what supplies it contains is anyone's guess, for the Emperor appears to have neglected to assign you a quartermaster. And you have four Roman army officers to advise you, several of whom, I'm afraid, are rather on the knavish side."

At this, Julian straightened out of his lethargic slouch and looked up at me with frank interest.

"Perhaps," I continued tentatively, "this would be a good time to discuss the qualities of your 'advisers'? At least as far as I know them?"

"And how far do you know them?"

"I confess that it is largely by observation, rather than firsthand acquaintance. But I am a physician, Julian—I have some skill at diagnosing men, both body and temperament. I have lived at court, I have heard the eunuchs and courtiers whisper, I have seen whom the Emperor trusts, whom he despises—"

"Enough!" Julian interrupted with an uneasy chuckle. "No need to display your credentials, I'm convinced. By all means—tell me about my 'advisers.' "

I looked curiously at the litter-bearers, whose hooded

gazes betrayed no interest in our conversation, but who were within easy earshot nevertheless.

"Perhaps we should speak in Greek," I suggested, to which he nodded his relieved consent.

"The first two of your advisers," I continued, "are Pentadius and Gaudentius. If I did not already know that Constantius has no sense of humor, I would think that these jackasses had been assigned to you as a joke. They are utterly worthless as officers, though they have on occasion proven their skills at pandering and pimping for the generals they have served. I can't imagine that the Emperor thought they could be of use to you, so I can only conclude that he sent them to relieve himself of the burden of maintaining them in Milan. In any event, they're yours now, until you decide how best to chase them off."

Julian sighed. "Another fine omen for beginning our journey. Who else do we have?"

I paused. "The third man is Paul, who is not actually an officer, but rather a sycophant of Constantius, and a spy."

"You mean the Spaniard, the one they call the Chain? He looks innocent enough but I notice he always seems to be whispering in the Emperor's ear."

"The same," I confirmed, "much to your ill-fortune."

"Oh? Why that epithet, the Chain?"

"He gained it several years ago, when the Emperor sent him to Britain to fetch back certain officers who had been accused of conspiracy. He went far beyond his original instructions, and descended like a whirlwind over the entire province, seizing goods and chattel and even entire estates in the name of Constantius. He placed a huge number of free men and citizens in handcuffs, and patched together a fabric of false accusations. He finally returned to the Emperor's palace steeped in blood, and trailing a chain of prisoners behind him in squalid misery. When they arrived, he even advised the executioner as to which types of hooks and instruments of torture would be most effective on which prisoners to make them confess their imaginary crimes. Since then he's been known as Paul the Chain."

Julian stared at me. "Unbelievable. This is a man my cousin has sent to accompany me?"

I nodded.

"So what am I expected to do with him?"

I shrugged. "Keep him as far from you as possible, I suppose."

He turned and gazed straight ahead with a shocked look on his face. "So we have two pimps and a spy. Who is the fourth man, Caesarius?"

"Him I do not know. He joined us in camp only last night. A nobleman by his bearing. He keeps apart from the other three when traveling. Perhaps that is a good sign."

"Indeed." Julian pursed his lips and thought silently for a moment. "Call him over here, please. I should like to have a word with this man."

I dropped back to fetch the stranger from where he was riding in the very last ranks, seeking out stragglers who were attempting to sit at the side of the road, and swatting them with his sword. He was a tall, thin man, almost gaunt, with piercing blue eyes and a long ridged nose that betrayed a non-Roman heritage. His skin was dark and leathery, like that of a peasant who has spent his entire life outdoors in the weather, yet his bearing was graceful, and his clothing, though plain, was of a quality and fit indicative of a cost far beyond the means of a mere officer. He was a silent man, preferring the Roman nobleman's habit of communicating orders by a mere finger gesture or a flicker of a glance; when he turned to my summons I noticed his entire body poise and tense, like that of a finely trained boar hound on the scent of his quarry. He spoke Latin with a stiff ease and a slightly lilting foreign intonation that was barely perceptible, and impossible for me to place—one of those foreigners who have been so well schooled that they speak Latin better than native Romans, thereby betraying their foreign origins by their ability to speak *too* correctly. He heard me out, and then, reluctantly it seemed, spurred his horse up to take his place at the side of the Caesar's rocking sedan chair, while I followed close behind.

When he arrived, he reined in his horse and saluted elegantly.

"You summoned me, Caesar?"

Julian looked at him. "You are the man who joined our party yesterday, just before we separated from the Emperor? I don't even know your name."

"Sallustius," the man said simply. "Secundus Saturninus Sallustius."

"Sallustius," Julian repeated thoughtfully. "An unusual name. Are you Roman?"

"I am. My father was a Romanized Gaul, a citizen and a nobleman, and I have been in the Emperor's service my entire career."

"Grew up—in Gaul?"

"Yes, Caesar. My father's estate was outside Marseilles."

"You are different from the other men my cousin has assigned me. What horrible crime have you committed to be given the pleasure of this feeble company?"

The man smiled sardonically. "I volunteered."

Julian almost choked. "Volunteered? Good God, why?"

The man looked carefully at him for a long moment. Finally, his gaze turned to its habitual position on the far horizon and he shrugged.

"Because I believe, I suppose," he said, switching effortlessly to Greek, much to Julian's surprise, "I believe that new blood is needed among Rome's command in Gaul. I believe that a man who comes from outside the standing school of plunder and abuse is needed to tame the province. If that means the Emperor's inexperienced young Greek-speaking cousin—then perhaps all the better."

Julian stared at him. "You know that is not my mandate from the Emperor."

Sallustius did not miss a beat. "I also believe that the Fates do not intend you to be a mere figurehead. And moreover, that you do not intend to be one either."

"So you feel there may be a purpose in this madness."

Sallustius shrugged again. "I don't claim to divine a purpose. I just don't see the situation as hopeless—yet. Beyond that I can express no opinion."

"Sallustius, assume you were in my shoes. What would you do now?"

The man spoke as if he had been waiting for precisely that question.

"You are the Caesar. You have been legitimately appointed, duly invested. Regardless of your experience, or lack of it, you have been given command of a province. You must identify your opportunities, seize the authority due you, and fill your role—the role of a *Caesar*."

Julian stared at him, wide-eyed, in silence. "That's the first time anyone has honestly said, in so many words, what I myself have felt ever since I was appointed to this wretched post."

"Because it's the truth. Your very survival depends upon it. And what is more—so does Rome's."

Julian took a deep breath and straightened his shoulders. Already, I could see, he was beginning to like and, more important, to trust this stranger. A hint of a smile appeared at his lips.

"Since you seem to have no qualms about speaking frankly, Sallustius, I will ask you again, and perhaps this time you will be more specific: If you were in my place, what would you do?"

Sallustius met his gaze and spoke quietly and evenly.

"First, make this mob march like a Roman cohort, or we will be meat for the barbarian wolves when we descend through the Alps."

"Can you do that?"

He thought for a moment. "I am not a professional military man, but yes, I have served my tours of duty. We will need to take some time off from the march to train. I'll need three weeks."

Julian scoffed. "It will soon be December. The passes will be closed by snow in a matter of days. I'll give you one week."

"Fair enough."

"And what would you have me do—be a soldier as well?"

"That, Caesar, is up to you. If you order me to, I will."

"I order you to. A good, solid Roman soldier. What should I do?"

"You may not wish to hear it."

"I am a philosopher. I take what life gives me."

The man paused and took a deep breath. Then he turned directly to Julian.

"Very well. First, get your ass out of that chair."

Julian stared in astonishment, and then the wry smile crept back to the corners of his mouth. Reverting to Latin, he called out to his bearers to stop and set him down.

With a collective sigh of relief, the entire procession stopped immediately, and the ascetics collapsed to the ground in exhaustion, praising God all the while. Julian stepped out of his sedan chair. I noticed the curtains on Helena's chair part, and her gauzily veiled face peer out curiously.

Sallustius dismounted and stood before him, towering over him by a full head.

"Next, remove the toga."

At this, Julian himself breathed an audible sigh of relief and stripped off the fussy ceremonial garment, with which he was forever fidgeting and tugging to keep properly aligned on his shoulders. He called to one of the sedan-bearers, who rummaged around in the duffel bag inside the compartment until he located an old, threadbare school tunic and a wool cloak, which Julian donned as protection from the air's coolness.

Sallustius stood appraising the Caesar's body critically, noting the thin chest and legs, the beginnings of a paunch.

"Are you fit?" he asked, somewhat doubtfully.

"I travel with my physician," Julian answered confidently, nodding at me. Sallustius looked briefly at me and snorted.

"That's not what I asked," he said. "I need to know how

strong you are. A weak body burdens the mind. The art of medicine has caused more harm in the world than all the sicknesses it claims to heal. I don't know what illnesses physicians are capable of healing, beyond binding up battle wounds, which I can do myself. But I do know the diseases they cause: laziness, credulity, fear of death. I don't care if they can make cadavers walk; what your crew needs is men, and your physician can't give us that."

Julian stood thunderstruck at this diatribe. He glanced at me with uncertainty, though under Sallustius' fierce glare he seemed unable to pronounce a challenge. Finally he found his voice.

"Homer said that one physician is worth many men."

"Then let Homer lead your troops."

Julian sighed in resignation. "What next?" he grumbled.

"No court sandals."

He looked down in surprise at his feet. He had worn the thin-soled, loosely strapped footwear his entire life, and it had never occurred to him that any other might be necessary.

"I can't go barefoot."

Sallustius looked back down the train and spied one of the supply wagons stopped a short distance away. Trotting over to it, he conferred briefly with the slave driving its mules, who flipped back a tarpaulin and began rummaging in some crates in the back, finally locating what Sallustius was seeking. He then trotted back to the Caesar, who was standing rather sheepishly before the staring crowd of ascetics and his wife, and handed him a pair of Roman army sandals.

Julian whistled audibly as he hefted them: a full half-inch of tanned ox hide, stiff as a board, with dozens of hobnails protruding from the sole for a better grip. Brass fittings protected the toe tips, and thick, pliable leather straps wrapped the ankle and calf almost to the knee. He tied the straps, then stood and stomped a few steps, stiff-legged.

"They feel like boats on my feet. Heavy boats." Then he slowly smiled. "Roman boats."

"You asked me what you should do."

"So I did. Now what?"

"Now march."

III

Thus began peaceful, scholarly Julian's ascent as a soldier, and it is doubtful that there had ever been a more inauspicious beginning to a warrior's career since Telemachus, who was denied the firm guidance of his kingly father Odysseus until the day he was suddenly thrust into battle against Penelope's hundred thirty-six suitors.

His training under Sallustius commenced, and the difficulty of the master's regime was exceeded only by the student's stubbornness. The Caesar had never in his life experienced the slightest physical hardship. Until this time, all his training had been of the mind: courses of philosophy, rhetoric and composition, Greek literary works of good authorship. You may have heard it sometimes argued that children of lesser parentage should not be educated, on the grounds that their best hopes for advancement are in the military. As the old saying goes, "A scholar made is a soldier betrayed." Such people point to the most fearsome of the barbarian nations, the Franks and the Huns, whose leaders are all soldiers by training and custom, and who denigrate book learning as unworthy of their skills. To my knowledge, however, in almost all cases truly successful military leaders are educated to at least some degree, or if they are not, they are ashamed of their ignorance and seek to remedy it.

Certainly Julian's education had not neglected the military classics, such as Thucydides' recounting of the war of thrice nine years between Sparta and Athens, and Themistogenes' shameless embellishment of Xenophon's Persian campaign. Nor was he ignorant of the devastation that had been wreaked on the Roman people by the Germanic tribes over the centuries: the loss of five entire armies, all commanded by Consuls; the destruction even of the supreme general Varus and three legions; how though the Germanics had actually been defeated several times, by Caius Marius in Italy, Julius in Gaul, and Tiberius and Germanicus in their native territories, it had been accomplished only with great difficulty and enormous loss of Roman life. Julian was well versed in strategic theory, the uses and benefits of diplomatic policy and coercion to facilitate military aims, and other such grand issues as are discussed at length in the classics. But when one's entire marching force in hostile territory consists of three hundred sixty footsore ascetics, and one's very survival is at stake, such lessons in international political theory and strategic military alliances are of little import. What Sallustius would seek to impress upon him both now and in the years to come were what I might term the lesser military arts: drill and basic tactics, military protocol, use of the bow, lance, and sword, and effective riding; and what Sallustius began with first was marching.

Dear God, Sallustius drilled us ceaselessly, and it was not a matter of doing so at leisure in a well-tended Field of Mars, for it was still necessary to make sufficient progress each day on our way to Vienne. For a solid week we practiced the Pyrrhic march-step and its related maneuvers to the maddeningly monotonous beat of a drum pounded by Sallustius himself, and the skirling of a pipe played haltingly by one of the hermits who had once as a boy, while working as a shepherd, taught himself a single tune, which he now repeated incessantly. Sallustius' only concession to the exigencies of travel was to allow us to halt our progress through the Alps perhaps one hour earlier each day than we otherwise would have, at which point he drilled us for another three hours under sodden, iron skies until the weaker ones collapsed with trembling knees, whispering prayers or curses under their breath, and Julian's face was drawn and ashen. The physician Oribasius refused even to watch after the first day or two, his pudgy hands fluttering helplessly and his balding head bobbing in distress. I marched every step of every drill along with the troops, if only to better perform my duty of monitoring Julian's health. The whole scene was the source of much hilarity to Pentadius and Gaudentius, who strove to do as little as possible to assist with Sallustius' efforts. Paul the Chain, for the most part, confined himself to his own tent, depriving us of his company, which few seemed to miss.

Happily, within two weeks of late-afternoon drill sessions, the ragged mob had begun to imitate a reasonable semblance of a Roman military detachment, at least in their marching order and discipline, which had naturally been Sallustius' first order of business. The older man's initial fear had been that if the Alemanni scouts we frequently saw spying on us from ridge tops had noted a chaotic, bedraggled band of civilians wending through the foothills in a long train, we would be ripe for attack and slaughter. This danger was now allayed, and as is often the case when discipline is established, morale increased as well. Indeed, I would even venture to say that this period may have been the happiest in Julian's entire life—for what young man would not be happy, after having been set free from a virtual captivity in a city he detested, by a man he loathed, to travel to new lands with a new wife, bearing the ring of a Caesar no less?

When after a month we finally arrived at the Roman city of Vienne, the capital of Gallia Viennensis, a hundred miles up the Rhone from its spill into the Mediterranean, it was to shouts of joy by our troops that could not have been more heartfelt than those exclaimed by Xenophon's men upon their first glimpse of the sea. And to the surprise and delight of all, their elation was matched by that of the people of the elegant city, who greeted Julian's arrival as if he were the answer to their prayers. They thronged the streets, flocking from the countryside miles around, like the crowds in Jerusalem that fateful day three centuries before, swelling the population of the city to thrice its normal size. They paraded before him on his route, singing the praises of the young commander who would rid them of the barbarians and restore them to their former prosperity. They gazed the more eagerly on his royal pomp because he was a lawfully invested prince; and they were amazed and delighted when his soldiers spontaneously broke out in a perfectly modulated hymn of glory and praise sung in ecclesiastical Latin, rather than the obscene camp ditties and rough marching tunes they were accustomed to hearing from entering soldiers.

That afternoon, Julian's warrior monks celebrated a solemn service at the Church of Saint Stephen in thanksgiving for their safe arrival, and Sallustius gave us our first reprieve in a month from his nightly drills, with the stern warning that they would recommence the next day. We then participated in a citywide banquet sponsored by some local patricians, consisting of five hundred roasted winter lambs, the first fresh meat we had eaten since departing Milan. The occasion was indeed historic—for even Sallustius smiled.

Later on, long after the last soldier had said his prayers and retired, Helena sent a messenger to the barracks where I was sharing a room with Oribasius, to fetch me to the Bishop's palace, where she and her husband had been temporarily lodged upon their arrival. I rode breathlessly on the horse the messenger had brought, concerned that Julian had somehow injured himself or become indisposed from his unaccustomed feasting that evening. Rather, it was she who was feeling out of sorts, with symptoms that would not normally have occasioned any alarm in a person experiencing them, but which were a source of concern to her, for being an exceptionally robust and healthy girl, with a naturally hearty appetite, she had never in her life felt even a twinge of indigestion of any kind.

I performed a cursory examination of her, familiar as I

was with her family history, and sooner than I expected, I left the bishop's residence smiling in relief, and with Helena blushing deeply at the results of my palpations and questioning.

The Caesar's wife was with child.

IV

News travels quickly in the Empire, and personal gossip more quickly still; one would have thought that the tidings of Helena's pregnancy had been transmitted by fire signal from tower to tower all the way to Milan, for not two weeks after my examination of her, Julian received a note from the Empress Eusebia—the first personal contact he had had from her since their unfortunate interview at the palace. It was a mere three paragraphs, actually, stating that she was just leaving to attend a state function, and was dashing this off to meet the deadline for the military courier's departure, but that she had heard the wonderful news that Helena was expecting a child, and wished to be the first from the imperial court to congratulate the happy couple on their good fortune. The letter was signed with broad strokes in a delightful flourish. After recovering from his initial surprise, Julian hastened to show the paper to his wife.

Helena, naturally enough, was proud and delighted, and quickly snatched the parchment away to be carefully preserved in an illuminated missal bound in carved ivory, which she carried with her on all her travels. Julian's fears as to Eusebia's ill will toward him were now dispelled, and he replied to her letter in tones as effusive as her own, praising her matronly guidance of the court, and extolling her wisdom and influence on the Emperor's decisions. His concerns about political intrigue at the court of Milan were now over, he felt; and with a clear mind, he was able to shift his focus to the matter at hand—establishing his position in Gaul.

Despite the general havoc the barbarians had been wreaking in the surrounding countryside, Vienne was an extraordinarily appropriate center for him to continue with his military and political education at the hands of Sallustius. Here, though it was only a provincial capital, Julian found a court and administrative center of quite some sophistication. It was the major city of the province, and through it flowed all the trade moving up and down the Rhone. The city was served by a well-maintained military road that passed through Lyons in the north and split into branches serving Reims and Paris in the northwest, and Strasbourg, Mainz, and Cologne in the northeast. The Roman army of Gaul was now in winter headquarters at Reims under General Marcellus, a cavalry officer whom Sallustius secretly scorned; and old Ursicinus, Marcellus' predecessor as commander of the army, whose well-deserved retirement Constantius had delayed in order for him to act as an adviser to, or observer of, his successor. As of yet, Julian had under his direct command in Vienne only the warrior monks who had accompanied him from Milan, and the garrisons of Vienne and several other nearby cities, a force which, if consolidated and pulled from their current duties, might total two thousand heads. And he had no illusions as to what the veteran commanders in Reims thought of the new Caesar who had been appointed to serve over them. The word "figurehead" passed many a lip in describing his position in those days.

If, as Socrates once said, it is a wise man who realizes how little he knows, then Julian was the wisest of all, for he soon came to the conclusion that he was as ignorant in matters of civil administration as he had been of marching in step to a cadence; in this regard, fortunately, silent Sallustius was as capable an adviser as he had been a drill instructor. Though of Gallic origin, Sallustius was nonetheless fully a Roman citizen in education and taste. He was cultured, honest to a fault, loyal to his duty, and through his previous positions as an officer and district governor under Constantius' predecessor, he was much experienced in matters of administration. Most important, he looked upon Julian as an eager student, one whose survival, indeed the survival of Rome's very presence in Gaul, depended upon the skills Sallustius would be able to impart as a wise mentor to the young Caesar.

At the top of Sallustius' list was the need for Julian to familiarize himself with the province's sources of revenue, which consisted chiefly of three types of taxes, each differing to a degree in their effectiveness, but relatively similar in their cruelty. The first was outright requisition, by which those who worked small farms, that is to say, the vast majority of the province's inhabitants, were compelled to feed the Roman army through contributions of provisions. Under this system, the size of one's contribution was not necessarily calculated with a view to meeting the pressure of the immediate crisis, but rather to suit the whims of the tax collectors, who scarcely bothered even to determine whether a farmer actually owned the provisions he was called upon to contribute. When a farmer came up short, which is to say, most of the time, the poor devil was forced to look elsewhere to find the required food and fodder, often purchasing them at ruinously inflated prices from far-off locations, and then carting them to wherever the army happened to be. The net effect of such requisitioning under Constantius had been to bankrupt many who owned farms, having the perverse result of driving them off their land, thereby yielding the army even fewer provisions than it would otherwise have had.

The second method of taxation was the "impost," and it applied to those unfortunate souls who had been driven to the brink of starvation from the previous requisitioning, or who may have already gone under. It was a tax that fell out of the blue on those same owners to penalize them for lands that had been abandoned or taken out of production, and it remained payable even by any subsequent buyers who might attempt to take possession of the land and restore it to working order.

The third application was the "special levies," which might be described very quickly. These levies applied to freeholders in the cities, and were imposed seemingly at random in both timing and amount. As if this tax were not vicious enough, a few years earlier, when a pestilence had swept through the cities of the region, leaving a trail of death and vacant properties in its wake, Constantius had showed no mercy toward those freeholders who were ruined. Even then he demanded annual payment of the tax, and not merely the amount that each individual was assessed, but the amount that his deceased neighbors owed as well. This was in addition to all the other demands falling upon those residing in the walled cities, such as having to vacate the best rooms of their houses in order to accommodate troops, and wait on them like slaves, while they themselves were relegated to sleeping in the most wretched toolsheds and outhouses on the property.

As Julian was soon to learn, the province was in a virtual state of bankruptcy, with tax revenue having fallen to near zero, and enforcement actions by Constantius' normally ruthless collectors at a standstill. This, in turn, was due to the security situation: the fall of Cologne had, in fact, been symptomatic of far deeper troubles. Over the past two years, forty-five flourishing cities—Cologne, Trèves, Worms, Spires, besides uncounted towns and villages—had been pillaged by the Germanics and largely reduced to ashes, a figure that did not even include citadels and minor fortifications. The barbarians had taken control of the land on the Roman side of the Rhine from its sources at Lake Constance all the way to the ocean, and had established settlements and farms as far as thirty-five miles on either side of that river. In doing so, they had driven out Roman settlers from an area three times again that distance, within which citizens could not even pasture their cattle.

Possibly the only saving grace, if one could truly call it that, was the barbarians' peculiar territorial strategy. For after invading a civilized area, they routinely failed to occupy the cities, preferring instead to simply destroy the walls and leave them abandoned or sparsely inhabited by terrorized squatters from the countryside. Strangely enough, the Alemanni preferred to camp on the outskirts or, even better, in the surrounding woods and fields. This was due to the fact that the majority of the barbarians were, in truth, savages accustomed to living only under the open skies or hidden in dense forests, and they viewed cities with a combination of fear and repulsion. As Julian was to find later, this custom, like many others, could be used to great advantage by a thinking general when reconquering a region, for it meant that although the enemy occupiers might be destructive and dangerous, they were not deep-rooted; they merely lodged in fallow cornfields rather than barricaded behind walls or entrenched in cellars.

But enough of history and geography, Brother. I find I am beginning to sound like an old schoolmaster, and part of the reason may be that I find it difficult to launch the next phase of my story. I would note, however, that if Constantius had expected his cousin to be the most pliable and unassuming of underlings, one he could appoint to an empty post and promptly forget about, Julian flatly rejected any such plans for himself, nor did he allow such a notion ever to be conveyed to the Gallic and Roman administrators over which he was the titular head. From his earliest arrival in Vienne, with Sallustius' overt encouragement, he requisitioned the quarters, supplies, and servants he needed to create a staff headquarters worthy of a newly appointed Caesar on campaign. Not lavish, mind you, for luxury and ostentation were traits that Julian despised in other men and fled in himself—but sufficient as to project the image of power and authority he felt his due.

His days were exhausting, but he did not let up on the demands he placed on himself even at night. After a brief, plain dinner with Helena, he would retire to his offices to spend the remainder of the evening, sometimes until dawn, dictating correspondence to a team of secretaries working in shifts. This he would intersperse with extensive readings of philosophy, particularly Plato and his beloved Marcus Aurelius. He was the only man I ever knew for whom the revolutions of the sun and moon meant nothing—he rarely slept more than two or three hours consecutively, and this whenever the need might hit him, several times during the course of a day. This strange habit he kept as long as I knew him, and I once even witnessed him drop off into a short nap only moments before he planned to send his generals with twenty thousand men into battle. The advantage was, of course, that there was never a time the enemy was able to take him by surprise, for he worked and thought at even the most abandoned hours of the night. The disadvantage was that when he needed to consult with an adviser or friend, that person was summoned forthwith, regardless of his state of wakefulness.

And so it happened that just in the darkest hour before sunrise, when the only souls awake and abroad were sentries or other men bound by duty, inclination, or suffering; in the hour when a man feels most abandoned to the loneliness of night and the forces of evil and temptation; when God Himself seems to disappear in that dreadful, seemingly unending hour before sunrise; just before saffron-robed Dawn hastened from Oceanus' streams to bring light to immortals and mortals alike, there came a knock at my door.

For a physician, a knock at the door in the dead of night is not something to be taken lightly, particularly if his only patients are the Caesar and his wife, though even these were merely half-patients, if you will: Julian was still undecided as to the relative effectiveness of Oribasius' ancient Asclepian healing techniques, as compared with my more scientific, Hippocratic approach. Though I was dismayed at being roused from my warm bed at such an hour, I was nevertheless gratified that he had seen the sense of relying on my own practices, rather than on the superstitious nonsense of my friendly rival. I hurriedly dressed and followed the messenger through the deserted streets, sweeping past the sleepy palace guards with a quick nod and a whispered password, down the silent, darkened corridors to the small room that Julian had taken for his office.

The space glowed almost with the brightness of day, by the light of thirty or forty candles and small oil lamps set on every available shelf and sill, forming long stalactites, as in a cave, from the drippings over the past several months. An unshaved, pasty-faced scribe sat slumped on a small stool in a corner, his quill dropped from his hand to the floor beneath him, his head fallen onto his breast, exposing a pink, round bald spot in the midst of a thick shock of unkempt black hair. Julian paced back and forth, muttering to himself as if composing a letter in his mind, ignoring the snorting and snoring scribe in the corner.

"Good morning, Julian," I greeted him, unsure whether it was his health I was to inquire about, or Helena's.

He paused in his pacing and looked at me, his own face drawn and pale, his hair mussed, as if he had just awakened from one of his thrice-daily naps. Without a word of greeting in return, he stalked up to me.

"Caesarius, do you believe in spirits?"

The question was so strange I could not help but burst out laughing, which annoyed him. He resumed his restless pacing. I composed my face and sat heavily on a bench in the corner, opposite the scribe, hearkening back in my mind to the children's stories I had heard long ago.

"Spirits, Julian?" I asked, still chuckling. "Ghosts and vampires of fable, werewolves that wander the roads at night? I'm going back to bed."

"Yes, yes . . ." he muttered in some embarrassment. "No, that's not exactly what I meant." At this, Julian stopped and looked at me meaningfully for a long moment. I paused, not knowing precisely what to say. This was why he had awakened me?

"I had a vision," he said, and paused again.

"Perhaps your irregular sleeping habits are distressing you?" I inquired, puzzled.

"No, no, no. I called you, Caesarius, because this evening I had a dream, from which I have just awakened. A beautiful woman approached me, a smile on her lips and love in her eyes, in a diaphanous gown that trailed behind her. Her hair was in a style that I have seen only in the sculptures of the wives of the ancient founders of Rome. I watched as she came close, bearing in her arms a burden, which I took to be a baby."

I stifled a yawn, for dawn was just beginning to redden the sky.

"It was merely anticipation at your prospects of becoming a father, Julian," I said reassuringly. "There is nothing to be concerned about."

He shook his head at me in exasperation.

"No, Caesarius, you didn't let me finish. She came close and as I stood there she held the burden out to me, smiling. When I took it, I noticed it was uncommonly heavy, and I found it was a cornucopia—a horn of plenty, bursting with ripe fruit, figs and melons, wheat and barley, the empty gaps filled with gold coins, dried fish, fragrant herbs, spices from all corners of the earth—everything needed to sustain life."

I stared at him, still puzzled but increasingly disquieted. "Julian," I said calmly, "such dreams are unholy, unworthy of your concern. All men have them, but only naive pagans, seers and oracles and the like, would place any stock in them at all. If you read the Scriptures before you sleep, you dream of Christ's works. If you read fables—you dream of ghosts."

He glanced at me quizzically and, I thought, somewhat disdainfully, and his eyes lingered on me for just a moment before he continued with his story, ignoring me as if I had not interrupted him.

"I looked at her more closely," he said, "and she smiled sweetly, and I knew inside that she was the *genius publicus,* the guardian deity of Rome itself, in the form of a goddess; Caesarius, I saw her so clearly, so vividly I could describe her to you in every detail, every hair, every eyelash—you would think she was in this very room with us! This was no dream, I assure you. It was truly a vision. And then after leaving in my arms all the riches of the Empire, she slowly turned away and vanished."

At this my drowsiness, too, had vanished, and I looked at him with sharp rebuke.

"Nonsense. You're asking me to interpret a dream which I believe is simply the product of an overheated imagination and a dyspeptic stomach. I'm not a soothsayer, Julian, I'm a physician. We are Christians, not worshipers of the old gods. Eat some meat, get some strength into your muscles, and stay away from silly tales before bedtime." I saw that my lecture was having little success, for still he stared at me, his face as white as when I had first arrived this evening. "What could you possibly be frightened of?" I continued. "At worst, it was only a dream."

Ruefully he turned and renewed his silent pacing, as the white plastered walls of the room gradually turned a rosy pink with the light now slanting through the small ogive window. A tiny cross, seemingly placed on the wall for the specific purpose of catching the sun's earliest morning rays, gleamed from a polished stone set in the middle. The gathering brightness and airiness of the room was in stark contrast to the dark circles forming under Julian's eyes, and the pained expression on his face.

"I'm not frightened," he said in a calm voice, as he waved his hand at me in dismissal. "I simply wished to tell you of my vision. I see that was a waste of time."

V

"Oh, sweet Jesus," he moaned.

"Don't take the Lord's name in vain."

"I'm not, Caesarius—I'm praying."

I rolled my eyes and continued massaging the mint oil into the growing goose egg on the back of his head, which I had already shaved and stitched up with cat gut.

"Praying. That's a bit of a novelty for you, isn't it?"

He turned his head slightly to eye me balefully, one eyebrow raised. "And that's a rather impertinent manner you have of speaking, especially to your Caesar." He chuckled and tried to turn his head farther, but winced.

I remained silent for a moment, concentrating on cleaning up the dressing, then began straightening my instruments. "Where else are you injured?"

He sighed ruefully. "Every muscle in my body. Caesarius, I've spent more time in these past few weeks looking up from the ground at a horse's pizzle than I have riding."

This, at least, was true, for Sallustius had embarked Julian on an intensive training stage in horsemanship, at an isolated farm outside the city that afforded us privacy from spectators curious to watch the Caesar's progress. Frankly, however, little progress was being made. Even worse, in my own training alongside Julian, I was turning into a rather talented student, magnifying his own ineptitude. Our boyhood bareback riding on horses in the neighbor's paddock, Brother, was bearing fruit! The problem was that Julian had never actually ridden a warhorse. Oh, naturally, he had traveled sedately on mild transport animals, usually supervised carefully by a watching colleague or groom, and even then rarely accelerating beyond a calm trot. But a true warhorse, under battle conditions? Never, and at his age, the ripe, old, out-of-shape age of twenty-four, it was like trying to learn a new language after reaching puberty—seemingly impossible.

Merely mounting the beast was a skill he was having difficulty mastering, and any confidence he had had before embarking on this venture was now severely shaken. He stood only head-high to the shoulders of the Frankish chargers that Roman officers in Gaul ride, and Persian-style mounting, using a slave known as a *strator* to hoist the rider up onto the horse's back, did not meet Sallustius' standards. You've probably watched soldiers in the field, Brother—the trick is to approach the animal on its left side, and seize the reins loosely along with a good handful of mane from near the horse's ears. Then with your right hand on the middle of its back, you pull yourself up high enough to flop across on your belly and swing your leg over into a sitting position. It can be a daunting task even for a skilled rider, though my own height made it relatively easy for me. While Julian was at first given the gentlest old nags on which to practice, he consistently overshot his flop; or inadvertently kneed the animal in the ribs, causing it to start; or slipped his grip and ended up jerking the mane out by its roots, with predictable results. Sallustius grimaced and shook his head in disgust, forcing Julian to mount again and again, disdaining even to help him up and dust him off after he fell beneath the animal's feet—"You'll have no one in battle to do that for you," he stated matter-of-factly.

It took Julian days to master the technique, practicing from both sides of the horse, mind you—and then Sallustius threw him another one.

"On the run!" he shouted. "Go!"

Julian just stood and looked at him blankly. "Mount the

horse while it's running?" he asked, astonished.

Sallustius paused, as if unable to comprehend the difficulty. Finally he spoke, slowly, as if to a dense child. "Not the horse," he said. "You. Chonodomarius is within your sight, there, in front of you. You've been caught off your animal, but so has he, and you can catch him if you can mount quickly. Now run and vault onto that horse!"

Julian tried gamely, every way he could—leapfrogging from behind over the horse's haunches, side-vaulting as if scaling a rail fence—and I can't help but say that for many days the results were pitiful, Brother, for Julian simply did not have the quickness or strength to make up for his lack of height, and would invariably slam painfully into the horse's side or rear, and end by clawing and scrambling his way up a by now thoroughly flustered animal. Sallustius shrunk from even watching him, as did I—I merely concentrated all the more fiercely on my own animal. Only Paul the Chain, who often slunk out of his quarters to observe the training sessions, continued to observe attentively and cluck his tongue after each fall, until Sallustius, in exasperation, ordered him to leave the premises. After several days of wincing at Julian's failure to mount, Sallustius admitted defeat, at least for the time being.

"We'll go back to mounting later," he grumbled, to Julian's infinite relief. "In the meantime, we'll work on actual riding. As far as mounting goes, for now you're a Persian," and he called over a hulking Gallic slave from the stables who bent his back for Julian to step on and more gracefully mount his horse.

When riding in battle, Brother, good form is of the utmost importance, from the carriage of one's head to the hang of one's foot. I have seen inexperienced riders in battle who grip their horses' sides not merely with the thighs, as they should, but with their calves and ankles as well, keeping their feet rigid against the animals' ribs rather than letting them dangle loosely from the knee. If their stiff leg strikes against anything hard, like a stump or a rock, or even the armored knee of an onrushing enemy rider brushing close by, it will snap like a twig just at the joint. This is an injury which, despite all the miracles that modern medical science is capable of offering, rarely heals properly and usually leaves the victim a cripple. If the leg hangs easily from the knee down, however, it will yield when struck, without moving the thigh or its rider from position.

Just so, there are proper ways of carrying one's weapons, of wielding one's shield, even of draping one's mantle over the shoulders and dropping one's visor over the eyes, so as to most effectively ease one's own efforts while increasing the threat to the enemy. For weeks Julian was trained intensively in hurling the javelin from horseback, two of which he carried in his left hand behind his shield, while Sallustius cantered alongside on his own mount, shouting out instructions step by step and handing him replacement weapons.

"Left shoulder forward, right one back—good! Eye your target—eye your target, damn it, Caesar, not your horse! Now, grip with your thighs and rise up for leverage.... No, not too high . . . NO!"

Thank goodness, Brother, for the back padding and safety helmet he wore in training, for he took a tremendous beating learning to stand erect on his thighs and hurl the javelin forward without allowing the horse to run straight out from under him—I lost count of the bruises and scrapes he received, though one corner of the farm's stable I had converted into a regular infirmary, where I spent a great deal of time treating him after his mishaps.

As Julian slowly progressed, Sallustius moved on to more dangerous techniques as well—stringing and firing a bow while riding, like the dark-faced Huns; rearing the horse into the air to allow it to kick out at enemies with its sharpened forehooves; and slashing Persian-style with a curved scimitar, a much more effective weapon for a mounted horseman than a straight stabbing sword. With this weapon, Julian practiced on a man-sized oaken post Sallustius had driven into the middle of the arena, which was later dressed up in Germanic clothing and armor, using a melon mounted on the top as a head. Scimitar practice on horseback was far too dangerous to practice with living opponents, as there is no practical way to shield the blows; but not so for lance practice. By placing a hard clay ball on the lance tip, these weapons can be rendered somewhat less deadly to one's sparring partner, though by no means painless when contact is made.

Sallustius himself charged at Julian repeatedly with the blunted lance, as Julian alternately attempted to defend himself against the attack with his shield, and took the offensive with his own blunted weapon. Again and again Sallustius' lance tip slammed into Julian's padded practice armor, though the skilled instructor was sufficiently deft as to divert the weapon at the last moment so that it would generally glance off Julian's side without knocking him from his horse, leaving him unharmed but for a weltering bruise or a cracked rib. One day, however, after Sallustius carefully glanced around to see if I was nearby, he rode down on Julian full bore, lance tip tracing tight, maddening circles in the air as it feinted and dodged Julian's wavering shield, and then slammed full into the middle of Julian's chest, lifting him clear off the horse into the air and throwing him hard onto his back on the packed ground. He lay still as his riderless horse cantered to the far end of the paddock, as if attempting to evade any blame for the mishap.

I rushed from where I had been preparing for my own sparring session with Sallustius, and knelt beside Julian. To my relief he soon began sputtering and gasping for air. The wind had been knocked out of him, and he was badly shaken, but was otherwise unhurt. He was still dizzy, however, and barely able to talk, when Sallustius rode up calmly on his horse. The man didn't even bother to dismount, and I glared up at him accusingly.

"Look at him! Were you trying to kill him?"

Sallustius glanced down at Julian impassively. "Yes," he said simply.

I bristled. "You had better be joking."

"Do you see me smiling?"

"You never smile."

"Nor do I joke," he replied.

Julian struggled to sit up. "I—I could have you arrested for that . . ." he gasped.

Sallustius looked down with an expression of mock puzzlement on his face. "For failing to joke?"

Julian's face turned red in anger as the breath rushed back into his lungs. "For trying to kill me!"

"So arrest me."

Now it was Julian's turn to look puzzled.

"You should thank me for trying to kill you," Sallustius continued coldly, "for if I don't try to do so now, and fail, someone else will surely try in the future and succeed. And you fault me?"

"Damn you, Sallustius," Julian muttered, staggering to his feet. "Where's my horse?"

In private, Sallustius shook his head in admiration as the young Caesar continued to make the long ride out to the farm every morning for further drilling, never complaining of his aching muscles and the knots on his head. To Sallustius' great satisfaction, once Julian finally developed a basic level of strength and dexterity, his military skills improved amazingly, and what he lacked in pure physical ability, he more than made up for in wit and cunning. His major frustration, however, continued to be mounting; here his skills continued to fall embarrassingly short, and this failure was having an effect on his confidence in all other areas of horsemanship and weaponry. After several weeks, however, the camp's head blacksmith arrived, bearing with him a stout cavalry lance with a curious supplement to it—a thick iron hook attached to the shaft by a sturdy band, about four feet from the butt end.

"This," Sallustius said, "is your *strator*."

The next day, as Julian prepared to ride out to the farm to resume his lessons, he asked with a wry smile that I *not* accompany him for a time. Though surprised, I presumed that it was to spare his dignity when learning yet another impossible technique, and so I agreed without protest. His uncommon cheerfulness upon his return from the paddock each day, however, kept me wondering, and when next I was allowed to accompany him several weeks later, I was astonished at the sight that met my eyes. There stood Julian calmly, in full cavalry regalia, stiff mailed tunic descending to his hips, thigh plates, mailed knee joints and greaves, crowned by a tight-fitting, open-faced bronze cavalry helmet, all of which weighed near sixty pounds. He had been fitted with a gilt-plated, full-sized Roman cavalry shield, a richly decorated scimitar, and a gleaming officer's lance, twelve feet long, its painted wood sanded smooth and enameled to a polished, ivory gleam. These weapons lay neatly against a fencepost, as they would be positioned while in camp, except for his scimitar, which he hung in a scabbard against his left leg. His horse pawed the dirt nervously at the far end of the paddock.

As I leaned against a rail watching, the stable slave gave a signal and then began loudly counting beats with a drum, measuring elapsed time. Julian rushed to his gear while simultaneously cinching his armor, and in a single, fluid motion that astonished me with its focused gracefulness, he hoisted the heavy shield onto his left shoulder and picked up the lance. He then began running toward his waiting horse, which was itself heavily mailed, even to the bronze faceplate and rounded iron blinders over its eyes to prevent it from seeing anything but straight ahead.

At first, Julian lumbered slowly in his heavy armor, then gradually picked up speed and momentum, as the slung shield slapped loudly against his back. It was then that I noticed something odd—the lance he was carrying in his right hand, which had been fitted with the strange hooked device, was backward—the tip was pointed to the *rear*. I sighed, and resigned myself to another embarrassing attempt by Julian to demonstrate skill at arms.

Just as he neared the animal, however, which was beginning to skitter and paw in anticipation as he heard his rider's clanking approach, Julian planted the thick butt end of his lance into the ground some four feet from the horse's left hooves, and drove his body in toward the shaft. The pole lifted to the vertical, flexing slightly, and he leaped into the air and swung upward with his two hands on the shaft. He then planted his left foot on the hook as if it were a ladder rung, lifted his right leg, and dropped easily and gracefully up onto the enormous horse's back, armor and all. In the same motion he kneed the animal sharply, causing it to rear back and paw the air as he calmly tightened his grip on the reins with his right hand and flipped his lance forward with his left; then deftly swinging the pointed head of the weapon forward, he braced the shaft squarely against the top of the horse's head, between its ears, and raced off like an arrow shot.

I was dumbfounded.

"Nothing like four hours of practice a day to improve your mounting," said a voice next to me. It was Sallustius, who had sidled up in silence as I watched.

"The lance hook is ingenious," I said. "I'm sorry I doubted you."

"Developed by the Spartans," he noted laconically, ignoring my apology, as we watched Julian canter confidently around the arena. "I've ordered one made for every cavalryman in Vienne."

It was Julian, naturally, who first demonstrated the lance-vault technique to the city's garrison and reserves at a ceremony held at the arena that spring to launch the campaigning season. The garrison's champion swordsmen first gave an impressive show of the bladework and shield technique for which they had trained all winter and in which they were now to drill their comrades. Boxing and wrestling then ensued, followed by demonstrations of feats of strength among the infantry companies. Finally, the cavalry squad, decked in heavy ornamental armor, divided themselves into two teams of twenty, distinguished by dramatic enameled masks depicting golden-coiffed Amazons and Olympian gods. At a signal, the two sides raised a shout, and raced toward each other across the arena at a thundering gallop, smashing into their opponents with blunted weapons and a blinding cloud of dust, fiercely striving to knock the opposing riders off their mounts. The ferocity of their charges was astonishing, and at the time, Brother, I could scarcely believe that actual battle with the Alemanni could have been any more brutal. Lance tips snapped in the foining and flew winging into the stands, shields split and shattered from the impact of the collision, and men who failed to grip their horses securely with armor-clad thighs were thrown twisting and grunting to the ground, where they rolled to avoid the horses' flailing hooves. Those who fell were disqualified, and had no recourse but to scramble stiffly from the sand and hobble to the edge of the arena, nursing their bruises and scrapes, to await the outcome of the match. A few remained writhing where they lay, and had to be dragged to safety by attendants.

Sallustius sat his horse at the edge of the pit as a referee, though bearing his own heavy shield and lance for protection against the wide-ranging riders who suffered from terrifyingly poor visibility behind their tragedy masks. Several times he was forced to spur his horse forward into their midst, shouting the men down and splitting them apart if tempers frayed and the teams refused to retreat to their corners after each charge. After a dozen fierce attacks, all to the raucous cheers of a thousand overexcited and half-drunk veterans, he finally awarded the laurel crown to the two horsemen still remaining on their mounts, both of them from the Olympian team—their shattered lances and dented armor attesting to their valor and strength.

Sallustius remained at his post while the arena was quickly swept and the obstacle course erected for the final event, the horsemanship demonstration, in which Julian was scheduled as the last of the riders to participate. His intent, of course, was to observe Julian's performance at close hand, and to shout out any instructions the Caesar might require, though as it turned out, such assistance was entirely unnecessary. When Julian's time arrived, he strode into the ring bearing gold-plated ceremonial armor even heavier than the set I had first seen him wear, and topped by another of the ominous enameled masks depicting a Greek deity with its mouth set in an awful grimace, and only two tiny eyeholes through which to peer.

Despite these encumbrances, his performance soon silenced the skeptical troops who had been led by rumor and past observation to expect at best a clumsy and simple demonstration. He first deftly demonstrated his innovative mounting technique from both sides of the horse, and with each clean vault he made onto the skittish stallion's back, I could almost hear the jaws dropping around me. He then delivered a stunning display of riding and swordplay, weaving through the series of oaken post-men that had been set up in a row among scattered pits, fire walls, and other obstacles. The troops, enthused now at the skill demonstrated by their Caesar, began a rhythmic stamping of feet that drowned out all conversation. Flawlessly Julian ran his spirited animal through its paces, leaping over high rails and sidestepping ground spikes, all of which had been placed so as to simulate true battle conditions as closely as possible. As he approached the mock enemy forces, he twirled his flashing scimitar in the sun and slashed fiercely from side to side, cleaving and demolishing the unresisting heads with his whirling blade, scattering pulpy, melon-seed brains over his legs and the sides of the horse.

The men roared their approval and delight, though Julian was still not without some skeptics. Just in front of me a watching centurion applauded politely, but his gaze continued to range over the obstacle course distractedly. "Why is he cutting at fruit?" he muttered to a colleague as the cheers died down. "Couldn't they find a cavalryman to spar him?"

His friend quickly silenced him. "He's the Caesar! Who would spar with the Caesar in the arena? If you win, you lose. If you lose, you lose. So he hacks at melons." The logic was impeccable.

Still, Julian's performance was impressive, particularly given his complete lack of skills only scant months earlier, and the troops' applause was genuine as he completed the

difficult course and cantered around the arena, acknowledging their cheers. For show, he even stopped his horse
suddenly and reared it back, waving with his sword in the
classic depiction of the victorious Roman general. At this,
Sallustius shook his head in disgust and began trotting
slowly off the field to the side stables. His work, for the
moment, was complete.

Suddenly, just as the raucous cheering had begun dying
down, Julian leaned forward, adjusted his mask, and kneed
his animal. The horse leaped ahead, eyes rolling in excitement, and the troops again fell silent at the prospect of
another display. He accelerated into a flat-out charge, lowering the blunted lance he had been carrying against his hip
to the horizontal attack position. At the loud thudding of
hooves behind him, Sallustius stopped his own mount and
turned around to see what foolishness Julian might be attempting. As far as Sallustius was concerned, the demonstration was over, but from the glint in Julian's eyes behind
his white-faced mask, I could see that this was no demonstration, and that Julian was now in earnest.

Sallustius spied the charge from half the arena's length
away, and with his practiced soldier's ease and a hint of a
smile he quickly unslung and mounted his own shield and
steadied his own ball-tipped lance while spurring his horse
forward to a sprint. Julian thundered straight and unhesi-
tatingly, his heavy bronze cavalry shield braced firmly
against the fulcrum of his thigh, swaying only slightly back
and forth as he countered the bobbing arc of Sallustius'
lance tip, while at the same time feinting and weaving with
his own weapon. In complete concentration he sought the
slight opening, the overplayed hand, that would allow him
to slip the balled point around his opponent's shield to the
face or chest behind.

The watching troops fell silent—to the point that I could
hear Julian's rhythmic breathing and grunts behind his
mask as the horses stormed toward each other. With a flurry
of dust and a loud CRACK! both weapons slammed into
the opposing shields, and a three-foot section of shattered

lance flew into the air and spun crazily into the crowd. With the brutal crash of the weapons, both lance-wood and men yielded and broke. The warhorses, reins loosened and riders' knees ungripped, continued forward in their own fierce momentum and smashed into each other, falling in a writhing, whinnying heap of hooves and snapping teeth. As the animals struggled to their feet and staggered off to the edge of the ring, both men lay still for a moment where they had fallen. I began pushing past the troops at my side, making my way toward the arena to treat the injuries I was certain to find there. This was unnecessary, however, for first Julian, then Sallustius, sat up and painfully rose to their feet, groggy and unbalanced under the stiff weight of the heavy cavalry armor.

Immediately, spontaneously, the troops stood and erupted in a loud roar, and Julian raised his mask and acknowledged their cheer with a weary grin and a wave of his hand, blood flowing from one nostril down his chin and dripping to the sand from beneath his helmet. Sallustius, too, face impassive as ever, nodded to the soldiers and accepted their praise. Julian then bent slowly and picked up his lance, the tipped end neatly broken off during the tremendous impact with Sallustius' shield. He examined it ruefully, and then held it high in his right hand in a kind of salute, raising another roar from the men at this trophy of his mock battle. Finally, turning to Sallustius with a sheepish expression, he advanced toward him with his arms wide, as if to embrace him in acknowledgment of his courage and skill.

He didn't make it far, though to his credit the judges deemed it a perfectly fair blow, and the men's raucous laughter afterwards would appear to confirm them in this ruling. For as Sallustius bent awkwardly in his stiff-kneed armor to pick up his own dropped weapon, Julian took careful aim, and with a robust prod of his broken lance, knocked the surprised Sallustius ignominiously back into the dust.

VI

That spring of the year commonly calculated as being the
three hundred fifty-sixth since the birth of Our Lord and
the one thousand ninety-first since the founding of the city
of Rome, Sallustius, Julian, and I spent daily in deep discussion at the headquarters, surrounded by an enormous
quantity of maps, crumpled parchment, and reference doc-
uments, planning the campaign for the year to come. Many
hours were spent in close consultation with the various tribunes and cohort leaders of the legions, devising strategy
and shuffling troop deployments, arranging supply drops
and reviewing prisoner interrogations. It was during one
such session that the old eunuch Eutherius entered without
knocking, eliciting an irritated glance from Julian.

This breach of protocol, so minor by any stretch of the
imagination as to hardly be worthy of notice in this chron-
icle, was, however, so extraordinarily out of character for
the excellent Eutherius as to beggar a short digression.

Like his old tutor Mardonius or his physician Oribasius,
there was not a time in the young Caesar's life when he
could not remember being in the near presence of this ancient eunuch, who was now well into his ninth decade. The
fellow had served Julian's uncle Constantine as head chamberlain forty years before, and Constantine's son Constans
after that, and it may sound incredible to say, but although
he was a eunuch, he was possibly the most honorable, gen-

tle, and trustworthy man I had ever met. Xenophon had
observed long ago that while castration in animals might
tame their wildness, it did not diminish their strength or
spirit; and he claimed that among men, those who were
separated by castration from the rest of humankind would
become even more personally loyal to their benefactor. My
own experience with eunuchs, this disruptive, meddling
breed, would seem to put the lie to such a claim. In fact,
it was once said that if the great Socrates were to speak
well of a eunuch, even he would be accused of lying. Old
Eutherius, however, was a pearl, far removed from the unc-
tuous, sneering, conniving sorts usually representative of
such men, a true example of how roses may grow even in
the midst of thorns.

Perhaps the quality of his manhood was so high because
he was not raised as a eunuch, but rather as a freeborn son
of free parents, who was captured as a young adult by pi-
rates, castrated out of sheer maliciousness, and then sold
into slavery. Far from falling into despair over this unfortunate turn of events, he made the most of his new condition, and his studious nature, rectitude, and intelligence
were soon recognized and brought to the Emperor's attention. Eutherius was found to have a prodigious memory and
the judgment of a sage, and as a counselor and mentor he
was perhaps the most valuable property that Julian inherited
from Constans after his assassination. Eutherius had been
allowed to recede into a gentle retirement only a few years
before, but when Julian was made Caesar, he called his old
friend out to Gaul, to serve as a reminder of his past and
to help him ground his decisions on proper judgment. The
man was loyal to a fault, to the point of being entrusted
with all of the Caesar's personal financial affairs, and Julian
would have happily staked him his own life.

In any event, on this day Eutherius entered the staff
room without knocking, and unceremoniously cleared his
throat. Julian looked up.

"My lord," he said, "forgive me for disturbing you, but

we have just received an urgent missive from the garrison at Autun. The barbarians have laid siege."

Sallustius and Julian stood up, their stools clattering to the floor behind them. The matter was serious. Autun was a noble and industrious city, an important trading center in the interior of the province. It was a stronghold, though the walls had been weakened by centuries of decay, and Constantius and his generals had not made the effort to rebuild them. It was inconceivable that the Alemanni could have strayed so far from their Rhine forests, for Autun was a good hundred miles from the previous limits of their invasions. In fact, it put them within striking distance of even more important Roman cities, Auxerre, Sens, and Paris to the north, Lyons and even Vienne to the south, which would block the entire Rhone river. The main body of the Roman army under Marcellus was still in winter quarters far to the north in Reims, and we could not be certain they had even received news of the attack. In any case, Autun and the besieging barbarians now stood between us and Marcellus, so with our direct line of communication to the main army cut, it would be impossible to coordinate effectively with them, even if Marcellus did receive word in time to take action himself. Julian began quickly ruffling through the stack of military maps on the table before him. Sallustius gazed down at him coolly.

"Gently, gently," he warned. "Neither battles nor women are won by rushing. Invite your worthy chamberlain to sit with us and explain what he has heard, and we shall devise a plan."

Though Sallustius moved calmly, encouraging lengthy pondering of the situation, Julian acted instinctively, issuing orders to the troops to mobilize immediately. In addition to the warrior clerics he had inherited from Milan, who by dint of steady and exhaustive training had become a formidable if somewhat reluctant fighting force whom he referred to as his Acolytes, he had available some two thousand other troops in various garrisons within two days' march of Vienne, as well as that many again retired veterans of the Roman army who had taken Gallic wives and settled in the area. Sallustius and Eutherius worked tirelessly, night and day for three revolutions of the sun, to mobilize and equip a fighting force. Julian himself dealt with the prefects and provincial administrators, promising future payment and honors, to obtain the equipment, road crews, and civil support he needed to accompany a Roman army on the march. To my great surprise and pleasure, though Julian still had little firsthand experience with administration, he was proving to be a master at improvisation. On the fourth day, he reviewed his troops, possibly the largest body of soldiers Vienne had seen in one gathering since Julius Caesar had passed through centuries earlier.

Helena wept. "You're only a boy," she sobbed, in unwitting condescension. "Send Sallustius to lead the troops and stay with me. Stay with your child."

Julian hesitated, knowing that the duty and the objective he had created for himself lay with the army, but uncertain how best to comfort his wife. I stepped forward.

"She'll be fine," I said, reassuring him. "There is nothing you can do for her here, until her time. Meanwhile I will continue to monitor her. She is having an exemplary pregnancy."

He looked at me with a hint of amusement. "I'm pleased she's doing so well," he said, "and that you're so willing to make the sacrifice. But there's no need. Oribasius will care for Helena in my absence."

My face must have registered my surprise at this news, for although Oribasius was considered one of the best of his profession, I still had little trust in his techniques. To me they smacked too much of witchcraft and soothsaying rather than the solid science I hoped to promote among Julian's family and the army.

Before I could protest, however, he explained. "Don't reproach me, Caesarius. I need my best men with me on campaign, not monitoring morning sickness—even for the

Caesar's wife! Oribasius is too unfit to accompany me into battle—and he has no experience with war injuries in any case."

"And *I* have experience with war injuries?"

He waved me off with a grin. "Bah, I've seen you dive into those autopsies. You yourself boast of your detailed knowledge of anatomy. Not like those butchers Constantius already has assigned to the army as physicians, who would just as soon saw off my leg to cure me of a spider bite. I'll trust my bodily safety to no one else, Caesarius."

After a forced march of four days, we arrived in Autun on the twenty-fourth of June. The barbarians, having espied our arrival from the fields surrounding the city's besieged walls, swiftly abandoned the site before we were even within view of the garrison. Julian had won his first battle, with a ragtag, improvised army, without letting fly a single arrow.

To my great surprise, however, he was terribly disappointed at not having encountered the enemy, for during the march he had taken pains to closely question Sallustius and veterans familiar with the layout of the land at Autun. He had devised a complicated plan of attack involving feints and counterfeints and was eager to try out his newfound military skills. Declaring this the beginning of the season's campaign, he resolved to set out for Reims, to combine his little force with the army's main body there. Accordingly, he gathered that portion of the local garrison that Autun could spare—a company of *cataphracti*, heavily armored cavalry troops, and a squad of *ballistarii*, soldiers in charge of the large rock-hurling machines. He also decided not to take the safest route to the army at Reims, but rather the shortest—a road that led him through Auxerre and Troyes, but which passed through some of the most dangerous country in the province, where his troops would be constantly exposed to ambush by the marauding Alemanni.

As at Autun, the mere appearance of a Roman legion was sufficient to drive the outnumbered barbarians away without mishap. Julian stood on the crumbling city walls and surveyed the lightly armored forces of barbarian raiders beating an expert, controlled retreat across the surrounding fields on their swift horses, shouting taunts at the Romans as they melted into the forests. He then continued on toward Troyes. This time, however, his troops faced the full brunt of an Alemanni force that attacked them on the way. The barbarians would have done better to strike sooner, however, for Julian's marching strength by this time was close to five thousand, from the additional troops he had picked up in Autun and Auxerre. With the discipline of his battle-hardened veterans, and some quick-thinking tactical maneuvers he devised on his own, to the quiet admiration of Sallustius, he was able to turn back the barbarians from two vicious attacks, even taking a quantity of valuable plunder and horses.

He arrived at Troyes a full three days before the besieged garrison thought it would be possible—so early, in fact, that the garrison at first refused to even recognize their new leader, fearing instead some ruse on the part of the Alemanni. It took a great deal of effort, and Julian's very best rhetoric shouted through a bullhorn, before the Troyes garrison could be persuaded to voluntarily open the gates to us. After a brief rest here for his increasingly enthusiastic troops, he collected another two thousand soldiers and veterans from the surrounding cities and countryside, and marched on Reims to meet his generals, with an impressive array of somewhat mismatched forces that scarcely three weeks earlier had hardly existed as a military body, except in Julian's imagination.

Arriving at the city after a three-day march, he was greeted at the gate by an honor guard of Roman soldiers, who led him and his seven thousand troops through the thronging streets of the ancient city under the watchful eyes of its curious citizens. At the gates of the palace that Marcellus and Ursicinus occupied along with their staff, the two generals stood on the front steps, in formal greeting of their Caesar, who was nominally their direct superior. The word "greeting," however, does not adequately describe their attitude, for the term typically implies a form of welcome, and, in cases involving a direct representative of the Augustus himself, should involve at least a certain degree of supplication. There was nothing of supplication, however, in the expressions and stances demonstrated by the two generals waiting for Julian.

The bulk of his troops halted and stood at regal attention, arrayed by company, in the enormous courtyard in front of the forbidding palace, which was actually the former outer walls of an ancient military fortress that had been overtaken and encompassed by the growing city around it. The walls and battlements, themselves no longer performing the defensive task for which they had been built centuries before, had had their outer stones redressed and artfully plastered as befitted the elegant administrative headquarters of a sophisticated major regional city; yet they still retained the imposing height and thickness of the fortress they once guarded.

Julian's coterie of "senior officers," twenty or thirty grizzled centurions he had pulled out of retirement from their allotted farms around Vienne and pressed into service with a promise of promotion and double wages, walked their horses to the foot of the stairs with him, where he motioned them to halt, but to remain mounted. He himself dismounted, as did Sallustius, and side by side the two strode up the long flight of stone steps to the portico, where the generals stood at attention, watching them coldly.

If ever I have seen the eye of a dead man, and I have seen plenty, it was nothing compared with the cold, lifeless stare of Marcellus as he observed Julian approaching him from below. A short, stocky man of middle age, with a dark shadow of beard showing beneath the cheek plates of his ceremonial helmet, he stood squarely, chest thrust, shoulders back, drawn up to his full height, and utterly motionless with the exception of his small, dark eyes. His twitchy gaze as it passed between Sallustius and Julian was all the more bright and disturbing as it gleamed from under the dark foreridge of the headgear.

Ursicinus, the former commander whom Constantius had ordered kept in his position as an adviser to Marcellus, was easier to read. Several inches taller than his younger colleague, he too was stocky and swarthy, though his weight appeared not to be of the hard-muscled variety, but rather of the softness of age, of one having served too long in the military in regions requiring little physical challenge on the part of the local garrisons. His face was paler and somewhat plumper, and his eyes, too, darted back and forth between Julian and Sallustius, though with more than a hint of amusement in them, and a slight upturn to the corners of the mouth.

"Hail, Caesar!" Marcellus said loudly when Julian and Sallustius arrived at the top of the stairs. I noticed, however, that the general was facing Sallustius when he said this, and that Julian even stepped slightly to the side, perhaps out of amusement. "As general of the Roman army in Gaul, I bid you welcome to the stronghold of Reims, which the barbarians tremble to approach and where the townspeople live in peace and safety under the protection of the twenty-five thousand troops serving the mighty Emperor Constantius. Greetings, Caesar, and all hail!" He then swept low and stepped to the side, beckoning for Sallustius to pass and enter the Great Hall.

To my amazement, I realized that General Marcellus had somehow confused the two men, though upon further reflection I admit that this is not as astonishing as it may sound. Sallustius had spent most of his career in the eastern theater of operations and was unknown to Marcellus, and of course Julian had never had any exposure to the military ranks at all before arriving in Vienne a few months before. Marcellus had most likely been apprised of Julian's promotion through a dry military dispatch, which lacked any sort of physical description of the new Caesar. Believing him to be a mere figurehead, there is really no reason why Marcellus *should* have been concerned with the prospect of meeting Julian personally. And when the occasion did arise, he simply assumed that the more regal-looking of the two men—Sallustius—was the Caesar.

Sallustius stared at Marcellus silently for a moment, deciding how best to disabuse the general of his misplaced identification, and then glanced slyly over to Julian. Julian gave Sallustius a quick, expressionless, almost imperceptible wink.

Sallustius nodded slightly to the two generals and strode imperiously past them into the Great Hall, and Julian began to step into place behind him. Marcellus and Ursicinus quickly closed ranks with their own bodies directly behind Sallustius, however, and marched him into the palace, leaving Julian to trail in the rear. As he disappeared behind the enormous, bronze-sheathed doors guarding the palace's entrance, he gave a quick look back at the troops, his face betraying only the slightest hint of amusement. Scattered titters rose from those in the front ranks on the steps below who were able to see and hear the brief ceremony of welcome, and then the palace guards stepped back into their places before the doors and snapped to attention, glaring haughtily down the steps at the battle-stained men before them. The troops broke formation and sat where they were in the middle of the forum, trading loud wisecracks with the starched and polished garrison, who remained at attention around them. The garrison troops' shining armor, clean-shaven jaws, and immaculately tanned strap leather were in sharp contrast to the grimy, sweat-drenched veterans who had accompanied Julian from routing the barbarians in three cities.

I regret, Brother, that I was unable to be a fly on the wall at this initial meeting with his army's two top generals, though I later heard snatches of what transpired from comments dropped by Sallustius. Although Ursicinus wisely remained silent for most of the conversation, in his role as observer, Marcellus, apparently, made a regular fool of himself. He spoke endlessly without letting the others get in a word, alternately fawning on Sallustius as the presumed

Caesar, and patronizing him as the militarily ignorant cousin of the Emperor, who would be learning under the expertise of himself, the *true* military strategist.

The truth became apparent only when Marcellus stopped to catch his breath, preparing to dismiss his presumptive superior and the casually dressed young lackey tagging behind. At that point, Julian stepped forward.

"Thank you, General, for your warm welcome of both myself and my adviser Sallustius," he said, and Sallustius bowed to Marcellus as the general stared in astonishment. "I am indeed grateful for your military preparedness, though I might have been more impressed had you used your twenty-five thousand soldiers to rid your territory of barbarians, which I have somehow been able to do with a handful of retired veterans over the past four weeks."

Marcellus mouthed silent protests like a fish gasping out of water, and the meeting only further degenerated from there. After an hour, I heard scattered shouts as the men around me began to gather their weapons and stand, and looking up I saw that the four leaders had emerged, though in quite a different order of appearance than before. Julian marched first out the bronze doors, looking younger than before, if possible, his eyes flashing as he gazed down proudly at his troops. Sallustius stood just behind and to his right, his brooding presence impassive as ever, his dark eyes betraying no hint of any emotion as he stared calmly out at the men gathered in the forum.

Behind them walked Marcellus, stoop-shouldered and with a haggard face, like one whose diet consists of too much lard and insufficient fruit. His gaze avoided his own wondering troops lining the outside of the forum. He focused instead, with an expression of muted fury, on the animated face of Julian, whose arms were now raised as he motioned the troops to silence. Ursicinus, standing beside Marcellus, bore an expression of slight bemusement.

"Soldiers!" Julian shouted, and the men's shouts and calls gradually died to a subdued murmur. "Soldiers! I address you not as 'gentlemen,' as did Xenophon when exhorting his troops, nor as 'countrymen,' as does the Emperor, but with the proudest title a Roman can bear: 'Soldiers'! "

The men cheered lustily. Julian sought out my eyes in the crowd and smiled slightly. His stance and gestures as he stood before the troops were somewhat awkward and contrived, the pose of a student calmly debating a belabored point of sophistry before a like-minded crowd of academics. Still, I noticed as he raised his hands to quiet the troops that he consciously mimicked the broad, sweeping arm motions and commanding jut of the chin that had so well served Constantius, who himself was a master orator. Julian's trump was his youth and confidence, his open sincerity with his men. With a little practice and coaching, I reflected, young Julian would be giving even the Emperor a run for his money.

"For too long," he continued as the men gradually fell silent, "you have been serving inside your walls; for too long you have been on the defensive; for too long you have been eating preserved rations from the quartermaster, polishing your armor, maintaining your fitness by combat among yourselves, unable to prove your superiority against the barbarians just outside your gates. For too long, soldiers, the Alemanni have failed to feel the fury and the might of the Roman army. They have strayed with impunity beyond their borders, ravaging the countryside and occupying the lands—Roman lands, for this is Gaul, this is land your ancestors conquered under Julius Caesar four hundred years ago, this is land as Roman as Sicily—and it shall remain Roman!"

The cheers increased in volume, with scattered clanging of shields on knees. I felt a terrible unease, however—Julian had stepped far beyond the role to which Constantius had assigned him. Julian would ascribe his actions to a greater cause, to the task of saving a diminished Roman Gaul from attacks by savages and the incompetence of its own military leaders. True, patriotism is a cause that is difficult to reproach. But overriding those same military leaders without orders, as he was so blatantly doing—at what point does patriotism become treason?

"Tomorrow, lads—tomorrow, *soldiers*!—by the grace of the Almighty God we shall emerge from our walls fighting, and we shall not stop until we have reached the Rhine and cleared it of the infernal barbarian presence, from its source in the Alps to its mouth in the North Sea! We have marched from Vienne to Autun, from Auxerre to Troyes, routing the Alemanni and reclaiming Gaul for Rome and the Emperor. We will continue our march of death and salvation. Tomorrow, by God, our forces will have been combined under the joint command of General Marcellus and myself, and woe to the barbarians, who have never seen such fire and steel as we will give them in the bellies, who have never felt such muscles as we will flex—whose memories of mighty Rome, their rulers and masters, have begun to fail them, but who will soon be reminded of the penalties to be paid for their insolence. Tomorrow we shall start!"

The forum erupted in a massive cheer, as Marcellus' disciplined forces lining the colonnade joined with Julian's rough-hewn veterans. The Caesar stood erect and still for a moment, and then stepping forward to the front ranks of his men, he seized a cavalry lance that had been fitted with one of the mounting hooks. Spying his horse, which a groom had led forward as if by prearrangement, he deftly flipped the weapon backward, raced several steps toward the waiting stallion, and vaulted flawlessly onto its back. The troops exploded. Never had they had a leader, much less a full Caesar, who was so much one of them. Julian drank it in, his lance raised in triumph and his horse rearing and prancing on cue, as Marcellus slumped, glaring in fury at the man who had so deeply humiliated him.

That night the air was heavy with the smell of burning flesh, as the worshipers of Mithras among Julian's troops celebrated their triumph over the Alemanni with a sacrifice of three oxen. The carcasses burned on an altar whose flames were visible for miles around, a stark repudiation of the attacks of the roving barbarians. It was also, I felt, a

repudiation of the victory of Christ over these obsolete and
satanic pagan sacrifices, and I sought Julian out to demand
that he put a stop to such rituals. I found him in the vicinity
of the altar itself, from which sizzling blood was still flowing down the makeshift gutters and forming in pools at the
feet of the priests who energetically tended the roaring
flames. He was surrounded by a company of his men, eating heartily of the charred meat they offered him from the
coals and laughing uproariously at the crude camp jokes
and ditties they plied him with in their drunken good humor. Unable to force my way through the crowd of troops
to catch his attention, I left in a foul mood.

That summer was one to remember, one of terror and victory. Though Sallustius continued to offer valuable advice
from his long years of experience, he no longer dominated
the late-night strategy sessions. Julian had gained much
confidence, and the student now surpassed the master in
craftiness and skill. Gathering together the bulk of his combined army, the Caesar marched east to the Rhine, leaving
sulking Marcellus behind to consolidate the earlier conquests of that spring. Despite the barbarians' best efforts,
their wiliness, their ability to appear unexpectedly in our
very midst or melt into the forests at will, Julian seemingly
had them stymied. With almost bewildering speed and precision, he divided his forces to lure the Alemanni into in-
defensible valley positions, where they were surrounded.
He routed their camps and destroyed their fortresses, capturing their scouts to prevent his presence and intentions
from being disclosed, seeming to be everywhere at once,
yet nowhere the barbarians ever expected him.

In fury they fled east before him to the Rhine, where
they resolved to make their pitched stand; yet in Julian's
cunning, he had sent divisions of troops racing ahead of
them through the Vosges mountains to intercept them before their arrival at the river, preventing them from consolidating their forces into a beachhead. The barbarians fled

across the river in disarray, commandeering any available vessels, sometimes riding nothing more than logs paddled out into the stream for the current to take them away, anywhere, as long as it was far from the Caesar's fury. After every victory, large or small, he ordered an immediate count and inspection of the enemy dead, even before the Roman victims themselves were buried, and it was always the same question he anxiously put to Sallustius:

"What of Chonodomarius, the Beast? Has he been captured? Killed?"

Sallustius would carefully scan the ledgers prepared for him by the parties detailed to strip the enemy dead, seeking any description that might indicate great physical size, or armor or body ornamentation more elaborate than that of the typical barbarian soldier—even evidence that uncommonly large weapons had been retrieved—but his answer was always the same.

"No, Caesar, I fear he was absent from the battle."

What Sallustius failed to mention was that his conclusion had already been drawn long before the accountants had calculated the numbers of enemy dead. For Chonodomarius' absence in a battle was simply assumed by default, by dint of the fact that the barbarians had retreated. The enormous king had seemingly vanished without a trace, like an ephemeral spirit, into the vast, black forests beyond the Rhine. Though the Alemanni were losing battles, Chonodomarius was holding back—feeding our confidence, lulling us, perhaps, waiting for the time when he could organize his hordes into the crushing blow he was surely planning in his dark, wooded fortresses.

Fall approached, the time for returning to winter quarters, and the cornered barbarians, we knew, would soon be breathing sighs of relief; still, Julian did not abate in his fighting. Upon reaching the left bank of the Rhine, the current speckled with barbarians fleeing in their makeshift craft, he paused no more than a day, just long enough to let his troops relish their triumph. He then struck north, aiming at the great Roman cities that had been lost over the past decade, and which he had resolved to regain for Rome. He met no resistance at shattered Coblenz, the city which since earliest antiquity had been known as the Confluence because of its location at the juncture of the Moselle and Rhine rivers. Tens of thousands of displaced barbarian farmers and soldiers retreated in terror and surrendered the entire city to a dozen of Julian's advance scouts before the main forces of his army had approached within twenty miles of the city walls.

Arriving effortlessly at Cologne, the city which only a year before had been a source of nightmares and terror upon his first learning of its fall to the barbarians, he gathered together at the single tower still left standing with the representatives of the united barbarian tribes. There, he dictated to them conditions that would maintain their peace and subjection through the winter, after which, he made it clear, his campaign would begin anew until all of Rome's former territory in Gaul had been returned to the Emperor's domains.

Leaving garrisons to man the cities and towns he had reconquered, he marched back to Reims with a skeleton force consisting largely of his Acolytes, as a personal guard. He gave an account of his actions to Ursicinus and the surly Marcellus, and then coolly retired to his winter quarters at Sens, which he had chosen in large part for the reputed vastness of its governor's library, and for the healing qualities of the sulfur baths to be found in the vicinity, which he felt would be comforting to Helena when recovering from the birth of her child. The library did not disappoint, though Julian's information on the baths was apparently out of date, having been gleaned from an ancient commentary on Julius Caesar's account of the Gallic Wars. The springs, it seems, had been dry for three centuries.

BOOK THREE

LIFE AND DEATH

Nescia mens hominum fati sortisque futurae
et servare modum rebus sublata secundis!

How ignorant are men's minds, of fate
And of their destinies; how loathe to keep
Due measure when uplifted by success.
—VIRGIL

LIFE AND DEATH

I

God, Brother, is not to be found in the bronze statues of Zeus and Apollo in the temples of Athens, which you, of course, will be the first to assert; nor residing on the heights of Olympus or in a palace in the depths of the wine-dark sea, or skulking in a cave surrounded by voiceless wraiths deep beneath the earth, all of which you again will laughingly dismiss as unworthy even of your briefest consideration. Nor, however, is He to be found in the tear-stained icon adorning the wall of the anchorite's cell, nor even in any of the myriad splinters and shards of the True Cross reverently traded by wealthy pilgrims and Desert Fathers alike, in such quantities that they would be capable of rebuilding the entire Ark of Noah. And it is only among those of the deepest faith in the Mystery of Mysteries that God may be found in the morsel of bread and drop of wine in the Eucharist. Among the vast majority of lesser mortals, belief in His presence therein ebbs and flows, rising and falling like the tides, with the swelling and shrinking of our faith, dependent as it is on the circumstances of our own lives and fortunes. I say this not to denigrate those favored ones, like yourself, who have been graced with the gift of unquestioning belief, but rather to acknowledge the reality facing the rest of humankind, who struggle daily in the quest for God and meaning in their lives.

For at the risk of descending into the *bathos* that the

Greek tragedians so wished to avoid, God is to be found not in so many exotic and obscure locations as remote mountaintops, or in the preserved finger joints of centuries-dead martyrs. Rather, He is here before us, every day, in the birth and miraculous presence of a baby, in man's constant capacity for redeeming the errors of his existence and creating himself anew, in a perfect, unstained, and sinless regeneration of himself, without lust or ambition or evil intent, a confirmation of the image in which he was created, and of his ultimate rightness with God. Chastise me if you will for my heresy, Brother, but I knew, as I saw Julian that evening by the flickering firelight, holding and gazing in rapture at the son that was the guarantor of his immortality, that God had descended into our midst as surely as He had in Bethlehem three and a half centuries before, as surely as He does so briefly and mysteriously into the Sacred Host that is the very lifeblood of our faith.

"What age so happy brought thee to birth? How worthy thy parents to have begotten such a creature!"

Still softly murmuring the lines from Virgil, Julian handed his son, only minutes old, back to Helena's midwife Flaminia, a well-known Gallic birther who had tended her and accompanied her on the journey north from Vienne. The midwife took the baby to a corner, carefully rewrapped him in his swaddles, and carried him into Helena's bedchamber. Oribasius, who as a rule disliked births, had scuttled back to his quarters as soon as the procedure was complete, leaving Flaminia to perform the cleanup and postpartum care, along with her daughter, who was assisting her. I waited where I sat, in the candlelit anteroom outside the chamber, hearing Julian's low voice as he talked softly to his sleepy and satisfied wife, and to the cooing of the midwife as she deposited the young prince onto Helena's soft breast. Matilda, the daughter, remained in the anteroom with me, waiting for her mother to emerge so they could return home. She was a frail, jittery lass,

scarcely out of girlhood, yet unlike her thoroughly professional mother she seemed unable to sit still, constantly fidgeting with her hands and face, picking at her chewed
cuticles. I observed her calmly, noting that with a disposition like hers, it seemed doubtful she would ever make a
skilled midwife, as her mother was training her to be. My
attempts at conversation were fruitless—it was difficult for
her to remain on a topic, her Latin was halting, and even
her Gallic, though fluent, was tinged with an odd accent.
Her father, apparently, was a Germanic immigrant and the
girl spoke his dialect at home.

I soon gave up trying to put the girl at ease, and peeked
carefully into the room where Flaminia was settling the
baby and mother. Moments later, Flaminia tiptoed out, bidding me good night with a tired smile as she and Matilda
gathered their things and slipped out the door to their temporary lodgings down the corridor, and then Julian too finally left the chamber, closing the door softly behind him
with a click. He settled himself down across from me, and
though his eyes were red-rimmed from fatigue, he nevertheless began rummaging in the small map case he had
ordered brought in from his staff office, and I saw without
surprise that he was beginning the next phase of his work-
day.

I asked him if he would mind some company, as my
nerves were too worked up to even contemplate sleeping
at that time, and he smiled happily.

"Of course not, old friend," he said. "It would be a welcome change from the shifts of dreary scribes who usually
accompany me at night. I'm afraid I'm not up to conversation, but if you can endure my silence, please stay."

I wanted nothing more, and having neglected to bring
any reading materials of my own, I contented myself with
merely gazing into the coals of the fire.

It must have been about two hours after midnight when
I was awakened from a light sleep I did not even realize I
had fallen into. I jerked my head up with a start and glanced
over at Julian. I assumed it had been the cry of the baby

that had awakened me, and marveled at how long the infant had slept between feedings. Julian looked at me expectantly, however, and I then realized that the sound in question was a soft rapping at the door, and that the Caesar, surrounded as he was by maps and parchments and with his quill dripping ink, was hoping that I would be better disposed to get up and answer it. Shaking my head groggily I stood and stretched, then walked the three steps across the small room to open the door.

Two sentries stood before me, a spitting, struggling woman standing between them with her hands bound in front of her and a heavy woolen cloak over her head and shoulders. In the flickering torchlight behind them I was unable to make out her identity.

"Beg pardon, sir," said the sentry on the left. "We seek the Caesar."

I heard Julian quickly rise behind me from his stool and stride to the open door, where he stood looking quizzically at the strange trio. "Yes?" he inquired amiably.

The men shuffled awkwardly. "We disturb you only because we know you keep late hours, sir," the first one said tensely. "We just came off our shift at the outpost, sir, five miles beyond the city walls on the south road, when we came across this woman, ridin' hell-for-leather on a horse from your stables, sir, and with no baggage to speak of but her little kit, and a pouch of new coins. We found it passing strange, to say the least, at this hour of the night, and thought it best to bring her back and confirm she has leave to borrow the horse. Another woman was with her, sir, but slipped past us in the dark."

Julian stood perplexed for a moment, blinking in the dim light, and then stepped away from the door.

"By all means," he responded. "Bring her in, but quietly, if you please."

The two sentries, looking uncomfortable, stepped into the room, pushing the woman in front of them, who stumbled slightly as she stepped over the threshold and cursed under her breath. Julian led her over to the light of the candles he kept burning brightly around his desk, and ordered her to remove her cloak so he could see her face.

The woman threw back her head defiantly, letting the hood of the cloak slip off, and as she did we froze. It was Flaminia the midwife, her kindly, patient expression now replaced by one of ill temper and exasperation.

"Caesar, these men have unjustly accused me and disturbed your rest," she began loudly, knowing as well as anyone present the reason to keep our voices down. "I received word that I was urgently needed for a birth in an outlying village, and had simply borrowed the fast horse to make greater speed."

At ill-mannered Flaminia's loud words, I sighed and stepped over to Helena's door, intending to enter quietly and put her mind at rest, for assuredly all the commotion in the anteroom had awakened her and the baby. Ignoring the midwife's hoarsely whispered protests that I would be disturbing the mother's sleep, I stepped inside. As the light from the anteroom flooded across the bed, Helena's eyes fluttered open sleepily and she lifted her head in befuddlement and with a slight grimace of pain.

I saw with relief that the baby was lying quietly at her breast in the crook of her arm, precisely where the midwife had placed him earlier that evening, and I stepped forward to apologize to Helena for disturbing her at such an hour. She smiled contentedly, and I reached down absentmindedly to stroke the baby's tiny head, and to gently feel the pulse through the soft spot at the top where the skull was not yet fused.

The pulse was not there. The baby's head was stone cold.

I hesitate to describe the horrible scene that ensued, Brother, for whatever you can imagine, it was ten times worse. Thinking I had made some mistake, had somehow lost my touch, I placed both hands on the infant's head and palpated frantically, then pried him from Helena's arms and lifted him to the light to examine him more closely. The skin was deathly white, the eyes rolled back into the head, the joints stiff and hard; such symptoms are terrifying enough when seen in a man who has fallen in battle, perhaps unconscious and facedown in a pool of his own blood. But in an infant, in a tiny vessel of Almighty God Himself, the effects of it are perverse, the very image of evil. I let out a cry, and Helena struggled to a sitting position, reaching for her baby at the same time as Julian rushed in and saw me clutching the infant in horror. He snatched the tiny creature from me and brought him into the light of the anteroom, where he collapsed to his knees, holding the baby to his chest.

"H-how can this be?" he stammered questioningly at Flaminia, his eyes filled with confusion. Helena struggled out of bed and stood leaning against the door frame as I supported her on the other side. "Help my son," he pleaded to the midwife, "he's not breathing."

Flaminia looked sorrowfully down at him. "Your wife must have rolled over and suffocated him in his sleep, Caesar," she said. "It happens often enough to first-time mothers. I should never have placed him in her arms this night and then left. My God, I intended to return later and check on them, but I received this urgent message. Lord knows what has become of the other baby I was called upon to deliver this evening."

Julian stared at her uncomprehendingly, and then turned to look at Helena, who had straightened up in wild-eyed astonishment, clutching her belly in pain and rocking back and forth on the balls of her bare feet. Tears coursed down her cheeks as she contemplated the implications of what the midwife had just said.

"Please, my lord, it will be daylight soon," the midwife pleaded. "I first left the palace over two hours ago—I have an urgent assignment that I must attend."

"Urgent assignment . . ." he muttered, then he looked up fiercely. "Begone with you, then! I'll not be the cause of another . . ."

Flaminia smiled triumphantly at the two sentries, who quickly stepped forward to cut her bonds. My mind raced at the thought of what had happened, as the midwife's ropes dropped free. She stepped quickly to the door, massaging the feeling back into her numb hands that were white where the tight knots had bound them, knots that had slowly cut off the flow of blood . . . the flow of blood . . .

"Wait!" I shouted, and everyone in the room jumped. Flaminia stepped quickly out the door and I could hear her steps as she began racing down the corridor. I leaped away from Helena, who was only barely able to brace herself in the door frame on her own, and ran out the door. I skidded around the corner into the polished-marble corridor and saw Flaminia running pell-mell toward the staircase and the exit. The two sentries, after recovering from their initial startlement, themselves raced out the doorway to follow my strangled cry.

"Hold that woman! Hold the midwife!" I shouted, and there was no contest, for although I was tired, I was still a young man, and it cost me little effort to catch up with a woman twenty years my senior. I was not gentle, however, and seizing her about the waist I tackled her as do boys playing a game of chase in the dust. We fell heavily onto the marble floor, where she hit her jaw hard, and narrowly avoided being trampled by the sentries following close on our heels.

"What in God's name?" shouted Julian, himself emerging from the anteroom and running to where we had all gathered around the moaning midwife. "What are you doing, Caesarius? Are you mad? Will you cause the death of another infant tonight?"

"My lord," I gasped, "this woman must be held until I can examine the baby. I assure you," and I gulped hard, thinking of the white skin and already stiffened joints, "I assure you that Helena did not kill your son."

Julian stared at me, wild-eyed, then whirled on Flaminia in a fury. By now half the palace had been awakened and was in an uproar. Servants were running into the corridor in their nightclothes, hair bedraggled, and a trio of household dogs had set up a mad yammering, running through people's legs and leaping at the soldiers as they struggled to lift the writhing midwife, blood pouring from her broken teeth and split chin, and place her again in fetters.

"Throw her in the cellar, and may God damn her," Julian shouted at the guards as Flaminia spat and clawed at him frantically. "I want a full confession!" His voice was choked and his breathing labored now, and he glared at the woman with an expression as crazed as I had ever seen on the apoplectic Constantius during one of his own fits of rage.

"Julian," I began, trying to remain calm. "Julian, I must examine the baby first. We can't know what happened until—"

"A full confession, damn her!" he screamed at the guards as they dragged their prisoner away. He whirled on me. "Caesarius!" he barked. Despite the wild commotion around us and Flaminia's frantic screaming echoing down the corridor, I jumped. For a moment I was afraid he would order me to extract the confession, for a physician's knowledge of pain centers and joints was sometimes used for just such a purpose. My fear on this score, however, was quickly allayed, as he paused for a moment, still staring at me, trembling in rage. Then his face softened slightly as, struggling, he gained control over his emotions, and turned away, slowly but still shaking. "I have an assignment for Paul the Chain," he muttered, to himself more than anyone, before sweeping past the pandemonium of hysterical maidservants to return to his sobbing wife.

Minutes later, the reluctant Oribasius and I examined the body of the baby, much to my colleague's distaste, as he had little use for autopsies, particularly on infants.

"The midwife was probably correct," he said laconically before we began. "Helena simply rolled over on him in her sleep. She's a big girl, Caesarius. It happens all the time."

I was not convinced. "I saw her myself, Oribasius," I countered. "Helena sleeps soundly, without moving the entire night. As her physician, I have witnessed this many times in the past. When I found her and the baby, they were in precisely the same position as when the midwife had left them. Besides, the baby was white, not blue as he would have been had he suffocated."

Oribasius shrugged. "Proceed, then," he said. "I will observe your efforts, but don't ask me to participate."

As it happened, an autopsy was unnecessary. When we unwrapped the swaddles, we were surprised to find not the normal two layers, but five full sets of wrappings—the outer ones hiding the inner layers, which were soaked in blood.

"The infant's cord was not tied," I noted grimly. "He bled to death."

Oribasius peered at the bloody little corpse in astonishment.

"But I saw her tie it off!" he exclaimed. "I held the cord in my fingers while she knotted the string—it was still pulsating!"

We stood staring at the baby in silence.

"And then," I began slowly, "and then you left, and Flaminia gave the baby to Julian to hold." I thought hard, straining to remember all the insignificant details of the past night. "A few minutes later she took him back, and then she and her daughter went to the corner and changed his swaddlings, before taking him in to Helena."

"Changed his swaddlings? So soon?" Oribasius asked, puzzled.

"To murder him. She clipped off the cord above the knot, then wrapped extra cloths around him to hide the bleeding. My God—for a newborn, just losing a small cup's worth of blood would be fatal."

He had died in his sleep in his mother's arms, losing blood so quickly as to be unable to sustain life in his little body for more than an hour or two at the most, or even to gasp in distress to his sleeping mother—but long enough for the culprit to make her escape.

As Julian had ordered, Flaminia was placed in the cellar

below the palace, where in times past noble hostages who had been captured in battle were kept in relatively comfortable surroundings while awaiting ransom payments from their relatives. Prisoners had not been kept in those cells for two centuries or more, however, and the quarters now were far less accommodating. Her unceasing shrieks and howls, like those of a maddened dog, jangled our nerves that entire night and most of the next morning as Paul applied his instruments and techniques of interrogation. The sounds wafted up through the kitchen flues and ash drops, anywhere there was a vent or duct communicating with the cellars, and they trebled in volume a few hours later when Flaminia's husband and several other immigrant men were brought in, after being captured while attempting to flee disguised as beggars. The prisoners' incessant wailing drove all of us to near lunacy, and their cries were joined periodically by those of Helena, who herself drifted in and out of lucidity in her madness and grief. The only thing worse was the sudden silence from the cellar shortly after sunrise, almost at the peak of one of Flaminia's screams, leaving only the howling of the men, which itself was cut just as abruptly, one by one, moments later.

Oribasius looked at me and sighed, realizing the implications as well as I. We had just finished our own investigation and now walked slowly down the long hall to Julian's office, the same anteroom where I had left him the night before. He sat disheveled, his clothes unchanged, his face unwashed, a few of the candles still sputtering on the sills where he had left them lit, most of them dissolved into stinking masses of tallow. Papers and books were strewn on the floor where he had swept them off the tables in his misery and fury. Muffled sobs could be heard from the adjacent room where Helena lay, mixed with the soft voice of her Gallic nurse attempting to soothe her. In the midst of the chaos stood Paul the Chain, clean, freshly shaven, with a hint of perfumed scent and a faint, condescending smile on his lips as he calmly surveyed our rumpled clothes and hollow-eyed faces. He was flanked on either side by

Pentadius and Gaudentius, looking somewhat less prim.

"The court physicians have arrived, Your Majesty," he said unctuously, though Julian scarcely looked up from his vacant stare at the wall. Then casting an apologetic glance at us, he continued, "I was just about to report the results of my investigation into the mat—"

"Our suspicions were confirmed, Caesar," I hastily interrupted, wanting to avoid hearing the details of Paul's report. "The child was murdered, by the midwife. If you wish me to explain how, I will be happy to do so."

There was a long pause, during which the silence was broken only by the unremitting, choking sobs emerging from behind the thick oaken door of the next room. "I do not," Julian finally replied almost inaudibly, without moving. "It is enough for me to know that she has been found and caught, the murderous bitch. Now all others involved in the conspiracy must be uncovered."

At this Paul, as if on cue, stepped forward. "Indeed, Caesar, they already have."

Julian slowly turned his head, not yet facing us, for like anyone who has suffered a soul-crushing loss, he was not yet capable of looking another man directly in the face. He maintained his silence, however, and Paul continued.

"The midwife's husband was a German, who, though a permanent immigrant to these parts, was clearly bent on revenge at your defeat of his people. He was assisted by several Germanic cronies, relations of his, and they had infected the woman Flaminia with their hatred for Rome. Obviously they were in the pay of Chonodomarius' agents. Their gold, which the woman was carrying, has been sent to the imperial treasury, and the woman, her husband, and their collaborators . . . dispatched. We are still seeking the daughter." Pentadius and Gaudentius, silent as leeches, nodded vigorously.

Julian remained motionless for some time, looking as wretched and careworn as any man I had ever seen, having aged twenty years in a night. Finally, he stood up with a motion slow and deliberate, facing us all and straightening his shoulders from their habitual slump with what seemed a mighty effort.

"Chonodomarius will die for this. Slowly and painfully. I shall make it not only my personal goal, but the mission of the entire Western Empire, and this I pledge: Chonodomarius will die."

Matilda, the daughter, was captured several weeks later, purely by accident, when she was recognized begging in the city by one of the palace staff—she had returned after her escape, knowing of no safe place to hide. Since Paul had by then been recalled to Milan, and Julian could not be approached about the matter, Sallustius ordered that she be quietly executed. At my remonstrance, however, as to her youth and to the fact that the wretched girl was probably innocent of her parents' crimes, he shrugged dismissively and demanded simply that she be imprisoned outside the city walls, away from our sight. She was, and promptly forgotten.

II

During the winter, the season when officers are most often given leave to attend to their private affairs at home or in Rome, and the common soldiers simply hunker down to rest and recover their strength for the rigorous spring campaigning to come, Julian worked himself brutally, spending the mornings stripped bare to a loincloth in Sens's garrison camp, exercising with his own soldiers. He was completely absent of any shame of the fact that his physical skills and strength in the soldiering arts were barely equal to those of his bottom rankers, but he garnered the admiration of his troops for his relentless determination. His thin, common soldier's cloak, which he wore even in the bitterest wind that whistled down out of the north woods, and his unkempt hair were a familiar and welcome sight around the camp in the mornings. After his strenuous training at swordplay and the lance, and his physical conditioning with a boxing coach, he could often be found limping over to a campfire, throwing a blanket over his shoulders to spend a few moments savoring a bowl of soup and some hardtack like any infantry grunt, listening to the gripes and joking of his men.

In the afternoons he spent long hours huddled in his drafty, unheated quarters with Sallustius. One by one, he summoned each of the commanders of all the garrisons of Gaul and the Transalpine to meet with him personally over the course of several days during the winter. During these private meetings he and Sallustius grilled them mercilessly: What is the disposition of the barbarian troops in your area? Their numbers? Their weaponry? Their training habits and discipline? What is the level of fitness of your own troops? Your garrison's ability to withstand a prolonged enemy siege? Its ability to apply a siege to the enemy? What are the levels of cooperation between you and your neighboring garrisons? Frequency of communications? Sources of rivalry? Instances of incompetence? Each interview ended with the most important question of all: What of Chonodomarius? What of the Beast? But the barbarian king, with his unmistakable weapon and physique, had seemingly disappeared.

Indications of weakness or indecisiveness were immediately seized upon by Julian and derided as unworthy of the magnificent Roman army he was building. Relative troop strength was relentlessly debated, and thousands of men, from Spain to Britain to Gaul, were placed on the march that winter, as he and his advisers identified gaps in defenses that needed to be filled, officers who needed to be retired, dismissed, or promoted, and underutilized garrisons to be scheduled into routine rotation. The icy roads that winter witnessed a constant stream of shifting divisions, shouting officers, and infantrymen shivering and blowing vapor as they marched on the cobbles and flagstones in their standard-issue military tunics and cloaks. Dismissing such garb as impractical for a Roman fighting force, Julian insisted that the men be issued thick, woolen trousers, leather jerkins, and well-tanned ox-hide boots, to be equal to the winter-ready barbarians.

A low pall of smoke hung over the fields as the garrisons and camps on the front lines of the Rhine territories filled with soldiers newly transferred from the reconquered cities in the rear. The forum rang with the men's cheers in response to Julian's patriotic exhortations, and the workshops rang with the sounds of the armorers' anvils as they reshod the long-neglected battle horses, and restocked the quartermasters with spare javelins, swords, shields, and helmets.

The smithies created length after endless length of thick, sturdy chain, which we strung across every road and minor river to inhibit the passage of all persons except those authorized by each local garrison commander.

But although he spent his days in constant motion, his nights offered little respite, for in the hours after dark, when the rest of the city and the camp lay in exhaustion from his demands, he paced and watched, preparing himself for the bitter cold of his shirtless morning training sessions with his men, only a few hours away. He never used his bed or even a camp cot anymore, but preferred to take his rest for only an hour or so at a time, his head down on his arms at his study table, or leaning back against the hard stone wall as he sat upright on a stool. Fearing the effect on his health, I would try to force him to rest.

"Rest?" he asked questioningly. "Impossible. Idle hands are the devil's tools. You know that old saw, Caesarius."

"And what does that mean? Exhaustion and sickness are the devil's delight as well. You drive yourself too hard."

He shrugged it off. "If building an army means losing some sleep, then I will lose sleep. I could not forgive myself if Rome's borders were breached because her Caesar was sleeping. When preparations are complete, then I will slow down."

His nights he spent with his beloved philosophers, Plato and Marcus Aurelius foremost among them, and passed hours discussing with me the subtleties of thinkers such as Plotinus and Iamblichus. He took much delight in my ability to pick up on the neo-Platonists' closely reasoned arguments, though he laughingly derided my opinion that such philosophies were unworthy of an enlightened Caesar in the new Christian age. God, however, he had relegated to a tier far down on his list of priorities, as he attended Communion services only when required for reasons of state, and read Scripture almost never. It was almost as if, rather than seeking out comfort from Christ during times of torment, he avoided Him out of a sense of betrayal. I often kept Julian company during his long hours in the dark

library, distressed that the jewel-encrusted, illuminated codex of the Gospels Eusebia had sent him that winter as a
gift had been carelessly relegated to a corner shelf. On several occasions I artfully arranged to leave it lying open to
passages I thought might be appropriate to his mood that
day, but he ignored or refused the hint, impatiently returning the heavy volume back to its place.

By February, after almost six months of turmoil and
movement among the armies of Rome in Gaul and the West,
Julian and Sallustius finally seemed satisfied with the arrangement of their forces and their preparations for the
spring campaign. The barbarians had begun testing the resolve and strength of the Romans with predatory raids in
eastern Gaul, but had been repulsed by the reinforced garrisons on every occasion, confirming Julian in his thinking
that he had effectively anticipated the strengths and weak-
nesses of both his and the enemy's forces.

And then disaster struck.

Stupidly, blindly, he had been so focused on building
effective bulwarks for the Empire against the Alemanni
massing on the far side of the Rhine that he had neglected
his own base of operations. The local commander at Sens
had not been subjected to the exhaustive weeks of probing
and discussion that every other commander in the province
had suffered. The city's walls were collapsing in some
points, and crumbling nearly everywhere else; worst of all,
the local garrison had been reduced through reassignments,
leaving Julian even without the services of the *scutarii* and
gentiles in his personal bodyguard, the shield-bearing Gallic
infantrymen and mounted lancers who were traditionally
assigned to support high-ranking Romans when visiting
Gaul. Only his Acolytes and a skeleton garrison remained
in the city.

And the Beast noticed.

He arrived on precisely one of the endless nights that I
have described for you, Brother, just before Dawn stretches
forth her rosy fingers to light the face of the heavens, the
coldest part of the night when even the sentries on watch

are beginning to nod in their drowsiness. An arrow, whizzing silently through the frigid air in the midst of a cloud of such angry missiles, slammed into the face of one of the watchmen, an enormous man and a crack wrestler from Phrygia nicknamed Helix, "the Creeper." The arrow pierced his cheekbone and knocked him off the wall, but incredibly, the man survived the twenty-foot fall with full consciousness, and true to his name, he crawled to the next sentry post dragging a broken leg behind him, the arrow shaft lodged deep in his face, and sounded the alarm.

The Acolytes were immediately roused, as were the two hundred men of the garrison, and Julian, who was naturally already awake, quickly called the city magistrate and ordered him to summon the local militia. The old man did so immediately, gathering together a thousand merchants, tradesmen, and farmers lodging within the walls for the morrow's weekly market to assist in defending the city. It was only with great difficulty, and the loss of some forty Acolytes and garrison soldiers, that we were able to repel the fierce barbarian attack that night. I confess that our success in doing so was due not so much to our own skills and training as to the barbarians' astonishing misfortune: During a clever feint on our main gate, they had sent a large body of crack assault troops to a point on the other side where our walls had crumbled so far that the local urchins routinely climbed through the rubble to steal fruit from the orchard on the other side. It was only by the merest chance that one small boy happened to be doing just that when he spied the band of barbarians assembling for the rear attack. The brave lad was able to rush back and sound the alarm in time for Julian to divert his forces to that sector, and thereby save the city.

Daylight revealed our precarious situation. Sens had been ripe for a bold stroke, for the barbarians to effect a lightning raid to capture the Caesar and all his staff in one fell swoop. God's grace had prevented this for the time being, but when I peered over the walls that morning I surveyed ten thousand Alemanni massing just out of our arrow range, their officers racing and prancing up and down the lines on their horses. In their midst was a single, enormous German, shirtless in the cold and brandishing a *harpoon*, as my old acquaintance at the palace in Milan had put it. My blood ran cold. All I could think of was the fate of Lucius Vitellius and his men at Cologne, and I sought out Julian to inform him that his prayers had been granted: he was about to face the Beast.

Julian, however, was not to be delayed by my morbid warnings; the man had become a tornado. Despite having taken no sleep the night before, he and scowling Sallustius seemed to be everywhere. The city's gates had attracted his first attention, just as the attack was getting under way, and were barricaded in time. Sections of the walls that were threatening breach were immediately repaired as well, though not without loss of a considerable number of men to arrow wounds, as they were forced into exposed positions low on the walls to replace the missing stones. For two days and nights he stalked the ramparts ceaselessly, pressing into service every man and woman in the city above the age of twelve. The youngest and least skilled he assigned to the menial tasks of hauling hods of mortar and collecting spent barbarian arrows from the streets; the oldest men and women were made to prepare food in their own kitchens for the soldiers and workers so they would not have to take the time to do so on their own. Within two days, two normal weeks of defensive works had been accomplished, and Julian, at my persistent urging, allowed himself to take a nap, one of an unthinkable duration for him, five hours—at which point he rose, refreshed, and recommenced his urgent pacing of the walls.

Night and day he strode the battlements and ramparts, grinding his teeth in fury at his stupidity in retaining for himself such meager numbers of troops, which prevented him from breaking the siege. Below the walls fumed Chonodomarius, in equal rage that his plans for a swift blow against the Caesar had been thwarted, and that he was now reduced to besieging a large, walled town with troops that were insufficient in either number or patience to do so successfully. For hours every night we could hear him bellowing in pidgin Latin in his great voice, taunting Julian with harsh words:

"Come down, little Greek, and fight like a man! Come down, you show me what Greeks are made of, you tiny-dicked dog! A pole I have for your comfort, great Caesar, as big as my own, the same pole that Lucius enjoyed. . . . !"

I raged loudly at his obscene prattling, but Julian merely stared from the tops of the walls, his eyes glinting murder and hatred, his expression reflecting the frustration he felt at having the killer of his son so close as to see his very face, to hear his voice—yet to be unable to emerge from his own harried defenses. He forced himself to study the maneuvers of the attackers, occasionally commenting to Sallustius on the discipline and arrangement of the Alemanni forces. It took a supreme effort of will to prevent the Beast's taunts from rattling him.

He later told me that he concluded the barbarian's bluster was less for the sake of rankling us than for maintaining the cohesiveness of his own restless forces. Chonodomarius was the leader of a huge collection of families and clans, but the ties of fraternal kinship among barbarians extend only so far, and in that, Brother, the Alemanni are not much different from us civilized men, truth be told; for just as the sons of the Emperor Constantine slaughtered each other mercilessly, real love between brothers is a rare occurrence indeed. Whether this is because of the sins of Adam or, what is more likely, the effects of primogeniture and the inheritance laws, I cannot say. The Beast's strengths, to us, appeared formidable, but within his own clans his position could be precarious.

Fortunately, Sens was well stocked, due to the fresh influx of supplies for the farmers' market to have been held the day of the attack; and water was abundant, from the large number of springs and fountains inside the city walls. Defensive weapons, too, were readily available, for Sens had long been a regional distribution center for military provisions. Apart from each soldier's plentiful complement of arrows, bows, javelins, and spears, the walls were well supplied with more powerful devices, often requiring several men to operate: "wolves," which are a type of crane set up over gates, with tongs for grasping the head of a battering ram as it strikes, and a winch to haul it sideways; "scorpions," portable devices designed to hurl stones by applying the crank-twisting and sudden release of a rope of hemp or human hair; and "wild asses," which are rather larger and more unwieldy scorpions.

It was the catapult that was particularly fearful, from the standpoint of damage to humans and animals. The device is a huge mechanical bow designed with grooves fitted with thick bolts with wooden fletching, which can be shot with murderous force. It is operated by three men, one the "spotter" to sight the target and place the bolt in the horn groove, while the two others wind the crank. The spotter then releases the catch and fires the heavy bolt to astonishing effect, at such a speed that no sloping of the arrow over distance even needs to be taken into account. On one occasion I watched as a barbarian cavalry officer was selected as the target. The spotter took careful aim, and upon firing, the bolt whizzed invisibly across the field and slammed into the officer's thigh, neatly piercing his thick armor and penetrating all the way through the horse's ribs. The impact was so strong it actually lifted the animal's hindquarters into the air before it fell, the man's near leg pinned to it by the bolt, and his far leg crushed under the fall of the horse. With that, I thanked God that I was not the barbarians' camp physician.

The garrison would be able to hold out for several weeks at full provisioning, twice that long if rationing were imposed, perhaps indefinitely if the civilians were ejected and thrown to their fate with the barbarians. It was simply a matter of waiting for Marcellus to arrive with reinforcements from Reims. But as day after day passed with no signs of salvation from that quarter, and with the barbarians becoming bolder, Julian's confidence in Marcellus' ability to lift the siege began to flag. On the day of the initial attack he had sent several pigeons, with identical messages, ordering Marcellus to bring assistance. He received no response. Runners were then dispatched, a riskier proposition given the likelihood of their being seized and tortured after slipping outside the walls; yet at least two of them successfully made it past enemy lines, as we were informed by the small signal fires they set that night on a vacant ridge just to the northern limits of our view. The messages, however, were as if scattered by the winds of heaven, puffed into the clouds unheard and unread. Marcellus did not arrive, and Julian boiled with anger at the delay, suspecting the worst of the commander.

It was soon apparent, from our vantage point high atop the walls and from the loud, unguarded voices of the barbarians wafting through the still night air, that Chonodomarius would not be able to keep his men in check much longer. When we could see that an all-out attack was being prepared, Julian ordered the city's smiths, both army and civilian, to work night and day on the manufacture of primitive and forgotten devices he recalled from his readings of Plutarch—caltrops. These consisted of iron balls, each fitted with four sharpened spikes a foot or so in length, equidistant from each other on the sphere. They could either be carefully positioned, or simply tossed on the ground from atop the walls; but however a caltrop lands, it always rests upon a firm tripod of spikes, with the fourth aimed straight up in the air. The troops called them the Devil's burrs. Hundreds of the devices were quickly crafted and by darkness strewn thickly on the ground outside the walls around the main gate, and on the narrow stone bridge leading to the entrance, where Julian had judged the enemy's attack would come.

This measure was none too soon, for the very night the caltrops had been placed, the enemy mounted a massive assault. It began with a feint by a smaller detachment that Chonodomarius had shrewdly directed toward a weak point in the walls on the far side of the city opposite our main gate, diverting a large number of our troops to that area. Just as we succeeded in fending them off, however, shouts rose from the sentries manning the entrance and we rushed back, fearing the worst.

The worst had occurred. While the bulk of the Acolytes and the garrison were defending the rear of the city, a half dozen traitors within the walls had made their way to one of the towers at the main gates. There, they overpowered the crew manning the massive oaken gate bars and pulled the winch, raising a beam and allowing one of the two enormous gates to swing open. With thundering, slashing hooves, a squad of torch-wielding Alemanni cavalry plunged toward the open door, followed by a mob of howling infantry, their bodies naked and streaked with flame-colored paint, like that of their barbarous leader. We ran breathlessly along the tops of the walls, still several tower lengths distant from the defensive bulwarks over the gates, watching their approach in despair. The Germans' terrifying size and the ghastly paleness of their skin, an infernal vision if ever I had seen one, struck all of us with dread; as the ancients knew, in all battles it is the eyes that are conquered first, and if the outcome of this engagement had depended upon what we saw, we would by now all be laboring in some frigid, northern iron mine with brass slave chains pinning our manhood backwards by the foreskin.

As the Germanic horse troops stormed onto the narrow stone bridge, unable to see clearly by their wavering torchlight but trusting in the smoothness of the path that funneled them toward the open gate, the animals caught their hooves in the spikes of the caltrops lying thickly on the flagstones. Screaming in pain, they stumbled and fell, impaling themselves and their riders, raising howls of rage from those falling upon them from behind. We had not yet fired a single shot above the milling, moaning horses, and the barbarian infantry, running just behind the horsemen, must have assumed that the collision and piling were due merely to the riders' incompetence at trying to force too many horses simultaneously onto the narrow bridge. Bellowing in reproach at the writhing cavalry and animals blocking their path to the open entrance, which they could see only yards before them, they swarmed over the mounds of horses and men, leaping down the other side onto the caltrop-studded bridge—and impaled themselves in turn, in the feet and groin, on the evil spiked spheres awaiting them there like patient, ravenous spiders.

The nature of a caltrop, unfortunately, is that it can penetrate only one man, after which it has been neutralized; so by their sheer numbers, the barbarians charging blindly up the mounting piles of dead and wounded soldiers and down the other side were slowly, but effectively, making their way closer to the entrance. The caltrops had bought us sufficient time, however. The traitors wielding the winch that had opened the gate, seeing Julian's troops racing back to the entrance, lost heart in their task and dodged outside the gates to join their fellows. There, they were themselves pierced painfully and fatally through the feet and buttocks by the caltrops placed before the door. The open gate was quickly slammed shut and the Roman troops, taking their customary places on the wall up above, began raining missiles and stones down on the infuriated barbarians below, making short work of those who had had the misfortune to become impaled but had not yet died. The enemy retreated in disarray, and the remainder of that night was filled with the sounds of their howling, in pain and mutual recrimination, with the frustrated bellows of the Beast sounding loudest of all. Again and again he issued his obscenity-laced demands that the Caesar meet him personally to surrender the city. By morning, however, the barbarians had dispersed into the hills, leaving a thousand smoldering campfires as their only trace.

And what of poor Helix, you might ask, Brother? I daresay he is not in heaven, nor is that because he has made his lodgings in hell. After the chaos of the initial attack, he found his way to me with the help of a comrade, for the garrison was so understaffed it did not even have a camp doctor. Appalled at his grisly appearance, with the arrow still emerging two feet from the front of his face, I resigned myself to his imminent death and resolved simply to make his last hours more comfortable. Surprisingly, his greatest source of pain was his broken leg, and seeing that this was also the injury I could most easily fix, I ordered his comrade and a passing slave to hold the man down while I set it and splinted it. This Helix endured with nary a grimace, distracted, no doubt, by the strange sight of the arrow's fletching hovering before his eyes wherever he looked. Then as an academic exercise, I took a closer look at the arrow.

Having apparently been shot from rather a long distance, it had fallen into his face at a downward angle, and was aimed toward a point in the back of his neck. I walked behind him as he sat erect on the stool, and pressing his neck there I could actually feel a hard lump, which made Helix wince in pain as I touched it. Borrowing a pair of tin snips from a smith, I clipped off the shaft close to his nose, and then carefully cutting into the back of the man's neck, I located the arrowhead, grasped it with a pair of surgical pliers, and drew the entire arrow cleanly through, barb and all. Helix fainted from the pain and had to be supported by his comrade, and at first I thought he was dead, as the blood hardly flowed from either hole. Amazingly, however, he came to his senses an hour or two later, sat up in his cot, and weakly asked for water. When I handed him a cup I half expected it to flow out the back of his neck, but it did not, and after I had cleaned and sutured the injuries he stood and limped dazedly out of the room of his own accord, leaning on a crutch. Though weak of leg for many months afterwards, he eventually recovered completely and survived to fight more battles for Julian. As far as I am aware, Helix creeps still.

Julian's first act was to order the arrest of Marcellus. When Sallustius heard this, he was livid, despite Marcellus' undeniable treachery. Striding into Julian's library, where he and I were assessing the procurator's report on the damage to the city, Sallustius closed the door sharply behind him.

"By the gods, Julian!" he protested, waving a copy of Marcellus' arrest order in our faces. "He was appointed by the Emperor! You may outrank him on paper, but you are defying the Emperor himself by arresting his general! This is *not* your mandate!"

With his face reddening and eyes flashing, Julian stood up slowly and snatched the paper away from his mentor. "Damn the Emperor!" he said deliberately, with calm but unmistakable fury. We immediately fell silent. After a moment, Sallustius let out his breath.

"I'd advise you to hold your tongue," the older man said quietly, staring hard at Julian. "The rank of Caesar has never before stopped Constantius from eliminating a rival who defied him."

Julian held his gaze, clenching and unclenching his fists in pent-up emotion. "For a year you've known me, Sallustius," he said, his voice barely controlled. "And you, Caesarius, for longer than that. With your help, I have built up the armies of Gaul. I have campaigned from the Atlantic to the Rhine. I have resisted every German assault and we have reconquered territory the barbarians had held for years. I have reformed the tax system, the state's coffers are overflowing, government administration has never been more efficient."

"This we know," I interjected. "Why recite it to us?"

His eyes remained locked on Sallustius. "You tell me," he said. "What was my mandate?"

Sallustius glared at him in silence.

"What was my *mandate*?" he roared.

Still we said nothing, though Sallustius dropped his glare.

"By God, my mandate was to do *nothing*! To let the state continue to rot, to see Gaul fall piecemeal to the barbarians while the Emperor's incompetent generals cowered behind their walls. My mandate was to be a *figurehead*!"

Julian strode around the end of the table to Sallustius and laid a hand heavily on his shoulder, placing his face within inches of the older man's.

"*You* trained me, Sallustius!" he shouted hoarsely, his eyes full of emotion. "*You* made me march, up there in the Alps above Vienne! *You* have watched every step I've taken since I arrived in this bloody province! Where in the hell do you think my loyalties lie? With an emperor who would just as soon have me dead as see me take any initiative beyond feasting and protocol? My ruler is Rome itself! Rome! All that I've accomplished, all that *we've* accomplished, Sallustius, has been for the glory of Rome! Caesars are beheaded, emperors die, but Rome lives forever—and Rome will *not* be stymied by a petty general in Reims who refuses to come to the aid of a besieged garrison!"

Sallustius stared thoughtfully at the floor for a moment, then nodded, composed his face, and strode out without a word. In the hallway I heard him barking orders to a centurion of military police to send a squad to Reims immediately to arrest General Marcellus. Julian slumped back down in his seat, exhausted, his hands over his face. I sat in silence for a moment, observing him, then quietly stood to go out myself. Just as I approached the door, however, he stopped me.

"Caesarius," he muttered, and I turned to face him. "We are doing right, are we not?"

I thought for a moment before answering. "Can you have any doubt?" I asked. "Have faith, in both God and yourself." I took the heavy codex of the Gospels and set it on the table in front of him. "Count on this," I continued. "And count on me."

He put his hands down, and his face looked years older from tiredness and strain. He ignored the book I had set in front of him, but instead looked up at me steadily, and smiled with genuine warmth.

"Sometimes," he said, "the hardest battles to be fought are within one's own camp."

When the military police arrived in Reims several days later to discharge their duty, they found that the commander of the Roman army of Gaul had already anticipated them, and fled days before to Rome. By this time, Sallustius' anger had cooled, and he strode into Julian's room to announce the unfortunate news.

"Marcellus has fled to the Emperor, Julian," he said impassively. "It is his version of events, now, that the Emperor will hear first, not yours. The first rule in court politics is to control the flow of information—and in this instance we have failed."

"We have not failed, Sallustius," Julian said, glancing up from the parchment he was reading. "We have the power of right and the good of Rome on our side, and with Marcellus gone we now have the entire army of Gaul at our disposal. With assets such as those, are Marcellus and the Emperor really of such concern?"

Sallustius shook his head in frustration and raised the subject no more. The barbarians were continuing to mass in the East, Chonodomarius was still at large, and our work had just begun.

III

As for Helena, it was as if the thirty days' siege of Sens had not even occurred, for she neither left her rooms nor acknowledged Julian's daily visits to her. Since the baby's death, she had maintained her own apartments, and had now become a virtual stranger to her husband, locked away in her own mute misery, accompanied only by an ancient Gallic slave woman. Julian had at first tried to bring her comfort—insisting they would have another child, that it was the fault of the evil midwife, that families even of the Roman elite often required the birth of eight or ten children to ensure the survival of even one to adulthood. The Emperor and Empress themselves, he pointed out, were unable to conceive at all. But Helena was inconsolable, half-mad from the loss of the infant she had carried for nine months and loved as her child even while in her womb. She constantly recalled the look of accusation that Julian had cast at her upon realizing the baby had died, when Flaminia had blamed her for smothering her own flesh and blood.

Oribasius had been assigned to Helena's care, but was at a loss when faced with her indifference to life. The physician hovered about her in frustration, offering various potions and herbal extracts, burning incense to the healing god Asclepius, and finally despairing as Helena began even to refuse food. At this he took me aside and asked my counsel.

"Caesarius, perhaps your methods would have some effect where mine have failed? I am losing my patient."

I shrugged. "What ails the Princess is a sickness of the soul. For that I am as helpless as you are. Have you brought in a priest to talk with her?"

Oribasius shrugged in turn. "That was the first step I took. He *confessed* her—strange custom you Christians have—which seemed to comfort her for a day or two, but she relapsed afterwards. Since then she has treated even the priests with the same indifference as she does the rest of us."

I considered this. In Milan, the prescribed remedy for cases of severe melancholy is a trip to a healthier clime outside the hot, dusty city. Ironically, the preferred destination is often Gaul, where the mineral springs and the cool mountain air are considered ideal. Here Helena was, in just such an environment, but suffering from the same distraction as I had seen among wealthy matrons in the court of Milan. Perhaps it was a problem not of place, but of people.

"The Princess hasn't seen her brother and friends for over a year now," I offered. "She's in a foreign land, surrounded by war, with a husband away half the year campaigning and obsessed with training even when at home; she's just lost her first child, to apparent murder. Even low-ranking officers are entitled to a leave of absence once a year; perhaps the Princess would benefit from a return to her family for a short time?"

Oribasius thought this an excellent idea, if only, it occurred to me, because it would remove the blame that would fall to him if a royal patient were to die while in his care. I raised the idea with Julian the very night he was informed of Marcellus' escape.

He thought carefully. "A coincidence you should raise the subject, Caesarius," he said. "In fact, Eutherius is just now preparing a trip."

I looked at him questioningly, for Julian was highly dependent upon the old eunuch for keeping his household affairs in order, supervising everything from the quality of the cooking to the legibility of the accountants' figures.

Julian would not be sending him away lightly.

"Marcellus is heading straight for Rome, where Constantius and the Empress are spending the winter. He will no doubt bring charges against me, that I have improperly usurped his powers as commander of the army. His version of events must not be the only one to reach the Emperor's ears. There is no one in my circle more well-spoken than Eutherius, nor more highly trusted by the Emperor, so I have asked him to go and to explain Marcellus' conduct. Not only would it be convenient for Eutherius to take Helena with him, but her views would bolster his defense before the Emperor—she, too, witnessed the siege."

Although I doubted very much that mute, stricken Helena would be of much assistance to anyone, I heartily concurred with his idea of allowing the Princess to accompany Eutherius on his mission. Within two days a proper traveling party had been arranged, the dazed Princess's luggage packed, her now considerably depleted bulk eased into a sedan chair, and Julian's blessing bestowed upon her. She seemed not to know, or even care, where she was being taken. The party was accompanied by a hundred cavalry and six hundred heavy infantry, sufficient to dissuade all but the most vigorous of barbarian attacks.

Helena's absence meant that Julian was no longer fettered with household cares, and he dove into his military duties with a gusto that surprised even his officers. Within a week of her departure he had collected fifteen thousand troops from their winter quarters in the various garrisons, including those of Marcellus' abandoned center of Reims, and had set off for the Vosges mountains. There, a number of recent raids by Alemanni on local farms and villages seemed to foretell a larger, better-planned movement by Chonodomarius in the near future. At the same time, the Emperor informed Julian by letter that he was preparing a new strategy, one that would crush the barbarians once and for all. He would be sending a newly formed army of twenty-five thousand men into Gaul from the southeast, to meet up with our forces at the Rhine. They would sweep the various barbarian tribes before them in a pincer movement, trapping them as if in an enormous net, and then destroy them or roll them up north to the far hinterland, where they would be dealt with by the Huns, never again to pose a threat to Gaul.

Thus, our familiar General Barbatio reentered our lives, he who had previously been the commander of the household guard under Julian's doomed brother, and who had been the officer responsible for Gallus' arrest and murder. At the Emperor's orders, Barbatio advanced through the Alps with his legions as far as Augst. Rather than crossing the Rhine as planned, however, and pushing north to meet up with our troops in the vicinity of Strasbourg, he settled down on the far side of the river to wait. This was either, as he claimed, because of the unexpected resistance of the barbarians opposing his river crossing, or rather (as Sallustius charged) because of his own perverse negligence.

In any event, Julian's intelligence about the barbarians' intent in the Vosges was wrong, for in fact the isolated attacks in the area were nothing more than another of the Beast's diversions. As soon as he saw that the Caesar had committed himself to Strasbourg, and that Barbatio had settled at Augst, Chonodomarius led a flood of barbarians pouring out of the Black Forest directly between the two Roman armies, driving a wedge through them. Moving with the force of a landslide, they raced across the plains of central Gaul to the very walls of Lyons, cutting off all communications with the coast. The gates of the city were barred just in time, however, and Chonodomarius, again thwarted in his plans to take a major city by surprise, in frustration ordered his forces to disperse throughout the region to pillage and plunder.

When word of the debacle reached Julian he reacted swiftly, sending three cavalry squadrons racing south and taking the looters on the flank. The barbarians retreated into the woods and fields, leaving behind some dead and much of the booty. Enormous damage had been done, however. Barbatio's scouts had been watching the operation closely, and the general immediately began sending a series of reports back to the Emperor complaining how easily our lines had been infiltrated by the wave of Laeti storming out from the Black Forest, and how Julian had unwisely split off his cavalry to chase them down. When one of Julian's squadrons pushed even farther south in its pursuit, it was actually stopped by a larger contingent of Barbatio's cavalry, who claimed that the Caesar was not authorized to interfere in the territory assigned to the general. The fleeing barbarians were allowed to melt through Barbatio's lines and escape to the Rhine with impunity, and the general reported to Constantius that the true objective of our cowardly officers was to corrupt the soldiers under his command.

Julian resolved to continue the operation on his own. The barbarians hindered us from chasing them through the already dangerous mountain roads, however, by an ingenious technique: They would first cut a row of enormous trees along our route in such a way that they remained upright, supported by only the slenderest layer of uncut bark. They then moved a hundred feet deeper into the forest and did the same thing with another row of trees, aiming their arc of fall at the first row carefully balanced along the road. Lastly, they hid in silence until our troops passed through the trap on their march, at which point, from deep in the woods, the barbarians used cunningly prepared ropes to pull down the farthest row of trees, which crashed in turn onto the huge trees nearest the road and sent them toppling onto our terrified troops. We lost a large number of men and wasted untold days clearing the roads after several ghostly attacks of this nature before we finally fought through to the Rhine.

Here, however, the barbarians sheltered their raiding parties on sandbars in the middle of the river. To gain access to them we required boats, of which we had none. Barbatio, however, had many at his camp upstream. Julian sent a courier to him asking for a mere seven, and in response Barbatio burned all he had, much to the delight of the watching barbarians. Chonodomarius, in fact, even took it upon himself to offer us assistance by sending the half-burned hulk of a captured Roman grain barge floating downstream, draped with the crew's mutilated corpses and painted with obscene Latin epithets in huge red letters on the outside of the hull for all to see.

Julian ignored the insult. By moonlight, he sent the scout Bainobaudes with a squad of auxiliaries to attempt access to the raiders' islands, using anything that floated. The first wave of troops, using rafts and dinghies hastily constructed from the timbers of Chonodomarius' gift vessel, reached the nearest island and actually took the barbarians by surprise, slaughtering them in their sleep. Then discovering the dugout canoes the barbarians themselves used to move about, they seized those as well, and continued their raids on the other islands over the next several nights. After a week, Bainobaudes returned from his expedition loaded with Roman booty recovered from the barbarians, to the acclaim of the worried soldiers waiting on the banks. The remaining barbarians in the vicinity, seeing that they were no longer safe even on the islands, retreated with their possessions across the Rhine to the right bank.

Barbatio, however, continued his obstruction and harassment, absconding with supply columns carrying provisions to Julian, burning crops that were intended as forage for our animals, and rejecting all pleas for cooperation. The troops on both sides, as well as the barbarians, watched the rivalry between the two commanders with a great deal of interest, though ignorant of the motives behind it. Their confusion, however, did not prevent the soldiers from drawing their own conclusion, which was logical enough: that Julian, a novice in military matters though increasingly perceived as a potential threat to the Emperor's rule, had not really been sent to reconquer Gaul, but rather to meet death on the battlefield. Wrong though this deduction might be, it only further increased the loyalty of his men to the cause.

Even Barbatio, however, could not simply remain an impediment forever, and he eventually received orders from Rome stating in no uncertain terms that it was imperative that he cross the river, establish a presence on the left bank of the Rhine, and meet up with the army of Gaul. Our couriers reported signs of increased activity at Barbatio's camp in preparation for a major movement, and a message we received from Eutherius about that time noted that the Emperor and his advisers were eagerly awaiting news from Barbatio of a major victory against the barbarians without help. Julian felt this tactic was senseless, and that a successful strategy would require the combined forces of both armies. One afternoon, however, as we walked back from a review of the troops, he confessed to me his frustration at being unable to effect this collaboration with Barbatio.

"What is worse," he concluded, "I am running short of ambassadors. I've already sent my own household steward to Rome, and all of my military couriers to Barbatio have been insulted and ejected from his camp. I must resort to asking a personal favor of you, Caesarius—particularly since you and Barbatio are already old acquaintances."

I listened to him in silence and some consternation. As you know, Brother, ever since we were children it has always been you who has been the public speaker in the family. I myself have always been wholly incapable of putting two words together coherently in front of strangers, and it is fortunate that you found your calling as a priest and a polemicist, for I am much more comfortable silently examining the dead than verbally cross-examining the living. We strode over to Julian's camp tent, where Sallustius was waiting impatiently, reviewing a sheaf of reports from the scouts.

"Explain to Caesarius the mission on which we are sending him," Julian said.

Sallustius scarcely looked up. "Just this," he replied tersely. "Convince Barbatio to stop seizing our supplies and obstructing our affairs, and rather to concentrate on destroying any barbarians the Caesar's forces might drive his way. All he needs to do is cross the Rhine and stay put, with his eyes open and his legions ready, while we beat the bushes for Chonodomarius and his men. Barbatio will get the pleasure of the killing and credit for the victory, and can retire happily back to Rome, leaving the province free of Alemanni. Don't worry about your luggage, physician. Your bags are already packed."

I took a deep breath and looked at Julian. He smiled at me confidently and slapped me on the shoulder, wishing me a successful trip, and in less time than it would have taken me to say a paternoster slowly, I found myself on a military courier horse with a guard of six cavalrymen, galloping to Augst.

BOOK FOUR

THE CROSSING

*The death of earth is to become water,
and the death of water is to become
air, and the death of air is to become
fire.*

—HERACLITUS THE OBSCURE

I

We arrived several days later, shortly after the noon hour, after talking our way past Barbatio's guard outposts and across the river on a rickety supply ferry. Even this far toward the Rhine's source, and in the low waters of summer, the river was wide and sluggish. Trotting north along the well-traveled road, signs of Barbatio's camp became evident miles before we actually arrived. For yards on either side of the road the land had been laid bare—clear-cut of its enormous, centuries-old fir and pine trees, the terrain shorn and denuded of all but the slenderest of saplings. Limbs and brush had been dragged into mounds and burned to charred heaps. Skid roads and wagon ruts crossed the land at all angles where the huge logs were still being bucked and dragged away by Gallic drovers using enormous teams of oxen—twenty-four, sometimes thirty-six or more, enough muscle power and raw materials to build an entire city.

Upon rounding the final bend before Barbatio's camp, I drew up my horse in astonishment. There before me lay not the small, temporary trading post and river docks I had been led to believe would be the site of the Roman encampment, but a veritable fortress city, constructed entirely of wood. For months Barbatio's army had been here, and the general had spared no effort or expense in securing the comfort and safety of his troops. Wharves extended far out into the river, braced sturdily on pillars of the same straight, heavy trunks I had seen dragged on sledges from the forests upstream; broad storehouses and depots were built directly on the piers, with others lining the riverbank for a hundred yards, all sided with sawed planks nailed on sturdy posts and beams; and the troops' barracks, hundreds of identical, flat-topped log huts neatly arrayed on carefully measured quadrants, each capable of sleeping eight or ten soldiers. The blocks of houses extended up the slope for a quarter mile, with the officers' quarters nearest the river somewhat larger and more luxuriously appointed. Surrounding the whole was a high palisade, the tips of the logs hewn to rough points, the walls fronted by a deep and broad ditch.

There was clearly no fear of attack at the moment, however, and the guard posts were minimal. The few men in the city itself were calmly going about their daily tasks, the sick and injured were recuperating on their litters by the street in the warm sun. The entire population, it seemed, both legionaries and hired hands, was swarming over the quays and docks, for it was here that the most amazing structure of all was to be found.

At this point the river was some five hundred yards across, at first glance a placid stream. But beneath its smooth surface, it bore a rapid current capable of carrying even the heaviest boats downstream at a man's jogging pace—in fact, the heavier the vessel, the faster. A deeper keel reached currents that would whisk the ship along at a speed that far surpassed that of lighter rafts and dinghies bobbing at the calm surface. Here Barbatio was constructing his bridge, one capable of sustaining the march of five Roman legions with their wagons and supplies, and their subsequent return loaded with barbarian plunder.

Pairs of huge pilings had been laboriously driven into the river a hundred feet apart across the entire expanse of the water, while across each such span heavy hempen ropes were stretched securely, forming the solid bracing for what was to follow. Stretched in a gently curving train from the right bank was an enormous line of barges and rafts—not of uniform length or width, but a motley assortment of craft, including grain and supply barges seized from the Alemanni and rude pontoons assembled locally by the soldiers. These were lined up end to end, the bow of each vessel securely lashed to the stern of the next, with the entire column passing between each pair of pillars. The sturdy ropes stretched between these pilings prevented the lateral movement that would have caused the entire line to shift downstream from the pull of the current.

The bridge was complete but for a short space in the middle, with room for perhaps two or three vessels, which were being poled along the existing portions of the bridge, readied for insertion into their places. Along the entire length hundreds of soldier-carpenters labored like ants, carrying flat-planed boards laboriously cut by teams of naked troops along the bank, working in pairs at crosscut saws. The planks too were laid end to end and nailed securely along the line of craft, lending rigidity to the entire structure at the joints between vessels, and forming two parallel tracks precisely the width of wagon wheels. This would provide a uniform surface on which the troops could march during the crossing the next day and, more important, stability for the hundreds of supply wagons to follow, drawn by skittish horses and oxen that would rebel at any more than a gentle swaying of the craft beneath their feet.

I stood on the low ridge above the encampment for an hour watching the unhurried but relentless labor below, one of the greatest examples of Roman military engineering I had seen. Finally, feeling the fatigue of my journey, I urged my horse into a slow trot and made my way along the hard-packed street to the general staff building, a two-story, frame-sided structure with legion pennants fluttering at the door.

This I was not even permitted to enter, for when the sentry was informed that I came from Julian, he curtly called into the doorway, summoning his cohort commander.

"General Barbatio is occupied with final preparations for

tomorrow's crossing," the man stated in a matter-of-fact tone. "He cannot see you now."

"May I at least make an appointment to see him later?" I inquired wearily.

The officer looked at me more closely. "Are you an army officer?" he asked suspiciously.

"No, sir—the Caesar's personal physician and his envoy. I have an important request for your commander. I need a few moments of his time."

The man paused and stroked his chin thoughtfully. "Come by this evening," he said. "I'll see what I can do. In the meantime, take your rest in the officers' barracks behind us. There are several empty cots. You can eat with us in the staff commissary while you're here."

I nodded gratefully, and leaving my horse I walked slowly to the barracks, the weariness now weighing on me like a leaden blanket. Seeing that the first cot at the door had no baggage and appeared not to have been slept in, I dropped my bag at the foot, collapsed onto it, and immediately fell asleep.

I awoke with a start. The hut in which I lay was still empty, but from the darkness I judged I had slept for hours, and the night was now well advanced. Standing hurriedly, I strode to the doorway and stepped into the street, dismayed to see by the height of the moon that the time must have been near midnight. Still, the sawing and hammering continued at the same steady pace I had heard at midday. Dodging shifts of soldiers carrying long planks through the street, this time by the light of torches and camp lanterns, I walked over to the staff headquarters. There I found the cohort commander standing outside, chatting with the sentry.

He looked at me with a wry smile. "And so the dead have risen."

I returned his gaze with a surly expression. "You could

have awakened me so I wouldn't miss my interview with the general."

"Wouldn't have done any good. The general hasn't been in his quarters all evening. Even now he's inspecting the bridge and conferring with his engineers. You did well by sleeping."

I shrugged. "I'll wander over to the bridge myself. Maybe I can corner him there."

Stepping back into the street I followed the sounds of the heaviest activity and made my way to the foot of the bridge, which consisted of a massive wheat barge, fifty feet wide and two hundred feet long. A soldier told me the Alemanni had scuttled it in a swamp nearby, but Barbatio had ordered it raised and patched. Lashed securely fore and aft to two pairs of gigantic pilings, it formed the rocklike base for the entire right-bank side of the bridge, with room to spare for warehouse structures and toolsheds along its sides, sheltering the narrow plank road that had been constructed in the middle. A similar massive craft had been installed on the left bank.

The bridge, I saw in the moonlight, had been completed while I slept. The train of craft swept in an unbroken line the entire width of the river, the linked vessels swaying downstream slightly in gentle arcs between each set of pilings, like festive ribbons draped over an archway. In the middle, carpenters were completing construction of the plank road and further securing the crucial joints between the last craft that had been inserted.

The full moon shone bright and peaceful, rising high south of the bridge and casting beautiful shadows and glimmers the length of the river, a pale, liquid light that reflected almost effervescent on the water, illuminating its course for miles in either direction.

It was while peering at the moon's reflected gleam, its long white tail rippling playfully in the gently swaying surface, that I saw them.

Far upstream, they appeared almost as waves or shadows, perhaps merely the strange diversions of currents

caused by the underwater shifting of sandbars or the remains of a bevy of stumps. I stared at them absentmindedly
for a time, until I noticed that they were not stationary, but
rather drifting steadily closer. A flotilla of boats perhaps?
No, not boats, for they rode too low in the water. I strode
out onto the bridge and trotted along the grain barge to the
next vessel, which was not encumbered by the large warehouses obstructing my view upstream. Arriving at the end
of the structures, I looked again.

They were closer now, not more than a half mile distant.
Something more than ripples but less than ships, bearing
down on the bridge with the relentless speed of the river's
current. I looked around somewhat nervously, and seized
the arm of a nearby centurion. He looked at me with irritation, but I merely pointed to the middle of the river upstream of the bridge. He followed the direction of my
finger, and his expression changed from annoyance, to
questioning, and finally to complete understanding—and
fear. Suddenly he whirled, stepping onto the plank road and
racing along the boards to the middle of the bridge.

"Logs!" he cried. This produced no response from anyone, as the city and bridge were surrounded by logs. "Bearing down from upstream!" he shouted. "Clear the bridge!
Clear the bridge!"

I looked back upstream. Logs, enormous specimens,
seven, eight, and nine feet across, were riding low and menacingly in the water like huge marauding sea creatures,
bearing down upon the very center of the bridge with all
the speed the irrepressible river could offer. Thirty of them,
no, fifty, a hundred in all, on a front a hundred yards wide,
in perfect true to the current, pointed like arrows at the heart
of Barbatio's structure. Now the din rose as men saw them
coming, and as they realized the consequences of being on
the bridge when the massive missiles struck. Soldiers and
carpenters dropped their tools where they stood, tossing
planks to the side or into the water, rushing forward or
back, some on the far end losing their heads and running
back to the near side so as not to be stranded away from

the Roman encampment. Men pushed and jostled, tripping over one another and bottlenecking at unfinished sections of the planking, all eyes fixed upstream at the silent black shadows bearing down on them.

The initial impact caused a sickening crunch, and a shudder snaked through the structure from center to ends, like a rope that has been sharply snapped. Timbers groaned and creaked as the huge logs smashed ponderously into the vertical pilings, loosening them like tent stakes kicked from the ground. As the logs hit, the force of the current rotated them sideways, and their rear ends swung around, slamming their full length and weight against the slender ties of the bridge.

But that was all. After the shudder and groan—silence. The bridge had held, barely, although it was bowing out dangerously where several of the support pilings had been uprooted. Yet still the bridge held! The men on both ends broke into a spontaneous cheer of relief, echoing across the silent river—yet their jubilation was short-lived.

At first I thought it could only be shadows, the trick plays of moonlight on overwrought eyes. But pushing my way through the crowds of men to the front closest to the center, I soon realized I was mistaken.

"Barbarians!" someone shouted. "It's the Alemanni!"

It was pandemonium. I stood rooted to the spot as the unarmed men behind me rushed again to the ends of the bridge for safety. First dozens, then hundreds of dark, shadowy figures, their naked bodies painted black with grease, clambered over the logs under which they had been hiding, some still clutching the hollow reeds through which they had been breathing as they had floated beneath and beside the missiles they had aimed at the bridge. Working rapidly and nimbly, they drew long knives and swords from their belts, and with trained strokes began hacking at the support ropes strung between the pilings, sawing at the lashings linking together the rafts and barges, using sticks and levers to pry up the planks that had been so painstakingly smoothed, fitted, and installed.

Within moments the middle of the bridge had been broken, and the first loosened vessel began floating away down the stream. With the structural tension released, the two ragged ends in the middle also began bowing out, and as the surface current began rushing through the breach, the jam of logs too began exerting inexorable pressure on the weak spot that had been opened.

Another cry rose up from Barbatio's men, this one of outrage at seeing their work destroyed by a handful of greased apes. With a roar that was echoed by their counterparts on the left bank, men seized tools lying about—axes and adzes, pry bars, boards, even the occasional sword or bow, and rushed in an angry mob toward the middle of the bridge, which was now swaying ominously, the ragged ends drifting steadily away from the linear into a curve down the stream.

"Don't let them get away!" I heard someone cry, and looking up I saw an officer in full dress armor bearing a crimson cloak—General Barbatio. "Seize those criminals!"

But the Alemanni had seen us coming. With white smiles glowing eerily in the moonlight from their blackened faces, they pried and slashed at the ropes until just before the lead Roman carpenters, wielding woodcutting tools, had reached their position. Then, each one pausing only long enough to seize a loosened plank, they leaped back into the water—this time *downstream* of the bridge—lay with their bellies flat on the broad boards beneath them, and serenely paddled off with the current, the moonlight reflecting for a long while on their glistening backs, as the Romans raged impotently on their now broken and wandering bridge.

Those who receive a second chance at life are often far tougher for it. Yet the first failure still rankles.

Although not a man had been killed or even injured on either side, the bridge had been utterly destroyed but for a few sad-looking vessels on either end. The planed planks that hung off their bows to link with the craft ahead of them in line now protruded forlornly like the tumescent tongues of the dead, and soldiers and engineers took turns standing on the end to stare with melancholy down the river whence the bridge's middle sections had disappeared. On the far side, across the immense distance now remaining to be spanned again, equal numbers of frustrated soldiers gathered. Barbatio was furious. Plans for the crossing had been set back weeks, for the timber required to build new rafts and road planks now had to be hauled considerably farther across the denuded slopes surrounding the encampment.

In the end, the army swallowed hard and did what Roman armies do best: cinched its belt, flexed its muscles, and hunkered down for more.

Barbatio was determined that a handful of Alemanni lumberjacks and suicide swimmers would not get the best of his legions, and in this regard he had become much wiser: Before commencing the rebuilding of the bridge, he posted detachments of soldiers every mile upstream for five miles, each outpost supplied with a quantity of small rafts and dinghies. These were assigned the duty of intercepting any further flurries of floating log missiles the barbarians might send down. In fact, Barbatio's instincts were correct on this score, for on three separate occasions, all in the dead of night, we were awakened by breathless runners reporting that flotillas of logs had been sighted upstream and that the Roman interceptors were at that very moment paddling furiously into the current with their pikes and ropes to seize the logs and guide them ashore before further damage could be wreaked.

On all three occasions, Barbatio sent additional troops from the camp racing into the water with their own rafts to head off any logs that might have slipped past their brethren upstream. For this very reason, a narrow gap the width of perhaps two or three vessels was left in the middle of the newly constructed bridge until the last moment, as an opening through which any rogue logs that might have escaped could be guided without damaging the existing span. But the men upstream performed their tasks efficiently, indeed magnificently. No log made its way through to the bridge.

Strangely enough, however, not a single black-greased, reed-breathing barbarian was ever caught; unlike the first destructive volley, the three subsequent releases of logs from upstream were all unmanned, as if the Alemanni were actually expecting us to counter their efforts on these occasions. I had my suspicions as to their motives, but I held my tongue in the midst of the general exuberance and back-slapping that reigned in the camp after each attempt had been successfully turned back. Why spoil the party? Besides, Barbatio had refused all my requests for an interview, though he had no objection to my lodging in the barracks and even taking meals in the staff headquarters with his officers. I lingered in camp to witness the final crossing before reporting back to Julian.

Two weeks later the bridge was finally readied again, except for the last link in the middle, the safety gap. The three vessels to be inserted in that position had already been planked for wagons, and their length carefully measured so that at the appropriate time they could be quickly placed into position, readying the bridge for use within no more than two hours after the order was given.

The middle link was to be lashed into place at dawn, and the first supply wagons had already lumbered across the near half of the bridge and up to the gap, awaiting the final signal to cross. That moonless night the entire army spent awake by the light of ten thousand torches, breaking camp and consolidating their provisions in the enormous warehouses at the foot of the bridge on the right bank, readied to be loaded onto the oxcarts and trundled across to the western side as soon as the first rays of sun appeared.

On the second watch, an upstream runner burst noisily and breathlessly into the staff commissary, where Barbatio and his officers were busily wolfing down a meal and agreeing on last-minute instructions for the crossing on the morrow. I set down my plate and edged closer to the center of the room to listen to the commotion.

"Sir!" he gasped. "The barbarians have made another attempt!"

The officers in the room leaped up in alarm, but Barbatio simply smiled confidently.

"Another load of logs, soldier?" he said quietly. "I trust that since you are not bellowing for assistance, this one, too, has been intercepted?"

"Not logs this time, sir," the man panted, now regaining his breath. "A fire ship."

Now Barbatio slowly stood up, his face darkening in anger. This was a tactic he had not anticipated. Fire ships were said to have been used occasionally by the Greeks in antiquity, as a desperate weapon to break naval blockades or destroy closely massed squads of transport vessels. They were older craft, deteriorated from dry rot and ready to be scuttled, that were soaked with a flammable substance, fired, and set adrift in the direction of the target. With luck, they would collide with a group of enemy vessels and set them afire as well, or at least cause them to scatter in chaos. Such a tactic, however, had never been used by the barbarians.

The courier hastily continued. "Our detachment five miles up was patrolling even farther upstream, anticipating that the Alemanni might plan a ruse. Three miles beyond our camp, we sighted a transport scow—a huge one, sir—heading downstream without lights. One of those deep-bottomed craft the Alemanni use for the ice trade."

At this, the men looked questioningly at one another until one of Barbatio's northern veterans explained: "Aye, sir, the barbarians collect ice in blocks from the Belgicae up north during the winter months, pack it tightly in sawdust, and pole it upstream during the summer when the water is lower. Must be one of the vessels they use for that."

The courier nodded. "The men caught it, sir. Boarded it without incident while the barbarians dove off the other side. It's riding high, no ice in the hold from the looks of it. The decks were stacked with barrels of turpentine and pitch. The Alemanni didn't even have a chance to pour it over the vessel, sir, before we captured it."

Barbatio stroked his chin thoughtfully and began to relax. "Seaworthy, is it? And empty you say?"

"Yes, sir—practically new. The barbarians must be desperate to be sending expensive vessels like that to be fired. The men are floating it downstream now."

Barbatio clapped his hands together and cracked his knuckles, grinning broadly. "Excellent, excellent. A bit of luck, wouldn't you say, gentlemen? A large vessel like that could speed our crossing. As it is, the weight of full oxcarts means we can't have more than six or eight vehicles on the bridge at any one time. If we ship our supplies over, however, we can send the carts and wagons across empty, and line them up nose to tailgate—it'll speed the crossing. When this vessel arrives, moor it at the warehouse and open the hold. We can load the grain and provisions in there. Save the flammables—perhaps we can offer our friend Chonodomarius a warm gift in return for his hospitality."

The men guffawed at the poor joke, and the group broke up, all to attend to their separate tasks. I myself wandered down to the main pier to witness the vessel's arrival.

I didn't have long to wait, for even in the blackness of the moonless night the ship could be spied far up the placid river. The triumphant Roman squad that had captured it had festooned its mast and spars with lanterns and candles. As it slowly pulled up to the pier, the men on the dock cheered, not only at their good fortune at averting another disaster, but at having acquired such an aid to conveyance. Dozens of hands reached to seize the vessel's ropes and tie it hard by the dock, while others began hastily cutting a large hole through the rough-hewn planks of the warehouse wall on the water side, under which the vessel's hatches could be positioned for the bulk grain to be more easily shoveled in. Other dozens of hands reached down to assist the grinning crew in climbing up onto the pier, and marching songs broke out spontaneously to celebrate the good fortune.

I peered over the side. Indeed, all available space on the

deck had been loaded with barrels and crates of tinder, turpentine, pitch, naphtha—any flammable material the barbarians could lay their hands on. Had the Roman detachment arrived just a few moments later, after the ship had been fired, it would have been impossible to divert—indeed, no boarding party would have been able to approach within a hundred feet and it would have drifted unimpeded into the bridge downstream—a terrible, and this time fatal, disaster.

Several smiths were brought up, bearing mallets, chisels, and saws, and were soon well on their way to cutting through the heavy bars on the hatches. As on all such vessels, its three oaken hatch ports had been fitted snugly to withstand swelling or shrinkage, maintaining an airtight seal and protecting the ice they covered. The workers, preparing to shovel the grain into the holds, crowded closer as the smiths' saws broke through the thick iron bolts.

"Stand back," called out a burly officer from one of the Germanic auxiliary divisions. Barbatio normally posted his allied Germanic cohorts with the construction and road-building crews, away from the front lines, out of his suspicions as to their loyalty in combat. The fellow was tall and commanding, and he strode across the deck on top of barrels, shouting in his harsh and heavily accented Latin, "Give 'em room to work! Here's a lantern. Clear out whatever's in the hold, make sure it's dry inside, and start shoveling that grain. You men—start carting these barrels off of here."

With some effort, the smiths slid the enormous bolts through the loops and seized the stout wooden handles. As the three ports were pried open, the officer approached the middle one with his lantern to peer inside, and a sudden thought came to me as I recalled my days in Athens, packing cadavers in sawdust for their protection, the smell like rotten eggs, the composting shavings steaming from heat, actually hot to the touch. I paused for a moment, thinking, sniffing the air venting from the hatches, and then . . .

"No!" I shouted, and leaped back a half dozen steps to

the other side of the dock. A hundred men went suddenly silent as all eyes turned to me with expressions of surprise and amusement, like a crowd watching an epileptic.

"No!" I repeated. "It's sawdust from the ice! Back away! Put out your lanterns!"

The hundred pairs of uncomprehending eyes filled with confusion. The smith crouched as if frozen, holding the hatch door open, while men edged away from the deck, not understanding my words, but sensing something was terribly amiss. I too turned, and began walking swiftly toward the foot of the bridge, but kept my eyes fixed on the hold, when I witnessed the bravest and perhaps most terrible act in my life.

The Germanic auxiliary, like everyone else, had stopped short just at the opening, holding high aloft his flaming lantern as his eyes flashed between me and the dark opening of the hatch. His face, and his alone, was calm and lacking fear—rather, he wore a fixed expression of dead determination. Pausing only a moment, he looked at the smith still squatting motionless at the hatch opening, and then with a loud cry of "Long live Chonodomarius!" he brandished his torch, took one step forward, and dropped feet-first into the inky darkness of the hold.

There was a brief pause during which time seemed to stand still. I turned my head toward the shore and began to run. Men looked at me in puzzlement and fear, unsure themselves whether to turn and flee or to step forward in curiosity as to what had set off my fright, and I tried to call out to them to run for their lives, but no words came from my mouth. My legs felt leaden and unresponsive, and in the end, my body leaning forward in an attempt to move faster, I stumbled, my fingers grazing the rough, wooden planks, picking up jagged splinters in my knuckles as my feet left the decking. I flew headlong into a crowd of surprised carpenters running up to join in the commotion, my shoulder driving roughly into the face of one of them and stifling the oath he had just begun to shout at my clumsy fleeing.

As I landed I felt the ground beneath me, the solid ground, tremble and rumble noiselessly for a moment. I then was hit by a rushing blast of hot air from behind. I turned and was almost blinded as an enormous ball of flame welled up from the ship's hold, fed by the naphtha-impregnated sawdust inside. It engulfed what had been the ice vessel, and expanded to swallow everything around it for a hundred feet, a hundred and fifty feet, more. I scrambled up again and began running, and this time I found purchase on the solid ground and sprinted headlong through the paralyzed crowds of men, who stared as the fireball swelled, grew, and then rose upwards, and we were hit by the heat as if from the open door of a blast furnace, a heat that blinded and toppled men not even touched by the direct impact of the flames.

I continued running until I reached the street and was able to pause behind the solid wall of a long building, and found myself praising God for the shelter of those overhanging eaves. The air was thick with a rain of flaming planks and shards of wood, support beams and molten nails, in such density that it appeared solid with steel and flame. These were followed by grislier objects—arms and feet, open-mouthed heads with hair aflame like screaming Gorgons, torsos and entire, intact bodies. Moments after these had landed, the air thickened again with flaming pellets and droplets of pitch, a fiery, hellish rain that stuck to the skin and burned like branding irons, impossible to shake off, or to be plucked without sticking to the sensitive tips of one's fingers—an excruciating pain impossible to remedy short of scuffing dirt onto the droplets to extinguish their flame. Finally, a sound as if of hail—the light sprinkling of six months' supply of grain for five Roman legions, raining out of the sky whence it had been blown in the destruction of the warehouse.

I stepped cautiously around the corner where I had taken refuge to survey what was left of the bridge, and was faced with an unspeakable sight. The warehouse had been obliterated, as had been the bridge for a quarter of its distance into the river. The span beyond that, which had not yet been connected to the missing center section, had come unfastened from its moorings in the blast, and now drifted slowly down the river, spinning lazily in the current like a piece of driftwood tossed into a stream by an idle boy. Charred bodies lay everywhere amidst smoldering stacks of timbers and overturned oxcarts. Several of the hospital barracks and houses nearest the foot of the bridge had collapsed in the blast and were now burning fiercely, and invalid men crawled slowly out of the wreckage, moaning in pain, some with their clothing and hair aflame. Even my physician's instincts had deserted me for the moment, and I stood frozen at the sight.

From far across the river, where the still-intact bridge of the left bank stood, faint shouts came drifting over the nearby groans, and fearing the impact of another fire ship, I clambered atop a pile of smoldering wreckage to better see across the dark expanse of water. There, too, were fires, though no explosion, and no ship. The shouts grew louder and more distinct, however, and as the flames rose higher I could see that the entire far end of the bridge was now engulfed, and that men were leaping over the side of the structure into the dark waters to escape. How did the flames from the blast reach even that far? And then after a moment, I saw the answer.

At that end of the bridge, a full five hundred yards across, a small sister encampment had been constructed to feed and house the soldiers building the bridge from that end. There, I saw new flames shoot up, and in front of them the silhouettes of horses and riders—only a few at first, then dozens, then hundreds, lances raised, riding and shouting shrilly in triumph. Racing back and forth, they clubbed and struck down the unarmed men on foot whom I could see attempting to race into the darkness or leap into the water, until all the screams from the far side of the river had been silenced. An enormous steed then trotted calmly into the water by the light of the flaming barracks on the far side of the river, ridden by a man whose tremendous breadth of shoulder and waist-length hair tossing loosely in the fire-whipped breeze was visible even from where I stood. He raised his gigantic harpoon far above his head and slammed it point first into the surf beside him, where it stuck, its haft quivering like an arrow that has just found its bloody mark. His shrill, mocking cry came drifting over the groans of the dying: "Death to the Romans! Death to Rome!"

The river continued its slow, implacable journey to the sea, washing clean its bloody banks, carrying away the detritus of men's vanity, its immortal movements unstilled and unaffected by the actions of the puny beings along its shores.

II

*Here, Your Holiness, I might interject my own brief obser-
vation, as my brother's isolation in Gaul rendered him
fairly ignorant as to events much beyond his immediate
circle. Since I myself had some contact with Constantius'
court at that time, I might more easily enlighten you as to
General Barbatio's fate. For as Roman armies are un-
daunted by defeat, so too are their generals undeterred in
their opinions of their own greatness. Barbatio did as his
instincts led him, for reasons of both expediency and blindness as to the true situation—he declared a great victory
and retreated his army to winter quarters, while announc-
ing his own glorious retirement.*

*Soon afterwards, as hapless as he ever had been when
building his bridges across the Rhine, General Barbatio
died in a fitting manner. It appears that just before he had
departed on the Rhine campaign, his house had been visited
by an enormous swarm of bees, which caused him great
anxiety. He consulted experts in the interpretation of
omens, who warned him that the swarm foreshadowed
great danger in war. This unfortunate event, and its foolish
interpretation, somehow led Barbatio's wife, Assyria,
whose ambition was exceeded only by her stupidity, to become mentally unhinged. After her husband left on campaign, she labored under the illusion that Constantius was
about to die, and that her husband was destined to succeed*

him as Emperor, but she worried that Barbatio might cast her off in favor of a marriage with the beautiful Empress Eusebia. Assyria's fears were so great that she wrote an exceedingly ill-advised letter to her husband pleading with him not to do such a thing after he assumed power.

Thus God makes all things to be as they should, though it need cause no surprise that men, whose minds we sometimes believe to be near to the Divine, distort God's intent. Man confounds and confuses place, time, and nature. He destroys and disfigures everything and loves all that is deformed and monstrous. He will have nothing as God has made it, but insists on shaping the world and his destiny to his own taste. In this regard, Assyria would have been much wiser to trust in the benevolence of God and to remain silent. As it happened, her tearful letter was intercepted by Constantius' spies and brought to his hands, and in retribution the Emperor caused both Barbatio and his wife to be decapitated.

So much, then, for these things.

On another topic, I offer belated apologies, Your Holiness, for my brother's rather florid writing. Many times in the past I attempted to instill in him a joy in the purity of God's creation and an optimistic hope in the future through simpler verbiage. How difficult can it be for him to forgo his overwrought descriptions of sunrises, for example, and simply note that another day had dawned? In this I may have failed, though whether it was due to a defect in his faith or to his persisting rebellion against his older brother's authority, I leave to your superior insight.

Let us return to Caesarius.

BOOK FIVE

STRASBOURG

Ubi solitudinem faciunt pacem appellant.

When they have wrought desolation, they call it peace.

—TACITUS

I

It was the most oppressive of the summer's dog days, a day so hot that trees and men alike wilted and drooped—the trees from the sheer effort of enduring the shadeless heat, the blinding glare of the sun until nightfall finally arrived to bring some relief, but the men—the men, my Lord. I had to keep reminding myself why exactly it was that we were marching in that heat and dust, voluntarily and obediently, no less, some of us even with determination and ferocity, as we picked our way slowly and carefully across the unnaturally empty and silent landscape.

The road wound low between two gentle ridges, as if centuries of tramping by countless Roman legionaries, barbarian invaders, and the daily collections of peddlers and princes had somehow actually sunk the road several feet into the surrounding countryside, as a gently babbling rivulet over time gouges deep fissures into the solid rock beneath. The fields on both sides were dense with ripening wheat, interspersed with occasional thick hedges centuries old, or low walls of stone picked from the fields by the farmers, or by their grandfathers or great-grandfathers in Trajan's day or earlier. The stillness and silence bespoke a permanence about the place, an unchanging persistence, a stubborn certainty, if you will, that the march of a mere thirteen thousand men on a single day, in that particular year out of hundreds or thousands of other years, would not affect the land in the slightest.

Not a farmer was to be seen. The houses were abandoned, boarded up, some burned and still smoldering. Cut hay lay untended and scattered in the fields. The pastures, normally studded with bemused, dully observant livestock, lay open and empty. The sense of abandonment was overwhelming.

Barbatio's shameful retreat the week before had outwardly caused little effect on Julian—he was loath to demonstrate any disappointment or anger at the performance of his colleague in the presence of his men, as this would simply add fuel to the rumors that had been circulating of outright hostility between the two generals—but in private he was seething. The loss of Barbatio's twenty-five thousand troops was a severe blow to Julian's ambitions to rid Gaul of the barbarians—and the news brought by riders from his border garrisons only days earlier was of the worst sort.

Seven powerful Alemanni clan chieftains, led by Chonodomarius, had assembled at Strasbourg on the Rhine. Even more troublesome than the gathering of these barbarian leaders, however, were the thirty-five thousand armed men of various tribes they had brought with them, some of them serving for pay, others under the terms of family alliances, and all of them eager for plunder and Roman head. Without Barbatio, Julian's chances for success against the gathering enemy forces seemed meager, and several nights before, he had called Sallustius and his generals and captains into council to discuss the matter.

"We have less than half the troops they do," Sallustius pointed out without emotion. "We'll be fighting on unfamiliar ground, with a long supply line to defend. I don't like the odds."

Bainobaudes, the Cornuti tribune who had defeated the Alemanni river raiders a few weeks earlier, scoffed. He had been admitted to Julian's inner council only recently, after his impressive victory, and his Frankish mannerisms, which had not been effaced even by his long service as a Roman auxiliary, were still crude and lacking in all deference.

"They're barbarians!" he growled. "They're strong, but they've got no discipline. It's each man for himself. Our legions have tactics and training. I'd throw even our auxiliaries against the Beast's men any day."

Several others weighed in with their own opinions, for and against attempting to force a battle under the circumstances, as Julian listened silently, pondering each man's words carefully, and then dismissing us all from his field tent. As usual, his lamp could be seen glowing through the canvas walls far into the night. I, too, remained awake and was therefore not surprised when a guard peered into my tent only several hours before dawn, summoning me back to Julian's quarters.

I arrived to find him flipping through a well-thumbed travel codex of Marcus Aurelius and occasionally jotting quick notes in his cramped, minuscule hand. I began to greet him, but he stopped me with a quick glance, indicating for me to wait a moment as if he was in the middle of something of the utmost importance. I wondered at his seeming lack of concern over the issue of whether or not to take his army into battle, when he suddenly set down his reed with a gesture of finality and looked up at me with a half smile on his face.

"Only a friend such as you, Caesarius, would adapt his very waking hours to match my own," he said.

"Nonsense," I rejoined with a smile, brushing off his compliment. "I was about to drop by anyway. Oribasius gave me a package of smoked pheasant before we left. We should enjoy it before it spoils." And I pulled the little bundle from out of my tunic.

He glanced at it indifferently, then stood up and began pacing. I watched him for a moment, then shrugged, opened the bundle myself, and picked out a slice of the delicately flavored meat.

Julian stopped his pacing and looked at me hard. "I've

been thinking," he said, "that a philosopher's training is precisely what the army needs."

I stared at him in puzzlement for a moment, but he sat down and returned to his book, as if having lost his train of thought. I stood there wondering, but after a moment he looked up at me again.

"Who deserves greater admiration, Caesarius: Socrates, or Alexander the Great?"

I paused, unsure of his expectations. "In view of the fact that Alexander crucified his own physician," I said cautiously, "I believe I would have to vote for Socrates."

He looked at me briefly, then continued, as would a teacher before a dull student.

"Correct. From Socrates came the wisdom of Plato, the courage of Xenophon, the boldness of Antisthenes, the *Phaedo* and the *Republic,* the Lyceum, the Stoa, and all the Academies. Socrates changed the world! From Alexander came . . . nothing. Who has ever found salvation or comfort through Alexander's victories? What city was ever better governed because of them, what person's life was ever improved? Of course, many men were enriched by his conquests, or by the slaughter afterwards, but no one was ever made wiser or more temperate. More likely, men became even more insolent and arrogant than before. All men who have been saved through philosophy, all countries who are better governed because of it, owe their salvation to Socrates."

I shrugged. "So . . . you perhaps intend to teach the troops philosophy?"

He looked up, surprised, and then smiled briefly.

"No, of course not. I only meant to show that philosophy must be the basis for all our deeds. All my tacticians and advisers and specialists can counsel me only on specifics— comparative troop counts, locational deployments, lay of the land, procurement status—you saw that tonight. In the end, it almost helps to be ignorant of such matters when making the decision, and let information on road conditions and whatnot have a bearing only after deciding whether to fight or flee."

I looked at him in astonishment. "What criteria do you intend to apply when deciding?" I asked.

He looked up again, in surprise. "You have to get down to first principles," he said. "And the first principle of all is that we are Romans. We have no choice."

"No choice? I don't understand."

"As Romans, we cannot fail to attack. If we flee instead, then it is not only the Alemanni massing along the Rhine who will pour into Gaul, but every middling tribe from the Alps to the northern sea and from the Rhine to the Black Forest will pour out their hidden valleys and caves and rush like floodwaters into our cities. That, Caesarius, is a certainty. If we attack and lose, the same thing will happen. However, if we do attack, there is at least a chance that we might win. Logically, our chances in an attack are not good—but they are zero if we flee. If we flee, the Western Empire will be no more, and ultimately, the fate of Rome itself will be at risk. I have made myself a commander, and thus I am bound to take into consideration military variables. But I am first and foremost a Roman. I will listen to no more expositions on relative troop counts."

I pondered this. "That raises another issue," I said. "Constantius, as Emperor, is never seen at the front lines of his troops, actually fighting barbarians with his sword. His life is too valuable for that, and there is not a man in his army who would even think otherwise. Aren't you taking an unnecessary risk with your own habit of riding into the fighting and slashing away like a common soldier? Even if your physical skills were formidable—and let's be honest, Julian—how much can one man contribute, compared to the loss Gaul would suffer if you fell in battle?"

This time it was his turn to weigh words carefully.

"Caesarius," he said, "if God told you that you would die tomorrow, or at most the day after tomorrow, would it matter to you whether it happened on the second day or the third day?"

I smiled. "Not unless I were so wicked I needed an extra day to complete my confession."

He nodded. "Exactly," he said. "And between one day and the next, how small is the difference? I will die eventually. To me it is no great thing to die tomorrow rather than twenty or fifty years later."

I said nothing, but pondered his strange fatalism. To Julian, one day or two might be of no concern—but to the thirteen thousand legionaries marching under his command, whether their leader emerged from battle dead or alive made all the difference in the world.

"The Fates," he said, "will take me when they will."

Thus we found ourselves that day in late August, picking our way carefully across the silent plains toward the barbarians' stronghold at Strasbourg, twenty-one miles from our starting point that morning. The infantry advanced steadily along the road, the engineers and drovers marching in the van to remove the logs and other obstacles the barbarians had used to impede our advance. Our flanks were protected by roving squadrons of *sagitarii,* sharpshooting archers, who often disappeared into grain growing higher than their heads. The *cataphracti,* heavily armored horsemen led by a crack cavalry officer named Severus, ranged ahead and far to the sides to occupy prominent positions along the route and capture any Alemanni scouts they might encounter. I had the good fortune to be riding a cavalry horse, but it was unimaginable to me how the infantry troops were able to keep up their spirits in the deadly heat, bearing eighty-pound packs with their gear and weapons, on a diet which for the last two weeks had consisted largely of hardtack, gnawed stale when on the march, or softened in warm lard when in camp. Amazingly, morale remained high, as if Barbatio's retreat had actually removed a burden from our shoulders rather than created one.

As we crested a low hill, three mounted enemy scouts burst out of a hedgerow in which they had been hiding and raced away to the east on small Hunnish ponies that our cavalry were unable to run down. One enemy soldier on foot, however, whose horse had been lamed and who was found cowering in the hedge where his faithless colleagues had abandoned him, was captured. Under interrogation he informed us that the Alemanni had been crossing to our side of the river for three days and nights, a sign that the enemy troop strength was greater than we had feared. Julian called a halt at the crossing over a small stream, the water of which had been reduced to a brackish trickle, summoned in the scouts and snipers, and assembled the troops in the little shade that was available beneath a copse of sparse chestnut trees.

Climbing the low bank to a boulder protruding from the side to form a natural platform, he stood in the open sun and removed his battle helmet, then stripped off the woolen caul fitted to his scalp to protect his head from the inner seams and rubbing of the helmet. This he ostentatiously wrung out in front of the men, grinning as the stream of sweat poured onto the rock and steamed. Many of the troops did the same. His face then became serious, and rather than the orator's harangue he normally delivered before battle, he assumed an informal, conversational tone so soft that the men stifled their restless shuffling and edged forward to a close circle around him, to better hear his words.

"Men, hear me well; I tell you this only out of concern for your safety and well-being, for I do not doubt your courage. As your Caesar I offer you the advice a good father would to his sons: choose caution rather than risk. Warriors must be bold when the occasion requires, and you have proven your valor well; but when in danger they must be obedient and deliberate.

"I will tell you my opinion. Heed what I say. It is now noon. Already we have marched ten miles in full panoply under a burning sun, and we are tired and hungry. The road ahead of us to the river is even rougher than it has been thus far, and if night catches us still marching, there will be nothing to light our way, for the moon is waning. The country ahead of us is burnt up by the heat—our scouts report there is no water to be had for miles. And when we do overcome these difficulties, what we will face at the end of the road is a body of enemy three times our number—rested and refreshed, camped by an enormous river of cool, fresh water, and now warned of our approach by the enemy scouts who just slipped through our grasp. What strength will we have to meet Chonodomarius and his fellow giants, when we ourselves are worn out by hunger, thirst, and marching? I propose we set a watch and remain here tonight, where we have a broad view of the plains all around and protection in this dry ditch, with a bank of scrub trees for a rampart. Then at first light, after a good sleep and a hot breakfast, God willing, we will march our standards to victory. . . ."

His voice was drowned out by an uproar and the fierce clashing of spears against shields. The men were actually shouting him down, venting their impatience and even rage, roaring their determination to continue the march and attack immediately. He watched for a moment, expressionless, then raised his arms for silence, and the shouting gradually died down.

"Men," he cried, "strong arms are nothing if not supported by full bellies and stout legs! I seek only to make our victory all the more certain by . . ."

More shouts, and then Marius, an older centurion who was one of Julian's trainers in swordsmanship, clambered onto a small mound in the middle of the riverbed and raised his own hands for silence. The tanned, hard-looking veteran showed every day of his thirty-odd years of service to Rome in the weather-beaten lines of his face and arms.

"Caesar—you concern yourself with our safety, but by holding us back you keep safe the barbarians instead! The warning they are receiving of our approach is a chance for them to escape. If we wait until tomorrow, they'll have time to flee, and you will have deprived us of a certain victory. This, Caesar, we will not allow!"

Cheers roared up from the men surrounding him on the riverbank, and the troops surged forward to where Julian stood unflinching on his rock, facing Marius with an expressionless gaze. The men again clattered their shields with their spears, this time setting up a chant—"Vic-to-ry! Vic-to-ry!"—imploring their Caesar to lead them on to the invading Alemanni.

Julian raised his hand for silence. "Men! How often have I heard you, the bravest of you, exclaim 'When will we find the enemy? When will we fight?' Well, here they are, chased from their lairs. The field is open, as you hoped it would be. An easy path awaits you if you win, but know this—*know this!* You will have a terrible, uphill struggle if you lose. The miles of hard march behind you, the dark forests you have conquered, the rivers and swamps you have crossed—all these are witness to your bravery and determination, *but only if you win!* If you retreat, all these become deadly liabilities. You will die!

"We do not have the enemy's local knowledge of the area, nor their abundant supplies. But we have strong hands, and the swords they hold are of Roman steel, and we have the power and might of Rome behind us, and I defy any enemy to vanquish us with God on our side! No army, no general, can safely turn his back on the enemy— nor shall we! If you are determined to press forward now, we shall do so to complete victory or death. I yield to your obstinacy—I yield to your valor! Fall in by company and march out. God grant us victory this day, and the devil take the Beast!"

The men roared and scrambled out of the dry riverbed, pouring from the depth of the ditch onto the road like ants from a hole, sharpened spears held high, gleaming in the blinding sun. Incredibly, despite the heat, they set off in perfect company formation, not marching but *trotting*, reciting as their cadence an obscene old victory song about devastating the Gauls, and even the Gallic auxiliaries joined in with grins, in their sheer exuberance at preparing to rout the Alemanni. Julian sat astride his horse at the side of the road, his right arm outstretched in salute as his troops passed in formation, looking the men in the eye as they marched, nodding solemnly at those whom he knew. As the last company of auxiliaries strode by, cheering, he glanced casually over at Sallustius, next to him on his own mount.

"Well, that worked," he said simply.

Within three hours we topped a low rise, yielding a vast view of the horizons below us, with the Rhine not more than two miles distant and the great walled city of Strasbourg just before that. The tiny Ill River meandered across the foreground, through the walls and heart of the city, to emerge on the other side, a languid stream gliding gentle and smooth, like a slow trickle of olive oil. Before the stream, in a vast display of color and strength, was a heart-stopping sight. With an order and precision unprecedented in our months of fighting the Alemanni, Chonodomarius and his chieftains had arrayed their troops below us, thirty-five thousand strong, in a series of six dense, wedge-shaped units, forming a solid block of men across a distance of a half-mile, their backs to the river, their faces all turned expectantly and silently toward us as our column marched over the rise and down the other side.

Hundreds of pennants, each painted and embroidered with their family and clan crests in differing levels of crudeness or expertise, fluttered from cavalry lances. The men, in varying states of armor and undress and with their bodies, faces, and shields hideously painted, stood motionless and massive in perfect formation. Their broad shoulders and deep chests were awe-inspiring even from this distance, and their auburn and blond hair, loose or in braids, fluttered like so many offspring of the colorful pennants above them. Several paces in front of the barbarian troops, motionless atop an enormous war charger painted with fiery orange and gold flames across its broad chest and neck, sat the Beast himself, his great barbed weapon propped casually upon his shoulder as he, too, turned his face toward the sun where our army emerged over the crest of the hill in the west. Far from having been caught unawares, the barbarians had been long expecting us, for the precision of their deployment indicated considerable preparation.

Julian's men kept their silence, the column snaking over the top of the hill without so much as a waver in the pace of its march, the cavalry fanning out into the fields of ripening grain on the flanks, spacing the distance between their animals slightly to give the enemy the illusion of greater strength of numbers, even while the infantry involuntarily tightened its own ranks, each man seeking comfort in the proximity of the shield carried by his comrade to the right.

Julian galloped up to take his place in the vanguard, flanked by Sallustius and Severus and his cavalry guard, and he now rode resolutely forward, his chin held high, looking neither right nor left as the perspiration ran in rivulets down his cheeks and fell in hot droplets to the plate armor on his shoulders and chest. Beyond the rise over which we had just passed was a gradual descent of a half-mile or so, which itself terminated in another ridge, smaller by half than the first, but sufficient to hide our view of the enemy, and theirs of us, for as long as we remained in the shallow valley between the two ridges.

Sending a troop of scouts galloping forward to the top of the second rise to secure the height and monitor the Alemanni, Julian took advantage of the army's short lapse away from enemy eyes to form his own ranks. With barely a third the numbers of Chonodomarius' men, it was necessary to extend our lines along at least as broad a front as the barbarians to prevent being enveloped on the flanks by the wily German's horse troops. This meant, however, sacrificing any benefits of depth. There would be no opportunity for a unit to hide behind the company in front of it. Every squadron would be on the front line.

Julian divided his army into four equal units, one of which, chiefly comprising infantry auxiliaries from various Gallic tribes, he assigned to the rear as a reserve. Of the three remaining units, he himself assumed personal command of the two on the center and the right, the heavy infantry and armored cavalry, while the left-most unit, consisting of more infantry, scouts, and archers, was led by Severus. The formation had been carefully planned in advance with a view to confounding the enemy, who would normally expect Severus to lead the cavalry, and as the marching column reached the bottom of the shallow valley just beyond sight of the barbarians, a single trumpet blast signaled the soldiers to fall into battle array, and within moments the new formation had been completed.

With a second blast of the trumpet the army advanced up the side of the next small ridge, with Julian, Sallustius, and Severus now to the rear. Upon mounting the hill we found ourselves within the barbarians' missile range, and even before we crested, the air began whizzing and humming an evil song as a cloud of arrows descended upon us like a poisonous shadow.

At a quickly shouted command from the centurions, the troops, as one, knelt on their right knees, left knees forward. The front ranks in each wing extended their shields in an interlocking wall, to protect their faces and torsos, while the troops immediately behind them raised their own shields horizontally over their heads, sheltering themselves as well as the men immediately in front of them. A thousand arrows, five thousand, clattered onto the upraised shields with a deafening rattle like that of a hailstorm on a tile roof. Most bounced off harmlessly or shattered, yet others, falling from a great height in the arc the barbarian archers had aimed, gained tremendous speed in their descent and pierced straight through the wooden and oxhide shields, or found their way through cracks between the shield rims of a man and his comrade, and here and there scattered cries of pain arose from among the Roman ranks. Gaps opened as soldiers fell, to be quickly filled by the man to the side or behind.

Julian shouted for Severus to advance on the left wing with his archers, to relieve the pressure on our center from the enemy arrows, and they did so, letting loose their own deadly cloud of missiles upon the barbarians. The Ale-

manni, despite their impressive formation, had not the training or the discipline to interlock their shields and protect
themselves as the Romans had done. In a single volley a
hundred barbarians fell screaming; their lines wavered and
gaps opened; and at Severus' bellowed commands the Roman archers advanced methodically, firing volley after volley, pinning the Germans in a disorganized squat under
their shields and halting the murderous storm that had been
falling on our center. Our heavy infantry rose back to their
feet and resumed their steady march, shields swinging hyp-
notically from side to side, a relentless, rhythmic tramping
designed to strike fear into the enemy with its throbbing
cadence.

Julian galloped his charger back and forth through the
lines, accompanied by the two hundred armored cavalry of
his personal escort, shouting at his troops to maintain order,
to advance steadily, to keep their pace. My position, as
always, was as near to his side as possible, ready to assist
in any way, even to defend him with my own raised cavalry
sword and shield, but I was not needed—the man was
golden, untouchable, arrows whizzing past his head and all
around him, landing with a *thwack!* in the shields of the
men close by, sometimes even grazing his skin, but never
striking him.

The steadily advancing Romans, protected by the withering onslaught of arrows from the left wing, were now
only yards from the enemy front lines. Closer they
marched, the war cries of the barbarians rising to a terrifying pitch, and with a final roar the opposing ranks of men
smashed into each other, muscles straining as Roman and
barbarian slashed with sword, parried and slashed again,
each man seeking to find the gap between the protective
wall of shields that would allow him to drive the blade
home through skin and bone to tender, bursting organ.

The Germans fought like animals, their long, flowing
hair streaked with sweat and blood and whipping about
their heads, their taunting screams making the blood curdle
as they swung their great broadswords in fury. Our own

short blades were murderous at close range, light and deadly, easily handled and able to be thrust precisely between shields and into the soft space under a man's jaw unprotected by any armor; yet it was a terrifying task to advance within range of a barbarian to deliver such a stroke. The enormous Germans whipped and swung their five-foot blades like windlasses, with such momentum as to lift a man completely off his feet into the air even if struck on the shield, and with force enough to slice cleanly even through thick mail or armor, to break a half dozen ribs with a single stroke, to crush a helmet with a man's skull inside.

The barbarians' strength and fury were overwhelming; our only defense was to increase our precision and discipline. Our soldiers determinedly protected their heads by raising their shields, each man sheltering himself and his neighbor, forming an impenetrable barrier beyond which the barbarians could not see, pressing inexorably on to the enemy front, denying the giants maneuvering room for their terrible weapons. They bore down on the Germans, closer, closer, shield boss against shield boss, until swinging blades and battle-axes became useless, and it was simply the weight of each enormous barbarian straining mightily behind his shield against the weight of his shorter, lighter Roman adversary—yet the Roman was not alone. Behind him were his comrades, pushing him in turn, and behind them still more, formation intact, until the enraged barbarian slipped in the gore beneath his feet, or until his ankle turned, or until, for a split second, he looked pleadingly and fruitlessly for assistance from the man at his side— then the swift and deadly Roman sword was thrust like lightning around his shield, into his neck or shoulder, and the man would give way, trampled ruthlessly beneath the hobnailed soles of the advancing Roman legion, and another naked barbarian, flowing mustaches soaked with sweat and blood, would leap bellowing into his place.

From my vantage point behind the lines, racing my horse from one flank to the other with Julian and his guard, the conflict looked fluid, though visibility was worsening. A terrific cloud of dust rose from the thickest part of the fighting, hovering malevolently over the combatants, refusing to disperse in the thick, still air. Rather, it spread slowly like a disease, swallowing legionaries and barbarians as they were drawn into its midst. The sun had nearly reached the horizon behind us, and the small hill's shadows were creeping inexorably toward the fray, creeping as they had a thousand or a million times in the past over the still fields and the languid Ill, moving like Morpheus' shroud over the howls of the victors and the moans of the injured. Tomorrow, regardless of tonight's outcome, tomorrow the shadows would creep once again over still and silent fields.

Severus' archers continued their deadly rain of missiles into the midst of the dense cloud, guessing the location of the enemy line by the pennants stabbing up through the swirling dust. The Roman infantry in the center advanced against the furious barbarians, relentless as the tide, slowly driving them back by sheer brute strength and discipline. The cavalry on our right, however, deprived of Severus' steady hand and unexpectedly seeing one of their captains slump on his horse after being pierced through the neck by an arrow, suddenly lost heart, and began falling back in disarray. The barbarian cavalry opposite them wasted no time. Quickly organizing a charge ordered by Chonodomarius, they swept into the ranks of our horse troops, their terrifying war cry piercing through the groans of the wounded trampled underfoot. Our cavalry turned in terror and began galloping back to the foot of the hill, threatening to trample the infantry in the center, who were blocking their path, or, even worse, to leave them unprotected as the Alemanni cavalry ran them down with their heavy German chargers. Our right wing was about to be routed.

Seeing the panicked condition of his cavalry, Julian wasted no time. He seized the standard carried by his personal escort, a purple dragon on a golden field which had been fixed to the top of a long lance. Followed by his own guards, he put spur to his horse and raced straight through his center column, intercepting the cavalry just as they were beginning to burst through in panic from the front.

His standard was immediately recognized as it fluttered streaming in the air like the cast skin of a snake, and the Roman tribune of the squadron leading the retreat pulled up short, his face pale and lips trembling. He stared at us with a pleading look, and when I glanced at Julian I saw his face purple with fury, the expression in his eyes for a moment that of an animal beyond reason. The shouts and clashing of battle surrounded us, and he stood in the midst of his advancing infantry, whose front lines were already forming to stand their ground against the attacking German horse pounding down upon them, their faces blackened by the hot dust that had settled on sweat-drenched skin. For a long moment he stared, furious, at the line of Roman cavalry stopped short before him. And then the light of reason gradually came back into his eyes.

"Where are we off to, Romans?" he bellowed, in uncustomary harshness. The tribune's mouth worked soundlessly. "Before you retreat any further you'll have to run me down, and I defy you to do it! Turn around and look, *damn you!* Your comrades on foot are doing the duty of a cavalry, stopping the barbarian horse with their own shields and spears, sacrificing their own bodies beneath the enemy hooves to protect their Caesar—and to protect you! If you wish even a share of their glory . . . Hah . . . If you don't want to be hanged as traitors, you will turn back now and prove you are Romans and not old women on donkeys. And you will follow me!"

The Roman cavalry looked at one another in confusion and shame, but with the barbarians' furious troops fast approaching them from behind, still they hesitated. Julian watched them for a moment, his face reddening again in anger, until he could abide it no longer.

"Soldiers," he roared, "when you are asked by your grandsons where you abandoned your Caesar, tell them it was at Strasbourg!"

And unbelievably, Julian, the young man who but two

years earlier had been a quiet philosophy student in Athens, speared his dragon banner into the ground and spurred his horse forward into the fighting, slashing in fury with his curved cavalry scimitar, until his escort was able to surround him in protection and draw him away to relative safety, as he sputtered in anger at the performance of his cavalry.

Having been held to a stalemate on both his right and left wings, Chonodomarius now directed all his attention toward the infantry in the center. The carnage was horrific, with gaps in the smothering cloud of dust revealing mounds of bodies heaped like cordwood in the center of the field, writhing like a nest of snakes as the arms and legs of those fallen but not quite dead twitched and groped helplessly for relief from the weight of those who had fallen on top. The layer of bodies, however, was *behind* the front line of the Romans—our troops were steadily advancing over the killing line, leaving a trail of death in their wake.

Momentum stalled, however, as Chonodomarius moved all his resources to the center to concentrate a wedge point of his forces and drive a breakthrough, dividing our thin line into two halves. The Roman legionaries' interlocked shields were wavering, individual gaps opening up here and there, widening to the space of two and three shields as men dropped moaning to their knees, not from injury but from sheer exhaustion. They were unable any longer to press against the fury and enormous physiques of the opponent, with no more troops behind them to step into the fray and fill the gaps. Still, barbarian troops continued to pour into the center, summoned furiously from the stalemated flanks by the frantically bellowing Chonodomarius, and slowly the line began falling back toward us, back over the bodies of the maimed, as another layer of Roman bodies began forming under the feet of the barbarians.

And then Julian pounced.

For the entire length of the battle, his Gallic auxiliaries, the Cornuti and the Bracchiati, had held in restless formation just beyond the crest of the hill behind us, out of sight of the barbarian leaders. Now, at his signal, the three thousand fresh auxiliaries behind us exploded in a terrifying imitation of the Germans' own battle cry. The sound, as it reached us, began as a low murmur in the distance that quickly increased to a mad bellow as the troops sprinted over the crest and down the hill, polished armor flashing and faces ablaze, until their cry's rolling wave smothered all other noise of battle, like breakers dashing upon a cliff. The barbarian lines visibly wavered as the sound washed over them, and the spent Romans before them straightened and cheered with the approach of reinforcements.

The auxiliaries hit the exhausted barbarians like a troop of war elephants, with a crash like a thousand chariots colliding. Screams from speared and dying horses rose to the sky, followed by the weaker and more plaintive moans of injured men, all still overwhelmed by the shattering battle cry of the Gallic auxiliaries. The barbarians stood their ground bravely for a few moments, for a quarter of an hour—but for them, the battle was lost. They were built like Titans, those Germans, with arms like ships' masts and legs like tree trunks. Their weapons were enormous, and their valor unmatched. But now their massive arms were numb with fatigue, their knees trembled and spots floated before their eyes—oh, I know the signs of exhaustion, I have studied them well and observed Julian steel himself against them every day in the agonies of his training—and the onslaught of fresh troops, light of arms and fast of step, was too much to bear. Worn-out and broken, barely able to even lift their battle-axes, the barbarians collapsed in despair on the spot or turned weakly and stumbled away in flight, pursued by the fresh troops, who plucked up the Germans' weapons where they had dropped them, replacing their own shivered javelins and bent swords, and plunged them into the barbarians' necks as they ran them down.

It was a rout, a total collapse. Forty thousand men or more suddenly emerged from the far side of the enormous cloud of dust and began running and staggering toward the banks of the river, some of them pursuers, most of them fleeing in panic. As the leaders reached the water, a few splashed in, those few who could swim, and waded frantically out thigh-deep before clumsily paddling into the current, burdened by their armor and heavy boots. The remainder stopped short at the water's edge, wading out to knee depth, no further, howling in rage at being caught between the dark river and all the unknown creatures it contained within—and the Roman auxiliaries storming behind them, arms laden with the blood-encrusted swords and battle-axes the barbarians themselves had dropped in their rush to flee the field.

The Alemanni in the rear pushed and strained against those who had stopped at the water's edge, an unwitting phalanx rushing not at the enemy but away from it, forcing the lead warriors ever deeper into the black waters. Those most desperate to avoid being shoved into the current turned and began fighting their own countrymen to make their way back to the dry land, using any weapons they still held, daggers and helmets, even fists and teeth, but to no avail. The Romans slowed slightly in their approach to the river as the crowds of panic-stricken barbarians ahead of them compacted, by their very mass preventing the attackers from advancing more quickly—yet though the main body of Romans had not yet reached the water, a dark red stain began spreading out from the growing numbers of men forced into the stream. Men fought wildly with one another to escape the slashing Romans behind them, and the terrifying current in front.

Julian raced across the battlefield, which was now quiet and devoid of life but for the weak moans of the dying, and the cries for water from a thousand parched and dying throats, men suffering terribly in the still-oppressive heat and settling cloud of dust. Here and there exhausted Roman soldiers knelt on one knee, chin on chest, shoulders and back heaving, concentrating all their energy on the mere act of gathering their breath, striving to muster sufficient strength to stand. Some, I saw, were sobbing, in the emotional exhaustion and release of victory, or in mourning for a dead comrade. One, in the same half-kneeling position, was calmly tying a scrap of sandal thong around his right wrist using his left hand and teeth, to stanch the flow of blood spurting from his severed limb. I longed to leap off my horse and run to assist him, for within minutes of bleeding at that pace he would be dead. My duty, however, lay in staying at Julian's side, and against every instinct I continued my gallop, sword extended and at the ready. As I passed, the injured man glanced up at me briefly, and in his eyes I saw a calm acceptance of his fate, whatever it might be, his entire life riding on his ability to tie a simple knot with his teeth and the stiffening fingers of his left hand. He nodded at me, casually and almost imperceptibly, as one does to a passing acquaintance in the street, a gesture as if to comfort me for the torment I felt, and unaccountably I felt reassured, almost justified in my decision, as I hurried on.

Julian raced as near as he was able to the rear of his auxiliaries before being himself blocked by the mass of men at his front, the Romans with their shields up, pushing on their comrades before them. The effect was like hitting a stone wall, impossible to pass through; easier would it have been to surmount it and walk to the river on top of the heaving heads and shoulders. He wheeled his horse in frustration, turning this way and that, churning up a gory spray and pocking the slurry of sand and blood, searching for a gap through which he could charge. Finally he gave up, reining in his animal and bellowing at the top of his lungs:

"Romans, hold! Don't advance into the water! Hold! Hold!"

His officers picked up the cry and soon fifty voices in the rear were shouting "Hold! hold!" in unison, and then a trumpeter too caught up with us in the chaos and blew the signal to halt. Slowly, imperceptibly at first and then becoming increasingly visible, a gap opened between the Roman front line and the rear of the fleeing barbarians, a gap precisely matching the water's edge at the bank, as the message wended its way through the lines and the soldiers themselves realized the foolhardiness of pursuing a desperate enemy into deep water, burdened by armor and weapons. Better to let the broad, flowing river do the Romans' work for them.

This it did. The barbarians, even those unable to swim, chose between the certain bloody fate facing them behind, and the cool, liquid death beckoning them in the fore, and the outcome was preordained. Throwing themselves into the corpse-choked stream, they thrashed in the water, tearing off their armor and loosening the heavy sandals that dragged them beneath the current a mere twenty feet from where the blood-spattered Romans stood staring and taunting. A few Alemanni who had kept their wooden shields were able to use them as floats, but they were quickly submerged as five or ten other frantic men grasped them and sought to pull themselves on as well, all of them sinking to the pummeling of fists as they fought for possession. The water deepened to a blackish crimson, staining the feet of the Romans a streaked red, and bits of flesh and armor leather floated on the surface where they had been cut away from their barbarian owners by the slashing of the troops on the land or their own comrades in the water.

After surveying the slaughter for a time, Julian turned away, complete victory in his hands. Dismounting and leading his horse, he threaded his way back through the lines, through his exultant troops and jubilant captains, making his way to the crest of the low hill from where the Roman auxiliaries had made their victorious charge. There he found a low, flat rock, and sitting down he faced not east, toward the site of his victory at the river, where for a hundred yards out into the middle and for a mile downstream could be seen the bodies of barbarian soldiers, floating immobile or paddling weakly as they made their way across to the far side of the Rhine; but rather toward the west, where rosy Apollo dipped his weary horses into the Iberian Sea, toward the last rays of the sun setting in a gloriously purple and orange sky. Narrow shafts of ebbing light shot through the faint and dispersing dust cloud that had risen from the tortured land, bringing on the coolness of the night. With his shoulders slumping in exhaustion, he buried his face in his hands.

II

The medical and burial squads that night reported two hundred forty-three Roman soldiers and four officers killed in the battle, including the brave tribune Bainobaudes. The Roman dead, however, were difficult to find on the field, lost as they were amongst the beaten and torn bodies of the six thousand barbarian dead, nameless and unidentifiable, covering vast tracts of land as thickly as a heaving, oozing carpet. No estimate could be made of the numbers drowned in the aftermath of the rout, but undoubtedly thousands were carried off by the river.

With every report and update from the scouts and burial parties, however, Julian, sleepless as usual even after the exertions of a day such as this, had only one question: What of the Beast? Where is the Beast? No one could answer.

Several hours after dark, one of the burial parties raced up to the general staff to announce that as they had approached a heap of cadavers, a man had leaped up from beneath a body where he had been lying and raced into a nearby copse, adjacent to the river. This in itself was not an unusual occurrence, since it is a favorite tactic of deserters and cowards on every battlefield to feign death until the heat of battle has passed by. This man, however, had caught the Romans' eyes for his sheer bulk, which, even accounting for the deceptiveness of the torchlight and shadows, was enormous. The fact that his face was bound in a dirty rag, as if to prevent recognition, was also suspicious. Julian, his eyes flashing, raced to his horse, calling as he ran for his personal guard and his Acolytes.

Thundering to the grove with some two hundred armed men, they dismounted and spaced themselves evenly into a line several hundred yards long, and then at a command, cautiously entered the thick undergrowth.

We had not taken more than a half dozen steps into the dark woods when there was a sudden shout from nearby, and suddenly thirty or forty men burst from the trees in front of us and raced through our line, knocking over and trampling our men, who were so startled at the sudden onslaught in the dark that they did not even have time to raise their weapons. Screaming their battle cry, the barbarians raced to the horses we had just left behind us, untended but for a few unarmed battle squires, who leaped away like a terrified troop of monkeys. The blood-darkened giants bore down like demons, Chonodomarius foremost among them, and leaping upon our horses they spurred them up the steep slope away from the celebrating Roman camp, into the darkness and emptiness of the woods beyond.

Julian and his men raced back to the remaining horses and took pursuit, determined not to lose the trail. The gods of the barbarians, however, false as they are, had turned their backs on the Alemanni. Before the Beast had raced a half mile, his horse, frightened by the strange rider and unaccustomed to the heavier load, slipped in some loose gravel and threw him heavily to the ground. He lay flat on his back, grimacing in pain, as Julian and the others thundered up, dismounted, and aimed the points of their lances at his neck. To their credit, the Beast's companions, though likely to have been able to escape on their own, also pulled their horses up short, and cautiously walked them back to our group, surrendering without protest.

The Beast himself, whose arrogance and daring had struck fear into the hearts of Roman commanders for a decade, laboriously stood up, wincing from pain after his hard fall to the stony ground. Straightening his shoulders he looked quickly around him and identified Julian, who stood only as high as the naked barbarian's bearlike chest. Three Roman guards moved forward to bind the huge German, but Julian signaled them back with his eyes and they reluctantly retreated. Chonodomarius took a step toward the Caesar, Roman lance points pressing upon him from all sides, and as he approached, Julian stood stone-still, his head tilted slightly to the side in observation, almost in curiosity, as if seeing for the first time a new creature brought forth from the wilds of Africa. The Beast moved slowly forward, expressionless, though his eyes darted warily from side to side behind the filth-caked hair obscuring his face. He stopped directly in front of Julian, dropped deliberately forward onto his knees, rested his forehead on the ground, and without a word slowly reached out with one hand to grasp the blade of Julian's sword and guide the tip to the back of his neck. The other barbarians in the group immediately did the same, dropping to the ground at the feet of the nearest Roman and signing with similar gestures to be executed.

We were dumbfounded, and for a moment we all froze, unsure precisely what to do. Had they attacked us, we would have killed them immediately. Had they fled we would have hunted them down like the dogs they were. This, however, was unanswerable.

Julian alone was prepared. With the barbarian lying prostrate on the ground before him, he carefully spread his feet and placed both hands on the sword hilt. With the tip of the blade, he prodded the neck of his son's killer, deftly parting in two the mass of matted and encrusted hair, exposing the white flesh of the nape. All eyes, barbarian and Roman, were fixed on Julian's sword, all lips fell silent. He set the tip into the groove of the neck, just at the base of the skull, and paused.

"Caesar," I whispered, from close at hand. He remained unmoving, his eyes locked on the sword tip. "Caesar," I rasped hoarsely, slightly louder, and I could see the tendons in Julian's forearm quivering. "Do not have this blood on your hands, Caesar. Send him away—send him to the Emperor. As a credit to you, and a burden to Constantius. The Beast's fate is sealed in either case."

Julian looked up at the silent men around him, then focused on me. His eyes had a strange light—as of intense feeling or turmoil, but uncontrolled, with a gleam of perhaps something like madness. "This man is a scourge," he said throatily, adjusting his fingers and tightening his grip on the handle. "With one thrust I avenge thousands of innocent Romans killed, with one stroke I prevent thousands more from being murdered in the future. What is the life of this wretched . . . *killer,* compared to the souls of all those he has destroyed, compared to the life of my own son?" He spat out these words in a kind of muted sob, and Chonodomarius froze in his position on the ground, not understanding the words but surely gathering their meaning, waiting for the swift thrust that would end his life.

I stepped closer, locking my eyes on Julian's wild gaze and speaking evenly. "Your justice requires a rule of law—even in times of war. That is what separates you from *him.* He is unarmed and helpless. It is never right to execute a man this way. Your son's soul would not be avenged. God would see it not as justice but as cold murder, no better than the barbarian's own crimes. In God's name, let him up."

Julian stared at me grimly, composing his face into an expressionless mask. A hint of a smile curled at the corners of his mouth and he leaned slightly forward over Chonodomarius, again adjusting his fingers on the grip. I saw he was going to do it, he *would* do it, if I did not do something, did not risk something.

"Julian—" I urged once more, using his given name even though we were in the presence of his troops. "*Julian.* As a favor to me, in the name of our *friendship*—let the man stand."

Julian's stare remained locked on mine for a long moment, weighing my words, the burden I had placed on him. For that instant I felt as if his hate were directed at me.

Then looking away, he slowly straightened his back, lifted his sword away from the man's neck, and sheathed it. The terrible gleam disappeared from his eyes and they returned to their former depth and intelligence, though they were not without a sharp flash of anger—at the actions of Chonodomarius, or at the terrible toll I had charged on our friendship. He set his mouth in a narrow grimace, turned impassively, walked to his horse, and mounted.

The pattern was now set by Sallustius. Expressionless and cool as ever, he bent down to the barbarian that had prostrated himself before him, a large fellow of a height equal to his own, and seizing him by the hair he lifted him bodily to his feet in a single, swift motion. Cutting the reins of his own horse, Sallustius roughly tied the man's wrists behind his back, jerking the knot tight until the barbarian winced in pain.

The rest of us swiftly followed suit, until the only barbarian remaining unbound was Chonodomarius, who still lay motionless at the place where Julian had stood. As the rest of us watched in not a little trepidation to see how the Caesar would handle the prostrate king, he walked his horse over and stood staring at the huge body for a moment. Then, with a terse "On your feet!" he ordered Chonodomarius to stand and walk behind him. To the surprise and wonder of all, the Beast did his bidding, and the entire party walked slowly and deliberately back to the camp. The procession was led by a grave Julian, walking his horse calmly in front of the towering, unbound Alemanni king, his long auburn hair and mustaches flowing, his heaving chest still painted with the flames of war and destruction, his cheeks flushed with frustration and shame.

In a subsequent search of the woods, an additional two hundred barbarians, many of them Chonodomarius' personal escort, were rounded up and taken back to camp. Three of his closest allies, including Serapion, his son, were among them. After several days of deliberation, it was decided to spare their lives and to send them to the Emperor in Rome, as the ultimate trophy of war: the Beast, who had troubled Constantius for so many years, with a troop of his fiercest warriors.

Again, Your Holiness, if I might supplement my brother's narrative with a touch of additional background: Chonodomarius, though treated with mercy by his fellow blasphemer Julian, nevertheless met a tragic end. In Rome, the so-called "Beast" was looked upon with awe and fear, not only for his great size but for the devastation he had wreaked among the Roman armies over the years, and out of deference to his military skills he was treated as something of a prisoner of honor, held in the castra peregrinorum, *hunkered between the Caelian and Palatine hills. Tradition has it that it was at this very site that Saint Paul had been held in custody when sent to Rome in chains three hundred years earlier, though far be it from me to make any comparison between the two. From the windows of his confinement, the barbarian king would have had a clear view of the Coliseum and the Arch of Constantine, and no doubt his last contact with his kinsmen would have been as they were later led in chains through that very arch as prisoners of war, surrounded by jeering women and pelted with rotten fruit. These barbarians would then be thrown to the wild beasts for the entertainment of the crowds, or to be matched against the* murmillones *and the* retiarii, *the swordsmen and the net-minders, in the bloody gladiatorial combats.*

There, in the darkness of his damp, stone cell, far from the fragrant pines of his shady Germanic forests and lost in the blackness of his own soul, wretched Chonodomarius died of consumption, coughing up his own lungs. May Our Most Merciful Father forgive him his wicked deeds at the last.

BOOK SIX
PARIS

*All things that happen are as common
and familiar as the rose in spring and
the apple in summer; for such is sickness and death, calumny and treachery, and whatever else delights fools
or vexes them.*

—MARCUS AURELIUS

I

That winter was the first of several Julian spent at his new military headquarters of Paris. This city, before Julius Caesar's time, had been little more than a flood-prone fishing village clinging to a marshy island in the middle of the Seine and inhabited by the now vanished tribe of the Parisii. In the intervening centuries, however, it had become an administrative and cultural center of the highest repute, Brother, as you are aware from your contacts with your fellow bishops of that Christian urb. It had long since expanded beyond the confines of the miserable river island, and the walls had several times been extended outward along the left bank to encompass a magnificent forum; a large arena, capable of seating sixteen thousand people and hosting gladiator spectacles and mock naval battles; and what was the greatest comfort to Julian, appealing to those slight sybaritic tendencies that remained in his soul after having been largely driven out by his Christianity and Stoic philosophy, a series of most magnificent baths.

These were wonderfully high-arched facilities of glowing reddish brick, lit by broad expanses of high windows and skylights of glazed glass. They had been completely rebuilt by the best Roman architects several decades before, after the depredations of an earlier barbarian assault on the city. The ample *frigidaria* and *tepidaria*, as well as the ingeniously floor-heated hot pools and all the intervening interior waterfalls and fountains, were generously supplied, but not by the swampy Seine, which flowed lazily a mere thirty feet below the level of the baths. Rather, they were served by a massive stone aqueduct ten miles long, constructed of limestone cut from the underground quarries at the foot of the Montparnasse and sealed to a watertight impermeability by a rubbery mortar mixed of fig milk, pork tallow, and sand, which brought vast quantities of cold, crystalline water from deep in the surrounding forests.

Here Julian passed his morning hours in gymnastics and swordsmanship, training to which by this time he had arrived at quite a level of accomplishment. Here also he retreated at later hours whenever his public duties would allow, after the baths' official closing at sunset, to rest his mind. I lost count of the number of occasions I accompanied him through the dark, cobbled city streets in the very dead of night, to the house of the key-master adjoining the baths. This good fellow, tipped generously with a gold *solidus* or two, would open the facilities even at that unlikely hour and stoke the underground furnaces, that the Caesar might spend some quiet time alone with his muses and demons.

Such demons as he had were of both the domestic and official variety. Since the death of their child, his wife had become a source of torment and puzzlement to him due to her complete lack of regard for things of this world. Like her namesake in the *Iliad*, Helena came to Paris, after her long sojourn with the Emperor and his wife in Rome. But she had returned in body only, her mind having long since fled its physical confines. Her figure was restored to its former plumpness, though she lacked the sweet expression I so clearly recalled as decorating her homely face upon her earlier arrival in Gaul four years before. Her dignified bearing, too, had returned, for she no longer appeared as Julian's giggling bride but had reverted to her original state as the Emperor's unapproachable sister, a matron cold and distant even to her husband, for whom she had become a wife in name only.

She was not scornful and haughty—on this I must set the record straight, Brother, for I am certain that she made no conscious attempt to humiliate or bewilder Julian; it was simply as though there were a piece missing—some indefinable part of her soul that had been buried along with the baby, that part of her that had formerly made her capable of love and affection. Without that part she was able to function only adequately, not normally, like a disturbed child one occasionally sees who shrinks from the prospect of any human touch, even from her own parent. Thus did poor Helena make her way stumblingly through life, the inward flame eating away at her vitals, the silent wound bleeding in her breast. She ignored, even fled, any relations with her husband or other humans.

From Julian I heard never a word of complaint at this state of affairs; indeed, he rarely even mentioned the matter. Nor did his head ever turn toward any other female face or form, though the palace and official facilities were full of lovely Gauls, both slaves and noblewomen, who would have willingly bestowed their favors on the not-unhandsome young Caesar. He was so conspicuous in his chastity that even his closest servants, or those who had been dismissed by him for cause, never accused him of any hint of lustfulness. It was as if he had renounced all desire for commerce with the female race and with his own physical passions, and, indeed, he often quoted Marcus Aurelius' rather off-putting description of the act of love as being a mere "internal rubbing of a woman's entrails and the excretion of mucus with a sort of spasm." Instead, he masked his passions by an even more energetic application to his morning training sessions and his marathon nights of study and philosophy. Still, whenever the topic of conversation touched upon domestic issues, his expression assumed a sad wistfulness that could not but lay bare the true feelings he had for the wife he obviously still loved.

Despite the drubbing of Chonodomarius the summer before, the barbarians were not yet defeated, and Julian still had much work to do before his victories were completely consolidated. As a result of his campaigns over the past several years, the upper and middle courses of the Rhine, from its source in the Alps to the vicinity of Cologne, were entirely in the hands of Rome or its allies. The lower regions of the Rhine, however, to its discharge in the North Sea, were still in the hands of various barbarian tribes. These regions were of the utmost concern to Julian, for not only would securing them provide additional buffer against the barbarians' periodic marauding from the East, but would also open an alternate line of provisioning, from Britain across the sea and up the river. To take advantage of this route, however, two conditions needed to be fulfilled, the first being an adequate fleet, and the second free passage along the entire course of the Rhine to the sea. Both of these were lacking, and it was to these objectives that Julian devoted much time huddled with Sallustius and his other military advisers that winter. Indeed, many sessions were held in the steamy, torchlit baths, as soft snow fell on the sleeping city outside the high-vaulted chamber, and the vengeful barbarians plotted in their drafty huts many miles away on the banks of the Rhine.

The first requisite he succeeded in fulfilling himself, through a combination of outright audacity and brutal labor. A fleet of six hundred ships was assembled over a period of several months, beginning with the coordinated and closely timed seizure of two hundred vessels along the hither coasts of Britain and the navigable stretches of the upper Rhine. Their owners had been a combination of foreign merchants lax in the safekeeping of their property and Roman citizens delinquent in their tax payments, whom Julian decided had the patriotic duty to contribute their vessels to the Roman cause in lieu of the cash debts they otherwise would have owed. Upon inspecting his booty, however, it was determined that most of these vessels were in a rather wretched state of repair, being mere grain barges and fishing boats with the occasional rotting hulk formerly used in the Germanic and Britannic fleets, scarcely fit for use. As a result, he mobilized all his troops not on active garrison duty for the winter, marched them to the Rhine, and embarked on a massive shipbuilding campaign, resulting in the creation of an additional four hundred vessels by the next summer, which, if not masterpieces of craftsmanship, were certainly sufficient to transport quantities of men, horse, and grain the length of the river and across the channel.

The second requisite at first promised to be somewhat more difficult, but in the end proved to be an easier task than expected, when Julian's hand was forced by the Roman prefect Florentius, a sycophant of the Emperor Constantius whom Julian openly despised. This man, in his capacity as civil administrator of the province, took it into his own hands to engage in secret negotiations with the barbarians on the lower Rhine, and obtained their consent to allow the free passage of Roman boats in exchange for a one-time payment of two thousand pounds of silver. When the Emperor was informed of the treaty he ratified it and ordered Julian to pay the sum. I happened to be with him at the baths one freezing night in late November, reading official correspondence aloud to him while he soaked in a hot pool, seemingly dozing. When I came to Constantius' payment order, buried in an otherwise innocuous piece of droning bureaucratic drivel, he sat up with a start, swallowing a mouthful of water in his astonishment.

"Caesarius—read that again!" he spluttered. "A *ton* of silver to those filthy barbarians, for allowing us passage on a river that is ours by right?"

I returned to the offending passage and reread it aloud. " ' . . . in exchange for a one-time payment of two thousand pounds of silver . . . ' Indeed, that is what it says, Julian."

"This is how he informs me of Florentius' dealings, by ordering me to pay two thousand pounds of silver in a treaty with which I was in no way involved?"

Julian was outraged. He clambered out of the pool and paced dripping wet along the side, naked in the frigid air, his furious expression ill-disguised by the dim light of the torches. He was still slight of build, but the stoop with which he had trudged as a scholar had been replaced by a springy, almost nervous bounce and the ramrod straightness of a soldier. So too, his physique had developed a hard, well-defined musculature and a series of scars resulting from his daily physical training and strenuous living on campaign. The boy Caesar now had a coarse coating of hair on his chest and shoulders, and a hard, determined look in his eyes, and his demeanor was far more impatient and demanding than when I had first come to know him. In fact, I reflected, there was very little left of the Julian I had first encountered years ago in Athens. I reexamined the letter.

"Here," I said, "the Emperor perhaps anticipated your resentment at being informed in this way of Florentius' agreement—in the next sentence, he softens his command by adding the phrase, 'unless it seems absolutely disgraceful for you to do so . . .' "

"Disgraceful? It's an outrage! I refuse to submit to Florentius' bullying, and his preying on Constantius' ignorance of conditions here. Is he so uninformed of my goals? Does he believe this is how we restore Gaul to prosperity? This is how we recapture Rome's lost glory in the eyes of the barbarians? It is scandalous, an outrage! . . ." And for long moments afterwards he muttered in fury, until he finally realized the discomfort of pacing in that temperature outside the confines of the hot water, and slipped back in.

I did not even inquire at the time what he found so disgraceful about the payment: whether it was the high price or the manner in which it was presented to him. I suspect, however, that even if the outlay had been nothing more than a pound of dried cod and an old shoe, he still would have been infuriated with Florentius' back-dealing.

"And what do you imagine the Emperor's reaction will be at your refusal to pay the negotiated settlement?" I inquired evenly after he had calmed somewhat.

Julian glanced at me slyly and then slid under the steaming water till his head was completely submerged, where he remained motionless a long while, only a trail of bubbles rising to indicate he was still alive. After a moment, he slowly rose up again, now with a faint smile on his face as he wiped the water from his eyes with the back of his hand.

"He will have the same reaction as he did when I sent General Marcellus packing, when I reconquered Cologne, when I defeated the Alemanni without assistance from Barbatio, when I *exceeded my mandate*: nothing."

I was not impressed. "Julian," I said, "for four years you have been walking a very fine line as far as Constantius is concerned. You are perceived in the court as a threat to his sole rule. He has killed many rivals for much less worthy reasons."

Julian snorted and, climbing out, began toweling himself off. "Of all the things I should fear, that is the last," he said.

"Oh?"

"Think, Caesarius. His eunuchs may perceive me as a threat—but clever Constantius knows better. For the first time in decades the province's treasury is full and tribute is pouring into the Emperor's coffers. The Alemanni are on the run, freeing up his legions for the Persians. And his troublesome young cousin is apparently quietly satisfied in his provincial little cities in Gaul, safely out of the Emperor's hair in Rome. Constantius could do much, much worse than to keep me alive and content in my position, don't you think?"

Thus in answer to the Emperor's missive, Julian's first order was to the city's bakers: since the season was still long before the snows would melt in the passes and his spring campaigning rations arrive from Aquitania, he ordered all the army's reserve stocks of grain to be mobilized from the surrounding depots, and the ovens to be operated day and night until a sufficient quantity of *buccellatum*, hardtack, had been baked to be distributed to each soldier to last twenty days. Their rucksacks filled with these crusts, he marched the army out of winter quarters two months before the traditional spring campaigning season was to begin. As planned, he encountered the barbarians still lolling in their beds. Within a matter of weeks, he had carried out such a number of lightning raids as to leave every barbarian king who had not submitted after Strasbourg, including King Hortarius, King Suomarius the Beardless, the brother kings Macrianus and Hariobaudes, the legendary King Vadomarius, King Urius the Harelip, and even the far-off kings Ursicinus and Vestralpus, begging him on their knees to accept hostages and allow their people to retreat back to the far side of the Rhine.

Even this Julian did not accept, however, for to him it was not sufficient that the Rhine serve as a mere boundary between Rome's empire and the barbarian lands: the river must henceforth be subject to free passage for all of Rome's ships and supplies, and so he demanded not only that the barbarians transfer across the river, but that they move far beyond, leaving a wide buffer zone between their own lands and the thither bank. When Urius the Harelip complained at what he viewed as excessively harsh treatment in forbidding his people from their ancestral lands, and refused to vacate his villages and farms, Julian deigned not even to respond to his envoys, but merely sent his legions across one of the new pontoon bridges he had built and put Urius' homes to flame, with all plunder and prisoners packed up and sent immediately to Rome. After that, there were no further challenges to Roman authority from the Alemanni.

During his years of campaigning against the Germans, Julian crossed the Rhine with his armies three times while under attack; he rescued and restored to their lands twenty thousand Roman citizens and their dependents being held captive on the far side of the river; and in two battles and one siege he captured ten thousand Alemanni prisoners, not merely ones of unserviceable age, but men in the prime of military life—the numbers of old men, women, and children he captured numbered probably thrice again as many. To Constantius he sent four large levies of excellent Gallic and Germanic infantry, an additional three more that were not so excellent, and two complete and remarkably fit squadrons of cavalry, a very attractive rate of return on the Emperor's original investment in Julian, which, as you will recall, Brother, consisted merely of a handful of singing ascetics; and most important, he recovered all the towns and cities the Alemanni were holding in Gaul upon his arrival four years earlier, strengthened their fortifications against any future attacks, and repopulated their deserted streets and farms.

Julian was right: Gaul was now at peace, and the Emperor could do much worse than to keep him alive and content.

II

As Julian had said, his goal was not merely to foster peaceful existence, but to restore Gaul to the prosperity it had enjoyed as the jewel of Rome's Western Empire. I mentioned to you that upon his arrival, he had found a state bureaucracy in shambles, bloated by nepotism and incompetence, yet fragmented by the attacks of the barbarian invaders. As a new Caesar, of course, he had as little experience in civil matters as he did in military ones, but once he had consolidated his army's victories and had given himself some breathing room, he was bound to become just as capable an administrator as he had been a general. In fact, merely "capable" is not the best description of his performance. Under the initial tutelage of Sallustius, and then with his own innate ingenuity and determination, he soon became the most brilliant governor Gaul had seen in generations.

Just as four years earlier he had spent the winter interviewing and strategizing with each of the garrison commanders under his control throughout Gaul, so now did Julian call in all the city prefects and tax supervisors, reorganizing the collection and expenditure system from top to bottom, stemming the sources of fiscal evaporation along all the numerous conduits by which revenues were conveyed to state coffers. Many longtime tax collectors quit their positions in protest at his heavy-handed approach, and he promptly replaced them with new ones, appointed not on the basis of blood relations or bribes, but rather on administrative competence and loyalty to himself and Rome. With Sallustius and other trusted officials, he undertook a personal audit of the province's finances, a task to which he dedicated two entire winters to poring over accounts and assessment minutiae for nights on end. The fairness and ability he demonstrated in tax matters, Brother, has been noted by authorities far and wide, both secular and religious, as you yourself have pointed out and as even the sainted Ambrose of Milan, despite his abiding hatred for the Caesar, has grudgingly admitted. For it was to the benefit of both the Roman state as well as to the common people that such fiscal matters be regularized. He diligently ensured that no one should be overburdened by more than their share of taxes; that the wealthy not seize the property of the poor; that no one should be in a position of authority by which he could profit by public disasters; and that no public official could break the law with impunity.

Most important of all was his elimination of two exceedingly harmful practices by which the prefect, Florentius, had negligently succeeded in bringing the province of Gaul almost to its knees. The first was the arbitrary awarding of "indulgences," which is to say, the cancellation of taxes in arrears, which in the sight of all fair men might be considered beneficial. This was not the case under Florentius, however, for such a practice was to the advantage only of the rich, who by various methods involving gifts, bribes, and threats were best able to convince the tax collectors to waive the amounts due on their estates and income, at least until such time as a new indulgence was granted. As for the poor, as is generally the case, they were constrained to pay all the taxes they owed, without exception or deferral, immediately upon the tax collectors' arrival. Needless to say, such a practice resulted in tremendous losses to the treasury, and great harm to the people's well-being.

Florentius' other technique, which was quite the obverse of the indulgence, consisted of the *augmentum*, the supplementary tax, which a decree by Constantius several years earlier had allowed to be applied at the discretion of the prefect. This highly irregular tax provided that any amount owed by those unable or unwilling to make payment would fall upon those who had already paid their own taxes, as an additional payment. When Julian heard of such effrontery his eyes flashed and he muttered "Tyranny!" before declaring that so long as he ruled Gaul, no such tax would be permitted in his province. He had only to point to the regions where *augmenta* had been imposed in the past—Illyria, for example—to show how the population had been reduced to misery and poverty because of it. Only the rich, of course, were sufficiently influential as to be able to declare themselves "insolvent"; consequently, the burden again fell upon the poor.

Furious at the challenges thrown at him by Julian, whom he considered a rank amateur in matters of civil administration, Florentius stormed back and forth between Julian's palace and his own opulent headquarters for the entire winter, bearing figures, log books, and tax registries in hand. Julian deigned not even to read them, and on one occasion when I was present he even threw the books to the ground and ordered Florentius out of his sight. The prefect fired off a series of angry missives to Constantius, complaining of the impertinence and ignorance of his young ward, but the Emperor, unwilling to pick this issue as a battle, merely attempted to amicably reconcile the two, privately entreating Julian to be more trustful and yielding with his prefect.

In the end, Julian's obstinacy held, and Florentius was forced to give in, much to the benefit of the province. For by eliminating exemptions and strictly enforcing assessments on all amounts owed, Julian was able to swell the state coffers to a degree unprecedented during Constantius' entire reign. Indeed, during the course of Julian's administration, he even succeeded in reducing the *capitatio,* the assessment per head, from twenty-five *aurei* to only seven, an amount which nevertheless, after the efficiency measures he implemented, still allowed ample budget for the functioning of the State. The key was that the funds were not only assessed on taxpayers, but actually *paid*, for the first time in perhaps centuries. Such measures as these were almost unheard of, not only in Gaul but throughout the entire Empire, and due notice of his methods was beginning to be taken in the capital.

Just as significant, perhaps, were his legal reforms, which were in sharp contrast to accepted practice. Exasperated in his attempts to find a sufficient quantity of judges and local governors whose abilities conformed to his standards of education and fairness of mind, he finally resorted to trying cases himself. This began to be a burden, however, for his time during the winter months began to be increasingly taken up with the settlement of minor property disputes and dowry claims. Toward springtime, when it was known that he would be departing on a certain date for a season of campaigning against the barbarians, individuals seeking redress would throng to the palace, imploring him to hear their case before he left, lining up in the corridors and down the steps into the street. They left him no peace even by night, when particularly brash or desperate claimants would sometimes station themselves close to his windows, and shout or sing their pleas and defense in carefully crafted verse, in an effort to attract his attention to their cause.

Since he clearly had no time to make personal investigations of each matter, he would often refer cases to the provincial prefects and governors, and then upon his return follow up on the outcome of the various suits. It did not help his privacy when it became known that he would often mitigate the penalties that had been handed down by his appointees through sheer kindliness.

Finally, out of pure desperation to regain a bit of his former privacy and time, he limited himself to hearing only cases that were of extreme importance or prominence, and since these cases were naturally the most widely followed, his reputation for personalized sentences became even more widespread. I recall specifically the case of Numerius who had recently been the appointed governor of Gallia Narbonensis, on the southern littoral. He had been accused by his enemies of embezzlement, and Julian determined to hear the case himself, which he allowed to be open to all. In an effort to set an example, he conducted the hearings and testimony with unusual severity, often grilling the witnesses himself. Numerius put up an airtight defense, however, and was ultimately acquitted, to much rejoicing among his supporters. The sharp-tongued prosecutor Delphidius, who had traveled all the way from Rome for the chance to participate in such a famous case, became exasperated at the lack of evidence in his favor, and at one point of the trial addressed the bench with a bitter question. "Mighty Caesar," he said, "how can anyone be found guilty if it is sufficient for him merely to deny the charges?" A hush fell over the crowded courtroom as Julian flushed red in anger at the man's impertinence. He stood up and stared imperiously at Delphidius, who for a moment stood his ground and then began to shrink back against the wall behind him. "And how," Julian thundered, "can anyone be acquitted if a mere accusation is all that is required to convict him?"

It was about this time, when his involvement in the functioning of the courts was at its height, that old Eutherius the eunuch made a remark that, as much as any, may have contributed to the subsequent unfolding of events. He had returned from Italy after spending much time quietly absorbing all the palace gossip and intrigue surrounding Constantius' court, and had resumed his position as Julian's chief steward.

"My lord," he noted casually, as if it had just occurred to him, and indeed it very well may have, "forgive me for raising an unpleasant subject, but one unfinished affair remains to be completed."

Julian looked up, startled at first, but with a hint of amusement in his eyes. "Eutherius, you old dog, what are you talking about?"

Eutherius maintained his customary grave demeanor.

"Again, forgive my presumptuousness, sir. But the woman Flaminia, the . . . er . . . midwife, had a daughter who still lives. She has languished in a solitary cell these past four years without trial. You have had other governors and judges demoted for treating their prisoners so harshly. She is said to be half mad, but perhaps you should put the matter to rest. Hostile tongues have been raising the subject of her imprisonment—Florentius in particular has been talking about it rather liberally—and such gossip could cast doubt on the impartiality of your judicial reforms."

Julian stared at the old man in confusion for a moment, hardly remembering even the existence of the girl, and then looked inquiringly over at Sallustius, who avoided his gaze as he absentmindedly shuffled papers at the worktable.

"Several times I have tried to assign the case to an appropriate judge," Sallustius said quietly. "All of them recuse, however. They fear your wrath were they to find her innocent, and they fear your accusations of cowardice and sycophancy if they were to find her guilty. Most of all, they fear having to call Lady Helena and yourself to testify. It is an extremely awkward situation, and I would urge you to settle the case privately and quietly, perhaps simply by sending a trusted centurion to her cell with a sharp blade."

Julian exploded. "A trusted centurion! And what's to stop that centurion from discussing the matter with another trusted centurion, and another? Have I studied philosophy all these years to so flee my own responsibilities? Is it so difficult, then, both to afford the girl a fair trial and to seek the truth in the matter? By no means. I shall conduct the trial myself, as the greatest test of my objectivity and self-control. Let it be done."

Dear God, what a nasty affair that was. I still shudder at the recollection. He had the foresight to first send me quietly to Sens, accompanied only by a single guard, with instructions to visit Matilda in her prison and determine whether she was fit to travel to Paris for the trial, and if so, to make arrangements for her transport forthwith. In the meantime, Eutherius, in hurried counsel taken with Sallustius and myself, pointed out the scandal that would ensue from a public trial of the girl, presided over by Julian himself as chief judge. The harm that would be caused to the Caesar's reputation for fairness, by trying a defendant while serving as both judge and plaintiff, would be incalculable. Not to mention the fact that the appearance of the dreaded midwife's daughter in Helena's presence would most likely only further unbalance the Princess's fragile state of mind. We resolved that I should delay as long as I reasonably could in fetching Matilda up to Paris, to allow them sufficient time to convince Julian that the notion of a public trial was folly, and that it was a matter to be settled privately.

Their efforts were in vain, though not for the reasons one might at first think. In accordance with the eunuch's and Sallustius' instructions, I tarried five days in arriving at Sens, on what would normally be an energetic two-day trip, first by feigning illness, then by slipping my horse a pinch of arsenic with his grain to render him colicky, and finally by pausing in one of the villages through which we were passing to surreptitiously inquire as to whether anyone in the vicinity might need medical assistance. I then arranged to treat a needy family on an urgent basis, which, as events would have it, involved nothing more than a case of childhood scabies and pinkeye. This treatment I was unable to stretch out for more than two hours, but by that time it was too late to take to the road again that evening. My guard and I were therefore forced to sojourn the night in the house of the sick child, where my own guard, rather fortuitously, as it turned out, managed to contract pinkeye, delaying our arrival yet another day. So much for these things.

Upon finally arriving in Sens, I repaired straight to the remote prison on the outskirts where the girl was being held, reluctant to delay in the city itself because of the number of people who knew me there and who might ask inconvenient questions. Upon arriving at the entrance to the cell, a windowless stone hut, really, hard by the city walls near the municipal rubbish heap, I was surprised to see that although it was locked, it was completely unguarded.

Peering inside past the two iron bars that almost completely obscured the high, narrow air slit in the side of the wall, I was unable to see anything, though when I called inside I thought I heard some faint rustling, perhaps of rats. Furious not only at this dereliction of duty on the part of the guards, but also at this ill-treatment of a prisoner, I sent my own guard galloping back to the city garrison to make inquiries, while I settled myself down by the cell door to wait.

It was not long, less than a half hour, perhaps, when a decidedly ill-looking soldier, an ancient Gallic auxiliary, shambled out from the vicinity of the rubbish heap, pale, unshaven, and tottering slightly on his feet like a sailor just landed after a three-week voyage. He stared at me with slightly unfocused eyes, and asked me in broken Latin what I wanted.

I stared down my nose at him haughtily. "What do *I* want? You drunken ape. I am a physician, sent by the authorities to check on the status of your prisoner. Is this how you maintain the guard?"

The man stared at me insolently for a moment, sizing me up to determine whether I might truly have some authority over him, before he looked away and shrugged his shoulders in resignation.

"Were that it were only drunkenness, sir. It's the cholera, sure as can be, spread through the fetid parts like this dump, and sure to move on next to the city proper. I've been back of the latrines, pukin' and shittin' my guts out, sir, and I'd be happy to give you a sample of the results here and now if you like, for there's plenty more where that came from. You'd be better off saving your treatment for the likes of me than for the bitch what's inside the cell, for if she's not dead of the sickness already she will be in a day or two." And leaning against the wall weakly, he managed to elicit a trickle of bile out of the corner of his mouth, and a mocking grin.

I stared at him in horror. In my wanderings of the past few days I had heard nothing, no reports of plague, and was unsure whether to give credence to the man. But if what he said was true, that Matilda was on her deathbed, then I had very little time. I backed away cautiously from the man as he watched me curiously, still smiling, then tossed him a gold piece, which landed on the ground at his feet.

"Let me in to see the prisoner. I have my orders."

He kept his eyes on me, not even glancing down at the coin. "I have my orders too, which is to let no man see her, and for four years that's the way it's been. Only way I know she's still alive is that each day the bread disappears and the slop is flung out that window above you."

I glanced warily at the air slit just over my head, and sidled a few steps away. I tossed him another coin.

"Treatment for the cholera's expensive, my lord," the man said quietly, almost threateningly.

Exasperated, I untied the small coin pouch from my belt and flung the entire parcel at him, which landed with a satisfying thud against the wall at his feet. He nodded silently, and without deigning even to pick it up, he brushed past me roughly, drawing a large, rusted key from a ring at his belt. He fumbled for a moment at the lock before it clicked and the door swung inward on rusty, long-unused hinges. I entered and heard the metal shriek in protest as the door swung back and closed behind me.

I stood still for a moment, adjusting my eyes to the darkness, which was broken only by the narrow beam of daylight streaming down at a steep angle through the barred and cobwebbed slit above. Thousands of tiny dust motes floated lazily and aimlessly through the bridge of light, as if undecided whether to stay in the known environment of the cell or to make their way up the shaft to the freedom beyond, the only beings herein allowed such a choice. On the far wall where the narrow beam fell, a tiny lizard sat motionless, bathing itself in a brightness that to it must have felt the ultimate luxury. Before my eyes had entirely focused, however, and while still unwilling to tear my gaze from the familiarity and safety of the floating particles, I felt a hand on my ankle, and a wheezing voice floated up to me from the ground.

"So, the great physician Caesarius stoops to visit his colleague and accompany her in her death sentence."

I paused. The voice in the dark was expected, though the words were not. There was no need to enter into a debate with this madwoman, for she had been unable to keep to a thought even when in her right mind four years before. My orders were clear, to ascertain her physical condition and ability to travel.

"I am not your colleague, and I am not under a death sentence. Nor are you for that matter, yet. I'm here to examine you."

At this there was a weak sigh. "You are a trained physician, though in your career you have had perhaps three patients. I was merely a midwife's apprentice, but have delivered thrice that number in a single day. You bring life, and you bury it as well. So too did I, though among the humble and unwashed rather than among caesars and emperors, and in exchange for a basket of eggs rather than a palace sinecure. Who are you to deny your affinity to me— *colleague*?" And she drew a deep, rattling breath that broke in mid-gasp into a racked series of coughing and retching.

I listened silently to her gagging, gauging the depth from within her chest that the phlegm was rising, judging by the bitter, ironlike smell the quantity of blood and sloughed-off lung tissue she was spitting up with each hacking bark. Cholera, hell. She had pneumonia. And it would be a miracle if she lasted the night.

I knelt on the ground beside her in the darkness, and with dismay felt my knee sink into a soft, moist substance, and I reached out my hand to palpate her chest. There have been very few times when I have actually felt utter repugnance for a patient or a medical procedure, even during the autopsies of my most heavily fermented research subjects, though on this occasion it was difficult to feel anything but revulsion. I grasped her thin shoulder, the dry, scaly skin barely covering the birdlike bones, and I could feel death resting upon her like a shroud.

"I have buried no emperors," I muttered absentmindedly, "except for the future one your mother killed, and there is no sentence of death hanging over me."

Another spasm of breathing broke down to a fit of sobs and coughs. I rested my palm lightly on her emaciated chest, feeling the spasmodic gasping and heaving of her fluid-filled lungs as she struggled to regain her breath.

"You're still . . . young," she retorted with great effort, gasping with every word, "like me. We have our entire lives before us, do we not? There is ample time . . . to bury emperors aplenty. As . . . as for the one you say Mother killed—you are mistaken, dear colleague. You are blaming the knife . . . for the deed of the butcher."

Plague or no plague, the woman was disgusting to the extreme, but she was my patient nonetheless, and I had sworn an oath, both on the spirit of Hippocrates after my studies, and on that of Christ during my baptism, to do everything in my power to help unfortunates such as her. I opened my kit, which I had inadvertently set down into another suspiciously odoriferous substance, and began rummaging in it with one hand for something that might relieve the pain of her congestion during her last few hours. More with a view to making idle conversation to soothe her than to performing any serious inquiries, I pursued her last remark.

"And who might the butcher be?" I asked, instantly regretting the question for fear that it might provoke in her unhinged mind another lengthy coughing attack, this time fatal. I would be forced to live with the sin of killing a woman by having engaged her in small talk.

But the coughing, this time, did not come. Instead, she lay in silence for a moment, grasping my hand, which still lay on her heaving chest, in her own thin fingers, with a strength surprising for one so fragile. So long did she lie there clutching my hand that I thought perhaps she had drifted into unconsciousness before I was even able to slip her the draught, and I was about to stand up and step away when the rate of her breathing changed, and I could feel her clearing her throat to say something. I paused where I was.

"Better to have examined the coins than the body," she said simply, and fell silent but for her wheezing breath. I was puzzled. The coins? The only coins I could think of were the gold pieces in the pouch Flaminia was carrying when she had been captured fleeing the city. I had had only a fleeting glimpse of them in the soldier's hands before Paul had confiscated them to the treasury. The girl was raving.

"What are you talking about?" I asked softly, all my senses on edge now. "What coins?"

"The blood money," she whispered back. "The Julians . . . the bloody Julians."

I strained to recall the events of that horrible night; a glimmer of understanding was beginning to form. The "Julians"—this was the term used to describe the gold coins minted by Constantius to honor Julian's crowning as Caesar of the Western Empire. But I was not a numismatist—what did they have to do . . . ?

Suddenly it all became clear. The coins had been minted almost five years ago in Milan. Julian had received a proof set inlaid in a special box shortly afterwards as a gift from the Empress Eusebia. But due to the normal slow pace of production and the gradual spread of currency throughout the Empire from its original place of minting, the coins had only recently begun to show up in general circulation in northern Gaul—within this past year. This was a fact I had noticed because of the remarkably good likeness of the Caesar on the obverse of the coin. But where had Flaminia obtained an entire pouch of the new coins almost four years ago, and why had Paul not noticed or investigated their origin, unless . . .

A searing pain shot through my head as I seized Matilda's face between my two hands. Her cheeks were wet with tears.

"Matilda—where did your mother get those coins? Who sent them to her? Tell me, girl, you're dying, you know that, you must tell me who sent those coins. . . ." But my words were drowned out again by her moan of despair, and a fit of harsh, gurgling coughing from which I knew, this time, she would not recover. For long moments she hacked and choked until she could breathe no more and then, wheezing, gradually sucked in sufficient air to begin another round of spitting and croaking. Great globs of fluid and tissue bubbled from her mouth and down the side of her face as I stared at her dark form in the shifting shadows. The fading shaft of light still made its way through the high slit, its angle flattening as it climbed inexorably up the side of the inner wall, the lizard following it imperceptibly like a lost woodsman following a trail home, like a released soul following the path of light to its reward.

Matilda's coughing finally subsided to a harsh wheeze, a belabored breathing that brooked no attempt at voice, so she whispered the final words she would ever communicate to a colleague: "The arms of Eusebia are long."

When I left the cell in the late-spring twilight, the lightness and effervescence of the air, compared with the fetid heaviness in the cell, almost overwhelmed me, and for a moment I felt dizzy and bewildered, my eyes dazzled by the colors and the clarity of things, and I thought perhaps all I had just heard had been a dream, a terrible dream. If only, I thought, if only I had been born at Mount Atlas of ancient legend, where dreams are said to be unknown. Then I looked to the side, where again I saw the grizzled old Gaul slowly limping toward me from behind the rubbish pit. I stared at him, more in my own inner confusion and shock than at anything specific about him. He stopped at a distance when he saw me, then slowly raised an earthen jug from behind his back in a kind of salute, and grinned at me with rotting, blackened teeth.

III

Julian suffered a terrible blow at discovering the Empress's unspeakable treachery. Out of naivete or pure blindness, he had failed to recognize what everyone else in the Empire knew: that any son of the Caesar would be heir to the throne, and would thus endanger childless Eusebia's position. For rather than accepting Julian's son as his heir, the Emperor could simply declare a divorce and take a new wife who could produce a son—hence her betrayal.

Julian bid me tell no one of what I had learned from Matilda. I lied, or rather told only part of the truth in response to Eutherius' questioning, when I said simply that the girl had died of natural causes, and that her case was closed. The shrewd old eunuch suspected something more was amiss, I'm sure, but said nothing. Julian, though shaken, remained outwardly composed and efficient, with a face that had seemingly become granite. His path, however, was to descend from one hell to another, for the week after my return from Sens, news arrived that certain enemies of Julian's in the Emperor's court, including Florentius, Pentadius, and Paul the Chain, had succeeded in gaining Sallustius' recall to Rome, on the grounds that he was exciting Julian against the Emperor. Sallustius was said to be spreading the word that the Caesar, not the Augustus, was the greatest military and civil leader of the Empire, and that he alone was the savior and restorer of Gaul.

The charges were ridiculous, of course, as silent Sallustius rarely expressed a personal opinion on anyone or anything, much less the Emperor himself. The Emperor's sycophants, however, jealous of Julian's success against the Germans as well as within Gaul against the ancient and hidebound Roman bureaucracy, attributed his effectiveness to Sallustius' efforts. Indeed, they saw no better way to trip the Caesar up than to remove his access to his longtime adviser and friend. Their clever accusations to the suspicious and paranoid Emperor, couched in the form of eloquent praise and eulogies of Julian's abilities, had the effect of coarse sea salt being rubbed into an open wound.

Julian received the news at first with shock, which was reciprocated by Sallustius in the form of an even moodier silence than usual. The latter, however, even knowing he was being sent to his death rather than to the honorable and wealthy retirement he deserved for his long years of service to the state, kept his chin high, and within a day had packed a few belongings in a leather soldier's kit, slung it on his shoulder, and arrived to bid farewell. Julian was disturbed at the alacrity of his departure and the simplicity of his belongings, and delayed an additional day to arrange an escort of thirty mounted legionaries and a gift of his own personal armor, hurriedly refitted by the city's best smith, with a small coffer filled with gold Julians. When all was finally ready, however, and Sallustius had sorrowfully mounted his horse to depart, Julian's expression became surprisingly placid. Sallustius looked at him suspiciously.

"Julian," he said, "I forbid you to take any action on my account. I'll not have you endanger yourself, or the province, by angering Constantius in this affair."

"Not to worry, old friend, not to worry. I seek only the good of Rome."

Sallustius continued to stare at him. "It's precisely words like that that make me worry."

Julian smiled sadly, and slapped the horse's haunches lightly. "Off you go, Sallustius. Stay alive." He paused as the horse began to trot off. "We will meet again." The older man turned and glared at him from the saddle.

During these dark times, Julian had few comforts and motivations—indeed, if one were to quantify them, there would be at most three, by my count. The first and most fundamental, indeed the very salvation of his soul, was in stripping down his life to its most austere, to its barest core. While other men under such circumstances might seek retreats for themselves, houses in the country, seashores, or mountains, and though he might have desired these things very much, Julian was of the opinion that such external needs were altogether a mark of a common, shallow type of man. Indeed, he prided himself on his power to retire into himself whenever he wished. Nowhere, he said, does a man retire with more quiet or freedom from trouble than into his own soul, particularly when he has within himself a store of thoughts that by looking into them, he may immediately fall into perfect calm.

As a physician, I would concur and go even further, by noting that such perfect calm is nothing more than a good ordering of the mind. Just as physicians always have their instruments and knives ready for cases which suddenly require their skill, so too does a man require principles ready for the understanding of things divine and human, and for doing everything, even the smallest thing, with a recollection of the bond that unites the divine and human to each other. A man can do nothing well that pertains to himself without at the same time having a reference to things divine. And falling back on his fundamental principles, Julian was able to cleanse his soul and arrange his life to be free of clutter and distraction, allowing him to focus clearly now on developing the plan that would take him so high, and sink him to such depths.

In this he continued with his routine of before, yet now with a severity and dedication that rivaled that of the most rigorous ascetics. He slept for only moments at a stretch, waking spontaneously without urging, and when fatigued would lie down again, not on a feathered bed or brightly colored silk spreads, but on a coarse woven mat which the local Gallic peasants called a *susurna*, under a worn, woolen soldier's blanket or, like Diognetus, with a mere plank bed and skin. Alexander the Great, it is said, used to keep his arm outside his bed over a bronze basin, holding a silver ball in his hand, so that when he fell asleep and his muscles relaxed he might be awakened by the sound of the ball's dropping. Julian, however, needed no such artificial devices to wake him whenever he willed.

He was utterly indifferent to cold or warmth; just as he ignored whether he was drowsy or satisfied with sleep, or whether he was spoken ill of or praised. I would go so far as to suspect that he would take only a mild interest even in whether he was dying or doing something else, for to his mind, dying was simply one of the acts of life, and it would have been sufficient to him merely to do it well, if that is what he had undertaken. His moderation in eating was legendary, limited mostly to a vegetarian diet, and he would sometimes go the entire day eating naught but a soldier's biscuit, as if the notion of feeding himself had simply slipped his mind. The common practice among banqueters of inducing vomiting in order to eat more, even during solemn occasions, was one in which he never indulged, nor would he countenance it in others in his presence.

Yet despite, or perhaps because of, the physical rigors to which he voluntarily submitted, I never saw him become ill, except on one occasion when he was nearly killed by a brazier that had been brought into his room. The winter had been severe, particularly in light of the normally mild climate of Paris, and the Seine was raising slabs of ice like marble, almost to the point that they could join and form a continuous path to bridge the river. Julian normally was strict in refusing to allow his domestics to heat his room, feeling that stuffiness and warmth induced drowsiness, which he could not abide, given all the other demands on his energies and time. On this night, when he relented and finally permitted them to bring in a few coals, his fears were realized, and he fell asleep. With the windows shuttered, he quickly became poisoned by the fumes, and it was only by a happy coincidence that a scribe reporting to him for duty discovered him sprawled on the floor, pale and scarcely breathing. By the time I arrived, he had recovered his senses and weakly waved me away, swearing he would never allow heat in his room again.

His quarters he decorated sparingly, a cross on the west wall to catch the light of the rising sun, and various dusty archaeological artifacts in which he had taken a recent interest heaped in the corners—strange, stonelike bones of giant creatures, shells of unknown mollusks that had been found on mountaintops, and, most especially, heads, torsos, and other body parts of various idols that had been found beneath the ground's surface when his engineers were excavating for new walls and buildings. Once, upon surveying an especially large deposit of what appeared to be pieces of sarcophagi littering his hallway and anteroom, I lost patience with—I'm not sure with what exactly, Brother, perhaps with what I viewed as merely the frivolity and futility of collecting and storing such vestiges of dead, or rather never-existent, gods.

"Julian," I said, striving to maintain a neutral but pointed tone to my voice. "Your collections are becoming a hazard to the guards. The corridors look like a pagan graveyard. Your Greek deities far outnumber the crosses."

"More pagan gods than crosses?" he echoed absently. "That is how it should be."

"How so?" I asked suspiciously.

He stopped fidgeting with the stacks of papers covering his desk and looked at me in puzzlement. "Just as one morsel of bread is sufficient when receiving the Eucharist, is it not? In fact, according to the Orthodox, even one crumb of the Host is sufficient for you to receive all of Christ's presence and grace. Grace is not doubled if you get back in line to receive two morsels, nor trebled if you receive three. Do you agree?"

"Of course. But what are you saying, precisely?"

"Only this: one cross in the room is sufficient for all God's purposes."

"And one pagan statue is not sufficient?" I inquired, somewhat annoyed. "You need thirty?"

"Ah, so your objection is not to the clutter after all." He surveyed the rows of mutilated godlets and body parts with what seemed, I thought, an expression of supreme satisfaction. "There are many pagan deities. And I . . . well, as you can see, I am a collector."

By candles and lamps he continued his studies of philosophy and poetry, and his intellect ranged widely over the long history of Roman domestic and foreign affairs. Though he preferred to speak in Greek with me and whomever else was conversant in his native language, he made a thoroughgoing study of Latin as well, becoming quite fluent over time. Julian's true life was spent in working by lamplight, like his ancient hero Demosthenes, whose adversaries had sarcastically claimed that his orations smelled of lamp oil. To the lamp he remained bound, even to the evening of his death.

So too did he develop his rhetorical skills at this time, declaiming endlessly by night in the echoing baths, engaging in mock arguments with himself or with a favored instructor or two, while I or another of his friends passed judgment and offered observations. In this his criteria for success was not that which would impress the savants, but rather that which would move the common soldier, the rough stalwart unencumbered by formal education yet blessed by an unerring degree of common sense. Consequently, such flourishes as might have left a professional rhetorician cold, he practiced and learned because of his conviction that they would strike to the heart of the common soldier. In response to my skepticism at the usefulness of these efforts, he reminded me that Aristotle, the greatest rhetorical theoretician of all, had been hired by the great Philip of Macedon to tutor his son Alexander, the greatest general of all, and therefore it had been recognized for centuries that eloquence went part and parcel with military success; he felt it to be a great shortcoming of modern education that this fact had been forgotten or ignored. He set his sights higher by aiming his rhetoric lower, at the men of arms who supported him.

His second driving force, after stripping his life to the bare fundamentals, was religion, and of the Christian faith he was a faithful supporter and financial contributor. The Bishop of Paris was a frequent guest at his dinner table and partner in animated discussions, particularly on the nature of the Trinity, which was a topic of much interest and concern to Julian. On the fifth anniversary of his appointment to the office of Caesar, a large celebration was held at the palace, of course, but he took special care in preparing for a solemn service of blessing at the Cathedral of Vienne, the first city in Gaul at which he had arrived five years earlier. In a rather belabored commemoration of the Caesar's skill at unifying the peoples and armies under his command, the local bishop, a passable amateur musician, herded together four disparate groups outside the cathedral to sing parts of the service in the four biblical tongues: Hebrew, Latin, the Greek of the Gospels, and that undocumentable dialect, the speech of lunatics possessed by demons. Under the bishop's skillful direction, the music of this combined chorus ascended to the heavens in perfect, otherworldly counterpoint and rhythm. The sequel, however, was less harmonious, as the three sane choruses proceeded into the church to continue their efforts in the nave, while the lunatics were enjoined to maintain beggarly silence outside. Several weeks later, at the feast of Epiphany, Julian celebrated another solemn Mass presided over jointly by the bishops of Vienne, Sens, and Paris, and arranged for a general absolution of sins, for which all those in attendance thanked him profusely. At this event he wore a magnificent diadem set with gleaming gems, in contrast to the beginning of his reign five years before, when he had worn only a cheap crown like the president of a local athletic meet.

That very evening, poor, troubled Helena died of the

stomach malady from which she had long been suffering. She departed this world, however, with a smile on her face, no doubt her last thought being that she would soon be united with the one of her flesh who had preceded her by four years into heaven, if indeed it can be said that the unbaptized, even if innocent children, ever can enter the Kingdom, a matter on which you, Brother, are better qualified to opine than am I. Shortly thereafter we received word that the Empress Eusebia had died as well, on the very next day, in Rome. Both husbands shed tears, I am certain, though what were the proportions dedicated to which wives it is impossible to say.

As for the third force in his life: I had no idea at the time, though I realized it much later, that his driving motivation, indeed his very essence, was such an ungodly one. That flame of determination that made him rise in the morning and work himself to exhaustion the entire day and half the night was so unworthy of a philosopher, yet perhaps so meritorious in a Caesar, that it could scarcely have occurred to me during those days in Gaul. Yet now as I write this years later I have the eyes and the wisdom to identify and name the obvious, his third drive, the very force of his existence.

It was vengeance.

I did not have occasion to reflect long on such things, however, for it was during these times, just after my return from Sens with the news of the midwife's daughter, that another event became of much more concern to me. One sleepless night I had gone to his rooms seeking company, knowing that he would be awake and most likely happy to talk. When I arrived, however, I found his door closed, and soft conversation coming from within. Not the dramatic pauses and cries of declamation, as when he practiced his speeches, but rather animated conversation, even argument, and I stood thinking, uncertain whether to knock. I resolved not to interrupt him, and so sat a moment on a bench in the corridor outside his rooms, until my own thoughts were interrupted by the arrival of the scribe who had been scheduled to take Julian's dictation for a shift.

It suddenly occurred to me that perhaps Julian had been dictating inside, and I spoke to the scribe.

"I believe he's busy with your predecessor," I said as he went to open the door. "Don't interrupt the Caesar until he finishes."

The man looked at me in puzzlement. "Can't be," he said. "I'm the first scribe he's scheduled for this evening."

I stood up, surprised, and followed the man into the room, finding Julian sitting flustered behind his table, his books closed and set to the side, and a vacant, almost clouded look in his eye. There was no other person in the room. It was the first of many evenings that I would find him talking to himself.

IV

Julian's jaw dropped in astonishment as he stared at the ancient Eutherius, who, for the first time I had ever seen, had lost his normally unflappable composure.

"Half my troops? *Half?*" he roared, as the distraught old servant stood shifting from one foot to the other, wringing his hands.

"Those are the orders brought by the tribune Decentius, my lord," Eutherius said. "And, it is not merely half your troops, but the best half. The Emperor specifies that the Aeruli, the Batavi, the Celts, and the Petulantes are to be transferred in their entirety, with an additional three hundred men to be taken from each of the army's other units. Furthermore, the best of the *scutarii* and *gentiles,* your personal bodyguard, are also to be sent at once to the Emperor. Decentius is lodged at the city prefect's palace, and is awaiting a response to this demand by . . . by Sintula."

Julian's head snapped up. "Sintula? The head squire? The orders were sent to my squire?"

"Not precisely, my lord . . . they were sent to the cavalry commander Lupicinus, although I informed Decentius that he is currently in Britain with the auxiliaries, putting down an uprising by the Picts. Instead the orders were delivered to the letter's secondary recipient, Sintula, whom I regret to say is now hastening to obey them and is selecting the finest troops from your legions as we speak."

Julian had been caught off guard, but almost immediately regained his composure. Naturally the Emperor, as the highest authority of the state, had every right to skip hierarchy and to pass orders to lower-ranking subordinates if he so chose, but this was unprecedented, unnatural, a case that the law books would refer to as *summum ius, summa iniuria*—a right pushed to its extreme may be an injustice.

He set his jaw. "Summon this Decentius immediately," he said simply and curtly. Eutherius' eyes widened, and he began hastily backing out of the room, but Julian suddenly called him back. "And, Eutherius," he said, thoughtfully and slowly, "summon the physician Oribasius also, for a consultation." At my questioning look he averted his eyes for a moment. "I have not spoken with my old friend for some time," he said quietly, before putting his head back down to his work.

Decentius apparently defined the word "immediately" differently than did Julian, for he was idling in his rooms when Eutherius arrived, and insisted that after his long journey he be allowed to take a short nap and freshen up before attending to the Caesar's summons. Besides, he said, his business was with Sintula, and he saw no need to respond to Julian's request—if he did decide to meet with him, it would be at his pleasure, not the Caesar's.

Six hours later, past midnight, he strode insolently into Julian's office, no doubt thinking to surprise him in a weary and impatient state of mind by arriving at such an hour—though in this case it was he himself who was surprised, for Julian had just wakened from his own nap a few moments before, was chatting with me, and was as rested and relaxed as a baby. The tribune hid any reaction he might have had, however, and after a cursory bow to the Caesar, sat down silent and uninvited, and looked around with clear distaste at the bare walls and shabby furnishings of the Spartan workroom.

Julian stared at him a moment as if sizing him up. The man was a senior courtier to Constantius, accustomed to being sent on sensitive embassies, and evidently bored with his duties at remote outposts like Paris, though not with the finer lifestyle that accrued to him while at home in Rome. He was a large man, gone soft from recent years of inactivity but still bearing a muscular frame and the stately posture of the senator he had once been. The fine linen of his toga and the exquisite, understated quality of the expensive rings on his hands were in sharp contrast to the Caesar's plain, unadorned, and almost purposefully unkempt appearance, which some might have attributed to his lingering mourning for Helena, but which was simply due to his refusal to waste time or money on superficialities. Finally Julian allowed himself a small, sly smile as he looked straight into the man's eyes.

"Thank you for your visit, Tribune. You are welcome to any of my services or facilities for as long as you stay in Paris. Perhaps I might even arrange for you a tour of our nearby garrisons and camps?"

This time Decentius found it impossible to hide his surprise, for he had clearly been expecting a hostile reaction. Though at first taken aback, he recovered quickly.

"I see no need to prolong my visit. I have delivered my orders to Sintula and will be departing as soon as the troops have been readied."

Julian nodded slowly. "I have been informed of the Emperor's orders, and I hasten to do all that I can to comply with the will of my ruler. As you know, however, over the past five years I have spent considerable time in the field, training and campaigning with my troops, and I feel a good deal of affection toward them, as a father toward his newly grown sons. And just as a father would, I feel a concern for their welfare which the Augustus, in all his wisdom, might perhaps not have anticipated. Might I therefore ask what the Emperor's intentions are for my men?"

Decentius stared at him warily, as if attempting to discern whether any treachery might be involved in his question, but seeing none in Julian's face, he finally shrugged.

"I see no reason why you should not know. The Emperor intends to place your Gallic troops at the spearhead of his campaign against Persia. King Sapor has recently attacked our eastern frontiers, and our legions in the East have a pressing need for troops. The Emperor has concluded that there is no threat of war in Gaul, as the barbarians have abandoned all their aggressions, apparently in fear of his reprisals. The fame of his Gallic troops has spread far beyond their region, even to the court of Sapor, who trembles at the thought of facing Constantius' courageous Gauls. Hence his determination to transfer unneeded troops from your command to that of his generals in the East."

Julian's eyes widened and he paused, absorbing this information. "Again, I hasten to fulfill the Emperor's orders. There is, however, a small legal matter to be overcome. When I first conscripted the Gallic soldiers the Emperor is demanding, it was on the express condition that they would never be taken to regions beyond the Alps. To them it is unbearable to be sent far from their homes. Not only would their transfer to the East be a violation of this condition, but my future ability to recruit Gallic auxiliaries would be compromised if they feared being sent to hot lands far from their families."

Decentius shrugged and stood up. "Your private treaties with the barbarians are not my concern, nor do they have any bearing on the Emperor's orders. It is perhaps for that reason that the demand was directed not to you, in any case, but to Lupicinus and Sintula. You have been relieved of responsibility, and, I daresay, you would do well to do nothing to impede the transfer. Good evening."

And without so much as a bow or a flourish, the man swept out of the room.

Julian sat smoldering in silence for a moment, then slammed his hand down on the tabletop, sending parchments fluttering to the floor. I stood up with a start.

"*Damn* his eyes, Caesarius! Invading Persia—with *my* troops! The man's mad, he's mad—what could the Emperor possibly gain from this venture?"

"He needs to make his mark, Julian," I said calmly. "Constantius has been in power for over a decade and he has yet to engage in war, to conquer significant territory—"

"So all this is just for the history books?" Julian interrupted, beginning to pace. "He's seizing my troops illegally to bolster his own reputation?"

"It's not illegal. He's the Emperor."

Julian whirled. "Even the Emperor is beholden to the good of the Empire," he hissed. "He is not Nero, for God's sake—he's the son of Constantine!"

"And does that exempt him from ambition?"

"No—but it does not exempt him from wisdom either. The western provinces are secure and at peace, money and trade are flowing, and the Persians can easily be contained in their current position with some deft negotiations and a bolstered garrison or two. He risks all these lives, all this treasure, all we have gained over the past five years by this insane venture—merely to put his name in the history books? Caesarius, that's insanity!"

"Yet you risk destabilizing the Empire by disobeying him. Would you compound his error?"

Julian sat down heavily in his chair, deep in thought, considering the distasteful options facing him. If he had learned anything from Sallustius, from his Christian faith over the years, it was that authority was to be obeyed—yet to what extent? To the point, even, of compromising one's values, one's patriotism? To the extreme of endangering the security of Rome itself?

The night was long and sleepless for Julian and his various advisers and courtiers, and I finally retired to my room, almost colliding on my way out with Oribasius as he scuttled in for the requested consultation with Julian. I questioned him good-naturedly, for it was unusual for the normally lethargic physician to be up and about, indeed to be looking so downright *energetic*, at such an ungodly hour, but he simply smiled mysteriously and slipped into Julian's office. Preparations were already beginning to be made for the departure of the troops, at the instigation of eager-to-please Sintula. The selected men, or at least those who suspected that their companies were to be selected, had already begun to assemble somewhat nervously. The worst thing, however, was the wailing. As you know, Brother, auxiliary troops do not serve in their own home region without copious numbers of camp followers, their wives and children, sometimes even mothers and other relatives, as well as large numbers of females involved in less licit but equally noisy relationships when the time arrives for the departure of their menfolk. Hence the wailing.

With daybreak, the wailing rose to a higher pitch even than during the previous night, for a reason that soon became apparent as I strode out of my apartments and into the streets. Unidentified parties had taken the occasion to churn out numerous copies of a secret letter in an astonishingly short period of time. It was addressed to the Petulantes and Celts and others rumored to be transferred to the eastern front, and was full of vile accusations against the Emperor Constantius, complaining bitterly of his betrayal of the faithful Gauls, and of his disgrace of Julian. *We are to be driven to the ends of the earth like common criminals,* the letter said, in crude camp Latin and equally crude Gallic written in Greek characters, *and our dear families, whom we have set free from their earlier bondage only through murderous fighting, will once again become the slaves of the Alemanni.* The letter continued with wicked and obscene slander of the Emperor that I dare not repeat here, and which gave such concern to Julian's advisers, fearful that he would be blamed for its libelous language, that both they and Decentius' cohort sought jointly to suppress it before it spread.

At first, a few copies of this letter had merely been tossed into the legionaries' camps, crudely tied to rocks, but the effectiveness of its language soon became apparent. It was read and then copied repeatedly by the troops themselves, then spread to the very city of Paris. That night shadowy figures were seen pasting hastily scribbled copies of the text on street corners and walls, even scrawling it in chalk on the bases of monuments when scraps of parchment became scarce.

The city was in an uproar. Julian remained cloistered in his workroom, now seeing no one except Oribasius, who slipped in and out of the closed doors as gracefully as his overtaxed frame would allow him. Julian ignored even Decentius when he returned to the palace in a fury, demanding in the strongest terms that Constantius' troops be selected at once and sent marching before similar letters were posted among the outlying garrisons. The Caesar replied simply, through Oribasius, that the Emperor's orders had been directed to Lupicinus, who was still absent, and to Sintula, who was by now overwhelmed and panicked at the troops' reaction, and that it was for them to take action—he was washing his hands of the affair. Decentius returned to his lodgings sputtering in anger.

Crowds of angry women and camp followers were now beginning to gather in the principal squares, and though it was broad daylight, many bore lit torches. The municipal guards of the city prefect were overwhelmed by the mob, and resigned themselves merely to protecting their own quarters, adjacent to the palace, surrendering the rest of the city to the belligerent crowds. Chants were shouted, carried from street to street by milling women, and effigies of the Emperor and Decentius raised and burned, a capital offense if their instigators were ever caught. Still Julian remained in his room, though the cries and wailing of the crowds outside could not have failed to penetrate even the thick walls of the palace, and the shouts of the frightened servants and the scuffling of their scurrying feet as they sought to barricade the outer doors could not have failed to attract his notice. Through Eutherius, he ordered only that the departing troops be accompanied by the massive wagons of the imperial post, bearing the Gauls' legitimate wives and children as far as their homes might be on the route east, to make the separation less painful for all and attempt to assuage some of their fury. This order, however, was met with derision and cries of mockery from the crowds, outraged that even Julian, now, seemed to be giving in to Constantius' effrontery.

Finally, at about noon, Decentius made his way back to the palace, in disguise and under a heavy guard, and burst into the office without announcement. There he found the Caesar calmly waiting for him.

"What is the meaning of this rabble?" he shouted. "Have you no control over this mob you govern?"

"Apparently I do not," Julian calmly replied, "for the Emperor has seen fit to take it away from me and hand it to my subordinates."

Decentius sputtered. "Paris is a mob scene, and will soon be a shambles. I demand that you restore order so we may assemble the departing troops and their supplies."

Julian stared at him thoughtfully. "You are blind if you think Paris can be so easily silenced while you break Rome's commitment to the troops. If you insist on fulfilling the Emperor's orders—and I repeat that I will do nothing to impede you in this task—I suggest you assemble in an outlying area. Go to Sens or Vienne, even Strasbourg, and avoid confrontation with the camp followers. If you do not, you will be courting disaster."

Decentius fumed. "Your words are traitorous, and will be duly noted to the Emperor. You are suggesting that Constantius run from a rabble of women and children, that he assemble a triumphant and conquering army from some collection of wooden huts in a remote village, that his legions fly Gaul in the dark of night. I will do no such thing. If, as you insist, you are bent on assisting us in this task, you will order all civil and military functionaries to gather before the palace three days from now, to officially launch the assembly of troops and collection of provisions. The presence of these officers will check the anger of the troops and they, in turn, will bring their unruly wives and offspring under control. If not, I will consider you as being in collusion with them."

Julian nodded obsequiously, and smiled. "As you wish, sir tribune."

Decentius glared at him in fury and, for the third and last time, swept out of the office. Julian looked over at me with a glance of resignation, and I marveled at his calm while the city outside was in an uproar. "I pray there is an afterlife," he said, "for this time tomorrow we, and half of Paris, may be there."

I looked at him in surprise. "Have you any doubt?" I asked.

"In the gods, no. In man, that is another question."

"The gods?"

Julian smiled, and gestured to the stack of dirt-encrusted deities littering an entire side of his room. "A figure of speech, Caesarius. Just a figure of speech."

Paris' uproar quickly spread to the surrounding suburbs, and then to the neighboring garrisons and encampments, and the slanderous letter, having by now undergone various manifestations and revisions, had within two days been posted in every village within a hundred-mile radius of Paris. As the troops were ordered to the city and abandoned their barracks and quarters, their families became panic-stricken, and attempted to intervene to stop them, acting as if they expected the imminent return of Chonodomarius' invasions. Soldiers marched along the roads with sullen expressions as their wives trotted breathlessly alongside them, holding up their babies and imploring their men not to abandon them to the rapine of the Germans. The letter was having an effect far beyond even the wildest hopes of its anonymous authors.

The first squadrons began to arrive in the city, fighting their way through the crowds of milling people and the beasts of burden barring their way. Julian roused himself from his closed offices and private consultations to ride out to the suburbs to greet them. This he did effusively, embracing those men and officers with whom he had campaigned or trained in past years, and praising them for the brave service they had provided under his command. True to his promise to Decentius, he entreated them to be faithful to their new commanders, whoever they might be, and assured them they would be amply rewarded for their sacrifice. On the two evenings before the official assembly, he held banquets for the arriving officers, toasting them in their new adventure, and asking them for any requests they might care to make, which he would do all he could to fulfill. His guests, puzzled at first as to Julian's calm resignation in the face of this enormous disruption to the forces of Gaul, left encouraged but saddened at being forced to abandon not only their native lands, but also such a noble general.

All went well, with even Decentius seemingly satisfied at the progress being made, until night fell, and the hour arrived that has been the undoing of so many well-laid plans. With the darkness rose the fears and imaginations of the troops, fed by the tensions of the populace, who for three days had refused to disperse but had continued to gather angrily in the now filthy and foul-smelling streets and forums. The gutters ran with the effluent of thousands of sleepless women who had followed their men in from the countryside, the night silence was broken by the squalling of hundreds of infants terrified at the torchlight and the evil spirits seeming to hover everywhere over that benighted city.

At about the fourth watch, the people could abide no longer, and whether at the instigation of secret ringleaders, or merely at the urging of their own self-fed fears, pandemonium suddenly broke loose. The Spanish guards stationed almost elbow to elbow around the palace to protect the Caesar were overwhelmed and trampled, and furious crowds surged to the palace walls, crushing between the stones and their bodies those unfortunate enough to be in the front lines of the mass of heaving, sweating females, who were soon joined by the thousands of sleepless auxiliaries only loosely barracked in their city quarters for the night. More torches were lit and raised, and screams ensued as the hair and clothing of some in the massed, milling crowd caught fire and the flames were swiftly extinguished, along with the lives of their victims, under trampling feet.

The palace was surrounded and under siege, and I raced from my own quarters in the north wing to Julian's office, bursting in just in time to see him staring up blearily from his reading, his eyes half hooded as if he were waking from a dream. Upon seeing me, he shook his head to clear his thoughts and made his way groggily to his feet.

"Thank God, Caesarius, you've come—such a dream I've had . . ."

I looked at him in exasperation, wondering how he could have been able to sleep in such pandemonium, and how, even now, his greatest desire was to recount to me one of his endless dreams. A chant, faint almost to imperceptibility behind the three-foot-thick outer stone walls of the palace and formidable oaken doors of his office, was beginning to seep through from the outside, like a noxious gas.

"Julian," I began, "the crowds outside—"

"Caesarius—the guardian spirit, the woman I told you about, appeared to me again. She appeared looking as she has before, carrying her burden, Caesarius, it was the same, the goddess . . ."

The chant began growing louder, more urgent, and I looked at him impatiently. "Julian," I said more insistently, "they're calling for you. The city is in turmoil, something must be done."

But he was as if in a trance, a half-smile on his face, staring straight past me as if it were I who was the shade, not the phantasm by which he was haunted. "She spoke to me, Caesarius, for the first time she spoke, and her voice was like light, like enchantment, but I didn't so much hear it as felt it, penetrating into me, and though she was rebuking me, her words felt comforting, as sweet as honey. . . ."

I saw by now that he was beyond me, that there was no dissuading him from this madness, and that the quickest way of addressing the urgent business of the mob outside was to encourage him to spill out his words as fast as he could.

"What did she tell you?"

"She scolded me, as a mother would a young and flighty son. 'Julian,' she said, 'long have I watched you in secret, wishing to raise you higher, but always being rebuffed. If even now I am unwelcome, I shall go away sad and dejected.' "

"I don't understand—" I began.

"That's not all she said," he continued, and I began to despair as the chant grew louder, more desperate, and the previously unintelligible syllables began to form words and meaning. "She said, 'Do not forget, Julian: if you reject me again this time, I shall dwell with you no longer.' "

"It was only a dream, a puzzling dream," I said.

"No, my friend, it was not, it was a vision, not puzzling in the slightest, as clear as any I have had yet. Listen!"

And for the first time I realized that he too was aware of the rising chant, the fearful sound, which had begun to make its way through and around the palace, rolling and echoing through the corridors and anterooms, gaining strength like a wave rushing unimpeded over an open beach, as more and more voices picked up the refrain. Within moments the sound was bellowed deafeningly from a hundred thousand tongues, roared from every street and corner of the city within a mile of the palace, torches and clubs rising and falling in unison with the rolling vowels of his name and the terrifying, traitorous suffix they had appended to it, to which only the Supreme Emperor was entitled: "Ju-li-an Augustus! Ju-li-an Augustus!" The thought of rebellion against Constantius was madness, it was suicide, for despite the might and loyalty of the Gallic army Julian had built over the past five years, it was but a small thing compared with the forces the Emperor could marshal from his legions of the Danube and the East with a mere twitch of his finger. Julian, however, was unperturbed, and as he passed out of his state of half-sleep, half-wakefulness, I saw his expression take on a hard, alert cast and he listened more closely to the shouts from outside.

The crowds roared his name and the forbidden title, they would not be put off. Within moments two officers burst

into the room, begging Julian to address the troops and the
camp followers from the balcony before the city was destroyed. The women, they reported, had begun dismantling
the palace from the outside stone by stone, and in their
frustration at being unable to reach the wall, the latecomers
and soldiers in the back of the crowd had begun tearing up
flagstones in the streets, and tiles and gutters from the roofs
of the surrounding buildings. Paris was being taken apart,
piece by piece.

He listened in silence, and nodded his assent. With the
two officers flanking him he strode out of the room and
down the corridors, followed by a small detachment of Petulantes archers who had also forced their way into the
building. I walked behind, to the grand balcony overlooking
the forum, where he was accustomed to receiving and greeting dignitaries and addressing the crowds for great proc-
lamations and religious occasions. Throwing open the wide
double doors, he was practically pushed out to the stone
railing of the balcony by his increasingly nervous guard,
who then retreated and stood at attention behind him as if
preventing the escape of a prisoner, though escape was far
from his intention at the moment. We were met with an
extraordinary sight.

The forum was filled from wall to wall, the front half
with thousands of women, their crying, tearstained children
hoisted onto their shoulders and heads, away from the pressure of the surging crowds but into the danger of the waving, thrusting torches. The women peered up in exhaustion,
their faces pale and haggard in the torchlight, hair disheveled and greasy, lips dry from three days of standing in the
square with only such food and water as they were able to
beg from sympathetic residents and bystanders. Behind
them, filling the far end of the forum and spilling into every
street and alleyway beyond, were the auxiliary legions, their
pennants flying almost as if the troops had marched in unison to join the riots. Men hung precariously on drain pipes
and downspouts, clambering and crowding onto the roofs
far over the crowds, clinging even to rough spots on the

sides of the walls that could afford a finger- or toe-hold to the most intrepid, all of them roaring the fearful chant as if with one voice: "Ju-li-an Augustus! Ju-li-an Augustus!"

When the balcony doors burst open and Julian emerged, the chant exploded and washed over us like a sudden downpour, and all faces turned toward us in the firelight. The crowd took a moment to realize who it was that had appeared on the balcony, and with cries of recognition and triumph, the people suddenly heaved forward, even though a moment before one would have thought them to have been already packed so tightly as to be unable to move. Scattered cries and gasps of pain rose to our ears from the stone walls below the balcony, out of our line of vision, but sufficiently close as to hear the agony of those being crushed below.

The chant rose to a deafening pitch, and the very walls seemed to shake with the reverberations. Julian stared out at the crowd, and though I was unable to see his face from my position behind him, I knew, as if I had been looking at him directly, that he had applied his inscrutable military leader's expression and was now surveying the crowd with an impassive face. As word of his arrival spread to the farthest corners of the forum and back into the side streets and alleys beyond our vision, the noise level initially increased. The mob's excitement rose to a fever pitch, and all shouted and pointed in the direction of the balcony. Within moments, however, as Julian stood frozen, staring at the crowd, a hush fell, broken only by the scattered and distant wailing of the frightened children held over their mothers' heads.

"The duty of a soldier is to obey his general," he pronounced in measured Latin, without preliminaries, in a clipped voice that carried easily over the heads of the silent crowd and resounded off the smooth stone walls of the buildings surrounding the space. "This my soldiers have always done, and they have been rewarded in their faithfulness to me by becoming the finest fighting force in the Western Empire, invincible, conquerors of the Germans and of all the barbarian peoples of the north." Scattered cheers erupted from the farthest corners of the forum, where the soldiers had gathered. Most, however, stood as immobile as Julian, waiting to see what further words he might have. The women beneath the balcony, filling the entire front half of the forum, wore expressions at best slack and unimpressed, at worst hostile.

"The duty of the people is to obey its Caesar," he continued, and now I saw where he was moving—testing the waters, as does a trained rhetorician, unsure of the level of attention or the sympathies of his crowd. "In this, too, the people of the Western Empire have acquiesced, building here for themselves Paris, the grandest city of Gaul, renowned for its libraries and public buildings and its *complete and utter fealty to Rome....* "

A murmur rose from the crowd, not yet loud enough or urgent enough to give one a precise idea of where they stood or where they might be led, but rather as of a rising tension, an anticipation for what they knew would be the concluding statement to come, the final installment of the trilogy of duty he was describing for his subjects.

"And the duty of the Caesar"—the crowd held its breath—"is to honor and obey the Emperor Constantius Augustus."

A roar ripped through the mob, high-pitched at first as the women nearest responded most quickly to his words, but expanding in volume and depth of tone as it surged to the back of the forum and Julian's words reached the ears of the soldiers and merchants whose lives most depended upon his acts. It was a bellow of fury, of exasperation and impotence, and the crowd surged forward and then swayed back as people tried to move, to run, to take some action, somehow, but were prevented and hemmed in by the press of the unwashed, cursing, roaring masses around them. Objects began to be hurled through the air—at first fruit, bread, bits of clothing and offal from the streets, but soon, as more rioters clambered to the tops of the buildings around the square and began ripping apart the rooftops and walls, more dangerous matter—clay tiles, bricks, and broken pieces of stone—began flying like missiles. Screams of pain and fury filled the air, and the women below looked up at us with expressions of terror.

"Julian," I shouted, pushing forward through the guards and onto the balcony. The majestic bronze statue of Julius Caesar in the middle of the forum begin to sway ominously on its pedestal. "They are destroying the city, and the army will soon be helping them. Unless you seize what is offered, you will have lost everything. They will kill you!"

His eyes shone strangely, firelike, and he stared hard at me for a moment. The corners of his mouth twitched and the veins stood out on his forehead. The man was under tremendous pressure, I reflected, more than any mortal should have to bear. Then he looked back to the crowd, and raised his hands high for silence.

Nothing happened, and I despaired. Only those in the front ranks of the crowd were even looking at him, while those on the rooftops and farther back in the forum had become crazed, rioting openly and willfully, hurling building materials down on their fellows and screaming blind insults at the Emperor Constantius. Julian raised his hands higher, shouted for silence, but in vain, for his words were unheard, as if released silently from a dry throat. The feeling was nightmarish.

Without hesitation, he stepped back for a moment, beckoned to the archers behind us, and six of them stepped forward, all that could fit side by side on the wide balcony. At a shouted order that only they could hear, they unslung the compact, army-issue crossbows from their shoulders and in one smooth motion strung the heavy gut cords and fitted the thick, ugly bolts that passed for arrows to their strings. These weapons I had never seen fired in anger or in battle, but I had heard tell of their capabilities—a practiced archer could pierce armor at a half-mile's range. The smooth, gray iron tips gleamed dully in the torchlight, round and barbless, the weapon relying on sheer force of impact, rather than the shredding effect of the warhead for its killing capacity.

Hesitating but a moment, waiting to see if the sight of the poised archers would attract the attention of the crowd, Julian shook his head in frustration, pointed out to the archers a tall, particularly active individual prancing on a rooftop with a large building stone held over his head, and made a short, chopping motion.

Simultaneously, as if from one hand, the six arrows leaped from the drawn strings with a speed that made them disappear from view by the naked eye. A second later, however, the results were clear.

Four of the iron bolts found their mark, while the fifth and sixth clattered noisily against the tile roof and caromed off into the streets beyond. The rooftop marauder, pierced twice in the chest, once in the throat, and once in the thigh, looking for all the world like the martyred Saint Sebastian, may God forgive me for saying so, froze suddenly on the roof, the building stone still balanced high above his head. A moment later the stone fell, glancing painfully off his shoulder and rolling down the roof and off the gutter, while the man himself sank to a sitting position, then lay back onto his shoulders like an exhausted stonemason settling down for a rest. He slid weakly down the steep pitch of the roof on which he had been standing, gathering speed and leaving a dark, glistening trail on the russet tiles above and behind him, before pitching feet-first, stone dead, over the eaves and onto the heads of the horrified crowd below. I was unable to determine who the man might be, and I prayed that he was not one of Julian's soldiers. Screams erupted from the onlookers near the building from which he had fallen, pierced by the high, frantic wailing of a woman, likely the wife or concubine of the man who had been struck—but elsewhere around the forum, a sudden, barely controlled hush fell upon the crowd, and all eyes turned back to the balcony, the expressions on their faces a mixture of terror and relief.

Julian waved the archers back inside behind the balcony

and again stepped forward, into the silence of the frozen crowd.

"The Emperor's duty, however," he continued calmly, as if having never been interrupted in his previous harangue, "is to guide and honor his subjects, and in my effort to remain obedient to the Emperor to the end, I have contributed to his dishonoring of his subjects, contributed to the breaking of Rome's solemn vow to its Gallic auxiliaries, and therefore made myself unworthy of your obedience."

The crowd was stunned and silent.

"We are told in the ancient myths," he continued calmly, his voice rising as he found his orator's rhythm, "that the eagle, when testing which of its brood are genuine, carries them yet unfledged into the upper air and exposes them to the sun's rays, that the god Helios may determine whether the brood are true born and destroy any spurious offspring. In the same way I submit myself to you, as though to the sun god himself. It rests with you to decide whether I am fit to lead you or not. If I am not, then fling me away as though disowned by the gods, or plunge me into the river as a bastard. The Rhine does not mislead the Celts, for it sinks deep within its current their bastard infants, taking fit revenge on the offspring of an adulterous bed; but all those it recognizes as being of pure blood, it floats on the surface of the water and gives back to the mother's trembling arms, rewarding her for a marriage pure and beyond reproach. Thus so, I throw myself on your judgment, to determine whether I am legitimate in this task, and to accept my due punishment should I fall short in your eyes."

At this Julian stopped short, his head bowed, as if waiting for the mob's judgment to be passed on him, prepared for whatever verdict might be handed down. The crowd stood silent a moment, puzzled and dismayed at his hesitancy to assume their command. Then a single cry rose from the back, from the area where stood the soldiers, the pennants drooping lazily in the still air.

"Ju-li-an Augustus! Ju-li-an Augustus!"

Instantly, the cry was taken up by all, and the forum

again resounded with the tremendous cry—this time, however, unbesmirched by rioting or violence. The entire crowd stood motionless, all eyes on Julian, lips only moving, a hundred thousand of them opening and closing simultaneously with the mouthing of the syllables as the words poured over us, reverberated off the limestone behind and above us, pounding into our heads—

"Ju-li-an Augustus! Ju-li-an Augustus!"

He looked up, nodded, and a cheer rose from the mob. The archers behind pushed me roughly out of the way and lifted Julian high above their shoulders on a military shield in the traditional posture of triumph, swiveling him slowly this way and that above the heads of the people, as he held his arm before him in a solemn salute.

After long moments of cheering, the women crying in loud wails of relief, knowing merely that their men would not be sent to the sweaty, painted harlots of Syria, the archery captain stepped forward and announced crisply that to complete the ceremony, the newly acclaimed Emperor had to be crowned. Julian raised his eyebrows in surprise.

"I am a soldier," he shouted to the man over the continued cheering. "I do not own a diadem."

The officer looked at me, recognizing me for the palace physician. I shrugged.

"I could run up to fetch a necklace or tiara of Helena's," I offered. Julian visibly shuddered.

"The omens would not be good," he said. I stared at him in exasperation and frustration that he could be so selective about his jewelry at a time such as this. "A cavalry frontispiece, then," I said unthinkingly, imagining the highly ornamented ironwork and jewels worn on the face of Julian's warhorse during ceremonial occasions. Julian scoffed.

"I take responsibility for my actions," he shouted, visibly affronted. "I shall not be portrayed as a horse led by the nose."

The crowd's cheering was dying down and an ominous restlessness was beginning to set in as the people watched the animated discussion being held on the balcony, wondering whether they should fear for the validity of their acclamation. Finally, one of the soldiers resolved the issue.

Stepping forward, he removed the thick golden neck chain he was wearing as standard-bearer of the Petulantes' cohort, and, without ceremony or permission, simply placed it on the head of the newly acclaimed Augustus. Julian looked back out at the crowd, the long chain perched precariously in a gleaming heap on the top of his head, one loop dangling lopsidedly off his left ear, and as the roar swelled for the last time, I saw now that the faces were smiling, and I knew all would be well.

Later that day, when Julian learned of the hasty, terrified departure of Decentius and Florentius from the city after the acclamation, Eutherius advised him to kill the latter's family and relations who remained in trembling disguise in the suburbs, and to appropriate his considerable wealth for the treasury. Instead, Julian ordered their possessions to be carefully cataloged and packed, and all to be sent in covered wagons to Rome, with the family to be carried comfortably, if not luxuriously, and safeguarded on the journey by the same cohort of Petulantes archers. It was a magnanimous act, one that flabbergasted and confounded Constantius when he heard of it; it was an act entirely in keeping with Julian's forgiving but crafty nature; it was an act that was his last as a Christian and his first as the disputed Emperor Augustus of Rome.

BOOK SEVEN

BELLUM CIVILE

Occasio in bello amplius solet juvare, quam virtus. Amplius juvat virtus, quam multitudo.

In war, valor is more useful than strength of arms, but even greater than valor is timing.

—VEGETIUS

I

What a terrible thing, Brother, is a civil war. One week
your dominion is at peace, the enemy on all borders has
been subdued, the army is draining marshes for farmland
and repairing fortifications, the Emperor is satisfied, and the
Church is expanding; then with one fell blow, one ill-
advised order from on high, all is a shambles. One's life is
uprooted and overturned, the Empire is on the brink of
schism, and death is all around. One week, within which
one day was the turning point, though I would be hard-
pressed to determine precisely which day that was, as all
seem to run together in an evil blur; and within that day a
critical hour, minute, and second. Before which point, if the
fatal order had not been issued, all would have remained
the same; after which infinitesimal lapse, all is lost, or
gained, depending upon the side you are on, and on that
side, depending upon whether you are a general who will
be allowed to retire peacefully to an estate in Pannonia, or
a mud-booted infantryman, in which case it hardly matters
on which side you fight, for the end result will be the same
either way, and the twenty years' service in exchange for
retirement, a thick-armed barbarian wife, and two acres of
bottomland for a garden are as impossible as Perseus' flight
to the sun. A week is all it takes, Brother, for God to create
the universe, for civil war to erupt, for a plot of beans to
sprout in the summer. A day is all that is needed to watch

the gladiator battles in the circus, for a baby to be born. An hour to attend a Communion service, or for that same baby to die. A minute to tell a joke, to say a prayer, to ask forgiveness, to utter a betrayal. A second for a wasp to sting, for an archer to loose an arrow, for a murderer—or an Emperor—to snuff out a life. Yet that insignificant period of time is impossible to predict in advance, or its inexorable progress to be stopped, and despite every good intent, that which God hath decreed is made manifest, and the wasp stings, and the war erupts.

Like the deified Julius four hundred years before, Julian had crossed his Rubicon, yet if the first Caesar had known what he was about when he took this fatal step, the same could not be immediately said of his successor. For though the Gauls praised and acclaimed him as the savior of their nation, and indeed of the Empire, this was because most of them had never been farther than twenty miles from Paris and could scarcely imagine an empire much bigger than their own country. There were very few rays of sun on the horizon; all of Julian's outlook was darkened by clouds. He could indeed boast of having raised and trained a crack army in the past five years, but so too had Constantius during his own reign, and his troops numbered four times as many as all that could be mustered in Gaul, and he had the treasure of Rome and Constantinople and all the mighty cities of the East to support him if any more were needed. If the Gallic people and troops could scarcely look beyond their own day-to-day existence, Julian and his advisers could; and our prospects were not promising.

For lack of a better strategy, he resolved to stall, to gain as much time as he could to solidify his local base, while softening Constantius, even dissuading him from his anger. He entered into direct negotiations with the Emperor, explaining to him in a respectful letter precisely how his acclamation of Augustus of equal rank to the Emperor's own had occurred, and stating his desire to come to an understanding. We spent days drafting and honing the wording of this missive, to convey a tone neither timid nor arrogant, continuing to recognize Constantius as senior ruler of the rest of the Empire, but requesting in return recognition of Julian as the Supreme Ruler in the West. In what I thought was an additional fine touch, he decided to have the letter personally delivered to the Emperor by old Eutherius, a man whom Constantius had long known, and one of the few men in Gaul whom he respected and trusted. He issued similar explanatory letters to the Senates of Rome and Athens, and in a characteristic anachronism, a nod to his desire to safeguard the ancient morals and customs, he sent copies to the Spartans and Corinthians as well, though it had been six centuries, at least, since their cities had carried any political weight in the world.

The gesture was wasted. Eutherius and his party were impeded and harassed every step of the way by hostile customs agents and other imperial authorities. After they finally crossed the Bosphorus and presented the letter to the Emperor, who was then visiting in Caesaria of Cappadocia, Constantius broke into a murderous rage, screaming at them and spitting from his flabby, unwieldy lips, sending his court diving for cover and causing even the stalwart old eunuch to fear for his life. Without even questioning Eutherius, denying him the right to explain the letter, the Emperor ordered him to leave, and Eutherius scuttled back to Gaul and advised Julian to prepare for war immediately.

The old adviser's haste, however, was not warranted, at least not yet. Shortly after the interview in Cappadocia, the Emperor came to his senses and determined that of the two threats arising on either side of him, the newly acclaimed Augustus in the West and the Persians in the East, the Persians were the more dangerous. Accordingly, he too adopted stalling tactics and engaged in his own exchange of letters, demanding that Julian immediately renounce his title of Augustus and retain only his early, subordinate authority in Gaul, and all would be forgiven, though no mention was made of the terms of service of the Gallic troops. This letter was delivered by a group of court officials, all of whom had been appointed by Constantius to various senior military and civil posts in Gaul, in an effort to deny Julian the right to fill these positions with men of his own choosing.

I shall make a long story short, Brother, for almost the whole of that year of Our Lord of 360, and half the next, was spent in these diplomatic skirmishes and thinly veiled insults. Constantius became bogged down with his diplomatic and military campaigns against the Great King Sapor, drawing new levies of troops to fill the gaps in his legions, increasing the numbers of cavalry, imposing heavy tax burdens on all classes without distinction, and drawing huge quantities of provisions, men, and treasure from Italy and all the other provinces under his control.

Julian, meanwhile, spent all his time strengthening his army, recruiting auxiliaries from both sides of the Rhine, tightening the collection of taxes to ensure that every copper due was paid, and assigning his troops to rigorous training and mock battles. The Gauls took this in good stride, indeed cheered him and encouraged him in these ventures, to the point of even volunteering for him large sums of silver and gold beyond what was due in tribute or taxation, which he initially refused, but eventually accepted when they practically forced him to take it.

Dozens of times, however, I urged him to caution. "Julian," I would say on a typical occasion, while reviewing correspondence from the garrisons with him, or studying our respective texts at night, "with the military you would do well to be discreet. Every company you add to your legions is fodder for the Emperor's spies to report. He already suspects your intent. You are eliminating your options, making it all the more difficult to turn back."

Normally he would nod in silence or simply ignore me. On the final occasion that I made such a warning, however, he slammed down the codex of laws he was reading and stood.

"Damn it, Caesarius, you underestimate me, just as General Marcellus and Sallustius and the others do!" His voice was controlled but tinged with anger. "You and I—we have fought together, grieved together—you buried my own son! Do you know me so little? Have all my efforts to preserve Gaul, to glorify Rome, passed over your head? You still assume I nurture the option of turning back. You are wrong. There is only one direction, forward to the end, and only God knows whether I will be Emperor or a dead man. But I will not rule jointly with Constantius. I cannot apply philosophy to a man who has none. There can be no more cohabitation with the man who killed my son."

"But, Julian," I protested, "the letters you have written him . . . the embassies you have sent. Surely something—"

"Surely nothing," he interrupted hoarsely, in a voice barely contained. "Don't mistake my delays for hesitation. I am building my strength, Caesarius. Time favors me, and I will not be rushed on this enterprise."

At this I was silent, merely staring at him as I pondered the implications. He breathed slowly and deeply for a few moments, his eyes locked on mine the whole time, and again I noticed their strange light, the fanatical gleam that had so disturbed me the first time I saw it, at Strasbourg, when he was contemplating the execution of the Beast. Finally looking away, he gathered his composure, lowered himself slowly back to his seat, and bent his head to the codex he had been reading before I had spoken. I sat thunderstruck at the transformation I had witnessed, from calm strategist a few moments before, to a man consumed by a furious hatred, and back again to studious analyst. I rose to leave, but before I made my way to the door, he had one more point.

"Caesarius." His voice was soft but penetrating, his gaze piercing.

I turned warily. He was my friend, but, yes, I feared. "Julian?"

"When you underestimate me, you underestimate Rome itself."

The following summer, Julian was told by his scouts that Illyricum, the province above Italy and just to the east of

Gaul, had been practically depleted of legions by the call-ups to the East, and that there remained only small garrisons to defend the major cities and military facilities. With his negotiations with Constantius at a dead end, and with the Emperor's forces on the verge of routing King Sapor in Persia, Julian felt that now was the time to act, before his rival was again able to return his full attention to the problem of Gaul. He made his move.

He resolved boldly, and his advisers said foolishly, to take all of Illyricum in a single pass, which would then give him a powerful springboard to control Italy to the south and even take Constantinople itself while the rival Emperor was still absent. Like a stage magician, his task was to pull vast amounts of material out of a seemingly empty sleeve, and I do not exaggerate when I claim his sleeves were empty: after subtracting the troops needed to be left behind to garrison the border towns along the Rhine against the Alemanni, his total forces amounted to scarcely over twenty-three thousand men—a laughable army compared with the resources at Constantius' command, and frightening to consider that with it he intended to conquer all the territories from Gaul to Constantinople and then swipe the most powerful city on earth from under the Emperor's nose.

In an attempt to give the illusion of a wide-ranging, sweeping attack across Europe by a crushing force, he divided his troops into three commands. Two each were of ten thousand men under his generals Nevitta and Jovinus. The third, a mere three thousand troops, the cream of his cavalry, the swiftest horse the Gallic forces could muster, he kept for himself. The three armies he assigned to three principal routes: Nevitta was to cross through Raetia and Noricum and descend along the course of the Danube into Pannonia. Jovinus' troops were to storm across northern Italy and then up to meet with Nevitta at the Danube. Julian himself would strike out across still barely charted territory, on the longest and most difficult trek of the three, through the heart of the Black Forest, which concealed the source of the Danube and in its northern reaches still harbored Germanic tribes hostile to Roman rule.

Of the three routes into which the army was split, not only was Julian's the most challenging, it was also the most frightening, for the Black Forest was a region into which Roman armies rarely ventured. It is said that there is no one who has even reached to the extremity of that forest, though men have journeyed through for weeks, to the point of madness, and in fact it is uncertain where the forest even begins. By so dispersing his forces, Julian was emulating a strategy employed to great effect by Alexander the Great, giving the impression of vast numbers of troops and spreading terror everywhere. The three armies were to meet at Sirmium, the capital of Lower Pannonia, a rustic, provincial city on a small tributary of the Danube.

It was determined, with much discussion and considerable regret on my part, that I would not accompany him in his attack through the Black Forest. There would be no occasion for medical treatment on his lightning thrust through Germany, he said—if wounded, he would either ignore the injury or die of it. Rather, it was decided that because of my own administrative and strategic skills, I would be attached to Nevitta's unit as a senior adviser. My role was to maintain the courier contacts and communications with the home base in Gaul, and coordinate the three armies' joint arrival in Sirmium, which we had scheduled for the ides of October.

Before departing, I took the time to visit fat Oribasius, whom I had not seen for several weeks. Though we were as unalike in as many ways as two men can be—of different generations, different schools of professional practice, different religions—still, I had always found his company enjoyable and his conversation stimulating, and I wished to bid him farewell. With the exception of the days leading up to the acclamation, when Julian had summoned Oribasius for a series of private consultations, I had almost com-

pletely supplanted my colleague in his physician's services
to the Caesar. This was ostensibly because I was more fit
to travel on the forced marches, though Julian had often
told me privately that he also mistrusted Oribasius' skills
because of his antiquated theories, and that he kept him in
his court merely for the sake of old friendship. Still, Oribasius seemed not to mind the diminishment of his duties
in the least, and always had a friendly word for me.

Knocking on the door of the field hut he maintained as
a small camp clinic for treating the garrison once or twice
a week, I poked my head in.

"Oribasius? I understand you're remaining in Paris. I
came to wish you well. I leave today."

He stood up, red-faced and startled, from the table at
which he was sitting, which was stacked high with dozens
of sheets of identical large-lettered texts. These he was sys-
tematically folding one by one and laying in the roaring
fire he had built in the small fireplace. The room was heated
to a stifling temperature. He limped over to me, his pink,
fat face perspiring, but wreathed in smiles.

"Good for you, Caesarius!" he said. "The adventure is
only beginning. Would that I myself could complete what
I started!"

What *he* had started? I paused in puzzlement and looked
over to the table where he had been sitting, with the piles
of broadsheets, all upside down to me so I could not read
them from where I stood. It occurred to me that I had never
actually seen Oribasius read or write anything—in fact, I
had often wondered if he was illiterate, and his talk of compiling a vast medical encyclopedia merely a sham. The
stacks of sheets were strange to find in the camp hut, and
it was even stranger to find him burning valuable parchment, but a light was slowly dawning.

"Oribasius," I said, pointing to the stacks of texts on his
table, "what have you been burning in here so diligently?"

He smiled mysteriously, but shifted his considerable
bulk slightly so as to hide my view of the texts. Though
upside down, their letters, I saw, were large and crudely

written, and it would be easy for me to make them out if I could just stand a little closer . . .

"Nothing important," he chuckled, attempting to disguise the slight wince of alarm as he saw where my attention was directed. "A few medical texts of your misguided Hippocratics," he joked.

I shouldered past him, attempting to mask my sudden suspicion with a lame joke of my own: "Oribasius, I didn't even know you could write! And here you are practicing your ABC's."

Moving to the side of the table I stopped short as I saw the top sheet on the stack, and the crude Latin words instantly jumped out at my eyes: *We are to be driven to the ends of the earth like common criminals, and our dear families, whom we have set free from their earlier bondage only through murderous fighting, will once again become the slaves of the Alemanni. . . .*

"Oribasius!" I hissed, barely containing the fury in my voice at finally identifying the author of the anonymous missive that had caused such an uproar. "You didn't . . . This is your work?"

His cunning smile never faltered, even as he shrugged his shoulders self-deprecatingly.

"My work—yes. And Julian's as well, of course." He sighed dramatically. "Though truth be told, the original idea was certainly mine. And the text of the broadsheet as well. Ah well—the secret would be out sooner or later. The crudity of the Latin was a nice touch, though, don't you think?"

"Do you realize this may be the death of Julian and of all of us?" I shouted.

Oribasius shook his head, his smile fading as his small, piggish eyes took on a look of dead seriousness. "Do not cross me, Caesarius," he intoned, though his voice was not threatening but rather that of a father scolding a dense son, "for by crossing me in this, you cross Julian himself, and through Julian your destiny is made. You are young, and your adventure is just beginning. I am fat and lame, I have now completed my duty to the Emperor, and I expect nothing from my actions, except . . ."

He paused.

"Except *what,* you fool?" I pressed angrily, seeing his focus wander off as if he were deep in thought.

He looked back at me.

"Just this," he said, "and you are the only man to whom I have told it: the fact is, I take great satisfaction in knowing that it was not the crowds, not the generals, not even the gods themselves, but rather fat, jolly Oribasius with his clever pen and ambitious mind—I, Oribasius—who made Julian Emperor. Oh, Julian knew of my actions, of course, for I proposed them shortly after the arrival of that buffoon Decentius—but the execution was all mine. History may forget me as a physician, Caesarius, it may even deride me as an encyclopedist; but as a king-maker, I rank among the best."

II

Of our march, Brother, I have hardly a word to say, for although we and Jovinus' unit constituted the first hostile armies in generations to pass those ancient Roman cobbled roads through the Alps, to Italy and beyond, we met not a single enemy, none of the ambushes and other obstructions we had anticipated, not so much as a stone thrown by a mischievous boy. You may doubt whether such a short description as the one that follows can adequately cover the story of a secret march of nearly eight hundred miles through hostile territory. Yet I truly cannot recall any events I have omitted that might swell this brief recounting to something more substantial. The troops were force-marched twenty miles a day and more, and the speed of the army's sweep and its surprise tactics created the intended effect, without need for us to strike a single blow. Panic ensued in the lands around us. Days before our arrival word had already been spread by Constantius' scouts, and cities were emptied, their garrisons scattered or force-marched farther south and east. The praetorian prefect for Italy, the most powerful civil official in the province, fled before Jovinus, taking with him the prefect of Illyricum as well. The speed and smoothness of our approach to the Danube was breathtaking, almost worrisome in its lack of impediment, as if Constantius were reserving his forces for some massive attack upon our arrival.

Smooth and speedy, I say, except for my own duties. As master of the couriers I worked day and night coordinating the messages and dispatches between Jovinus and Nevitta, as well as all the myriad details unrelated to official correspondence with the three armies—arranging advance supplies, resolving administrative issues back in Gaul, and promotions and transfers within the legions, but in one area, the most important of my duties, I failed miserably, and this I was sick about. For during the long, uneventful weeks of our march, not a single contact did I make with Julian— not a single order received from him, not a single progress report successfully sent to him. Every one of my post-riders returned to me weeks after having been sent off, unable or unwilling to enter far into the Black Forest in search of him, stymied in their attempts to obtain news of his whereabouts. The forest is big, I mused, huge—but large enough to swallow an Emperor and three thousand men without a trace?

At first I attributed the loss of Julian simply to my post-riders' incompetence, or to mine in giving them faulty instructions or incentive. Week after week of silence from one's commander, however, gives one pause. Nevitta was outraged, terrified at having committed his life and promising career to the insane venture of rebelling against Constantius with a meager force of ten thousand men, and with his leader consumed by wild beasts or tribes in the wilderness. All we could do, I told him, was to arrive at Sirmium ourselves to wait for him, pray, and hope for the best.

Limping sore-footed into Sirmium on the appointed day, with Jovinus' troops still two weeks' march behind us in their arrival, we were astonished to see the city gates wide open in welcome. Cheers erupted from the town walls and battlements as the population gathered to throw flowers down on our weary troops. We were met at the entry by fresh and rested Gallic troops, who escorted us to the central forum, where we were greeted smilingly by—who else?—Julian, who had, unbelievably, arrived two days earlier, having outrun every single one of my messengers along the way with his three thousand cavalry, and arranged the welcoming party for us upon our arrival. Our jaws dropped upon seeing him thus, and I wager that the only person more surprised than we was one Lucillianus, the Roman commander in charge of Pannonia before our arrival, whose story is worth a slight diversion to make up for the lack of events to recount to you of our own march.

Count Lucillianus was a veteran soldier who had fought bravely against the Persians and had recently been promoted to his present position. Several days before, he had received vague intelligence of Julian's approach, which, to give the man credit, was more than I myself had been able to arrange. Thinking, however, that he had several days or a week by which to arrange his defenses successfully and thereby garner great favor from Constantius, he went to bed that night content in the thought of his upcoming victory. He slept soundly until he was rudely awakened in the dim hours of the morning by the point of a sword against his throat and a crowd of evilly grinning men gathered about his bed. No answer was given to his shouts of protest, but he was bound, gagged, placed on the first available beast they were able to find in the barracks outside, which happened to be a donkey, and driven like a wretched prisoner past his own personal guard, themselves gagged and trussed like chickens, to the military quarters in the center of town. Upon being frog-marched into his office, Lucillian found Julian calmly sitting in his own chair, reading Marcus Aurelius.

It seemed that the Caesar had encountered an unexpected bit of luck in his journey. They say that as a harsh taskmaster, Alexander the Great was unexcelled—his idea of breakfast was a long march, and of supper, a light breakfast. Julian was typically somewhat more generous with his own breakfast, treating himself to an entire glass of water, when available, but in all other respects he followed Alexander's example in driving his troops and their horses mercilessly in their nonstop charge through the forest, fortunately having not met with any unicorns or other such creatures

that might have slowed their progress. When they gained
the Danube they captured a sufficient quantity of small
boats to transport his entire force straight down the current,
which was fast that fall, and which they augmented even
further by steady rowing. The superhuman labors of his
men at the oars, as well as a week of favorable, winds, had
carried his fleet over seven hundred miles in a mere eleven
days. Landing nineteen miles above Sirmium, Julian had
taken advantage of the moonless night to thunder his troops
straight to the city in a matter of two hours, silently overwhelming the guards before they had even known they
were under attack, and capturing the commander.

Lucillianus nearly died of fright, but upon recognizing
the Caesar, who was wearing the imperial purple and who
promised him clemency in return for an oath of fealty, he
decided to make the best of his situation, and even attempted to show his gratitude for the reprieve by offering
some timely advice.

"It is rash and reckless of you, Emperor, to invade another's territory with so few men," the Count proffered cautiously.

Julian answered with a bitter smile. "Save your wise
words for Constantius, soldier. You may kiss the imperial
purple not because I need your advice, but to calm your
own nerves."

Lucillianus did, immediately swore fealty to his new
Emperor, and was given a position of command in Julian's
legions.

III

In Sirmium, Julian spent but three days, for time was of the essence and momentum was on his side. Thus far he had moved with his entire army faster than Constantius' couriers and spies would be able to report his movements back. Conversely the Emperor, unaware of the speed of Julian's march, had been content to lumber slowly along on his return from Syria, stopping in each major city along the way to receive the acclamations of his subjects.

Julian paused only long enough to restock his supplies, stage a chariot race as a reward to the city for the favorable reception its people had given him upon his arrival, and secure the outlying garrisons. Reinforced now by Nevitta's troops, he resumed his rapid march on Constantinople. Advancing down the Danube, he entered Moesia, which was bordered on the south by Thrace. Thrace, in turn, was bounded on its southern coast by the Sea of Marmara, on which Constantinople, his goal, was located. He had therefore already accomplished almost half his journey without the loss of a single soldier or the death of a single Roman citizen.

The road ahead of him, however, was by far the most hazardous, for the region of Thrace was well fortified with strongly walled cities such as Philippopolis and Adrianopolis. These would have to be taken and passed before the capital could be reached, and the sentiments of the garrisons and citizens of those cities were anything but certain. What is more, like an eel trap with its spikes of sharpened reeds pointing inward to prevent its quarry from escaping once it had entered to take the bait, Thrace was an easy region to access, but almost impossible from which to withdraw under hostile conditions. The approach was a vast range of mountains running from east to west, with only a single pass across it, through the valley of Soucis. Although the valley was an easy march to anyone descending from Moesia, as Julian and his army would do upon their approach, it offered considerable obstacles to negotiate on a retreat north out of Thrace, even if there were no enemy troops defending it. And if a sizable garrison of the enemy were posted there, retreat would be virtually impossible. Recall, Brother, that eels are a delicacy to be flayed and fried while still alive, twitching and quivering in the pan.

After scouting the pass for himself, Julian concluded that with his meager forces it would be foolhardy to march further without first attempting diplomatic entreaties with the fortified cities below. He occupied the pass with a sizable garrison under Nevitta's command, and withdrew to the nearby city of Naissus, a well-stocked town in which he and his troops could comfortably pass some time.

That fall, things turned black. Though well entrenched and supplied at Naissus, his efforts to dissuade the surrounding fortified towns from supporting his cousin failed. The city elders hardly needed to consult with one another long to determine on whose side their destiny rested—Constantius' legions, fresh from victory in the East and supported by the treasure and resources of three-quarters of the Roman Empire, or Julian's tired, ragged band of men tenuously clinging to a remote mountain pass in upper Thrace. And even with this meager territory captured, our army was stretched untenably thin—military and political problems both locally and in Gaul were a constant source of vexation, and lines of communication with Paris were irregular. He made efforts to shore up his support in the region by lavishing attention on the general public welfare, restoring aqueducts and towers, reviving the city leadership, and lowering the taxes in some areas, as he had successfully done in Gaul the year before; and he spent countless hours attempting to rouse the people to his side through personal meetings and writings to influential officials. Still, the limp handshakes and slack-jawed smiles of a dozen city officials, though welcome, are nothing compared with the hard biceps and armor of a Roman legion, and in this Julian was sorely lacking.

The days became crisp in early November, and snow had already begun to fall during the cold nights. Julian grudgingly resorted to the leather Gallic leggings he wore to sustain him on his endless rounds of the encampment. The men had settled into their long winter routine, hunkering down to await the spring thaw that would allow them to resume their campaign, their critical march on Constantinople. For the time being, their fate would be in the hands of the diplomats.

Julian and I stood surveying the camp as it awoke one morning, the men emerging from the rows of crude log huts they had built as sturdier shelter against the cold than the campaign tents. For once, even Julian looked red-eyed and ill rested, and I marveled that he still had the energy to rise before his men, well before sunrise. The night before had been one of terror for the army.

Nevitta and the generals had been in council in the Caesar's own unprepossessing hut, which I attended as well. The generals had departed about midnight, rubbing their eyes and stretching. I dawdled for a moment in the hut, gathering papers and other items I had left lying about, and then made my way slowly to the entrance, some moments after the others had departed. Julian stood outside the door, gazing at the sky, and I began to slip by him, but he seized my arm as I made my way past. I stopped and looked at him, but he did not release his grip, and I saw that his gaze was still directed elsewhere, out toward the camp, but be-

yond it. I followed his line of sight, up into the inky blackness, studded with a million stars flashing brilliantly in the
cosmos like sparks from a roaring fire. Far in the distance,
above the northwest horizon toward which we were looking, shone the slow, searing blaze of a falling star, cleaving
the heavens in a broad arc with its fiery trail. I watched,
transfixed, for a long moment, before it disappeared as suddenly as a torch thrown into the sea. Julian stood motionless, gripping my upper arm tightly as scattered shouts rose
from the sentries around the camp who had also witnessed
the phenomenon, and the silhouettes of men roused by the
commotion appeared in front of the smoldering campfires.
Finally, he relaxed his grip and turned to me slowly, almost
reluctantly, managing an apologetic smile.

"Pardon me, Caesarius," he said, patting me gently on
the arm where he had gripped it hard. "A comet—well, the
omen is not a good one."

I brushed off his remark. "You mean that old saw about
portending the death of a ruler? We're educated men. Place
your trust in God, not the stars. All will be well."

Julian nodded. The camp, however, was in an uproar,
the men demanding that he appear before them personally
so they could witness the fact that he was still alive and
breathing. For hours they milled about in the cold, calling
to one another, doubling and tripling the watch to warn
against any unseen enemy, posting enormous detachments
of guards around his hut out of fear for his safety, despite
his protests. Their superstition disgusted me, their fear
aroused pity, their loyalty to their Caesar was humbling.

I remained at the hut with Julian for some time as he
reassured his nervous men, and I did not leave until he
finally lay down on his bare camp cot for some much-
needed sleep. As I slipped out the door, Julian scarcely
noticed me depart—he was again mumbling and talking to
himself as he drifted off, which he did increasingly during
times of stress. I had much to think about as I finally made
my way back to my own quarters.

It was several days afterwards, while he was again preparing for his morning rounds of the camp, that I fell flat on my face.

Normally, of course, this would scarcely be cause for comment, particularly to you, Brother, knowing as you do how bereft I can sometimes be in the way of physical grace. As it was, I had just finished conferring with Julian about something insignificant, some pulled muscle or other from which he had been suffering, and was walking him to his horse before he left to make the rounds of the camp. While giving him my hand to help him mount, however, my foot slipped in the frozen mud, and although he recovered and was able to rise easily to his horse, I, on the other hand, lost my balance completely and fell prostrate on the ground before him. Standing up ruefully and beginning to wipe the sticky filth off my face and tunic, I was surprised to hear no sound from Julian—no apology, no hoot of laughter, no reprimand for my clumsiness, all of which I would have been unsurprised to hear from his lips.

Rather, after clearing the mud from my eyes I looked at him and found him sitting stock-still on his restless horse, staring at me with wide eyes. "It's a sign," he said finally, unable to tear his eyes off me. "The man who raised me to my high position has fallen."

It took me a moment to understand what he had said, and that he was referring to my tumble as a prophecy of the fate of Constantius himself. I glared at him.

"First of all, a word of sympathy would be in order," I retorted, forgetting my custom of speaking deferentially to him when in public. "Secondly, I resent your inference. I am not an auspice, like a piece of entrail drawn from a dead goat, and Christians do not even believe in such superstitious foolishness."

He stared at me in silence a moment longer before finally shaking his head as if to clear his thoughts.

"Caesarius," he said, "let us talk. Take another horse from the stable and come with me."

The seriousness of his expression puzzled me, and the groom who had been holding his horse immediately left us for a moment to fetch another animal. This I mounted myself without difficulty, and we took a circuitous path along the inside of the city walls, which would eventually bring us to the open field in which the bulk of the garrison troops were camped.

As we trotted side by side he assumed a thoughtful demeanor.

"Caesarius, I meant to give you fair warning earlier, but was unable to, for lack of time as well as will. Your comment just now, however, leaves me no choice but to bring up a difficult subject."

"For almost six years I have been counsel to you," I said. "There is little you could say that would surprise me."

"This, I believe, may shock you. The men have not recovered from their fear at seeing the comet the other night. They have asked me to lead them in performing a hecatomb."

A burnt offering. Chanting to the god of war, reading entrails, an orgiastic devouring of bloody meat. *Shocked* is not the word. I was appalled.

"And you refused, of course, as a good Christian . . ."

He looked at me steadily as we trotted. "I did not. Caesarius, I have barely thirteen thousand men. Jovinus is facing an outright rebellion at my back, and I see a hundred thousand Roman veterans approaching me from the front. This is no time to embroil my men in a religious squabble."

" 'Squabble'! " I sputtered. "You're speaking about burnt offerings to pagan idols!"

He gently interrupted my outrage. "This is a Roman army, not a Christian one. First we do battle. Then we determine the army's religious direction, if any."

"I would think that as a Christian general you should do the latter *in order* to do the former."

He sighed. "Caesarius, this army is a microcosm of the Empire. As the army is divided by religion, so is the world, all the more so since Constantine legalized a new religion. Half the East is Arian Christian. I myself was raised Arian. Who am I to say whether they or their Orthodox rivals, such as *you*, are living a lie, based solely on semantic subtleties that I find incomprehensible? Half of Africa is Donatist, a type of Christian political party that Constantius has not prohibited, because it is not exactly a heretical view, though it is not Orthodox either; and only the other half of Africa is Orthodox. Should the Emperor tell half his subjects on that continent that they are wrong in their beliefs, and that they should be left to the murderous tendencies of the other half? And these are *Christians,* Caesarius! With divisions like these among the ruling religion, why would you have me stir up even greater tension by antagonizing the pagans as well, denying them a peaceful sacrifice? There will be plenty of time, when I am Emperor, to tread on toes and consolidate a state religion."

"*When* you are Emperor?" I rejoined. "With all due respect, Julian, you make it sound like a foregone conclusion. Any betting man seeing your situation and comparing it to Constantius' might think you had better spend your time elsewhere."

Julian's eyes narrowed as he pulled his horse up short. "I hope you are simply playing the advocate, my friend, and not speaking your true feelings."

I paused to consider my words, realizing now that I was walking a path as fine as the blade of a dagger.

"I am saying," I continued cautiously, "that you should first attend to your immortal soul, and only then to the opinions of others. Don't make me belabor the obvious. No man is immortal, no man can know when his time comes, and if you promote paganism among your troops now, and then fall in battle—"

"And if I don't allow this sacrifice," he interrupted darkly, "I may still fall in battle—but by a shot from behind."

"You exaggerate. These men would follow you to the ends of the earth."

"You overrate their loyalty. There are currents among the troops which you know nothing about, Caesarius, holed up with your books all day long."

I gaped at him. "*I* holed up with my books!"

"I certainly don't see you training in swordplay and drinking soup with the men every morning."

"I do not need to drink soldier's broth to know that by encouraging sacrifices you will offend every Christian in the army, and that *when* you become Emperor, you will offend every Christian in the Empire."

At my frank words his face flushed and he wheeled his horse, startling my animal into a whinny and blocking me from moving forward. He stared at me sharply.

"I engender far less hatred," he said coldly, by 'promoting paganism,' as you say—by allowing the harmless worship of Helios and Mithras—than by forcing Christianity, and thereby taking one side or the other in the Orthodoxy dispute. If you are worried about me dying, believe me, this course of action is far more prudent. Haven't you noticed? Christians are much more charitable toward pagans and nonbelievers, whom they hope to convert, than toward sects and heresies *within* Christianity. Pagans are tolerated. Heretics, however, are killed."

"You're mad!" I exclaimed, not realizing at the time how presciently I spoke. "Are you willing to lose your very soul for the sake of some primitive sacrifices to keep a few malcontents in the army from deserting? Julian, listen to me—this is madness! I know about Oribasius' leaflets—this whole campaign is madness!"

"Madness?" His eyes widened in astonishment. "Then you don't believe, do you? All this is a lark! Madness lies with Constantius, in leading the Empire to the brink of ruin in Persia! *That,* my friend, is madness! Don't you see how my hand was forced? To you, is the survival of Rome only . . . secondary?" At my silence, his mouth broke into a thin, mirthless smile, though the rest of his face took on an impassive cast. "*Semel insanivimus omnis,* " he intoned.

We have all been mad once.

Without a word, I backed my horse away from his, wheeled, and began trotting away. He paused for a moment in astonishment at my abrupt departure, and then cantered

up to my side and again placed his horse directly in front
of mine, stopping my progress.

"Caesarius!" he said loudly, his voice having regained
the commanding tone he used when ordering his men. He
had clearly taken offense at my brusque maneuver. For any
other man, such rudeness to a superior officer, a Caesar no
less, would have been grounds for demotion, or even dismissal from the service. At that moment, I didn't care.

I stared back at him in calm defiance. My horse stood
still, even as Julian's danced and shied, eager to be away.
Julian looked at me silently, as if debating with himself
how best to judge or punish me for my treatment of him,
weighing friendship against duty and protocol. Finally, he
found his voice.

"The hecatomb will be lit, Caesarius. And I *will* be Emperor." He then galloped off without further word. The matter was over.

I refused to watch the proceedings that afternoon, the
very idea of which was repugnant to me, though I could
not block from my ears the sounds of the priests, particularly the repulsive Gallic haruspex Aprunculus, as they
chanted their infernal cries to the demons, and the men
cheering when the omens were read. I was even told later,
to my utter disbelief at the time, that Julian himself had
participated in the role of a priest, personally slaughtering
an ox. The odor of roasting meat wafting through the camp
that afternoon rankled me, and at the same time made my
mouth water uncontrollably, which rankled me all the more.
I prayed to our Lord that He might make it as of a putrid
stench in my nostrils, and I rode off alone into the cold and
darkness of the surrounding scrub forests for the remainder
of the day, out of ear- and nose-shot of the offending ceremony.

IV

From the height of the Soucian pass, to which Julian rode every two or three days to check on his troops' placement and the progress of the fortifications, he had a clear view of the preparations being made in the valley below by the enemy. Constantius himself, of course, was nowhere near the vicinity; according to dispatches we read from several of his couriers our scouts had captured, he was still making his lumbering return home from the East after Sapor, the mighty King of Kings, had given up his impending attack on Roman territories without a struggle. The Persian justified the abandonment of his campaign by claiming unfavorable omens. Though not a drop of blood had been shed, nor an inch of territory gained or lost, Constantius had declared a great victory and was now returning to Constantinople in majestic, triumphal procession. From the comfort of his imperial city he planned to deploy all his unbloodied eastern legions to crush his disappointing upstart from Gaul once and for all.

He was reputed to still be as far away as Antioch when the valley below suddenly came alive before our eyes. Within a matter of days after our seizure of the heights, a large contingent of the Emperor's forces, part of the permanent Thracian legions under the command of Count Marcianus, marched leisurely in ominous procession into the head of the valley and halfway up the side of the pass.

They set up camp on the bank of a stream, posted sentries almost within shouting distance of our own advance outposts, and began methodically cutting the surrounding timber for fortifications, to prevent us from surprising and overrunning their troops before further reinforcements could arise. The notion of such a thing happening was laughable, of course—even this initial contingent far outnumbered the troops we would ever be able to spare for a surprise attack. The only positive aspect to these preparations that I could see was that the enemy apparently felt us to be much more powerful, and Julian's reputation much more formidable, than was actually the case. Therefore if we were somehow able to strike soon, before the enemy's troops were reinforced, their unwarranted fears might somehow work to our favor.

Julian, however, for the first time in years, was paralyzed by indecision—no, not indecision, for what options did he have from which to decide? The result was the same, however, a lack of action, endless and inconclusive meetings with his military advisers, entire nights of restless pacing through his quarters and among the encampment. Reinforcements were out of the question—the word from our rear was that Jovinus had become hopelessly tied down in northern Italy with various local rebellions and was scrambling to prevent the uprising of the entire countryside at our back. Julian was clearly suffering, though for what it was worth, I made my own peace with him after our earlier dispute. This was no time to be engaging in personal quarrels, and at least my conscience is clear on that score.

Two weeks after the arrival of Count Marcianus' troops in the valley, we noted further activity.

Shouts of drovers and the cracking of whips that could be heard as far as our entrenchments suddenly floated to our ears, and the forward sentries clambered atop rocky outcroppings and craned their necks to see what might be emerging in the valley below us now. At first far in the distance, and then slowly becoming more visible, teams of oxen appeared, yoked in sets of twelve and twenty-four, hauling enormous wagons with wheels the height of a man, bearing equipment or goods invisible to us because covered by heavy canvas tarps. For three days the beasts strained up the steep, rock-strewn pass, with the creaking, groaning wagons bearing their heavy burden, followed improbably by an additional two legions of light infantry, *lancearii* bearing their long, bronze-tipped weapons and *mattiarii* armed with their small javelins. These were the vanguard of Constantius' eastern army under the command of a general named Arbetio, who had rushed west to reinforce the Emperor's Thracian troops. Arbetio had only now arrived, just in time to become bogged down in the narrow road by the siege engines ordered up by Marcianus weeks before.

The contraptions were enormous, cunningly designed to topple or batter through the flimsy, stacked-rock fortifications our troops were rushing to complete before the first snows arrived. Huge *ballistae* to fling heavy stones at our troops as they worked, catapults armed with enormous iron-tipped bolts, quantities of other equipment, all intended to soften up our defenses and prevent us from strengthening our own fortifications. Why, you might ask, did we not build our own engines, and rain destruction down on our attackers from the heights with gravity as our ally, to prevent them from establishing a base so near our lines? I hesitate to place blame, Brother, but this was clearly an oversight on our part—for on our side of the pass for many tens of miles there grew no trees sturdy enough to support the enormous stresses caused by the whipping of the levers or the weight of the boulders, much less to construct the carts needed on which to mount such devices; nor did we have the manpower to send off into distant woods to cut and move such timber. The oversight? That Julian had failed to foresee this lack of materials, and remedy it by capturing territory in the valley on the far side of the pass, where the trees grew larger and in greater profusion, and where he could have set up a more defensible forward position, using the heights of the pass as a fallback.

All this our troops watched with wonder, their confidence in their leader's skills beginning to wane, despite the fact that several times in the past Julian had faced overwhelming odds but had returned victorious. All our past victories, however, had been against untrained barbarian troops. Now, for the first time, we were facing a *Roman* army, and the difference was clear, in the deliberation of its preparations, the ponderous inevitability of its movements, the sheer discipline evoked in the straight lines of the streets of tents laid out in the camp below, the simplicity yet impermeability of the log palisades, the hourly trumpet blasts we could hear from our heights, calling the troops to review, to dinner, to rise, to sleep, to parade and drill. We were facing a *Roman* army, each man worth any three barbarians we had ever faced before; and their loyalty to their own Emperor was unshakable.

Our men might have been able to endure this, even through the entire winter, had it not been for the enemy's letter. How much of this sad tale has been subject to the impact of a letter? A letter addressed not to Julian but to our men, and its effectiveness rivaled that of its twin earlier in the year, the one drafted by Oribasius, which had so fired up our own troops and their families as to acclaim him a new emperor. After the enemy had set up its first *ballista*, an enormous, ugly affair with a sling braided of the hair of Persian prisoners, and its wheels and stave painted jet black to appear more ominous, they took careful aim and fired a test round at our garrison on the top of the pass, containing not a boulder or incendiary pellets, but rather a sturdy wooden chest filled with hundreds of small sheets of papyrus, which burst when it landed upon the rocky soil of our fortification, strewing the papers about and sending them flying to the four winds.

Each of our two thousand troops on rotation at the pass that week seized one, of course, which turned out to contain the transcript of a speech Constantius had given to his assembled army on the eastern front several weeks before. Nor was it lacking in oratorical skill. In it the Emperor assumed the position of a disappointed father, one who had lavished favor and praises on his trustee Julian, who had returned this love with ingratitude tantamount to patricide. What Julian's actions amounted to, according to the speech, was not only an attack on the unity of the entire Empire, but on the very life of his mentor. Constantius, therefore, had entrusted his soldiers with the task of restoring sanity to the earth by punishing the ungrateful and clearly deranged young man, and by bringing his supporters to justice. All of this was to be meted out with the assistance of the Supreme Deity, whom Constantius, in his sagacity and knowledge of the mixed religious loyalties within his army, declined to identify. In what seemed a pointed reference to Julian's own love of Homer, the Emperor closed his speech with an uncharacteristic quote from the *Iliad* rather than the Scriptures: *A multitude of rulers is not a good thing; let there be one ruler and one king.* On some of the letters the scribes were even kind enough to describe the reaction of Constantius' troops upon hearing this vibrant speech, which naturally involved enthusiastic applause and demonstrations entirely analogous to those that had greeted Julian's own harangue to his soldiers the year before.

The effect on our troops was immediately clear. While desertions in an army under stress are a fact of life, the letter sparked a furor that Julian was unable to contain. The military guard around the camp had to be doubled, then tripled, not to repel the enemy but rather to contain our own troops, until even the guard itself began deserting in droves. The prison stockade that had been hastily assembled was soon filled, until as a gesture of mercy all of those convicted of desertion were released on condition that they not attempt it again. In vain. Within a fortnight of the letter's arrival, a third of our troops had disappeared, either into the cold scrub around us, or, what is more likely, to the enemy position below. Julian's army was falling apart before our very eyes, and Julian himself was increasingly exposed to betrayal or assassination. At this rate, Marcianus and Arbetio would be able to defeat us exactly as they had the King of Kings—without losing a man.

In the absence of any response from Julian, the opposing Romans in the valley became bolder. They had found their aim with the *ballistae,* and now launched random barrages at us, without so much as a warning from their trumpets. Our troops would be hunkered down in their blankets at night, or dispiritedly picking at their cold breakfasts, when suddenly the air would be filled with a rushing and humming sound, as if infested by a flock of gigantic birds. Dozens of stones, some as big as sheep, would come crashing into the camp, sending men diving out of their fragile tents and into the holes they had dug for such an occasion, where they would cower, cursing, festering in their own waste because they were afraid to emerge, waiting for the next volley, which might come five minutes later, or not until late the next day. Though few men were killed in such attacks, the very randomness of the volleys was wearing on us. It was a clear sign, as if we were still ignorant of it, that Constantius' legions were toying with us, knowing they could trample us any day they chose by sheer superiority of numbers, but preferring to wait us out, to risk as few dead on their own side as possible, until our untenable supply lines and our troops' desertions simply caused us to collapse.

Still, however, Julian took no action. Now he hardly emerged from his tent, and only rarely did he even confer with his generals, for there was little to discuss. His contacts were limited to his closest friends, and when I was with him his expression bore a tremendous strain, the tension between the improbability of his hopes and the inevitability of his fears. In the field, there was no movement from either side, with the exception of the continual jostling and blaring of the Roman troops in the valley, who were reinforced by the thousands every day as the eastern legions arrived from the Persian campaign. More leaflets were showered on us by *ballista,* more rocks and missiles, and our men's nerves were at a breaking point. I was sure we could hold no more than a few more days, since even with

the desertions there was insufficient food, and Julian had
ordered all men on half rations.

On a cold, drizzling day in mid-November two riders
were spotted picking their way carefully up the pass. They
were dressed in full ambassadorial regalia, and followed at
a respectful distance by a small squadron of armed cavalry.
Julian was not present at the pass that day, and so the captain in charge of the garrison, a Gaul named Honorius,
waited until they had come within easy earshot and then
shouted at them to halt, identify themselves, and state their
business.

The two ambassadors shouted back that they were
Counts Theolaif and Aligildus, that they had just arrived
from Constantius' court, and that they demanded to see the
Caesar immediately. Honorius had to think quickly. He was
under strict orders not to let any of the enemy cross behind
his lines on the pretext of negotiations or consultations, for
fear they would see how truly thin our defenses were,
though by now the enemy must have had a good idea of
our predicament from their interrogation of deserters. Nevertheless, although constrained by his orders, he felt the
ambassadors might not strictly be covered by the Caesar's
prohibition.

Shouting back that he would admit the two counts, but
not their bodyguard, the ambassadors quickly conferred
with each other, and then, nodding their agreement, raised
both their hands and rode slowly up to our lines, where
their horses' bridles were seized by our men. The Roman
guard stood still for a moment, watching, until the two ambassadors disappeared from view, and then slowly trotted
back to their own position.

Honorius raced ahead of the procession to Naissus to
inform the Caesar of his guests' imminent arrival, and as
the news was broken, a look almost of relief passed across
Julian's face.

"So it has come to this," he said after a moment, dismissing Honorius to await the ambassadors' arrival. "The
ultimatum I have been expecting. How go your prayers,

Caesarius? Be current with your confessions, because surely you will either die in the attack today if I refuse their demands, or be slowly flayed when you are brought before Constantius if I surrender."

Within moments of Honorius' departure Theolaif and Aligildus arrived and were ushered into the headquarters. Their faces were as inscrutable as those of peasants, and to their credit, I thought, they at least avoided the smug, victorious expression that Constantius would certainly have worn under similar circumstances. Julian stood up to greet them, and they cordially bowed to him, even then acknowledging his superior rank.

"Greetings, friends," Julian said magnanimously, though with his voice constricted with emotion. "A pity we were unable to meet under less . . . trying circumstances."

"On the contrary," said the taller of the two, whom I later identified as the Briton Theolaif, in perfectly inflected Greek. Where, I wondered, had a Briton learned Greek? "We find the circumstances quite propitious. Indeed, we have traveled from the Emperor's court as fast as the courier roads could take us over the past two weeks to find you, and we are delighted to have encountered you and your troops in this position, before any blood is shed unnecessarily. Clearly a battle under these conditions would be devastating."

Oddly, however, despite their gloating words of overwhelming military superiority, I saw no matching boastfulness in their faces. Nor did Julian, and as his eyes darted back and forth between the two a look of puzzlement came over him.

"Let us come straight to the point, then," he said finally. "May I ask the terms of the surrender you are demanding?"

Theolaif and Aligildus glanced meaningfully at each other.

"We ask no surrender," said Theolaif in his resonant voice. "Only your favor. Hail Julian Augustus. Constantius is dead."

V

He rode in triumph through the streets of Constantinople on a white stallion that had been groomed for Constantius' own planned triumphal entry, past the magnificent churches of Saint Sophia and Saint Irene, the famous library known as the Royal Porch, at which he gazed longingly, the colonnades of the jewelry makers, the Baths of Zeuxippus located between the Imperial Palace and the Hippodrome, and two miles down the length of the High Street. For the entire distance he was preceded by a thousand priests and bishops in the finery of their office, intoning a solemn hymn and asperging the genuflecting crowds with conifer sprigs dipped in holy water. The street was thronging with celebrating citizens, and had been decorated with thousands of wreaths and silken banners. Even the paving stones were strewn with petals. Children threw flowers and called to him, and women screamed at the sight of him, reaching out their hands to touch his foot or even his horse's braided tail as he rode by. The remainder of the thirteen thousand Gauls who had not deserted him on the cold mountain pass three weeks before marched proudly in formation behind, fitted with new bronze and polished leather, feted with the customary gift of five pounds of silver per man from the new Augustus, and basking in their appointment to his personal guard.

At each of the great forums through which we passed—

Arcadius, the Amastrian, Brotherly Love—the prefects of each city district approached with heads bowed, seizing his hands to make obeisance and offering words and gifts of welcome. At the Ox Market, he leaned down and picked up a small boy, perhaps five years old, who had run up to his horse and begun waving wildly to him. Placing him on his lap, Julian and the lad rode to thunderous cheers from the onlookers. I reflected that the boy was about the same age that Julian's own son would have been, and that had he lived he would have been riding in exactly that same position, on his father's legs, heir to the throne of the entire Empire. Upon finally arriving at the massive Square of Constantine, a fanfare of horns was sounded, the city militia marched out in a precision drill, and the Emperor Julian Augustus saluted Constantinople, the first city of the Eastern Empire.

The fame of his victories in Gaul, and the audacity of his break with his mentor, had made him a celebrity to the population, relieved at being spared the prospects of a civil war that might have destroyed the unity of the Empire. The capital was a whirlwind of celebration and well-wishing, despite the funeral services being held simultaneously for the dead Emperor, over which Julian himself presided as the deceased's nearest living relative, and for whom he even managed to squeeze a tear or two in a reasonable semblance of grief. As it happened, Constantius had suffered an untimely bout of fever at Tarsus, the birthplace of the Apostle Paul, and died shortly afterwards, at the age of forty-four, having reigned for twenty-four years. Julian's first significant act was to order a generous pension to be awarded to his predecessor's bereaved widow, Faustina, who had been married to him for only several months and who, against all expectations and without the assistance, it is assumed, of any intermediaries save for the saints, had managed to conceive by the former emperor. The baby girl was born early the following year.

His second act was to order the liberation and recall of Sallustius, who had been awaiting execution in a prison in

Milan, and to promote him to chief magistrate of the court trying political crimes under Constantius' administration.

As he entered the Imperial Palace for the first time as Emperor, he peered around at the magnificence of the marble and mosaics, the richness of the wall tapestries, the sheer, overwhelming opulence of all he encountered, and immediately requested that a small pantry off the enormous kitchens be cleared, in which he would prepare his unpretentious study. The crowds of fluttering eunuchs around us were aghast at such slovenliness, but at his insistence did his bidding. That night, as I settled in with some medical texts in a chair in his room, munching a piece of flat bread I had filched from the kitchen just outside the door, he leaned back on his hard stool and surveyed the small, dim space with as much satisfaction as if it had been the most lavish throne room of King Sapor himself.

"Caesarius," he said to my dismay, "now do you doubt the significance of your fall in the mud?"

BOOK EIGHT
EMPEROR FOR LIFE

I was once a fortunate man, but I lost it, I know not how.

—MARCUS AURELIUS

I

He was a very short man with the unlikely name of Maximus, scarcely taller than a dwarf, and I daresay there was much that was dwarflike about him, for his large head, overdeveloped torso, and short, spindly legs caused him to walk with a sort of swaying waddle that never failed to elicit snickers from the small-minded palace eunuchs as he passed. His clothes were old and patched, which is no sin, for I have no doubt that Our Lord Himself wore nothing better, though I hesitate to think that He might have washed and repaired His garments as seldom as did Maximus; for the latter's were perpetually stained with the unidentifiable contents of past meals and activities, some of them, I feared, *long* past. From what I could see, he never wore but the one tattered, brownish tunic and overlong mantle that dragged in the dust behind him when he walked, picking up the filth of Constantinople's streets and trailing it into any room he entered.

Though of a certain age, it was difficult to estimate whether Maximus was fifty, sixty, or even older. His dark skin was of the kind, like well-oiled leather, that resists wrinkling and prevents one from determining the owner's true age by mere appearance. His otherwise well-performing epidermis, however, was marred by a rather large patch of scaly, lichenlike growth below his left ear, of about two fingers' breadth and length, that threatened periodically to crack and even bleed and which thirsted for some healing salve, of which I had plenty and would have gladly applied had he even given the least indication of wanting any—but every time I even made an attempt to approach him regarding this or any other matter, his hard, hostile stare stopped me cold.

The most extraordinary thing about Maximus, however, was his demeanor, for in his way of talking, walking, and even entering a room, he acted as if there were only two people in the entire world—himself and Julian. The first time I saw this little man was the very day we had arrived in Constantinople, while the newly crowned Emperor was conferring with the palace steward about some matter or another in a corridor near the main entrance. In the confusion of the day, Maximus had somehow wormed his way through the crowd outside, talked his way past the overwhelmed palace guards, and strode imperiously straight through the gaggle of eunuchs who were desperately seeking a quick audience to ensure the preservation of their positions. Maximus walked quickly, his tiny legs churning and his head and shoulders bobbing like a duck's, straight to where the Emperor stood examining a plan of the palace and its dependencies.

It took a moment for Julian to look down and focus his gaze on the extraordinary little man who stood before him, but when he did, his eyes lit up, his mouth broadened into a beaming smile and he swept Maximus up in an enthusiastic embrace that astonished the queasy courtiers as much as it did me.

"Maximus, old friend!" he exulted, and I don't believe I had ever seen such joy on his face as I saw at that moment. He immediately excused himself from the steward and led the dwarf down the corridor to a private conference room on the side, the little man bearing a smug, haughty expression as he swept past the advisers and impatiently waiting retainers, into private conference with the Emperor.

Nor was it the only time I saw this occur during those first few weeks—for although the Emperor's effusiveness dwindled with the familiarity of having the dwarf constantly in his presence, the look of joy on his face upon seeing his arrival never did diminish. The same cannot be said, however, for the rest of the palace dwellers. The eunuchs and courtiers hated the little man, and their feelings were reciprocated, for when he was not ignoring them completely he muttered oaths at them under his breath and roughly shouldered them aside if they attempted to block his access, even if they were merely seeking to announce his presence. Even I, to my shame, grew to despise him, for the man's rudeness knew no bounds; he appeared to have no human feelings in him whatsoever for anyone but Julian. I once took Oribasius aside, after his arrival from Gaul, to ask him about the queer little fellow, about whom no one in the palace seemed to know anything, and even the voluble Asclepian took some convincing before he would speak freely.

"I avoid him like the plague," Oribasius told me. "The fellow gives me indigestion."

"But Julian must see something in him," I argued. "What is their connection?"

"He is an old teacher of his. A pagan, but not of the easygoing sort like myself. The man takes his worship of the ancient gods very seriously, almost, I would venture to say, murderously. He has performed astonishing feats of magic, raising spirits from the dead, causing inanimate objects to move, producing horrifying noises and smells from the empty air. Rumor has it he is skilled in certain black arts, poisoning and such, though I ascribe such tales to the malicious whispering of the eunuchs, who no doubt whisper about me as well. Still, several men who have crossed him in the past have died under mysterious circumstances."

"Mysterious circumstances?" I repeated skeptically. "Oribasius, you're a skilled physician, and so am I. There are no 'mysterious circumstances.' "

"That is true," he admitted. "Still, people have died for surprising reasons, people whose death he certainly did not regret. I recall years ago how one of his rivals at the institute at Ephesus died of cholera—"

"That is hardly mysterious," I interjected. "Thousands die of cholera all the time during the epidemics."

"There was no epidemic at the time." Oribasius sighed. "His was the one and only case that year, extremely unusual, you must admit. A bishop who had scolded him once suffered a stroke and was paralyzed—yet he was only thirty-five years old at the time. He suffered gravely for many days before he finally died of pure starvation, unable to eat. I could cite several others, but you get the idea."

"Wives' tales," I scoffed. "Call him what you will: hierophant, magician, thaumaturge, evoker of the gods—his techniques are nothing but sleight of hand. It's appalling that Julian has fallen for such utter foolery."

"Don't underestimate him, Caesarius," Oribasius said warily. "You may think Maximus a charlatan, but that word is not so easily defined. He calls himself a 'theurgist,' a worker of the divine. When he performs his 'miracles,' he uses every law known to science and to the gods—chemical, physical, optical—to achieve the effects he wishes to achieve. Since the gods made mirrors, or at least made men who made mirrors, he and his ilk see no contradiction in using them as props to obtain the desired theurgic effect. Blast it, mirrors are easy—he uses things that can't be easily explained, and convinces his followers that it is the gods' hand at work. Why are sparks created when certain rags of linen and wool are brushed against each other? Why does lodestone from Magnesia make iron jump through the air in its attraction to it? How do humble materials like saltpeter and charcoal, when combined, produce thunder and lightning? No one can explain these things, they believe them to be magic, and when Maximus uses them in his techniques they see him as a magician. You may think him a fraud, but since he employs materials provided by nature, indeed by the very gods, his tricks and manipulations are no fraud to his eyes. And you will make an enemy of him if you so dismissingly call him one. When Maximus is around I prefer to keep my mouth shut."

Still, the more I thought about Maximus' history and his crude behavior, and about how the entire palace staff was being upset by his presence, the more it disturbed me. I finally resolved to raise the issue at the first opportunity. Several nights after my conversation with Oribasius, I was studying with Julian in his tiny pantry office when he suddenly looked up from his work, rubbed his eyes, and stood as if to stretch. He looked around absentmindedly as if searching for something to distract him from his meditations for a moment and I seized the occasion.

"Julian," I said. "I say this to you as a friend, with only your interests at heart, and I pray you take no offense."

Julian smiled. "When have you ever minced words with me? Sometimes you're like the voice of my conscience, Caesarius, but I would have it no other way. Please—say your piece."

I hesitated. "Your comrade Maximus is . . . an unusual sort. He has rather affronted some of the palace staff and set the eunuchs unreasonably against him. Is he so important that he requires unrestricted access to the palace and to you?"

He looked at me cautiously for a long moment, as if seeking to guess my intent; then he slowly stood up, crossed the small room, and closed the door. A feeling of dread came over me, as one feels when about to be informed of a friend's death, and indeed Julian, as I knew him, died that day, in a way. He resumed his seat and his intense gaze at me, and then sighed.

"Caesarius," he said, "not everything an emperor does is public knowledge. My entire boyhood, for example, was a very private one, despite the fact that I was closely related to the Emperor and was a nephew of Constantine himself. I spent many years in seclusion, shuttling between banishment and acceptance, never for reasons of my own doing, but because of passing political winds. My tutor Mardonius and I moved several times, between Constantinople, Nicomedia, my remote estate at Macellum, back to Constantinople—"

"Julian," I interrupted, "your moves and your devotion to study are well known to all. You needn't explain them."

"Just so," he said. "But the following events you did not know. In my twentieth year Constantius sent me to the academy at Nicomedia, to distance me from the distractions of Constantinople. I quickly learned all I was able from the instructors there, and pleaded to the Emperor to allow me to travel further, to expand my horizons. In the end he relented, provided that I continued to travel with Mardonius, who was ordered to send in regular reports.

"During my travels I resolved to visit Pergamum, for I had heard of its famous center for Asclepian studies and I had in mind that I might wish to investigate the healing arts. You needn't furrow your brows at me that way, Caesarius, I know your feelings about the Asclepians, and in any case I ended by doing nothing to pursue that course of study. There will be plenty for you in a moment to make your brows furrow, and worse.

"In Pergamum I fell in with Aedesius the mystic. Aedesius was ancient, and at the time failing in bodily strength, but he had developed about him a circle of extremely vigorous disciples, including Eusebius and our friend Maximus. Caesarius, the first time I attended one of Aedesius' gatherings, I confess I couldn't leave; like those in the legend who are bitten by the 'thirsty-serpent,' I longed to gulp down huge mouthfuls of the wisdom the old man had to offer. Aedesius wouldn't allow it, however. He claimed that since he was so feeble, he would be unable to do justice to my thirst for knowledge, and he recommended instead that I look to his disciples to satisfy my questions. Perhaps he also feared the consequences if Constantius were to hear of my growing curiosity for mysticism. Yet the old man promised me: 'Once you have been admitted to their mysteries, you will rise above your base physicality, far beyond human nature, to become one with the spirits.'

How could I resist—could *you*, if you had been in my place, Caesarius?

"Thus at the old man's request, I took up my studies under Eusebius, as Maximus had gone away to Ephesus. I worked hard, though I was still dissatisfied with the fact that I seemed to have fallen in with Eusebius merely as a matter of circumstance, rather than because he was the most appropriate teacher. In fact, I learned that there were considerable differences between the disciples. Maximus, for example, was a student of the occult sciences and theurgy, while Eusebius claimed that such practices were the work of charlatans, prestidigitators, and the insane, who had been led astray into the exercise of certain dark powers. They were both students of old Aedesius, but they had rather poor opinions of each other's work. I asked Eusebius about the discrepancies between their beliefs.

" 'Maximus is Aedesius' oldest and most brilliant disciple,' he said. 'Because of his standing with the old man, and his own overwhelming eloquence, he feels he is beyond all rational proofs in these matters. Let me offer you an illustration.

" 'A short while ago,' Eusebius continued, 'Maximus invited several of us to visit him at the temple of Hecate, goddess of the moon and witchcraft, patroness of doorways and crossroads, the deity who delights in sacrifices of dogs. The temple was abandoned, practically a shambles, with all the furnishings long stripped by thieves but for the massive statue of Hecate herself. There Maximus boasted that he was one of the goddess's favored few, and how far he surpassed ordinary men in her eyes. As he talked, he burned a bit of incense, and even sang a hymn of praise in his own honor. And then, Julian, it happened, we all saw it. The enormous statue began to smile, even to beam at him, and finally to actually laugh out loud in joy. We were alarmed, but Maximus calmed us by saying he was in complete control of the situation, and as proof he would ask for more light, so we would not be trembling in near darkness. In a loud voice, he called to Hecate to provide greater light, and lo, the torches the goddess was holding in her hands burst into flame, casting a bright, dancing light on all around us. We were struck dumb, both by Maximus' power and by his mastery of such black arts, and we left the temple in great fear. I tell you this privately, Julian, out of earshot of my old master: you do not want to become close to Maximus.' "

"It was with good reason that Eusebius was skeptical of the man's work," I interrupted. "This Maximus is clearly a charlatan like those you have described. That is the nature of the theurgists, Julian. They pretend to be able to control the order of nature, to define the future, to command the loyalty of the lower demons, to converse with the gods, to disengage the soul from its physical bounds—but they are false, they abuse your credulity. Those old tricks of talking statues have been used for centuries to fool the simpleminded out of donations they could ill afford to make. They are nothing that can't be replicated with a length of copper tubing and a voice funnel."

Julian bristled at my skepticism. "Maximus," he declared, "has led me to the True Faith."

I was dumbfounded. "But, Julian," I said, "how can that be? Maximus is not a Christian, and you were already well versed in Christianity long before you made his acquaintance."

"I said he led me to the True Faith," he repeated, slowly and emphatically, his steely eyes fixed on me. "I said nothing of Christianity."

Julian's face was dead serious, and he had lapsed into silence, waiting for my reaction. I realized the abyss opening before me, and turned my face to the side. I was horrified, and grew only more so as the evening wore on and he impassively recounted to me his initiation into Maximus' mysteries.

"I set out for Ephesus and stayed for a year," Julian continued, "undertaking a regular course of study in theurgy and divination. Of course I still worshiped at the Christian churches, and counted many devout Christians among my closest friends. I could hardly have done otherwise, with Constantius' spies peering at me from every direction. Still, I found time and the occasion to meet secretly with Maximus and his followers, and in the end was officially initiated into the theurgic mysteries. You look pale, Caesarius"—he smiled, a combination of wickedness and indulgence I once saw on the face of an executioner when answering some pitiful procedural question from his victim before the deadly act—"have you heard enough to satisfy your curiosity, or shall I tell you more?"

I stared at him, open-mouthed, and nodded wordlessly, which he took as my consent to hear the remainder of his story.

"I am not permitted to recount to you the sacred mysteries themselves. The secrets of Mithras have been guarded for centuries, and I am bound by my vows not to disclose them. Initiation is a long and terrible process, subject to many trials and tests, though because of the circumstances, my own was a hurried, compressed affair. Maximus inducted me in a private ceremony, separate from all his other disciples, for which I was greatly honored and flattered. On a night of full moon, he descended with me into an underground sanctuary, a hole wherein spirits dwelt, of such kind as require complete darkness and the subterranean damp to thrive. We walked slowly through the stone tunnel, a cold, dripping place that smelled of mildew and death, lit only by an occasional sputtering torch, and there, Caesarius, I encountered terrors such as I never imagined in my life—terrors which only increased in their intensity as my fears grew. Earsplitting screams from empty corners, revolting exhalations from cracks in the floor, fiery apparitions, such prodigies as you can never have imagined!"

I sat rooted to my chair, Brother, speechless at what Julian was relating.

"Several times I held back, and my courage had to be revived by Maximus, but still we pressed onward, until the demons began to gather strength, floating objects in midair, even throwing them at me. I challenged them, and they backed away hissing like serpents, and my courage rose. I couldn't drive them off entirely, for they were returning faster and more furiously as I advanced deeper into the cave—but I had overcome their power."

"But of course you did!" I cried, standing up triumphantly. "How could you not, with Christ on your side?"

"Sit down!" he snapped at me, and I stopped short, startled by his vehemence. He glared at me a moment, and then continued.

"We finally reached the end, a tiny room cut directly into the solid rock, like a tomb—and indeed, in the far wall a narrow ledge had been cut, on which a long, white object lay. Maximus ordered a torch to flare, and it did so immediately of its own accord, and I could see by the light that the object was a young woman, wrapped in funeral vestments and lying as if dead. Perhaps, I thought, this was the source of the putrid odor that had been growing stronger as I advanced up the tunnel.

"Maximus pointed at her and issued a command in a strange and ancient language, and as I watched, the woman slowly rose from her ledge to a standing position and passed silently to the middle of the room, light and airy as if she were actually floating on a cushion of air. She was the most beautiful creature I had ever seen, her hair plaited in the ancient style and her face lightly veiled. Her eyes were open and she was gazing at me. In her hands was a large bundle, the cornucopia, and this she extended straight out from her body and advanced slowly to me, walking on the ground but making no sound, bodiless as air, like a fleeting dream. Just before she reached me, the torch sputtered out and she faded from my sight, much to my agony, for by this time I was no longer frightened, but enchanted, and longed to touch and caress her.

"I needn't tell you, Caesarius, that this was the same vision I had seen on those nights in Gaul, though this was the very first time it had appeared to me. The woman, Rome's guardian spirit, has appeared to me many times since, both visibly and . . . invisibly. Though I never touch her, I speak to her often, and she is a source of great comfort to me."

I was thunderstruck when I left his rooms that evening, struggling to focus on what he had told me, and the implications of it all. For thirty-five years the Empire had been a Christian one, or at least led by Christian emperors. During that time Christianity had experienced huge growth in its followers and in the numbers of churches dedicated to the worship of Christ, often through a reconsecration of temples to the pagan gods, the former sites of horrifying orgiastic festivals and sacrifices. Christ was winning the greatest battle for souls in history! Was Julian about to forfeit the victory before it could be counted? I was aghast at the lightness and ease with which he had cast aside his Christian convictions, even more appalled at the fact that this had happened so many years before and yet he had kept the secret for so long, from so many—from all, that is, until he had finally been proclaimed Emperor of all the lands that Rome ruled, and was now safe in the profession of any belief he chose.

II

For weeks I kept to myself except when absolutely needed, shocked at the implications of his conversion, and had not yet determined whether I could continue to serve an emperor who was no longer Christian. At least I had a choice in that regard; one does not, however, have the choice of *living* under a non-Christian emperor, when that emperor's dominions cover the entire known world. Word had spread quickly throughout the city of Julian's welcome of Maximus and his open apostasy, and the population was in an uproar, though a divided one. Bishops denounced him from the pulpit and Christian women openly wept as he passed in the streets, praying out loud for his salvation; but the city's pagans, who were still the vast majority, celebrated jubilantly and defiantly, and he was showered with invitations to attend the various celebrations of the ancient deities, and participate in the sacrifices, which he made every effort to do. He filled the gardens and rooms of the palace with statues and altars to the gods, to the point that they even resembled temples. Every morning he saluted the arrival of his titular deity, Helios the Sun, with the sacrifice of a white ox, and in the evening, at the moment the sun disappeared below the horizon, the blood of more victims was spilled. On days of public festivals the bloodletting was more extreme, involving sometimes dozens of bawling animals, and lasting throughout the entire morning until he had to be rushed from the altar by the eunuchs responsible for protocol, who washed him and changed his clothes in time for the more public ceremonies, when he received and rewarded his troops.

At these, as is traditional, his throne was encircled by the military ensigns of Rome and the republic. And while Christ's initials were surreptitiously removed from the *labarum*, the imperial standard which from Constantine's time had borne representations of those letters along with a crown and a cross, the symbols of pagan superstition were so cleverly embedded in the design and adornments of office that even a faithful Christian ran the risk of idolatry merely by respectfully saluting his sovereign. The soldiers passed before him in review, and each man, before receiving a generous donative from the hand of Julian himself, was required to cast a few grains of incense into the flame burning upon the altar. A few good Christians might refuse, or at the least confess and repent afterwards, but far greater numbers, attracted by the gold and awed by the emperor, entered into the diabolic contract. Since I myself refused even to view such atrocities, I found myself sadly contemplating a smaller role in Julian's inner circle—to his chagrin and wonder, as he could not imagine why I might be concerned with the religious beliefs of another, and to the evident pleasure of Maximus, who regarded me as a rustic interloper with a mere journeyman's education and culture. By now, the notion had formed in my mind of quitting Constantinople and finding my own path, yet I hesitated, thinking perhaps that Julian was merely passing through a phase, that he would return soon to his old self, and that I should not be too hasty in removing myself from his court.

Shortly after the new year, in an effort to combat the winter doldrums into which the city had fallen after the frenzy of the succession and the Christmas season, Julian determined to stage a series of games and combats in the circus. This prospect he at first looked upon with resignation, as a pastime unfitting for the mind of a philosopher. The entire time we were in Gaul he had never once attended the games, for in provincial cities such as Sens and Paris, in any case, only second-rate spectacles and gladiators would have performed. Even now, in the grandest city of the world, he was unsure whether they were worth his while. I reminded him of the danger of this attitude, for even the great Julius Caesar had once so offended the Roman people as to threaten a riot, when he demonstrated indifference by reading dispatches during the course of a race. Julian gradually warmed to the idea, however, and resolved to stage a three-day series of games, culminating in a gladiator battle that would be worthy of his accession to Constantius' throne.

And in this he begged my attendance. "It's time for a diversion, Caesarius, if only for a day or two," he said. "You're disappointed in me, I know. A change of view is what we need."

We were late arriving that day because of pressing business that had kept him at the palace—vastly late, to the irritation of the crowd, which typically looked forward as much to viewing the Emperor and his entourage in the box as the actual combat down below. The preliminary rounds had already been fought, and the mob had begun clamoring for the event for which it had paid, the battle between champions. It was only at this time that Julian arrived, followed by myself and a modest train of courtiers. The crowd erupted in cheers as he took his seat and nodded to the president of the circus to announce the climactic event.

There was at this time a Gallic champion with the unpronounceable nickname of Vercingetorix, in commemoration of the powerful Arverni chieftain who had so vexed Julius Caesar centuries before. He was said to have never been defeated in gladiatorial combat—which goes without saying, because all battles at this level were to the death. The man was huge—a good head taller than average, and solid muscle from head to toe, with long, auburn hair flowing loose to his waist and enormous mustaches streaming down the sides of his chin, a source of fascination to the crowd. As Vercingetorix was announced he sauntered into the arena to deafening cheers, as nonchalant as if returning from the market, his hands swinging freely at his sides, nodding casually up to acquaintances he recognized in the stands. He wore only a crimson loincloth and a dark, polished-leather helmet that obscured the entire top of his face, with openings for his eyes, serving the dual purpose of keeping his impressive hair out of his vision, and lending him a terrifying appearance, like that of an executioner. He wore sturdy sandals and a tiny string around his neck, which appeared all the more thin and fragile by contrast with the brawniness and rippling sinews of his shoulders and chest. A tiny object hung from the thread, which he kissed as if it were a talisman as he stopped short in front of the Emperor's box, his enormous sword hung casually at his right side from his broad belt. His shield, a custom-made affair of at least four thicknesses of ox hide over-layered with a sheet of bronze and studded with costly jewels and gold inlay, hung from its carrying strap across his shoulder, like a trophy on display. Although Vercingetorix was young, perhaps no more than twenty-five, one could tell at a glance that he was a showman as well as a supreme fighter, and he cultivated the appearance of a barbarian chieftain, much to the crowd's delight. He stood motionless before us, staring at the Emperor through his mask, his massive chest rising and falling slowly, and I marveled that a man could stand naked before a hundred thousand people, about to fight in combat to the death, and breathe so deeply and calmly.

"Where were men like that when we were fighting Chonodomarius, Caesarius?" Julian asked in a whisper, gazing in amazement at the warrior's sheer bulk. The sun glinted off the tiny talisman hanging from his neck, almost buried in the mat of reddish hair covering his chest, and I saw that it was a cross.

The president of the circus then announced Vercingetorix' opponent, a Romanized Syrian giant, taller even than the Gaul, though less Herculean in build, with long, rangy arms and a quick, nervous spring to his step as he trotted across the arena to take his place at his rival's side, facing us. This man was darker, with deep olive skin and a head almost shorn but for a layer of short, bristly hairs. He was older than the Gaul by some ten or fifteen years, and his face was scarred like one who has survived many such battles, with his nose lying lopsidedly to one side. Perhaps the most salient feature about his physique was the inordinate size of his right biceps and forearm, his sword arm; the forearm alone bulged to almost twice the size of its comrade on the left, with a swell almost like that of a thigh muscle, from years of exercise and training in swordsmanship.

He, too, was naked but for a loincloth and a large sword and shield, though his weapons were completely unadorned, lacking even in polish, as of one who refrained from all external frills or distractions that might burden him in the task at hand. He looked like a military man, and indeed, a courtier nearby whispered to me that he was a former legionary, plucked from his army duties in the East by imperial scouts who had been impressed by his size and fighting ability. His reputation was as a *scutarius,* a gladiator favoring the large shield and sword. Leo, for that was the name he had chosen, was famed throughout the Empire for his long reach and his lightning speed; and the cheers of the crowd when his name was announced were soon drowned by the cries of the bookies and the bettors as they adjusted their odds and placed their final wagers on the match's outcome.

Side by side they stood, Vercingetorix and Leo, staring hard at Julian, until with a nod from the president, an orchestra blasted a cacophonous fanfare and the crowd fell silent. At another nod, the two warriors simultaneously raised their right arms in salute, and intoned the customary greeting in clear, confident voices: *Ave, Imperator, morituri te salutant!* "Hail, Emperor, those who are about to die salute you!" They then retreated several paces in opposite directions to mount their shields, still keeping their eyes expectantly on the imperial box. At the final nod, this time from Julian himself, they drew their swords, turned away, and looked at each other for the first time.

A fever seemed to grip the stadium as the combatants warily circled each other, every man in the crowd standing and straining to see over the heads of those in front of him, bellowing at the top of his lungs the name of his favorite, or the action to be taken: "Strike, Gaul!" "Slaughter him, Leo!" "I've bet my house on you!" "I've wagered my daughter on your head!" "Kill him!" "Kill the bastard!"

The fighters clashed fiercely but cautiously, ducking and bobbing their heads right and left, performing half lunges with their swords, each testing the reflexes of the other, their eyes fixed only on each other's eyes, unblinking, focused with a concentration that blotted out all other sights around them.

Suddenly the Syrian launched himself forward, his shield held high in a tremendous lunge, landing with a crash on the Gaul's shield. The crowd's roar swelled as the two scuffled for an instant, their swords flailing and hammering, the Gaul suffering a glancing blow on his left shoulder that seemed to enrage him. Summoning all the force in his legs, he sprang forward against Leo, who was still bearing down upon him with his shield. The Syrian, overpowered by Vercingetorix' superior weight and strength, let the Gaul's momentum carry him forward, while he himself fell and rolled deftly on his back away from his opponent's rush. Vercingetorix, however, was too skilled to be fooled by such an old trick. He skidded to a stop and whirled just as Leo was again leaping to his feet. Disappointed that he had missed a chance to impale his enemy while he was down, Vercingetorix relaxed slightly to prepare for his next move, dropped his shield a few inches, and stole a glance at his bleeding shoulder.

That was the mistake the wily Syrian had been waiting for. During his entire roll and feint, Leo's eyes had never left those of Vercingetorix. Now, in that split second when he saw the Gaul glance away, when he detected the tiniest hint of distraction in his enemy's attention, he leaped.

The Gaul's glance shot back toward Leo, but it was too late. There was no time to brace himself for the assault, to set his stance and raise his shield to deflect the Syrian's outstretched sword. Startled, Vercingetorix momentarily lost his form, and had time only to take a clumsy step to one side to avoid his adversary's rush. This, however, was what Leo had anticipated. Rushing past him like a Spanish bull-leaper, his shoulder barely brushing the Gaul's, Leo reached behind with his sword arm as he passed, and with a single, clean stroke downward, he cleaved through the back of the Gaul's knee, severing the tendons that support the leg as easily as if they were taut tent strings. His lunge carried him forward, and he continued in an easy trot for several steps, waving his fist in a brief salute to the crowd, knowing from the frenzied roar that his plan had borne fruit.

I glanced over at Julian: he was transfixed, an expression of awe and fervor in his face as he surveyed the bloody sand of the arena. A strange light had come to his eye, an avid gleam almost of eagerness, a thirsting for violence seen only among men in the heat of battle, in the very act of killing. The Syrian champion slowly circled back to the center where the Gaul had sunk down onto his injured right knee, his left leg out in front of him bent at a right angle, a widening pool of black forming in the sand beneath him. Despite his desperate situation now, unable to move from his position, Vercingetorix seemed unperturbed: his massive shoulders were still erect, his huge chest barely moving. I saw beneath the leather mask that his mouth remained closed as he breathed easily through his nostrils. He gave his great mane of hair a shake to remove it from his shoulders and allow it to flow more neatly down his back—even then the man retained his vanity!—and slowly and deliberately he assumed the combat position with his shield and sword and awaited the Syrian's next move.

It was not long in coming. The Syrian circled Vercingetorix twice as he knelt in the sand, disdaining the easiest and most obvious maneuver of simply lunging at him from behind, whence the Gaul, unable to rotate quickly on his injured knee, could not defend himself. Instead he faced Vercingetorix full in front, his shield dropped at a lopsided angle, knowing that the Gaul would be unable to attack; and slowly, deliberately, he raised his own sword to aim directly at his opponent's chest, his long arm and weapon forming a single, straight, unified line of death. "Almighty Zeus, strengthen my arm!" he shouted, and the crowd roared. His knees flexed as he prepared to make the special spring and pounce that had given him his nickname, "the Lion."

That was the last time the Lion's mighty right arm would raise a sword.

Unbelievably, just as the Syrian was about to lunge, Vercingetorix, using only his single good leg cocked before him, sprang forward with the lightness and agility of a cat, lifting the weight of his entire body on the strength of his huge left thigh, his hamstrung right leg trailing behind him like the flailing limb of a rag doll. Caught utterly by surprise, and in a stance set to leap forward rather than to step back out of harm's way, the Syrian stood dumbly for a split second with his shield dropped as the Gaul brought his heavy blade down in a stroke that severed Leo's right arm at the wrist joint as neatly as a piece of cheese. Vercingetorix planted himself again on his knee where he landed, a grin now visible on his face beneath the mask and mustaches, as Leo straightened and backed away from the Gaul's range, staring dumbly at the flat stump of his forearm, the tips of the ulna and radius bones showing brightly amongst the red tissue surrounding them, seemingly too surprised even to bleed.

The crowd went wild. "Well washed! Well washed!" they cried, in their morbid twisting of the common bathhouse salutation, as the blood began cascading out of his severed limb onto his thighs. Those who had gone morose and silent with the hamstringing of the Gaul now erupted in an orgy of screaming and raving, of backslapping and gloating. The Syrian shuffled around the arena aimlessly,

staring disconsolately at his severed arm, which was now
spewing like a hose, his concentration gone as surely as
was his life. A senator in a box adjacent to us slid down
in his seat, holding his head in despair. "No!" he moaned.
"No, no, *no!*" The senator's wager must have been sizable.
Vercingetorix, in a mocking gesture, dragged himself on
his left leg to where his opponent's severed hand lay in the
sand, still gripping the sword. Seizing the white, bloodless
fist in his own thick paw, he held it and the blade up in the
air for all to see and appreciate, and then tossed them across
the arena to the Syrian's feet, as if daring him to reattach
the flesh and continue the combat.

The Syrian, visibly startled, looked down at the filthy,
blood-spattered and sand-encrusted weapon lying at his
feet, and a light seemed to come into his eyes as his face
regained a semblance of its earlier calm. Kneeling down,
he quickly slipped the shield off his left forearm, and
jammed the stump of his right arm into the strap instead.
This was a struggle, for the strap had been set to fit comfortably around the much smaller muscle on his left limb,
but after a few seconds of grimacing and awkwardness he
succeeded in stretching the thick leather of the strap sufficiently as to stuff his right forearm in up to the elbow—
and here I saw his genius. Now he would be able to bear
the shield with his right arm, though only clumsily because
he lacked a hand with which to hold the grip and pivot the
shield around the fulcrum of the arm strap. But more important, the extreme tightness of the leather strap around
his forearm served as a most perfect tourniquet. Indeed, as
he raised the shield triumphantly to the crowd, I could see
that the bleeding had slowed to a mere trickle. Leo bent
slowly to pick up the sword lying nearby with his left hand,
kicked his severed right fist carelessly out of the way, and
then calmly, menacingly, strode to where Vercingetorix still
knelt, dumbfounded.

A hush fell over the crowd, a silence all the more amazing and disquieting for the deafening roar of only seconds
before. There would be no more feints and jabs, no more

combinations and exchanges. The final blow would be struck in a moment, and all knew that one man, one of these of such tremendous strength and courage, would be dead.

This time, Leo had no patience for elegance in killing. He had lost a limb to that notion, and it would not happen again. Trotting directly to the front of the stricken Gaul, whose chest was now heaving in growing panic, he stopped and raised his sword deliberately, again pointing it at the Gaul's chest but prepared, this time, for the big man's leap. In this he was not disappointed, for he knew it was the Gaul's only defense. Springing forward on his left leg, Vercingetorix lunged desperately and clumsily at his opponent, who this time raised his shield deftly to ward off the blow and stepped neatly to one side as Vercingetorix landed off balance in front of him on his bad leg. Falling forward, the Gaul threw his shield down to catch himself, and at that moment the Syrian placed one hobnailed sandal in the small of his back, forcing the Gaul forward onto his belly, and balanced the tip of his sword firmly, but not fatally, on the back of the Gaul's neck, immobilizing him with pain. In this stance, the Syrian cautiously raised his eyes up from the trembling giant lying at his feet, and looked up to the Emperor's box.

In a case such as this, when one gladiator holds the life of another in his hands, it is the Emperor who decides the fallen gladiator's fate, which he pronounces in the form of a signal: if the fallen gladiator has fought bravely and valiantly, the Emperor may order his life to be spared by raising his thumb. Otherwise, the thumbs-down is given, and the fallen gladiator is dispatched.

Julian rose slowly from his seat, his face pale both from the shock of seeing such an extraordinary scene played out before him, and from the decision he was about to make. White handkerchiefs were raised around the stadium, and scattered shouts began to be heard :"Spare him!" "Kill the bastard Gaul!" "Thumbs-up, Emperor!" "Thumbs-down!"

The screaming multiplied, and within seconds the stadium had erupted into pandemonium, a roar of competing cries and oaths, indistinguishable one from the other. The Syrian stood motionless in the sand, staring patiently up at the Emperor, while the defeated Gaul lay prone and help-less, his right foot twitching uncontrollably from the excru-ciating pain of the severed tendons.

Julian held his arm straight out before him, his fingers curled in a fist, the thumb pointing sideways, neither up nor down, as he stared down at the warriors, silently deliber-ating. "What could he possibly be thinking?" I wondered. "Is there any doubt that they both fought bravely and are both champions?"

Still he stood motionless, and the crowd became almost frenzied in its impatience for judgment. Objects began fly-ing through the air—baskets and bottles. There was a dan-ger of riot, whichever way Julian decided.

"Please, Julian," I implored, though my voice could not have been heard over the crowd. I stood up. "Please, my lord," I shouted, "the Gaul, too, is a champion."

But it was as if he did not hear or see me, for he stared straight ahead with his mad gleam, his eyes on those of the victorious Leo, his lips mumbling words which only he himself knew, drowned as they were in the roar of the crowd. Slowly, deliberately, he turned his fist thumb down. With a trace of a smile, Leo plunged the sword deep into the sand beneath Vercingetorix and with a quick, sawing motion of the blade, sliced through his neck. As the head rolled to the side, ragged stump-end facing up, the right foot stopped twitching and the crowd settled into a sus-tained, less frantic cheer.

I sank back into my seat, horrified, as Leo, suddenly released from his effort, seemed to totter on his own knees. Letting go the sword, which remained standing upright and swaying slowly back and forth in the sand, the Syrian per-formed a shaky victory lap around the arena, weakly wav-ing the heavy shield which he dared not remove for fear of bleeding to death. An attendant dressed as Charon, the con-veyor of the dead, trotted out to Vercingetorix, removed the sword, and laboriously rolled the huge body over onto its back. He ostentatiously performed a short, stylized little dance of glee over his new customer, and then waved to his assistants to drag the body out of the arena by the feet, leaving a long, bloody trail as a wake. Additional attendants then ran into the ring and began hastily raking over the stained sand in preparation for the next bout.

The Christian was dead; Rome had prevailed over the barbarian, old over young, East over West. The vast trunk lies headless, without a name, in a pauper's grave on a foreign shore. I found a pretext to return to the palace before the next round of fighting began, and it was only much later that Julian himself followed suit.

III

Julian had made every effort to eradicate some of the most egregious examples of waste and excess in the court he had inherited from Constantius. The palace and its dependencies at Constantinople contained literally thousands of cooks, barbers, and cupbearers, and I do not mean thousands in total, Brother, but rather thousands of *each*. There were as many different wardrobe slaves as there were types of clothing: slaves responsible for the Emperor's palace garments and others for his city clothes, slaves charged with his military field uniforms and others his full-dress-parade uniforms, slaves responsible solely for his lavish theater garments. There were slaves employed only in polishing eating vessels, while others touched only drinking vessels, and amongst these there were subspecialists who focused on gold polishing, silver polishing, and crystal polishing. The slaves who cared for the jewels dared not tread on the authority of the slaves who monitored the pearls, and the bath slaves ceded ground to the masseur slaves, who in turn deferred to the hairdressers and barbers. At meals the usher slaves supervised the dining room attendants, who in turn lorded it over the waiters who carried in the dishes, and the different waiters who carried them back out. The cupbearers were organized into a complex hierarchy depending upon whether they held the flagon or presented the cup, while the most revered, though often most short-lived, slaves of all were the tasters, whose duty was to ensure the harmlessness of the Emperor's food and drink, and who were hoped to fulfill this task with more meticulousness than those employed by Claudius and Britannicus in generations past.

The numbers of eunuchs with no clear function whatsoever cannot possibly be underestimated, for they swarmed through the salons and corridors like flies in a latrine, though truth be told, there were precious few of the latter because of the vast squadrons of eunuchs employed in the palace toilets to keep them out. The excesses had spread even to the palace guard he inherited, who, though ostensibly soldiers, minced like dandies, to the vast amusement of Julian's rough-hewn Gauls. Rather than the traditional coarse soldier chants, the troops practiced effeminate music-hall songs; instead of sleeping on stone ledges, they demanded feather mattresses. Julian complained that while in the old days a Spartan soldier could be put to death for even daring to appear under a roof while in service, the palace guards in Constantinople drank from jewel-encrusted cups even heavier than their swords, and were more skilled at appraising the purity of a gold coin than at assaying the thickness of an enemy's shield. Rank cowards they were, who, as the comic poet says, considered it superfluous to use art in their thievery, so they plundered openly. Julian longed for the days of the common soldier he had once heard of, who was said to have stolen a Parthian jewel case laden with pearls while sacking a Persian fort, but who threw away the contents, not recognizing their value, preferring instead to keep the box because of his delight at its polished leather covering.

He dismissed all the *palatini,* the palace parasites, cutting a deep swath through the court's employment rolls, eliminating thousands of positions overnight, to the fury and desperation of the holders of such sinecures. By a single decree he reduced Constantius' palace to an enormous desert, wiping out entire departments of slaves and dependents, allowing no exceptions for age, length of service, or circumstances, even for faithful and honest retainers of the imperial family.

The immediate reaction of the people and the noble classes, however, which was one of outrage and even anxiety for the Emperor's sanity, was soon softened by his innate humbleness and simple common sense. The fiscal and judicial reforms for which he was well known in Gaul were immediately analyzed for applicability here, on the larger scale of the Empire's mightiest city, and their implementation was ordered, to the delight of the common people, who had long been overburdened by the taxes levied to sustain Constantius' excesses. So too did Julian immediately win over Constantinople's Senate, by granting it a number of heretofore unprecedented privileges and points of authority. In a gesture of perhaps even greater symbolic value, he reversed the previous Emperor's custom of summoning the senators to his presence and forcing them to stand uncomfortably before him while he listened to their deliberations. Rather, he humbly went to the Senate chambers himself, sitting at a vacant place in the assembly hall to take part in the debates as a mere one among many, and insisted that all those in attendance remain seated while in his presence.

Despite Julian's extensive reforms of the palace and the fiscal and judiciary systems, however, he somehow neglected to look closely into the workings of the palace kitchens. This was perhaps because, despite the proximity of his tiny pantry office, it was only during rare, mandatory occasions of state that he even sampled the extent of its services. Naturally, he had forbidden the staff from serving him dainty delicacies, such as the peacock tongues and sow's udders that Constantius had so adored; more often than not, he simply sent a steward to bring him a plate of fruit for his repasts, even then sometimes neglecting to eat or indifferent to what he did consume. It was for this reason, perhaps—his very indifference to food—that he allowed the dining facilities and budget to remain untouched and forgotten.

The far-flung and wasteful talent languishing in the kitchen, however, finally burst into full flower several weeks after the games about which I spoke earlier, when he was persuaded by his chief steward that it would be in keeping with protocol to host a banquet in honor of the newly elected senators who had recently taken office. Julian acquiesced absentmindedly, and pointedly asked me to attend and to be sure the steward arranged for me to dine on a couch beside him so that he would not be required to endure the blather of the puffing politicians. Otherwise, he left all else in the hands of the cooks. A black day that was to be.

The chief cook, a literature buff, apparently, had by unknown contrivances determined that that day was the two-hundred-fiftieth anniversary of Trimalchio's legendary dinner, and he resolved to replicate it morsel for morsel; a more obscene, puerile meal I have never seen in my life. For days beforehand, a vast army of slaves bustled merrily about the premises, between the massive kitchens and that part of the Imperial Palace known as the Brazen House because of its roof of brass tiles. It is in this magnificent structure that the four battalions of the Imperial Guards are quartered, adjacent to the state prison for men accused of treason and therefore requiring high security. Here too are the various throne rooms and vast colonnaded galleries in which the Emperor is expected to receive foreign dignitaries and heads of state. Most important, however, it is here that the state banqueting halls are located, and the entire focus of the palace's kitchen activity was for days centered on establishing the critical supply line to these halls, severely disrupting the quiet of Julian's pantry office with the shouts and laughter of the pastry cooks, sweetmeat makers, bakers, butchers, wine stewards, water-drawers, furnace-stokers, fish purveyors, and all the rest of the mob that Constantius had somehow found necessary to prepare a meal.

The evening of the banquet began smoothly enough: The guests had been happily if benignly entertained by a num-

ber of choristers and musicians presenting excerpts from
ancient classic dramas, and dancers in keeping with Julian's
austere tastes—no fire jugglers or nude Syrian girl acrobats
for him! Maximus, who attended with his usual stained tunic and unkempt beard, and whose position on the couch
was just on the other side of the host from mine, maintained
his customary sour grimace and piercing expression. This
was despite the fact that out of deference to the evil little
man's stature, Julian had taken care in advance to ban the
usual troop of comic dwarves and buffoons that Constantius
had often favored to lighten the mood of his guests. I stared
at Maximus as he smirked and whispered sycophantically
into the Emperor's ear, until he caught my glance and de-
flected it with a scowl. Despite my personal resentment of
him, as a physician I still bore some concern for the man,
for it seemed that his rash was spreading—the rough,
angry-looking patch of pustules I had first noticed upon his
arrival in the city had spread from beneath his left ear to
down his jawline and was approaching his left cheek.

When the music and entertainment began to grow tire-
some, and appetites had been appropriately whetted by the
small tidbits served by the bustling table slaves, Julian
looked up and nodded at the watchful usher at the door,
who turned into the corridor and clapped his hands sharply.
Conversation in the room fell silent in expectation, as a
long parade of richly dressed palace eunuchs filed in, bearing silver platters on their shoulders steaming with the incredible results of the past four days' hard work in the
kitchens. The head steward's and chef's repressed creativity
had taken on full bloom.

The theme of the meal was the twelve signs of the zo-
diac, with the arrangement of each of the twelve courses
focusing on a specific astrological sign. Julian looked on in
dismay at the inventiveness of the representations depicted
on the serving platters: for the Ram, headcheese of sheep;
for the Twins, matching pairs of stuffed kidneys. The majestic African Lion was represented by a delicate plate of
Numidian figs; Pisces by massive platters of poached mullet

from Corsica and the finest lamprey from the Straits of Sicily; and Capricorn not by a goat, as one might first expect, but rather by huge shelled lobsters garnished with fresh asparagus, and with their foreclaws mounted on their heads in such a way as to *look* like a goat. Virgo was rather tastelessly depicted by the paunch of a barren sow that inexplicably lay writhing and heaving on a tray in front of us, until the bearded slave who served it drew a hunting knife and plunged it into the foul-looking organ, whereupon a brace of live thrushes burst out, startling the diners. Sagittarius the Huntress was represented by plates of fresh game garnished by—what else?—bulls' eyes, which were nauseating both in themselves and in contemplation of the poor quality of the pun. Between each course, slaves dispersed among the couches with ewers and poured warm, perfumed water over our hands to remove the odor and detritus of the previous course. The palate-cleanser was Libra, an enormous pair of scales set in the middle of each table bearing sweet muffins on one side and delicate cakes on the other, white as snow and kneaded of the finest flour.

The dinner was concluded with the dessert: an enormous, dripping Priapus carved of ice, with cored apple slices chilling as they ringed his tumescent organ, and surrounded by peaches, grapes, and flavored ice. The effect, to my mind, was thoroughly disgusting, though received appreciatively by the other diners. Throughout, copious quantities of Falernian wine were consumed, so old the date had been effaced by the dust that time had gathered on the aged jars but which could not have been less than a century. The mix of water gradually became less and less substantial, "in order," Julian said, "to better appreciate the fine vintage," until against all custom, and particularly his own personal practice, almost the entire party was consuming it neat, with growing gusto.

Appreciative belches were politely emitted, in keeping with the philosophical doctrine that the highest wisdom is to follow the dictates of nature. Under Constantius this practice had been pushed to its logical extreme, and several of the more uninhibited guests engaged robustly in other emissions of wind, but a disapproving glance from the Emperor quickly put an end to music of this kind. Even Trimalchio had had the decency to leave his couch and exit the *triclinium* when pressed by urgent need. Even more flatulent than the reaction to the dinner, however, was the conversation of the immediate guests around Julian's table. It began with the most prosaic remarks about the new Emperor's liking of Constantinople's weather and his appreciation of various historical points of interest, and soon touched upon more sensitive topics of Constantius' past policies and the political stances of certain individuals not present at the dinner.

All this I politely ignored, smiling pleasantly and picking halfheartedly at my headcheese. It was when the topic turned to religion, however, that my interest was piqued, though I remained wary of entering into any serious discussion, for all present had by this time consumed ample quantities of wine and were not above spouting the first ill-considered thoughts that came to mind concerning such-and-such religious practices. Julian, too, became a more animated participant in the discussion, looking to me often for confirmation of his points of theology concerning Christian doctrine and increasingly attempting to draw me into the lively conversation, even baiting me to do so.

"What was it the Apostle Paul said?" he asked, looking at me, his words slightly slurred.

"My lord, I am no Scriptures scholar. Even had I memorized all of Paul's writings, would you have me repeat them to you now?"

He waved me off impatiently. "Ah, my friend, I won't let you shirk your conversational duties so easily. You know perfectly well what the great man said about salvation—you were raised among bishops as a child, just as I was. 'If you confess with your lips that Jesus is lord, and believe in your heart that God raised him from the dead, you will be saved.' Was it not that?"

"Indeed it was. His letter to the Romans, too. Very appropriate."

Julian chuckled as he saw I was warming to the topic—but still I remained chary. "And that statement is, in fact, the very essence of Christianity, is it not?"

"Of course."

"And one who acknowledges its truth and is witnessed to have accomplished those two things might rightly be said to be a proper Galilean, correct?"

"A proper *Christian*—yes, my lord."

He waited a moment, giving me an opportunity to expand upon my responses, yet all I could feel was the heat of the room, the uncut wine making my head swim, and I knew I had no desire to participate in a farcical discussion in the presence of senators and palace toadies. Julian's eyes narrowed slightly at my clear refusal to play along with his attempts at a debate.

"Then why," he said, feigning a look of puzzlement, "are Christians said to fear and despise me, and claim I am not one of them? Here, I shall say it: 'Jesus is lord.' Now am I saved?"

I felt all eyes at our table upon me, and noticed that all other conversation in the room had fallen silent. I spoke clearly and evenly. "I do not know of any Christians who despise you, though they might doubt your commitment to their faith. By merely speaking those words, you have fulfilled only half the requirement. You must also believe in your heart."

"Ah—so whether or not I am saved is contingent upon whether or not I believe. If I *believe* I will receive salvation, then I will receive salvation. Circular logic, is it not? What if I do not, or cannot *completely* believe—will I be partially saved?"

"No, my lord," I said. "You can no more be partially saved than can a woman be partially pregnant."

A few of the diners tittered appreciatively at the weak witticism, but were quickly silenced by Julian's stony face.

"So in other words, my entire fate is based on whether

or not I believe. Not on good works, not on charity, not on love. I need only utter the magic words and believe them, whether I am an illiterate peasant, a king, or a scholar, although, in fact, the more I am the latter, the less likely I am to believe. What kind of a religion are we establishing here, that is based so much on the vagaries of one's heart rather than on one's actions in the world?"

"My lord, you belittle our faith," I rejoined, striving to contain my anger at his mocking tone. "You cast it in overly simplified terms, to which no religion could stand up. This is not the proper venue for a discussion of this kind. If you insist, we shall talk of these things tomorrow, in private, when you are not so—"

"Calm, calm, Caesarius, I meant no offense," he interrupted, smiling lightheartedly. "I call our other guests to witness that I have said nothing vicious or untrue, have I?" Most of the others at the table diverted their gaze or laughed uneasily. "Here, on my honor, I confess my belief that God raised Christ from the dead, for I truly do believe that, Caesarius, as much as I believe that Athena appeared personally to Odysseus to assist him on his return home, and that Apollo spoke directly to Croesus through the oracle. Is there any disputing now that I am as much a Christian as the Pope himself? I believe those things!"

" 'The devils also believe, and tremble,' say the Scriptures." The room fell into shocked silence.

Julian's eyes narrowed again. "What exactly are you implying, Caesarius?"

"Only this," I said slowly. "The passage from Paul you cited presupposes that you have also acknowledged the verity of the Ten Commandments, the foundation of the Christian faith, the first of which is that you shall have no other gods. When you say 'Jesus is Lord,' you must mean he is *the* Lord of all, not *a* lord. Your belief in Athena and Apollo negates your profession of fealty to Christ."

I sat back in my seat, incensed at Julian for putting me on the spot in this way. He stared at me, smirking, and for the first time I noticed true malice in his eyes. "Ah," he said, "so there is a catch. An implied definite article modifying the noun 'Lord' in Paul's passage, which neither the Greek language nor its translations into the Latin were able to make explicit, apparently due to their linguistic and structural shortcomings, and which insightful Paul, writing in a language other than his mother tongue, was unable to clarify. Forgive me my denseness on this matter, Caesarius, in not recognizing what every Christian peasant across the length and breadth of Europe and Africa has apparently easily accepted. So there is only *one* lord, you say?"

I licked my lips, sensing I was being boxed into a corner, but not sure precisely how. "You *know* that is true, my lord," I said, and immediately bit my tongue.

Julian seized upon my words triumphantly, as he had been waiting to do. "Did you call *me* 'lord'?" he asked mockingly. "And I seem to recall your referring to the Emperor Constantius by the same term, did you not? And what will you call my successor, I wonder, should you be fortunate enough to continue your service under him? What has become now of your singular 'lord,' dear Caesarius? Or is there indeed a plurality of such eminences which you, in your wisdom, have not yet had the opportunity to explain to me?"

I was furious at his petty tone, and at the sophistic direction the conversation had taken.

"With all due respect, *Augustus*," I said, "you know as well as I that common court courtesy dictates that I refer to you by the title 'lord.' It is a linguistic convention. You are disputing semantics, not religion."

He smiled contemptuously and turned to the men seated around him, who were staring wide-eyed and gape-jawed at my challenge to the Emperor. They quickly, and nervously, smiled back at him, but failed to meet his gaze, and he stood up, draining his cup and holding it out to the steward behind him for a refill.

"The most notable example I have witnessed this evening of the pot calling the cauldron black," he said. "My dear friend Caesarius now claims that we must somehow *assume* that the Apostle Paul meant one lord, not many, and that we must somehow *assume* that Paul's definition of the word 'lord' was different from that used by any other man either before or since. Our Galilean here parses the meaning of Paul's simple phrase to support his own views, making Paul say something completely different from what the bare words of the text show. And when I ask an honest question about a discrepancy, as any honest reader should, it is *I* who am accused of disputing semantics. Is this a fair summary of our discussion thus far?"

The two rows of heads along both sides of the table nodded vigorously in agreement at Julian's assessment of my apologetics, and then all faces turned back to me. Maximus, I noticed, had perked up considerably and was staring at me with a broad smirk that exposed his crumbling teeth.

"My dear Caesarius," he continued, "if you and I, who have been friends now for many years, are unable to agree on a concept as simple as the definition of the word 'lord,' how then are we to resolve the disputes raging across the Christian world from Spain to Armenia, concerning the very nature of Christ Himself?"

My stomach had shrunken to a tight, hard little ball inside me, but I resolved to take a stand against this grossly unfair attack.

"Caesar Augustus," I argued, "religion is a matter of faith, not science, and it is in the nature of men that their differences increase in direct proportion to the strength of their faith. The divisions among Christians must not be viewed as a weakness in the core of Christianity, but rather as a sign of the strength of men's faith. The Greeks invented philosophy to take the place of religion, and were successful because our ancestors' pagan beliefs contradicted men's desire both for reason and for reasonable faith. In Christianity, however, the Greek philosophers have met their match, and have been defeated."

Julian stared at me bug-eyed, and I held his gaze a long moment, until finally, shaking his head groggily, he burst out laughing. A hard, brittle laugh that sounded alone and hollow against the smooth plaster walls of the dining hall as he looked down both sides of the room with humorless eyes. After a moment several of his tablemates joined him with hearty guffaws, and with the precedent set, all those present joined in, their hooting and coughing swirling around me like so many pestering starlings. I sat motionless and expressionless until he finally calmed himself and wiped a tear from one eye.

"So," he gasped, as the noise died away immediately, some of the men still with expressions on their faces indicating puzzlement as to' what they were actually laughing about. "Our silent Christian has balls after all, and a religion, he says, that is the rival of Homer, Plato, and Aristotle combined! Caesarius, my man of reason, my camp alchemist and anatomist, now professes faith over science. I'm not sure what to make of your medicine now, dear friend—perhaps it would be put to better use serving my horse rather than my own pagan heart and lungs!"

Here again he broke into another round of uncontrollable snorts and cackles, the others also joining in with their own strained and delayed versions of his mirth, some of them looking at me with dismay and, I believe, pity. I had had enough of Julian's public humiliation of me. I rose slowly from the table and addressed him with as much coolness and dignity as I could muster.

"My lord," I said deliberately, "I am not a trained philosopher or rhetorician as are you. Since it is God we are speaking of, we do not understand it. If we could understand it, it would not be God. We seek one unknowable, God, with another unknowable, ourselves, which in the end is impossible, a tautology that even a pagan philosopher can see: we cannot be understood, even by ourselves, because we are made in God's image. I limit myself to being an interested observer of the physical world and of men's actions within it, rather than of the obscure thoughts and reasons men may have for such actions. By attacking me this way, you attack the Church itself, and therefore you commit an unspeakable evil."

Julian's eyes narrowed. "And by killing my father and my brothers, by killing my wife and my son, by doing all in their power to do me in as well, what have the Christians done to me? That, too, was evil."

I recoiled, that he could attribute his family tragedy to Christians. "What Constantius did to you was not done in Christ's name, but rather in his own madness. You cannot blame his faith for his evil. You would certainly not allow me to blame the excesses of Hellenism on your . . . lapses. He will be judged by God. Vengeance on innocent Christians is not yours to take."

"Nor is your blind faith mine to have."

I knew then, Brother, that in the thickness of my tongue I had failed in the most important discussion of my entire life. I was through with that dinner, through with Julian's friendship, through with his obsession with Maximus, and if I had not been so blinded and distracted over the past year by all the events that had transpired, I would have recognized the irreparable breach that had opened between us long before, on that cold mountain pass in Thrace.

"My lord," I said coldly, "I refuse to be party to further mocking or abuse. I therefore beg to be excused from this dinner, as well as from my professional duties as your physician."

With that I stepped over my couch, nodded curtly, and strode calmly down the side of the long table to the door at the far end of the room, feeling every eye upon me, the very silence of the room seeming to magnify the soft, shuffling sound of my sandals on the clean-swept floor. It was the longest walk I ever made, a walk encumbered by the emotions roiling within me, of fury at the ordeal to which Julian had publicly subjected me, of pride at leaving the table and my position at the Emperor's side for the sake of principle, of relief at ending the confusion I had been suffering by serving a man whom I increasingly viewed as an enemy to Christianity—and of worry about my physical safety and that of my family, at turning my back on the most powerful man in the world.

As I reached the door, I looked back briefly and saw that Julian was smiling, and already leaning over to Maximus, engaged in a lighthearted conversation, while all along the table the conversation was beginning again to be animated. The clink of knives on serving plates resumed, and I knew that within a moment my presence would scarcely be missed, and it would be as if the dispute had never taken place—a dispute which to me had meant the end of a career, possibly the end of my life had it been carried to its logical extreme, but which to Julian and the rest at the table was merely a heated discussion abruptly cut off by an overwrought Christian zealot who, like all his co-religionists, took himself far too seriously for polite company.

I strode down the corridor in a blind rage, turning corners at random, entering empty halls, until I arrived at last at a tiny peristyle built into an unused space between two wings, a small, bubbling fountain in the middle embellished with a mosaic portrait of Jesus surrounded by the twelve Apostles. A small shaft of sunlight beamed down diagonally from the skylight onto one of the peristyle's fluted columns, illuminating the delicate pink and yellowish veins in the finely polished marble, showing it for all the world like a pale human limb, drained of blood and with the skin carefully peeled back as in an autopsy, each artery and vessel exposed for the physician's examination.

I walked to the column in a daze and stood staring at it, willing myself to clear away the rushing thoughts and confusion crowding upon my brain, focusing my eyes on the bright, sunlit stone, forcing myself to concentrate only on the essential of life. Emptying my mind, I brought my face closer to the stone, tracing with my eyes the meandering, bifurcating pink and yellow lines, following each to its tiny, indistinct end and then retracing my steps along the capillary until my vision began to blur from the strain and intensity of my focus and the sweat from my forehead burned my eyes. I closed them, and pressed my cheek, my whole body against the marble, which was cold except for the thin, narrow stripe that had been warmed by the beam of sun, and suddenly all the rage and frustration that had been built up in me by Julian's words and actions over the past year broke out. Struggling for control, I slid slowly down the veiny marble, sinking to my knees, still grasping the column with my arms for support, the trail of living perspiration on the fluting glistening and marking the path of my decline and redemption.

For a brief moment only, the moisture lent an aspect of life and suffering to the cold, dead skin of the stone, and then even it evaporated and was gone.

After Caesarius' courageous but ineffectual debate with the Emperor, he returned home to us at Nazianzus, a beaten, tired man. For many days after his arrival he scarcely moved, sitting despondently in the kitchen or praying for hours on end in the tiny chapel I had built on one end of our modest dwelling. Caesarius was so quiet, and moved so rarely, that though the house was small for three grown men and a woman, his presence was barely felt.

In time, he roused himself, seeming to have put behind him the events of Gaul and his long accompaniment of the Antichrist Emperor. He even began to apply some of the considerable medical skills he had acquired, treating the maladies of the poor folk and lepers of the town, bringing babies to light, even curing lame farm stock, though this was more of a psychological need for him than a financial one—he had returned from Constantinople bearing a considerable quantity of gold from his long service with two emperors, and over the previous few years had sent back even more to our father, who had distributed all but a few pennies of expenses to the poor. Caesarius resolved to settle down to the career of a small-town physician and, it was my fondest hope, eventually prepare himself for a life of holiness and meditation within a religious community, for which I believed he would be extremely well suited.

During that time he ignored what little news of the outside world filtered through to our small town—and such news was far from comforting. Julian moved his court to Antioch, and in an effort to purge himself of the mystic sign of God's promise he had received at his baptism, he washed his entire body in the blood of a bull during the diabolical rite of the taurobolium, *pledging fealty to the false god Mithras. Daily, it was said, he participated in ghastly sacrifices, slaughtering countless dozens of animals with his own hands, wrenching out their inner organs for interpretation by the seers of the gods' intent, reveling in the blood and gore of the foul ceremonies.*

And his apostasy was not limited merely to his own practices: for though professing freedom of religion for all in the Empire, he devised peculiarly clever atrocities to inflict on Christians. All religious sites, he decreed, were to be returned to their founding sect—which meant, in almost all cases, that converted Christian churches were to be restored to temples of the false pagan gods. Equally insidious was his conclusion that since Christians did not believe in the truth of the Greek gods, Christian instructors should be forbidden from teaching, and therefore profaning, any of the ancient Greek works of literature. He gave orders that Christians could not serve in the army, nor be appointed to government positions except at the personal whim of the Emperor himself. The ultimate intent was to remove Christians from the Empire's mainstream culture and political movements, resulting in a burdensome intellectual sterility and making our work much more difficult. So too did he permit open persecution of our faith. Churches in Syria and Phoenicia were desecrated by anti-Christian mobs. Priests were tortured, virgins violated. Victims had their abdomens slit open and filled with barley, after which the suffering martyrs were given to the pigs as living feed troughs.

Even old Marcus, Bishop of Arethusa, who thirty years before had rescued the infant Julian when other members of his family were being put to death, was not spared. He was ordered to repair a temple he had allegedly desecrated, but this he refused to do. Julian declined to hand down a death sentence, perhaps out of respect for his old guardian;

*instead he left Marcus' fate to the citizens of Arethusa. The
townspeople, possessed by the devil, applied mob justice,
dragging the bishop through the streets by his feet, tearing
out his beard and then giving him over to the cunning torment of wicked schoolboys, who amused themselves by
skewering him with their* styli. *Finally, half unconscious
and pierced with multiple wounds, he was smeared with
honey and exposed in the sun to the stings of insects until
dead. Each sting was an accusation against Julian.*

*Of even more concern were reports of the Emperor's
increasingly fragile state of mind. Upon his accession to
the throne it had been assumed by all that the era of unstable and paranoid rulers was behind us, and that the
Empire would now be led by a rational man who was firm
and constant in his philosophy and beliefs. Word began
filtering down to us now, however, of the Emperor's wild
mood swings and changes of policy; of his petty vindictive-
ness and an unwonted and unwarranted focus on irrele-
vancies; of bursts of energy followed by days on end when
he could do nothing but bemoan the death of his son and
could hardly muster the energy to rise from his bed.
Whether this was a result of his persecution of Christ's
followers—a kind of divine retribution, if you will—or
whether the guilt he felt at such persecution led to his increasingly unstable mind-set, I am unable to say. Which the
cause and which the effect? Or for that matter, which the
truth and which the lie? Rumor, as Virgil says, has as many
mouths and whispering tongues as eyes and waiting ears,
bearing falsehood and slander as faithfully as truth. Stories
and reports of his actions abounded, and were passed on
to us unfiltered by evidence and embellished by wild fancy.
As distant as we were from the royal capital, we were helpless to know what to believe.*

*Thus it was, until the arrival a year later of that obese
imposter, the physician Oribasius, who trotted into town
one day astride an overburdened, limping army horse,
flanked by a dozen bored legionaries and a pair of dis-
gustingly painted eunuchs, who looked around them with*

distaste at our humble community, and seemed to recoil at the very dust of the street. This man Oribasius I had never seen in my life, but I had heard of him from the stories told by Caesarius, and recognized him without a moment's hesitation. The same occurred to him as well, for as soon as he spied me in our tiny forum, he hailed me most heartily by name, though lacking in all the respect normally owed to a Christian priest and a bishop, and inquired into the whereabouts of my brother. So astonished was I at this appearance of a vision from Caesarius' past that, lacking in all presence of mind, I gave him directions to our house, for which he thanked me cheerfully. It was only afterwards that I regretted this action and wished I could have ripped my tongue out by the roots for the harm it had begotten. I hastened home as soon as I could to confront the flatulent fraud.

Oribasius was just preparing to leave when I arrived, and after nodding to me curtly, he was heaved onto his suffering horse by the sweating legionaries, and the entire party lumbered off to the east, whence they had arrived scarcely an hour before.

My brother refused to meet my harsh gaze as I demanded the reason for the foul Asclepian's visit. He demurred for a time, and then at my repeated prodding he admitted that Oribasius had, indeed, been sent by Julian, who was requesting, nay pleading, that Caesarius return to his service. The Emperor, in Antioch, was preparing to enter upon another military campaign, the most important of his life, he claimed. Oribasius' skills had apparently served him well during his sedentary court life in Constantinople over the past year, but although the gluttonous demon would be accompanying the army with the baggage train, the Emperor desired that Caesarius ride with him in battle, as he had always done in Gaul in the past.

"Naturally you flatly refused the Antichrist's entreaties," I said.

"Not . . . flatly," he replied.

"Were you merely being polite or does the Emperor's spell still seduce you, Brother?" I asked.

Caesarius lashed out angrily. *"I am under no spell but Christ's,"* he retorted. *"If I serve Julian again, it will be for the sake of his immortal soul. Christ said there is more joy in heaven over one sinner who repents than over ninety-nine just men. Would you deny me the glory of being the tool that dissuades that one sinner?"*

Against this argument I had no counter. Nevertheless, I feared in my heart that Julian's mind was set and that there would be precious little my younger brother could do to change him, surrounded as he was by his court of pagans and mystics.

"And you will accomplish this task how?" I persisted. *"By quiet persuasion? By force of arms? Brother, Christians are being martyred, and I fear you are testing God by placing yourself within the Emperor's grasp, even on the pretext of converting him."*

"If Julian is our greatest foe," he replied simply, *"then I would be derelict in not seeking to conquer his wickedness. The Lord will give me strength, and will guide me in words or in my right arm to dissuade him from further evil."*

I eyed him carefully. *"May both your words and your arm be used only for healing."*

He sighed. *"I have long prayed, Brother, for the gift of eloquence, for the grace of persuasive speech with which to win him over—"*

"You pray for the wrong gift, Caesarius," I interrupted him. *"Eloquence of speech is not yours to have. Simplicity is your true gift. It is by simple speech that you best express yourself, it is by simple words that you best convey your faith in the perfection of the Kingdom to come. Remember: 'The sun rose again on another day.' "*

Thus the last I spake with my brother before his departure for Antioch. His own narrative now continues.

BOOK NINE

REVELATION

If in this life only we have hope in Christ, we are of all men most miserable.

—PAUL OF TARSUS

I

"Your place has long been empty."

Julian pointed to the familiar bench, my battered shield still slung from the backrest where I had always kept it, ready to be used whenever Julian called for one of his spontaneous sparring sessions. The surroundings, however, were unfamiliar: a large, high-ceilinged, and lavish room, the walls painted with gaudy murals of frolicking satyrs and nude river nymphs, and an equally intricate mosaic on the floor depicting a vast pastoral scene. He, too, looked unfamiliar. Far from his typically casual, even shabby woolen garb, his formal court tunic was of a spotless white linen, the traditional broad purple band at the hem embroidered with gold denoting his rank. Even his beard, which mercifully he had retained or I would not have recognized him, was carefully trimmed to a self-conscious point and washed, and his normally unkempt hair was styled in the short, neat fashion of the day. The eunuchs of the court, I saw, had been exerting their influence, though I could not say, by these appearances alone, that it was for the worse. His eyes, however, were more hollow than I had remembered. More hollow, more wary, like those of an animal on its guard, or one about to attack. Only the bare wooden bench and shield in the corner remained of our old friendship.

I smiled wanly as I stood and surveyed him. "You've

changed," I said. "At least the eunuchs haven't convinced you to take off the beard. You still look Greek."

He chuckled. "Oh, they tried, believe me. The first time I allowed that doddering old fool Eutrapelus to give me a shave, he took so long that by the time he finished, my whiskers had grown back again. I have no doubt, Caesarius, that you yourself could have performed a neater field amputation than the job he did scraping my chin, but when I complained of the cuts, he tried rubbing my face with his depilatory liniment, some vile, secret *psilothrum* he had concocted out of ass's fat, bat's blood, and powdered viper that made my skin flower into a rash, not to mention making me want to vomit from the smell. Is it any wonder I let my beard grow?"

I laughed, but then became serious again. "You're the Emperor. You needn't take advice from anyone—eunuch or dwarf."

He paused for a moment. "There are many times I could have benefited from your common sense, Caesarius," he said softly.

"You said harsh things that night," I answered.

Julian shrugged. "It was the wine speaking. You know I meant no offense."

I sighed as I tried out my old seat on the bench. "You know I forgive you. It's my duty as a Christian. I think you may forgive yourself too easily, however."

"Others are unforgiving, Caesarius. I know what your brother has been preaching about me in his sermons. Gregory is a good man, but a misguided one, and a trifle hysterical."

"He has good reason. Is it true about the persecutions?"

At this question, he looked slightly taken aback, but quickly recovered.

"Caesarius," he said calmly, "the very fact that your brother continues to be allowed to preach against me, and not only to preach but to call me by all sorts of foul names, is proof of the . . . exaggeration of his accusations, is it not?"

"And Marcus?" I replied.

Julian sighed. "Marcus. I will admit there have been problems. Crowd control is sometimes difficult from continents away. Men misunderstand my words and intent. I do not seek to persecute Christians, Caesarius. Only to eliminate favoritism within the civil service, and the unfair exploitation of our Greek heritage by those who do not believe in the old gods or, worse, who mock them."

"So your goal truly is to restore paganism."

"Yes . . . I mean no. Caesarius, that's not the ultimate goal, but it does happen to be a result. And it's not a bad thing, if you would only pull off your damnable Christian blinders. Still, there's no other way to meet the objective."

"And what objective is that, precisely?" I demanded.

He assumed a bored expression. "Caesarius, you know the situation as well as I do. You saw it under Constantius. Treachery and assassination at the highest levels, corruption rotting the very core of government, nepotism, religious strife. And why?"

"Why indeed, Julian?" I said, knowing full well what his response would be.

"Because," he looked at me meaningfully, "the people have neglected their ancestral religion, the very gods who brought Rome to glory in the past. Is it any wonder we've seen barbarian invasions from every side? Jackals always attack the crippled and weak, and that's what Rome had become, my friend, crippled and weak. Caesarius"—he leaned forward, seizing me by the forearm, his eyes ablaze—"I know you don't support me on the religion side, but it's of no matter. We have the opportunity to redeem all of Rome's past errors! We have it! For the first time in decades, the Empire is capable of being great once again, of surpassing even its old glory! Undisputed control over the entire Empire is in my hands, the army is unified—Caesarius, there is nothing to stop us from restoring Rome, to making it the greatest empire ever to exist on earth, greater even than Alexander's! Nothing stands in our way, Caesarius, but lack of will!"

"Then why waste your time on religious squabbles?" I ventured. "Why not leave the Christians in peace?"

He relaxed his grip on my arms and laughed, though with his mouth only. His eyes remained hollow and mirthless.

" 'Squabbles,' you call them? Caesarius, didn't we have this conversation back in Naissus? I cannot restore Rome alone. I need Rome *itself,* I need its will, the united will of the entire Empire. There is but one thing that prevents that will from materializing, Caesarius: neglect of the gods. And there is only one source of dissent in the Empire—"

"And that is the Christians," I finished for him. He nodded almost regretfully and walked back around behind his table.

"Even the Persians are no obstacle," he continued. "They are cowering and pleading like stable slaves at the threat of Rome's might! But the Christians refuse to cooperate, to contribute to our efforts."

I moved to change the subject. "Julian, this Persian campaign you are planning—in Paris you denounced Constantius as mad for attempting the same thing."

"Ah, but he *was* mad," Julian said, smiling. "He planned his campaign with only half the Empire behind him. I, as you recall, was the other half, and he knew I would not support him, yet he embarked on the venture anyway. His motivation was pure greed and ambition. Mine is the glory of Rome. Our unity is Persia's defeat! So you see, he *was* mad."

"We have all been mad once," I replied quietly.

It had taken me three weeks traveling overland from Nazianzus to catch up with the Emperor at his new base in Antioch, where he was preparing for a final reckoning with Sapor, the King of Kings, the Persian who had for so long been a thorn in the side of the Empire. From Antioch, Julian was gathering men and supplies for the most powerful military expedition Rome had undertaken in a generation. Provisions were pouring in through Antioch's nearby seaport of Seleucia and from across the desert by way of Aleppo.

The supplies were intended not only for the army and the auxiliaries, but for the entire court, the administrators and the thousands of camp followers who were making of Antioch, already a great city, now one to rival even Alexandria, perhaps even Ctesiphon itself for opulence and wealth. Into Antioch's port poured the fruits and wines of Italy and the decorative tiles of Narbonensis; the wheat of Egypt and all of Africa, and the olive oil, silver, and copper of Spain; the venison, stout oaken beams, and soft, carded wool of Gaul; the marbles of Greece and Numidia and the cured hams of Baetica; the tin of Britain and the gold and amber of Dacia. From the vast caravans of ill-tempered camels flowed the dates of the oases and the porphyry and incense of Arabia; the ivory of Mauritania and the papyri of the Nile valley; glass from Syria and Phoenicia and silks from the Far East; and the gems, corals, and spices of India. And with the Emperor's arrival in Antioch, Antioch now eclipsed even Rome and Constantinople as the very center of the world.

Julian had arrived in the middle of July, while all the rest of the Empire was resting and escaping the heat in a somnolent torpor. He was accompanied by the recalled Sallustius, who stood always at his right hand, the side of Julian's sword arm, while Maximus kept to his left, the hand with which he wrote, the side of his intellect. They were his two principal advisers, dextral and sinister, and I was astonished and deeply concerned that Maximus seemed now to have attained influence as an adviser equal even to that of Sallustius. The Emperor was greeted at the ancient city by an enormous crowd, a fact partially accounted for by his fortuitous timing: his arrival coincided precisely with the ancient feast of Adonis, Aphrodite's lover, which was being celebrated throughout the city with the construction of small, artificial gardens and rites commemorating his death by a wild boar and his burial.

Nevertheless, despite the crowd's size, it was not necessarily one that enthusiastically supported the Emperor. Rather, the Antiochians seemed to prefer to defer judgment on their new lodger, for they had heard many things about him—that he was an ascetic, careless in his appearance, a scholar and a killjoy, a religious zealot—none of which endeared him to that city's hedonistic, worldly, cynical residents. And though the population was largely pagan, with some tepid acceptance of Christianity, or worse, of a pseudo-Christianity that blended certain of the ancient pagan rites with an adapted Christian liturgy, the citizens were not won over by Julian's enthusiastic leap into sacrificial worship of the ancient gods. In fact, they were badly put off by his excesses, for in a time of general famine (the harvests had largely failed that year), within the first weeks of his arrival at Antioch, he had engaged in an orgy of bloody sacrifices such as had never in memory been seen there.

In fact, Brother, Julian's actions were as extreme even as the exaggerated rumors we had heard back in Nazianzus, and worse—it was clear that in my absence his thinking had changed terribly, his taste for abomination grown, his capacity for refined and sophisticated thought deteriorated. I had accepted that he was no longer a Christian—indeed, he had made this clear to the entire Empire. But to have renounced even the subtleties of the philosophy he had so loved, which he had pored over for entire nights, all for the sake of these crude and humiliating pagan sacrifices was utterly beyond my comprehension. For hours every day, for days on end, the gutters of the temple precincts ran red, and Julian paraded from altar to altar with his hands and arms stained to the shoulders, at each one sloshing through a red bog of blood, surrounded by heaps of quartered beasts and reveling in the sheer quantity of animals put to the slaughter in the prodigality of his sacrifices. So insatiable was his appetite that he was said to rival even King Solomon, whom Scripture reveals to have offered such copious sacrifices that their blood and smoke must have infested Jerusalem for days.

To be sure, Julian felt compelled to remain in the gods' favor because of his plans to march against the Persians, and in order to maintain the love of his oldest and most trusted troops, the Celts and the Petulantes, who had accompanied him from Gaul and had remained faithful to him even during the darkest days of the winter in Thrace. Nevertheless, the constant feasting and orgies of the rude Gallic troops at the sacrificial banquets were an ongoing scandal to the refined and delicate Antiochians, who night after night suffered drunken, carousing foreign soldiers rampaging through their streets, and were unable to hide their resentment.

Yet the favor of the gods and of his men was more important to Julian than the private complaints of citizens in his host city, who soon resorted to less than honorable expressions in their jibes against him. He was a hairy ape, they said, bearded like a goat, buried always in his philosophical and sacred texts, with uncut, inkstained nails. He ate like a grasshopper and slept like a Vestal, and spent his days quartering countless hundreds of victims for his precious gods.

None of the ritual sacrifices did I see personally, of course, for still I refused to attend them, and indeed Julian granted me full exemption from doing so. This was a minor victory because he normally required all his troops and retainers, Christian and pagan alike, to witness his ceremonies. Nevertheless, there was one event during this period before the Persian campaign to which I was at least a secondhand witness, and which bears describing here, though I will refrain from applying any interpretation to it, Brother, in deference to your more accomplished skills in that regard.

Toward the end of that year, as I mentioned earlier, he resolved to rebuild the great Jewish temple in Jerusalem, which had lain as a pile of rubble for three hundred years since its destruction by the Romans in retaliation for the Jews' rebellion. For many years, in fact, Roman emperors had prohibited Jews even from visiting its ruins, which were left as a visible sign of shame, and, indeed, it was only in recent times that Jews were allowed to set foot in

Jerusalem again at all. The reconciliation measure was logical from Julian's standpoint: he carried no enmity toward the Jews as he did toward the Christians, and in fact was greatly desirous of earning their friendship. Jewish brokers held a great deal of sway among the grain merchants of Egypt and northern Africa, and exercised influence over the sources and prices of many of the luxury goods crossing the desert in the caravans from Persia. Moreover, to his way of thinking, the Jews' religion was actually not far distant from that held by the Greeks, differing only in minor details, its chief defect, of course, being monotheism.

More important, however, was the metaphysical benefit to Julian from reconstructing the temple: Christ's statement that not a stone of that great edifice would remain standing would be resoundingly refuted. The Augustus, the High Priest of Paganism, would humiliate Christians in their own house, making their god out to be a fraud. This last objective, of course, he did not discuss with me, and perhaps I exaggerate in even attributing it to him as one of his motives.

The entire reconstruction plan was couched in the form of a restoration of friendly ties between Rome and the Jews and in November of that year he invited me to travel with him to Jerusalem to witness the ceremonial unveiling of the temple's new principal gate, the area around which had been recently cleared of debris, and which, with the erection of new columns and porticos, was about to be completed. Already he had received encouraging news of the temple's progress; how at the announcement that rubble was to be cleared for the start of the construction, Jews of every age and from every region had set aside their disputes and converged on the holy mountain of their fathers to witness and assist in the great event. Men forgot their haughtiness and women their fragility; spades and axes were donated by rich benefactors, and rubble was carried by hand, even in mantles of silk. Purses opened up and the region's entire population was enthused by the pious commands of their new monarch.

Despite my mixed feelings as to his true motives, I eagerly assented to the trip, for I had never before been to Jerusalem and was delighted at the opportunity to visit the Holy City before the start of the Persian campaign in the spring. The night before we were scheduled to depart, however, a Roman naval trireme pulled silently into the port outside Antioch and disembarked its sole passenger, Alypius of Antioch, the former governor of Britain whom Julian had assigned to overseeing the rebuilding of the temple. He had left Jerusalem only three days before, paying bribes amounting to half his estate in gold to secure a fast ship that would take him to Antioch before our departure, and practically flogging the captain the entire journey to push the rowers to move faster. As Alypius rushed into the palace, accompanied by two sturdy, barefoot sailors who looked about in wonder and awe, I noticed that his face was ashen and his manner almost panicky. Julian was summoned, and in the moments before he arrived, I quickly poured out a large draught of uncut wine and offered it to the trembling architect to calm him, which he drank down gratefully in a single gulp. He then explained the reason for his hurried journey from Jerusalem.

"Your Highness," he stammered, until Julian ordered him to stand at ease. "All was prepared for your arrival and for the reception in a few days—indeed, lengths of sailcloth had even been draped over the new gate, ready for you to give the tug on a string we had rigged, which would send the entire veil billowing to the ground to expose the loveliest temple entrance in the East—"

"What is it, man?" Julian barked impatiently. "Get on with it!"

"There was a tremor."

"What?" I said. "An earthquake? We've heard nothing about one. Was there any damage?"

"Not to the city, no, my lord," the poor man answered me, afraid to look anyone in the eye.

"What, then?" Julian roared in exasperation.

"My lord," the hapless architect moaned, "the entire portico collapsed. Twenty workmen who were rigging the veil were buried in the rubble, and the remainder were only able to save themselves from the falling stones by taking refuge in a nearby . . ." He stopped, as if unable to go on.

Julian stared at him, motionless.

"A nearby *what*?" he asked, quietly and menacingly.

"A church," Alypius whispered.

"A church," Julian repeated, before spinning on his heels and storming out of the anteroom, muttering threateningly under his breath and gesturing with his arms, though there was no one nearby.

"What am I to do now?" the wretched Alypius asked me after a moment, staring around at the priests and guards who surrounded him, and at the malevolent Maximus, who had watched the entire exchange in silence. I had noticed, since my return to service, that Maximus' rash, if that was what you could call it, had spread several inches further and now engulfed most of the left side of his face and disappeared into the collar of his tunic, which he was constantly tugging and adjusting in his discomfort.

"I suggest you return to the trireme and await the Emperor's orders," I told the man gently. He looked at me as if I had just passed his death sentence, as in fact I very well may have, for he was jailed that next morning and killed later in the week by a fellow prisoner, a madman, apparently, who had become enraged at the unfortunate architect for reasons I never learned.

"It doesn't matter," Julian told me over breakfast two days later, in a calm after his earlier rage. "I will order the cleanup and lay the cornerstone of the reconstructed temple myself."

But the journey to lay the sacred stone was not to be. During the next several weeks, frightful reports filtered up to us from Jerusalem's temple district, which at first he dismissed in contempt, then noted in some disbelief. Finally, after summoning the Roman governor of Jerusalem himself to the palace at Antioch to give account for the strange happenings, he listened to them in utter astonishment. It appears that although at first the project to clear the temple site of the centuries-old accumulation of debris had been pursued with great vigor, not a workman in the entire city, Jewish, pagan, or Christian, could now be persuaded to set foot within a hundred yards of the site, for fear of divine punishment. During the first week after the initial collapse of the portico, as workmen had been in the process of removing the great stones and columns that lay in a chaotic heap, a series of terrible balls of flame had burst forth from the temple's ancient foundations, charring men into blackened skeletons. The fire had then disappeared without trace of an odor or a lingering flame.

The site foreman had at first attributed the phenomenon to some seepage of the black bitumen found in such abundance in the area of the Dead Sea, the ancient name of which, in fact, is the Lake of Asphalt because of the masses of that substance that periodically detach themselves from the bottom and float to the surface. A careless laborer, he concluded, might have ignited a pool of it when heating his supper in the shelter of the rocks, and thereby started the conflagration. He therefore sent a number of workers carefully into the underground vaulted cellars of the temple, some of which were still intact after the old Roman destruction, to investigate the matter further.

The second series of flames lit the evening sky like a lightning strike in a Dacian forest, and indeed many in the city of Jerusalem at first looked up to the heavens in surprise to see if they were about to be caught in the rain. They were even further surprised when the entire city was pelted with a barrage of dust, sand, and small pebbles. If only it had rained true water, it might have sooner ended the suffering of those poor ten or twelve souls among the cellar explorers who were still left alive after the explosion. They had rushed from the underground caverns shrieking and raving, their hair and extremities burned from their bodies. Most of them died hours or days later.

As I wrote earlier in this treatise, I have heard of fire issuing forth from dead bodies, and I myself have witnessed fire bursting from the storage of ice. Never, however, have I encountered fire emanating from cold, dressed stone, and I hope I may never live to see such a phenomenon myself. The rationalists among Julian's court speculated that terrible gases had somehow been released from where they had been building deep within the earth, perhaps from faults that had developed in the ground following the tremor that had first toppled the structure, and that these gases had, in turn, been ignited by the spark of a workman's chisel or the sputtering of an oil lamp. Others spoke more darkly of the wrath of the gods, be they the ancient ones of Greece jealous of Julian's favor to the Jews, or the mysterious bovine deities of Persia, infuriated at Rome's imminent march against the King of Kings. The Christians in the street claimed it as holy retribution against the Emperor for daring to question their Savior's divinity, while Maximus and the haruspices attributed it to still insufficient attention to placating Rome's guardian spirits through additional sacrifices.

I shall leave any final interpretation to you, Brother, for Julian wisely diverted his attention and energies elsewhere.

II

I have aged, Brother, faster even than the days that are passing me by, which tear the years off my life as does an infant the leaves of a book that has been left within its grasp. Over the past five years I fear I have aged ten, and over the next five years it will be twenty, and at this rate I shall soon catch up and pass you, and give even Father a good run for his money. Yet it is not in physical years that I am becoming elderly; by many standards I would still be considered a relatively young man, and indeed though my hair is thinning and growing gray at the temples, still my waist is trim, my bowels strong, my pace rapid, and my ability to turn a maiden's head now and then undiminished, though the desire to even tempt such a distraction is another matter indeed. No, of course it is not by fleshly standards that I am growing old, for all flesh must follow the laws of nature and only the steady passage of the days and nights can contribute to one's physical aging. I am growing old inside, for my spirit is tired, bone tired, if you will forgive the mixing of a spiritual metaphor with a carnal one, and this exhaustion, which does not leave me even now, began to be felt the day I arrived in Antioch and confirmed Julian's designs against the Persians. Despite the jauntiness of the soldiers, the cockiness and profanity of the sailors, the laughter and jests of Julian, and even the occasional excited grin from the pustulant mouth of Maximus, I felt a fore-

boding, a sadness about the expedition, perhaps as a result
of the shallowness of its motives. As we prepared for the
march, I felt like an old man with a very long way to travel.

The campaign against the Persians, let it be said, was
entirely unnecessary. Even Sallustius had tried to dissuade
Julian, to no avail.

"He believes it will resurrect Rome's ancient glory," the
adviser muttered, when I once cautiously asked him Julian's motives.

"So he told me, too. And will it?" I countered.

Sallustius grimaced, and sidestepped the question. "He's
following his vision, his goddess, and Maximus encourages
him. You know Julian as well as I do, physician. You cannot talk him out of something he feels is his destiny. And
Persia, he says, is his destiny."

"Every Roman emperor for four centuries has believed
that. Some have won battles, even wars, but none have truly
conquered Persia. Surely he doesn't believe Maximus'
claims for his 'destiny.' "

"Oh, he believes," Sallustius said resignedly, turning
back to the army's preparations for the march. "He truly
believes."

King Sapor was no fool. Indeed, I would even venture
that he was the wiliest monarch any Roman emperor had
ever faced. Though now in the thirtieth year of his reign,
he was still a young man, since by a strange fluke he had
held the title of Great King for longer than he had actually
been alive. His father, King Hormouz, had met an untimely
death while his wife was pregnant with their first child,
which had excited the ambitions of other princes in the
royal family who aspired to the enormous empire. To fore-
stall civil war, Hormouz' widow arranged immediately to
crown the prospective heir, even before knowing the infant's sex. An enormous royal bed was constructed in the
coronation hall for the ceremony, on which the queen lay
in state in the presence of all the courtiers and nobles. A
magnificent diadem was balanced on the spot assumed to
conceal the head of the future king, and all the satraps pres-

ent threw themselves prostrate before the queen's majestic belly and its royal contents. The infant ruler Sapor, with his official title of King of Kings, Partner of the Stars, and Brother of the Sun and Moon, was delivered several weeks later, and by that time his accession to the throne was a foregone conclusion.

King Sapor's spies in Antioch soon informed their employer of Julian's preparations. The King was well apprised of the extent of the military forces and foreign alliances being arrayed against him, and, most important, of the quality of its leader, the young, energetic emperor who had decimated the barbarians of the Rhine, crossed the Roman Empire like a lightning bolt, and seized the capital without spilling a drop of Roman blood. When Julian's preparations were confirmed, Sapor dropped all pretense at haughtiness and sent a polite letter to the Emperor, claiming kinship with him in their mutual capacity as great leaders, and suggesting that they negotiate their differences in a friendly manner.

Yet Julian's qualities and reputation, which had so terrified the King of Kings into suing for peace, were the same ones that prevented him from changing his course of action, despite the clear advantages and the saving of treasure and men. Julian's energetic efforts over the past year in Antioch had yielded an army of sixty-five thousand Roman legionaries, plus that number again of Arabian, Scythian, Goth, and Saracen auxiliary troops; an alliance with King Arsaces of Armenia to hold another sixty thousand Armenian troops in readiness to tie down the Persians on their northwestern front; a river fleet awaiting him on the Euphrates under the command of Count Lucillianus, consisting of a thousand transport ships laden with arms and provisions of every sort; and fifty massive ships of war for fighting, with an equal number of engineering barges for bridge-building and other riparian works. The wooden vessels, covered with raw hides and laden to the gunwales with an inexhaustible supply of arms, utensils, provisions, and engines, were so numerous that they crowded the entire Euphrates River from bank to bank. With a commitment such as that, what answer could possibly be given to King Sapor's diplomatic letter, offered in all humility by the lavishly arrayed uncle of the King himself, who presented rich presents, a fine Arabian stallion, the granting of territories Rome had long coveted, and peaceful coexistence between the two mighty empires as long as both rulers should live?

Unfortunately, in presenting the letter, the King's uncle did not stop with his humble entreaty, as a wise man would have. He also pointedly reminded Julian of the misfortunes of his predecessor, the elderly Valerian, during his own Persian expedition a century earlier, when he was captured and flayed and his wrinkled skin displayed as an "eternal trophy" at the Persian court. As Julian sat seething, the dim-witted ambassador went on to blithely describe the debacle of Galerius, so recent that it was still fresh in the minds of older veterans. His army had been almost destroyed and the general himself had barely managed to return to Antioch alive. Julian's eyes flashed in anger as he listened to the diplomat drone on.

And then he tore up the letter.

With a sneer, he flung the scraps in the face of the King's astonished uncle. "Tell your sovereign," he snarled, "to take heed, that I, Julian, Supreme Pontiff, Caesar, Augustus, servant of the gods and of Ares, destroyer of the barbarians and liberator of the Gauls, recognize no man's superiority over me, nor any empire's over Rome. Hasten, man, warn him, for I intend to deliver confirmation to him personally, at the head of my army!"

War was now not only possible, but inevitable, and the only conceivable destination for Julian's huge army was Ctesiphon, the royal capital of Persia itself.

The massive collection of troops set out on the fifth of March, a time that had been carefully planned to take advantage of the season, which was still sufficiently cool for comfortable marching. The normally arid, barren hills were this time of year still green with pasturage and liberally watered by a multitude of small streams. Our route took us due east across Syria, through the towns of Litarbae and Beroea, and on to Hierapolis, an important caravan center for the region, where additional troops and provisions were being assembled to join with us upon our arrival.

The omens were not good, however, and I am ashamed to say that perhaps because of my constant proximity to Julian and his augers, even I was beginning to take an interest in such signs. They would have been difficult to ignore by even Bishop Athanasius himself, however. Our entry into Hierapolis was staged to represent a triumphal march, preceded as we were by the vast arrays of colorful foreign troops marching in perfect unison, their polished armor gleaming in the bright sunlight. Just as we entered, however, a massive stone colonnade at the very gates of the city fell, narrowly missing Julian's chariot, which had just passed under. It killed fifty soldiers and severely injured untold numbers of civilians who had been standing near or climbing upon it, which was no doubt the cause of its toppling. Julian, however, unable to focus on any thought but the destruction of Persia, scarcely seemed to notice, even when the entire city threw itself into a frenzy of wailing and mourning for its dead. It was only with the greatest of efforts that he was convinced by Sallustius to pay a courtesy visit to the soldiers injured in the catastrophe, the first casualties of his campaign. His mind, however, was elsewhere, on troop counts and supply lines, negotiations with allies and terms of surrender for the Persians. He had no emotion to spare for the dead and injured.

Here we stayed three days, adjusting formations and marching orders, and then, rather than simply following the Euphrates downstream toward Ctesiphon, as King Sapor might perhaps have expected us to do, we crossed the mighty river on a pontoon bridge in the dead of night, and struck out again across the desert in a series of forced marches, twenty or thirty miles a day in full gear. The route took us through Batnae, where another unfortunate event occurred—a huge stack of grain collapsed at a supply station, burying and suffocating another fifty men who were gathering fodder. Still, however, we paused no longer than it took for Julian to perform a brief sacrifice for the care of the men's souls, a ceremony that left even the most ardent bull worshipers cold with the haphazard and absent way that Julian conducted it. Without lingering, we pushed on to Carrhae, an ancient town memorable as the scene of the destruction of a Roman army under Crassus centuries before. We were well on the road now to the mighty Tigris River, several weeks' journey distant, which also led to the same goal of Ctesiphon.

Ctesiphon had, in fact, been the mark achieved by the Emperor Trajan two and a half centuries earlier, in his victorious campaign against the Parthians. Trajan, however, had started from the north, in Armenia, and marched to the Persian capital along the more favorable course of the Tigris, leaving his secondary army to advance to the capital along the more difficult Euphrates shore. By marching well past the Euphrates and moving toward the Tigris with his huge army, Julian aimed to keep Sapor's spies guessing as to which of the two attack routes he intended to take; and perhaps he himself was unsure at this time which he would choose, as he attempted to monitor Sapor's own forces from afar. Ultimately, he decided to use the pincer tactic that had served Trajan so well in his assault, though with a twist: Julian's secondary force, under the command of his kinsman, General Procopius, would continue east toward the Tigris, joining with Arsaces' Armenians if called upon to do so, and then lay waste the districts along the banks of that river while advancing to Ctesiphon. Julian, meanwhile, with the bulk of the troops and supplies, would double back south to rejoin the massive Euphrates fleet at Callinicum, and then push forward to meet Procopius at Ctesiphon upon his arrival.

At Carrhae I was again party to a perceived good omen involving his horse. Ever since the embarrassing event in Thrace when I had fallen on my face in the mud, I had been particularly cautious, when invited for a ride with Julian, to plant my feet sturdily before assisting him into the saddle Persian-style, if his lance hook was not available. I was unconcerned here, however, for there was no mud.

He had invited me for a short ride to watch a detachment of Scythian slingers and archers at their target practice, and I had gladly joined him, eager for the excuse to leave the confines of the camp. On the way, however, Julian's usual stallion pulled a shoulder, and he borrowed a horse from one of the groomsmen accompanying us. We watched the practice for perhaps an hour, and were just mounting our horses to leave, when suddenly an errant stone from a slipped sling slammed into the side of the borrowed horse's face.

The weapon was not one of the deadly, lead, acorn-shaped missiles that the slingers use in actual battle, but rather simply a round, hard river stone that had been casually picked up by the slinger from the ground where he was practicing. Nevertheless, the speed of its impact knocked the poor beast's head to the side with a spurt of blood that bespattered the surprised Julian, as the stone penetrated its cheek and shattered the molars on that side of its face. The horse fell in agony to the ground, throwing its rider clear, but writhing and rolling in the dirt, its hooves flying in all directions, scattering its priceless silken trappings trimmed with gems and gold.

Julian was red-faced with fury. "Where is he?" he shouted, stalking toward the dumbfounded centurion who had been training the slingers, the crowd of confused soldiers clustering behind him in terror. "Where is the ass who felled my horse, and who damn near killed me?"

The centurion looked behind himself in consternation at his squad, wondering what he should do, as the groom and I rushed behind Julian to calm him before any damage was done. Rarely had I seen Julian in such a fury—even when his son had been killed he had been able to control his emotions, but his moods of late, swinging from utter apathy at the death of fifty soldiers, to sputtering rage at a mere injury to his borrowed horse, confounded me. I seized his shoulder to hold him back from launching himself at the centurion. Suddenly one young Scythian, scarcely a boy, stepped out from the crowd of slingers and made his way shakily toward the Emperor.

Julian watched, trembling with rage, and when he had approached near, roared, "Do you realize what you have done, boy? With your clumsiness, the horse is as good as dead, and it is only by the grace of the gods that I am not too! A fine horse, this . . . this . . . damn it all, groom, what was the name of the horse?" he said, whirling around to where I stood next to the trembling stable hand.

"Babylon," the groom croaked, and as Julian turned back to the boy to continue his tongue-lashing, he suddenly stopped.

"Babylon?" he repeated, in wonder. "Babylon. . . . Boy, Babylon has fallen!" and a broad grin suddenly wreathing his face, he threw his arm around the astonished slinger's shoulders and turned to stare calmly at the trembling, moaning horse struggling to stand to its feet, its rich trappings torn and hanging off its sides. "It has fallen, boy, stripped of all its wealth! You have killed Babylon!" And so saying he rushed to the horse, ripped off a strand of decorative gold chain that had been partially torn from its position on the saddle, and thrust it into the dumbfounded boy's hands. "May your aim never improve beyond today!" he shouted, and the wonderstruck archers and slingers cheered, though more with relief and surprise than in true support.

I returned to camp shaking my head in amazement that a man who professed such belief in the gods could ignore the signs given by disasters that had killed dozens of men in recent weeks, yet continue his campaign on the basis of a misguided sling stone.

III

Having split off Procopius' forces, the army continued its march to the south and east, reaching the fortified Euphrates city of Callinicum a mere three weeks after our departure from Antioch. Here Julian received homage from the chieftains of several groups of nomadic Saracens, who vowed obeisance to the Emperor on bended knee and offered him a golden crown. He received them graciously and accepted the military assistance they offered, since these tribesmen were known to harbor an abiding hatred for the Persians, and were considered to be excellent at guerrilla warfare. Here, too, we reunited with the fleet that had been slowly making its way downriver, and from this point on, the massive river and land forces advanced together into the heart of ancient Mesopotamia.

Over the next week the force covered ninety miles before arriving at Cercusium, a stronghold at the junction of the Chaboras and Euphrates rivers that Diocletian had fortified years before, because of its critical location in defending Syria from Persian invasions. Julian rotated and reinforced the local garrison, assigning four thousand troops from his own army, and ordered the construction of a pontoon bridge to cross the tributary. The fifty engineering barges, bearing pre-cut beams and pilings and stacked with miles of lashings, swung into action, to the astonishment of the sleepy local inhabitants, and within two days a magnificent bridge had been constructed across the half-mile-wide mouth of the Chaboras, over which the entire army, including supply wagons, camels, horses, and provisions, crossed in a matter of a few hours. The army cheered as the last of the ox teams bearing fodder and siege equipment lumbered over the solid timbers of the bridge, and the men stood by, aghast, as Julian gave orders to pour pitch on the timbers of the very bridge he had just built, and to fire it behind us. With the bridge destroyed, there could be no hope of turning back. His confidence, and arrogance, knew no bounds.

Evil omens followed as if by divine retribution, making the men increasingly nervous. During a sudden storm that had appeared out of a clear blue sky, a lightning bolt killed two horses and a soldier named Jovian, whose name derived from that of Jupiter, the king of the Greek gods; a flood caused several dozen ships to be driven through the stone dikes protecting the riverbank and sink from the damage; and a sudden tornado tore tent pegs from the ground and set the soldiers' tents flying, even throwing many of the men themselves painfully to the ground. Like the previous signs, Julian chose to ignore these, yet the men themselves could not, and in fact some even claimed that a Roman expedition so far east was beyond peacetime precedent and need. When we came to a place called Zaith, two days out of Cercusium, where lay the magnificent tomb of the Emperor Gordian, the muttering and lack of discipline had reached such a point that several legions of auxiliaries refused to march any further until the evil portents were addressed.

When informed of the troops' concerns, Julian was outraged at their lack of faith in him. His initial reaction was to order the mutinous troops to continue marching under pain of court-martial and death. His generals pointed out, however, and Maximus quietly concurred, that even if he were successful in forcing the men to march, they would not be supporting him in their hearts. A soldier who has lost confidence in his leader is worse than useless—he is, in fact, a positive danger, because of his propensity to lose courage and run, endangering the courage and lives of even staunchly loyal troops.

"Talk to them, Julian," I urged. "Put your skills to use. Remember Gaul, before the Battle of Strasbourg? You have always been able to fire up your troops."

He calmed himself, but remained indignant. "I refuse to believe," he said, "that Alexander had to coax his troops across the desert like so many blind puppies to their milk bowl. Still, if that's what it takes to make the Saracens march, let's go to it."

And without a moment's thought or planning, he strode over to a great mound of earth near the elaborately modeled, boat-shaped marble tomb in which Gordian lay, and stood waiting with his senior officers as heralds hastily assembled the troops. Within moments the army had gathered, all the centuries, cohorts, and maniples assembling in order, with those at the farthest reaches of the camp running as if to battle, for indeed the heralds had, at Julian's order, blown the call to arms to induce the troops to arrive yet more quickly. There, beneath a clear blue sky with scarcely a cloud to be seen, with the sun shining on rolling plains of low brown grass spreading away from the broad expanse of river like a vision from a pastoral of Virgil, he delivered the most, let us say, educational address I have heard, barring your inspired sermons, of course, Brother.

"Gallant men," he shouted, a promising beginning, "seeing all of you, heroes, so full of energy and eagerness, I have summoned you here to explain to you that, contrary to what has been suggested by certain rumormongers and malcontents, this is not the first time Romans have invaded the kingdom of Persia. Antony's general Ventidius gained innumerable bloody victories over these people, to say nothing of Lucullus. Pompey, after decimating so many hostile tribes that stood in his way, also broke through into this country and viewed the Caspian Sea with his own eyes. I will admit, however, that these were from very early times. More recently, Trajan, Verus, and Severus all returned from Persia crowned with laurels and triumph, and Gordian the Younger, whose tomb we here honor, would have done the same after defeating the Persian king at Resaina and putting him to shameful flight, if he had not fallen victim at this very spot to a wicked plot hatched by his own men. But justice weighed Gordian's enemies in her scales, and the dead Emperor's spirit did not long wander unavenged. All those who conspired against him, who plotted to thwart the Emperor's will while the army was vulnerable and distant from home, met agonizing deaths—as is right for anyone who conspires against their legitimate sovereign."

At this he paused, and stared pointedly at the companies of Saracens, whose grumbling had led to the calling of this assembly in the first place. They had fallen silent, and the Gallic legions adjacent to them eyed them coldly and almost imperceptibly sidled away. Having made his implicit threat, Julian continued, his voice rising fiercely and carrying effortlessly on the still air of the grassy plains.

"But all these emperors—all of them—were driven by base desires. Ambition to achieve great victory, a yearning for wealth, the quest for unchecked territorial expansion. Wicked motives yield corrupt results. Our own motive, however, is of the greatest nobility: We are here to avenge the shades of our slaughtered armies of the past. We are here to recover our lost battle standards and repair the damage done to the Roman cities Persia has recently captured, which under Persian rule are mired in wretchedness and slavery. Above all, we are here to restore the glory and civilization of Rome! All of Rome, both past and present, those who live and the spirits of those who are dead, are watching you now, gauging the extent to which they are avenged, based on your valor here. Be the heroes your forefathers are calling you to be! Do not let them down! We all, from Emperor to infantryman, are united in our desire to right these wrongs, to overturn past disasters, to strengthen the flank of the great Roman Empire. Posterity shall record the glories of our efforts and achievements!

"Soldiers, it remains only for you to check your greed for loot and plunder, to which Roman armies have so often fallen victim. Remain in formation as you advance. Follow your commanders, and when the time comes to fight, do so with every fiber of your body! In the end, any orders I give, any actions I take, any strategies I devise, are yours to follow, not on my authority as Emperor, but on my skills as general, and your trust in those skills. Our foe is wily and dishonorable, but I promise that any man who lags behind will be hamstrung, if not by the enemy, then by me!

"By the grace of the Eternal Deity, I pledge my honor that I will be with you everywhere. The front ranks will see me fighting among them, as will the cavalry and the archers, and the omens support me in my hopes. But should fickle fate strike me low in battle, I will be content to have sacrificed my life for Rome and for you, my heroic troops. Whatever fortune I may gain, whatever hopes I harbor, I now consign to you. Screw up your courage, in full expectation of victory. Know that I will take an equal share in any hardships you may suffer. And remember—a just cause always triumphs, and our cause is just! Be heroes!"

They applauded with an enthusiasm I had not seen since we had departed Antioch, though it fell far short of what I witnessed during Julian's early triumphant days in Gaul. The soldiers beat their shields desultorily on their knees, some of them calling for him to stand on his mound and salute them, which he did dutifully, though for too long after the cheers had died down. I noticed that he had masterfully skirted the divisive issue of religion in the ranks, referring only to the "Eternal Deity," and that his Christian soldiers as well as the pagans appeared to accept his encouragement equally. The Gallic troops alone demonstrated enthusiasm in their shouts of joy, remembering all those times, when Julian was in command and fighting at their side, that they had seen powerful barbarian peoples destroyed or forced to beg for mercy.

The men now marched in silence, forgoing the idle chatter and singing that often accompanies troops on the march.

The sun had become hot; each day's route was long; and though morale was now higher since Julian's harangue, the troops were tense and thoughtful, and preferred to conserve their energy for the task that lay ahead.

After two days we arrived at Dura, an important trading and caravan center, which at Sapor's orders had been completely deserted. Our hopes had led us to believe that here, in the heart of Assyria, we would encounter plunder that would well compensate us for our hardships thus far—for it is said that this region was personally chosen by the Great King Cyrus, Sapor's ancestor, as his principal source of supply. Four entire villages in those days had been assigned to providing subsistence for his Indian dogs alone; eight hundred stallions and sixteen thousand mares were maintained at the public expense for the royal stables. Yet in this regard we were sorely disappointed, for the granaries were empty, the kitchen gardens plucked, and the surrounding fields burned. Our only consolation lay in the great herds of deer that also inhabited the area, which, driven to desperation by the loss of their pasturage from the fires set by the King's troops, behaved wholly out of character for such animals. They would cluster together weakly even after sighting us, staring at us with eyes glassy with hunger, and would attempt only feeble flight as we approached, allowing us to save ammunition by capturing them with nets or even by beating them over the heads with heavy oars from our boats as they attempted to swim across the river to safety. Venison was a refreshing change for the troops.

It was here, during our brief rest, that Julian accepted an offer from a local Bedouin guide to visit an ancient temple to Apollo carved into the steep sandstone banks of a dry riverbed. The narrow path that wound down along the rock walls to the structure from the plains above had long since washed out. We were forced to take a detour of several miles to an appropriate descent down into the gully, and then retrace our steps along the dry bed at the bottom. We could see the temple high above us, appearing almost as a cave but with exquisitely carved fluted columns and age-worn stone figures adorning the entrance.

Through a complicated system of ladders and ropes that had been rigged ahead of time in anticipation of the Emperor's visit, Julian was hauled up to the opening. His eyes shone with anticipation as he ascended slowly up the rocks, and he glanced at me cheerfully—how long had it been since I had seen him thus, relaxed and happy, away from the pressures of command and the visions that haunted his sleep? Even the prospect of witnessing his abominable prayers at an ill-kept shrine to an unidentifiable cave deity did not seem as horrifying to me as it once might have— for where he was content, reason and calm prevailed, and many good things, Brother, can come of reason and calm. It is not for nothing that the devil prefers chaos.

We scrambled the last few feet along a crumbling ledge that had once served as a footpath for the caretakers, ropes still fastened securely about our waists. When we arrived at the cave, however, our eyes met not with the ancient statue of Apollo and the primitive murals from Homeric times that Julian's imagination had led him to expect but rather—a Christian church.

Actually, Brother, you should not raise your hopes, for out in that desert fastness it is unlikely that any such structure is deserving of the name of "church." It would be better-described as a hermitage, for it was inhabited by precisely one person, an emaciated, long-bearded old man wearing nothing but a dirty loincloth and as blind as a salamander from staring into the sun, which he did incessantly, seated in the entrance, facing the dry canyon before him. The room behind him was empty, scoured of all traces of past pagan presence, the only adornment being a single, tiny cross hung on the bare stone wall—which the hermit could not see, in any case.

Julian was at first dumbfounded, and then his astonishment grew to outrage. He stormed up and down the confines of the cave, poking his head and hands desperately into nooks and cracks in search of a carving, an engraving, anything that might bespeak the presence of one of his laughable deities. His Bedouin guides were terrified at his wrath, for being neither Christian nor Hellenist themselves, they had failed to understand the distinction between one Roman religion and another and had not realized that the Emperor might be offended. It was precisely at this time, just as Julian angrily gave up his search, that the ancient hermit's single daily meal arrived—dry bread and a lentil broth, brought by three Christian ascetics from a tiny community living among the rocks just below, and proffered in a bucket which the old man drew up with a frayed hemp rope.

Julian began harshly questioning the old one, though to no avail, as the man spoke only an obscure Syriac dialect which even our guides were unable to interpret. He then sent several of the guards that had accompanied us to intercept the three ascetics and haul them up to the temple for an explanation. They arrived trembling and bowing, astonished at somehow encountering a furious Roman emperor in their tiny desert chapel.

Grilling them angrily in the pidgin Greek that one of them spoke with difficulty, Julian finally turned away in disgust.

"Their motto, they say, is that old chestnut, 'Forsake all and ye shall find all.' That is why they live so wretchedly at this pathetic little shrine to their fisherman's religion." He paced back and forth a moment in the tiny room, fuming. "I have my own version of the saying to confront such nonsense." He turned to the three bewildered ascetics. "It's from Plotinus, whom you would do well to read, rather than your uneducated Galilean: 'Remove all.' "

And so saying, he ordered his guards to clear the church of everything, cross, hermit, and bucket, and prepare it for a cleansing sacrifice of blood on the following day.

I stood listening dumbfounded to his furious ranting, while the three ascetics huddled uncomprehendingly in the corner, pleading with their eyes to be let go unharmed, while the ancient mystic remained sitting where he was in the doorway, facing the dry riverbed and obliviously mumbling a prayer.

"Julian—this is madness!" I interrupted in the middle of his tirade. "The guides say the temple had been unused for centuries before the hermits found it. No one knows whether it had ever been dedicated to Apollo, or to some desert scorpion god instead. It is just as fairly used as a church as a pagan temple. You must stop this scandalous treatment of these men!"

Julian stopped and glared at me for a moment, but then ignored my argument as he continued his angry pacing.

" 'The ultimate sacrifice,' they call it, and this old blind man, their leader, they call him 'the sainted hermit.' The hypocrisy of it all!" he raged. "The old fool sleeps on the ground in a bare room and eats lentils and calls it a sacrifice! By the gods, I do the same thing! Yet at least I work for a living. His is not a sacrifice, it is the ultimate extravagance, for he relies completely on the service of these others. They are in his employ! They prepare all his food to be hauled up in buckets and his waste is let down the same way, and in some ill-begotten sense of holy sacrifice or just plain ignorance of basic sanitation, they use the same bucket for both tasks! What kind of a religion is this, Caesarius? Are they lunatics?"

I stood by in a silent rage, furiously clenching and unclenching my fists in an attempt to control the emotions I felt at that moment. The sullen guards carefully roped and carried the silent old man out of the room from which he had not set foot in thirty years, accompanied by the moaning and hymn singing of his distraught companions. Never again, I swore, would Julian commit such an atrocity.

This event, Brother, was unremarkable—though I can almost see your eyes widening in fury as you read that word. "Unremarkable!?" you bellow. "That a community of Christian ascetics be driven like dogs from their home by this . . . this Antichrist?!" Allow me to explain. Of course, Brother, it was remarkable *as a single act*, but when accrued to the sum total of all such remarkable outrages that Julian committed, which are too numerous to be recounted here, it was but a drop of water in the sea. In that sense, as the Sophists might put it, it was unremarkable in its very remarkability. And like a small wound that festers and suppurates for a time, but in the end reluctantly heals, the event would have remained small in my mind too, had it been small in Julian's—but such was not the case.

That night, still furious, I strode uninvited into his tent to reclaim some papers I had left there the day before. I found him slumped over his table asleep, yet dreaming fitfully and talking loudly and incoherently enough to make the guards restless as they paced outside.

"Demons!" he moaned. The events of the day were clearly tormenting him as much, in their own way, as they were me. "Demons, the Christians! *Devils!*"

Further such epithets sprang from his lips, but I ignored them, transfixed as I was by those initial words, and by the sight of him sprawled sweating and twitching across his table, his face grimacing in the imagined fears and torments reserved only for lunatics and the possessed.

God help me, Brother, murder came to mind, *murder!* And what is worse, the notion came in such a powerful rush, with such an infernal roaring, that I was unable to control the path down which my thoughts led me. I could not simply banish the notion as I have trained myself to do with other unworthy thoughts, by uttering a quick paternoster or a prayer to the Virgin. No, murder came to mind and murder stayed, and I froze as much in fascination at the sight of the Emperor of Rome spewing mad obscenities in his sleep, as in horror at the thought of what I might do, and at the pleasure I took in thinking it. How simple it would be to pick up a leather sandal thong, step over to the man and throttle him silently till he lay still. With a mere rag for a cushion around his neck it could even be done without bruising or abrasion—the Emperor would be found in the morning and thought to have swallowed his tongue in a fit of epilepsy! Or with only slightly more risk to my being caught as an assassin, I could, within seconds, crush his head with a quick blow from a brass candlestick, or simply slip his own dagger from his belt and thrust it into his heart, carefully placing his hands around the shaft to feign self-infliction. So easy it would be, mere seconds, and the course of this campaign, the entire future of Rome and Christianity, could be changed!

Has any man ever held so much power in his hands, so much unchallenged, world-cracking, empire-toppling power as I held for those few brief moments in the tent? Had Christ himself wielded such concentrated potential on that fortieth day in the desert, when Lucifer offered Him all the kingdoms of the earth in return for a mere act of homage? Was Lucifer tendering the same offer to me, here in my own desert—and if so, would it be more of a sin to accept the Evil One on his terms, or to place myself on the same level as Christ by refusing them, knowing that the man before me may have been Satan's own representative on earth? When Lucifer appeared to Christ as a man, would Christ Himself have been justified in murdering him? My entire life I had sought only to serve God, by serving and healing man—is this what it all came down to, a sordid decision as to whether to use a leather thong on the neck or a candlestick on the skull?

My mind swam, and the canvas walls seemed to close in on me, and, stiffly, like one benumbed with cold or with horror, I took two shuffling steps forward, my hand reaching out for the candlestick—and then stopped. Julian still lay awkwardly across the table, head to the side facing me, but now, and perhaps for some time, though I hadn't noticed from the effect of my own burning brain, he was silent and still. In the dim light I saw that his one visible eye was fixed steadily on me, wide and unblinking. How long he had been watching me, and whether he suspected the thoughts that had been racing through my mind, I did not know.

He slowly lifted his head and shoulders, sat back in his chair, and ran his fingers through his hair, reviving himself from his nap as I had seen him do so many times in the past. His expression was now calm, like that of the Julian I remembered from Gaul, and a faint smile was even visible on his lips from his embarrassment at having been caught napping. I stared at him, at my friend and companion for the past eight years, and a wave of nausea passed over me, of disgust that I could have so easily acted upon the terrible thought I had been contemplating. It is not for nothing that the name Lucifer may be translated as "light bearer," though the light he sheds is one that blinds rather than illuminates. Shaking my head in confusion, as if it were I who had just woken up, I stepped to the table to retrieve my papers and left the tent wordlessly, while Julian stared after me in puzzlement.

The next day, as we marched past the cliffs, I was told by the sentries that the bitter ascetics had left their community and dispersed into the desert in the night, God only knows where. May He keep them safe.

Continuing our descent down the Euphrates, we accepted the surrender of Anatha, a small, well-fortified island in the middle of the river. During the inspection of the prisoners, we were astonished to find an elderly Roman man, a century or more in age, who could barely speak Latin for having lived in these parts so many years. Doddering rheumatically up to the Emperor and his astonished advisers, he threw back his shoulders, peered as best he could through his cataract-thickened eyes, and barked out an order in a surprisingly clear and authoritative voice: "Take me to your general, tribune!"

Julian, taken aback at first, quickly recovered his poise, and solemnly placed his hand on the old man's shoulder. "I am the local commander," he said evenly. "How may I be of service?"

The ancient one stared long at him, then took a shaky step back and raised his arm in a creaky military salute. "Hail, tribune. Infantryman Cassius Rufinus reporting for duty, sir!"

With a faint smile appearing through the dusty tangle of his beard, Julian ordered the man to stand at ease, then after nodding respectfully to the crowd of overawed family members who had begun to gather, he invited the old soldier to accompany him to his field tent for a cup of wine. Cassius Rufinus assented to this with great dignity, and had I more time and papyrus than have been allotted to me, Brother, I could write an entire book of the old scoundrel's adventures, for over the next two hours his rambling story was allowed to spill out uninterrupted, a veritable living history of Rome's long-forgotten wars. He recounted how he had participated in the Emperor Galerius' campaigns in Persia seventy years earlier, had been abandoned by the legions in Anatha to die of fever from a wound, but had later recovered. There he ended up making his home, became prosperous, took several wives, and had many children and grandchildren, several of whom were called to the tent to witness a most extraordinary fact: that for decades Cassius Rufinus had predicted that he would be buried on Roman soil in his hundredth year.

Julian treated him gently and with great honor, attaching him and his huge family, laden with gold representing seventy years of back wages and pension, to a dispatch caravan being sent to the Roman governor of Syria. I was later told that the old man did, in fact, die there quite peacefully. This was a blessing, for as soon as the patriarch and his family had departed, Julian destroyed the town.

Following the river further we passed by the impregnable fortresses of Achaiachala and Thilutha without stopping, judging that speed of approach to Ctesiphon was of greater value than the destruction of these two minor strongholds. This was a wise decision, for the Persian garrisons stationed therein were so small as to be of little danger to our troops as we passed by them, yet it would have been enormously costly in terms of treasure and men to subdue them. At Baraxamalcha we crossed to the right bank of the Euphrates on a hastily assembled pontoon bridge, which, as before, Julian destroyed after its use. Seven miles farther downstream we encountered the large, beautiful city of Diacira, which like others we had passed had been largely abandoned, though this one more recently. In it we found large stores of grain and powdery white salt, which our quartermasters eagerly seized. A few women were discovered hiding here as well, but were found to be mad, and so put to death. We then continued our march along the dryer right bank of the Euphrates, passing a spring bubbling not with water, but with a strange, black, bitumenlike substance which we found to burn foully and unendingly with a thick black smoke when ignited. After much wonder at the strangeness and seeming lack of utility of some of the substances with which God finds fit to bless us, we finally arrived at the town of Ozogardane, a beautiful city of spas and pleasure facilities which was, again, deserted. Here we stopped for a much-needed rest and reorganization, though the troops could hardly relax: on every hill and rise around us, Persian cavalry scouts stood in silhouette, carefully observing our movements. The reason? This spot was a mere three days' march from Ctesiphon itself.

From here, the approach to Ctesiphon was guarded by a string of fortified cities, each more strongly garrisoned than the next. Unlike the fortresses earlier on our march, it could not be ignored. And though we were a mere fifty miles distant from our ultimate goal, the mere act of marching became an ordeal, for the Persians had summoned the rivers themselves to their aid. They opened the sluice gates to their massive irrigation canals, destroying their own lands and villages in a huge wash of water and mud, yet at the same time flooding all the fields and plains over which we were required to advance. The roads were covered with water, and our camp was inundated. Sloshing through the marshes for two days, the men assisting the oxen to drag the supply carts through the mire, we arrived finally at Pirisabora, the city whose name means "Victorious Sapor" and whose walls of baked brick laid in bitumen were bronzelike in strength. Julian's military engineers stared up at the battlements in dismay, but their complaints were useless; the city had to be taken.

Our missiles, large flaming rocks and ironclad bolts fired from close at hand by the ballistae and catapults the troops had painstakingly dragged all the way from Antioch, were of no avail. The besieged, whose courage even Julian's normally disdainful Gauls grudgingly acknowledged, had rigged curtains of soaked goat hides, awnings, and even family quilts and bed linens in front of the walls to cushion and dispel the impact of our weapons. Prince Ormizda, Sapor's exiled brother who accompanied us as a guide and who was sent to the front lines to negotiate the defenders' surrender in their own language, was greeted by them with jeers and abuse. Much to Julian's dismay, the taking of this minor city had degenerated into a drawn-out siege; yet time was of the essence. According to our scouts, King Sapor, who weeks before had marched up the Tigris in a fruitless search for our forces from that direction, had now realized his error and was marching rapidly back to defend his city.

The entire night Julian spent conferring with his generals as to the best means of achieving a quick victory. Ultimately, however, his strategy was decided not on the basis of military counsel, but from his reading of history. At dawn, bleary-eyed but excited at the solution he had devised, he summoned Sallustius, who entered the tent with his usual dignity and calm.

"*This* is the key to our victory!" Julian exclaimed enthusiastically. "This will have us in the gates by tomorrow without further bloodshed." They conferred quickly in low tones, the older man shaking his head slowly at first, and then forcefully, his face reddening in anger when he saw that Julian was refusing to listen.

"Madness!" Sallustius muttered as he stormed out of the tent a few moments later.

Julian smiled at me wearily. "He's no longer schooling a boy soldier," he said, a touch of defensiveness in his tone. "You would think that an Emperor's word would have counted for something in that old fool's mind."

Within an hour he had put his plan into play. He ordered the artillery and archers to provide a withering cover fire on the city's battlements, forcing the defenders to dodge behind their motley protective curtains for safety. He then stationed himself in the middle of a phalanx of a hundred handpicked troops, their tightly packed shields arranged over his head and to the sides of the wedge like an enormous tortoise, to protect him from arrow shots and other missiles. In this formation they awkwardly stormed the city's main gate, which consisted of a huge wooden structure reinforced with iron bars and fittings. Instead of weapons, the men bore only crowbars, chisels, and carpentry tools.

The army held its collective breath, praying to all its gods for the safety of the Emperor. The enemy, quickly realizing the identity of the daring raid's commander, in turn focused all its efforts on destroying the squad of makeshift locksmiths cowering under the shields below them. A deadly hail of arrows, bricks, and stones poured down upon Julian and his men, clattering upon the raised shields and staggering the soldiers beneath with the force of their impact. Several fell as their shields buckled from the weight of the rocks dropped from above, and when other men stepped in to fill the gap they too stumbled and swayed. Even to us standing in safety in the lines fifty yards away, Julian's voice was audible under the tenuous roof of shields, bellowing at his men. "Put your backs into it!" he cried as they worked to pry off the door's iron bars. "Burst the hinges, men, saw the boards!" To no avail. Try as the Roman artillery might to repel the defenders above the main gate, all the Persians' resources were being focused on the small Roman squad, for the winnings at stake were too great for them to ignore.

The effort was doomed. Several moments more, and the defenders began hauling up to their tower enormous rectangular building blocks, the kind that would crush a man's foot even if gently set down upon it—the effect they would have being dropped from fifty feet would be too horrible to contemplate. A shout rose up from the Roman army, urging the small squad to return before disaster ensued, and this time Julian heeded. Carefully retaining their formation, still sheltered beneath their dented and splintered shields, the wedge of men stumbled back to their lines, out of the defenders' stone-throwing range, dragging with them those who had been wounded in the ill-fated foray. The army cheered as if it had won a great victory, while the Persians on the battlements matched the shouting with their own hoots and obscene gestures.

Sallustius was furious as he strode back into the tent that afternoon, but Julian silenced him with a baleful stare before he had a chance to say a word.

"Are you going to dispute the wisdom of Scipio, Rome's greatest general?" Julian asked, pushing forward a battered scroll containing Polybius' history of the Carthaginian War.

Sallustius eyed the volume suspiciously, then looked coldly at Julian.

"Read it!" Julian ordered.

Sallustius remained immobile, still staring at Julian, coolly, calculatingly, as if seeking to assess what might be passing through his mind, to determine how far he might be pushed.

"READ IT!" Julian screamed, his voice cracking and his eyes bulging. The guards stopped their pacing outside and one of them peered cautiously in through the door.

Still Sallustius held his stare until Julian glanced away; then slowly and deliberately he stepped forward and picked up the volume with the thumb and forefinger of his hand, as if handling a bit of rotten carrion with tongs. He scanned the passage that had been marked in the margin with a bit of charcoal.

"I read here," said Sallustius dryly, "that the gate Scipio attacked was sheltered by a stone arch, and that he and his men were able to work on the door at their leisure while the barbarians above them were helpless to repel them, since their missiles could not strike. Scipio was indeed a wise general."

With that he turned on his heels and stalked out, leaving Julian glaring after him in silent rage.

In the end, the city Pirisabora posed no further hardship to us, once the proper resources were applied. Sallustius walked straight from Julian's tent to the quarters of the engineering brigades, and ordered that a machine the Greeks know as a *helepolis,* a "city taker," be constructed with all possible speed. Few in the army had ever seen or even imagined such a device, though Sallustius' own encyclopedic knowledge of military history allowed him to easily rattle off a description of the machines Poliorcetes had developed in Macedonia centuries before: an enormous tower constructed of strong wooden beams and covered with hides, green wicker, mud, and other noncombustible materials. Within two days it was complete, standing six stories tall, towering over even the city's ramparts. Twenty archers armed with flaming arrows and soot pots manned the topmost level, while ten feet below them a ramp was suspended by chains, to be dropped down onto the top of the battlements as soon as the device had been rolled close to the base of the walls. Fifty soldiers were picked to lead the rush from the tower into the city, and the entire army would follow close behind, either up the five flights of wooden stairs and over the ramparts, or through the city gates themselves if the attackers from the tower were able to open them from the inside.

At the mere sight of this terrible machine the inhabitants surrendered without further struggle.

The destruction of Pirisabora renewed the troops' spirits. With considerable hardship, but now eagerness to match, the troops floundered and sloshed again through the marshes and fields, commandeering dugout canoes and rafts from the inhabitants and running down and slaughtering the disorganized Persian defenders in the swamps. Fourteen miles we traveled this way, a distance that under normal circumstances would be scarcely more than a morning's easy trot, even with the crushing load of gear each man bore on his back. With the flooding and skirmishing, however, the journey took nearly two full days. Small bridges were constructed of planks cut from the spongy wood of palm trees, resting on rock pillars built in the waterways. Where the marshes were too deep, platforms were floated on inflated bladders cunningly sewn together of sheep hides coated with bitumen. We were so close to Ctesiphon we could even smell it; at times, when the wind was from the east, it bore with it faint whiffs of the spices and herbs of a marketplace, a marketplace so massive that only Ctesiphon could contain it. Julian knew that if he could reach the city before the King was able to reinforce its garrison, then its walls and all its wealth—indeed control of the entire Persian Empire—would fall to him.

It was fourteen miles, as I said, until we arrived at the ancient city of Maozamalcha, before which the army stopped and stared in awe. On every side rose steep, high rocks allowing only a narrow approach with winding detours. Huge towers rose over the outcropping nearly as high as the central citadel, itself standing on a formidable, rocky eminence. The land was slightly less severe to the rear of the city, with a slope leading down to the river, yet on these walls the defenders had amassed a fearsome array of artillery and other weapons that prevented attackers from forming up for a sustained assault. Spies informed us that the city's garrison was not the meager, underfed, and undertrained local militia that we most often found defending the battlements in such situations. Rather, the walls were defended by a large detachment of King Sapor's regulars whom he had assigned here before he departed up the Tigris, on the off chance that we might take this approach to Ctesiphon. For once, the hapless King had guessed right.

Julian slowly picked his way around the city on his horse, surrounded by a handful of generals, his deformed shadow Maximus, and a small coterie of light-armed guards, scanning the walls from all angles, careful to remain out of shooting range of the obscenity-shouting defenders on the ramparts. They stopped here and there to examine a landscape feature, the opportunity for an approach, a perceived weakness in the structure of the battlements—there were none. No city is completely impregnable, but it takes a trained eye to envision how a stronghold like this might be taken, and a strong stomach to imagine the consequences of doing so—or of failing to do so. If we were to succeed in our attack on Ctesiphon, this large garrison could not be left at our back.

Late that night, after consulting with Sallustius and his generals, Julian decided on a classic siege approach. He himself would direct the open assault and the placement of the artillery and siege engines. Just as we were leaving the tent after making this decision, the cavalry commander Victor galloped up with a small guard, their faces dimly lit by the sputtering torches they carried.

"What news, Victor?" Julian asked as the man stiffly dismounted from his foam-flecked horse. "If you miss another strategy meeting we'll assign you to the kitchens."

"A thousand pardons, Augustus," Victor mumbled calmly, above the snickers of Maximus and the others. "I went out last night on reconnaissance down the eastern road and was delayed in returning."

Julian's expression sobered. "No trouble, I hope? Any sign of Sapor advancing down the Tigris?"

Victor straightened his shoulders proudly. "No trouble, Augustus. On the contrary. I rode to the very walls of Ctesiphon and encountered no opposition."

The gathering went dead silent. Julian stared.

"To Ctesiphon and back, in one day? My God, Victor, that's seventy miles."

"Yes, sir. There are one or two more forts to be taken, but the garrisons are huddled inside like virgins, afraid to show. The roads are clear. Sapor is nowhere in sight."

Julian smiled thinly as he glanced around at his officers. "Men—Ctesiphon is ours."

IV

The instant the sun shot its first rays over the camp, like
bolts fired from a catapult, the long knife slid home. Steaming blood spewed forth in thick, ropy bursts, drenching the
spotless white folds and purple hem of Julian's linen gown
and pulsing into the large, wrought-silver basin at his feet.
The breathing of the quivering animal, stunned in advance
with a blow from a poleaxe, subsided into a choked gurgle,
and its huge eyes bulged and then clouded as the lifeblood
drained from its body. The assembled troops watched silently as the seers' florid prayers to the war god Ares rang
in their ears. A moment after the gash was inflicted in the
throat, the purple stream hissing into the basin lost momentum and subsided to a low trickle; the trembling head
flopped limply to the dust, and with an enormous shudder
the animal died.

Immediately the two Etruscan haruspices, dark, small-
framed men in conical hoods who had accompanied Julian
on all his travels since his apostasy and for whom I had no
use, leaped to their tasks with their knives held high in
enthusiasm. Slicing open the lower belly with a neat flourish, they beckoned Julian over. Well versed in his technique, he bent down on one knee before the still-quivering
animal, inserted both arms up to the elbow into the cavity,
which the largest of the two sorcerers struggled to hold
open for him, and, after a moment of grunting and tugging,

emerged with the glistening purplish liver clutched tightly
in both hands like the head of an enemy grasped triumphantly by a barbarian as a trophy. He knelt reverently before the haruspices and Maximus as the three solemnly
placed their hands on his head and then on the liver, pal-
pating it, testing its firmness, examining its color and the
thickness of its vesicles. Each man finally mumbled some
abomination to the gods and daubed a streak of blood on
Julian's forehead and temples. Standing erect he raised the
liver high above his head, blood pouring in rivulets down
his arms, dripping onto his beard and bared chest, staining
the sleeves and bodice of his ceremonial vestments, as the
assembled troops held their breaths.

"Thus ordain the gods," he shouted. "That like unto Alexander in ages past, the Persians must submit, both this
city and Ctesiphon itself. So their conquerors shall join the
ranks of the immortals, and by the holy blood of this sacred
ox shall you, my men, be strengthened and purified for the
triumph that awaits you. To conquer!"

"To conquer!" roared fifty thousand voices, a cry that
carried to the battlements of the doomed Maozamalcha.
"To conquer!" they repeated again and again, increasing in
pitch and volume, aiming to send their message, throbbing
and reverberating, to the gates of Ctesiphon itself. "To conquer!" the voices boomed, and Julian stood motionless, the
unspeakable, dripping organ held high over his head, staring at the heavens as the troops raged and raved before
him. The enormous pyre behind him, prepared in advance
with a stack of cottonlike palm wood smeared with pitch
to receive the sacrificial carcass, burst into a ball of flame
shooting into the sky, an acrid black smoke pouring in
pulses into the air and settling heavily over the men. Their
excitement had grown to a fever pitch with the rhythmic
chant, and as I glanced at the walls of the city looming high
over us, across the river flats I saw the battlements filled
with a line of silent Persians. The garrison and the city's
inhabitants, thousands of them, had been drawn from other
parts of the fortifications in their curiosity at the uproar in

the Roman camp below, the soldiers' polished mail gleaming starlike in the early rays of the sun.

Suddenly Julian dropped his bloody arms, passed the
liver to Maximus, and drawing a sword turned his back to
the men. He faced the lines of artillery and engines that
had been set up in the night parallel to the walls: a dozen
huge ballistae, their cords wound taut on the massive
winches and loaded with enormous, iron-tipped wooden
javelins; a row of "scorpions," each bearing a boulder the
weight of a man, poised in a long net to be whipped sling-
like over the top of the lever when the tension on the cords
was released; field catapults poised to let fly showers of
deadly, thick-stocked bolts; and a thousand archers, long
bows at the ready. He thrust his sword into the air in a
prearranged signal. With an earsplitting screech that silenced the roar of the men before us, the cords of the engines snapped to and screamed off their reels. Forty
massive levers from the engines shot up simultaneously.
Oak slammed against iron and iron against earth, and the
air became black with boulders and bolts, whistling toward
the astonished defenders. The mob of Persians on the wall
scarcely had time to blink before the stones slammed into
their ranks, each of them carrying away a dozen men at a
time. A huge wooden bolt shot completely through a Persian officer's chest armor and impaled three men behind
him, leaving holes in their torsos big enough to insert a
hand. One scorpion, misfiring from careless loading of the
boulder the night before, flipped into the air at the release
of its cord and hurled its chassis directly backward, crushing and mangling the body of an engineer so badly as to
defy recognition. But the worst terror was in the city itself.

Screams arose from the towers opposite us, and scarcely
had the dust of the initial impact cleared when Julian's
thousand archers, at a command, dipped the tips of their
arrows into the pots of flaming pitch that had been placed
at their feet and filled the air with a black cloud of smoking,
stinking missiles, aimed high over the heads of the defenders on the ramparts to land in the roofs and hayricks of the

city behind them. More screams of pain and terror rose into the air, this time from women behind the walls, and as the archers and artillery filled the sky with their whizzing, shattering hell, a pall of thick smoke rose from a dozen points within the walls and obscured our view.

At the first, massive eruption of artillery, the infantry troops at the sacrifice were shocked into silence and awe. Within seconds, however, a huge cheer welled up and the men broke out of the parade ground like water bursting through a dam, racing to their cohorts' assigned positions behind the artillery, prepared to leap forward at Julian's command to storm the city as soon as it had been softened by the barrage. The sun rose higher in the sky, the smoke behind the walls thickened, and the stench it carried to our lines carried the smell of death, of roasting meat, of excrement and vomit and all the unspeakable carnage and suffering of a city under siege. For hours the artillery attack continued, relentless, pounding, each stone driving into the granite-hard walls, forcing open fissures and cracks, toppling battlements—yet still the walls held, still the massive gates remained closed. The defiant defenders, during the occasional lulls in our hails of missiles, let fly taunts and obscene insults to our parentage or genitals, in ancient and crudely inflected Greek.

At first our troops, out of sheer nervous energy and anticipation of the pillage to come, were unable to remain still; when their offers to assist with the engines were rebuffed by the methodical artillery engineers, they put themselves to use hauling boulders and other ammunition for the machines to fire. Even so, the growing heat of the day under the blazing sun, and the thickness and stink of the black air began taking their toll. Frustrated and angry at the delay, the men collapsed in the dirt, tugging at their stifling armor and helmets, shading their heads under shields hastily propped on lances embedded in the ground. Shortly after noon, after a sustained artillery attack of such force that it would have leveled the walls of Rome itself, Julian rode through the ranks, furious and dripping with sweat, and issued the order to cease fire. The engineering companies collapsed exhausted on the ground, calling for water and food, and the support staff came running to assist them. Julian stood a moment watching the men eat and drink greedily but silently, and then, dismounting, he stalked wrathfully into his field tent, where he remained for the rest of the day.

Things fared no better the next morning, when our troops again watched in resentment and rage as the Roman engines and artillery poured a withering hail of missiles and boulders on the benighted city, still without fatal effect. Julian was almost crazed with impatience and fury. Five bulls he had sacrificed that morning to Ares, magnificent beasts that the haruspices argued the army could not spare for merely one offering, and for a minor city at that. He knew, for his whole life he must have known, that such offerings to false gods were of no more effect than a man's footsteps on the shifting sands, yet still he persisted in his folly. That whole day he refused to meet my eyes, the eyes of a man who would not have hesitated in calling him to task for his damnable obstinacy. He paced up and down the lines angrily, raging at the impregnable walls as a wolf prowling round a sheepfold howls at the gates, jaws thirsting for blood while lambs and ewes huddle fearfully within. He brutally abused the hapless engineers as they struggled to keep up the rate of firing he demanded, calling down the gods' curses on the steadfast Persians in their hellhole of a stronghold, refusing the entreaties of his advisers to drink water or to rest. Fear was developing in him that he would be unable to take the city without a protracted effort. What was worse: the first, early rumors had been received by his scouts that King Sapor was approaching with his massive army.

His mood broke when a short, slightly built legionary trotted up to him late in the afternoon, his hair not merely matted but encrusted with sweat and grime, flakes of drying dirt covering his torso like a skin disease, his eyes red and squinting in the bright sunlight. The watchful guard of sus-

picious Gauls at first refused to let him pass to address the
Emperor, until Julian glanced over and spied the commotion the small man was beginning to make as he raised his
voice indignantly. The Emperor smiled as he called the
guards back.

"Suffer the little ones to come unto me," he said calmly,
with a sly look my way, which I ignored. "Even the filthy
little ones. In fact—*especially* the filthy ones, if the news
this man bears is what I hope."

The trooper approached, his face still flushed in anger
at the guards, and there was no indication of obeisance in
his posture or voice as he stood before the Emperor. "It is
ready," he said simply.

"Good man," replied Julian, clapping him on his dirt-
laden shoulder without hesitation. "What is your name, soldier?"

"Exsuperius, my lord."

"Exsuperius. 'The overpowering one.' Your name is a
good omen, soldier, for this very night the Persians will
receive their comeuppance from one who is indeed overpowering. 'Exsuperius' will be our password this night, and
you, soldier, will personally open the gates of this foul city
to the Roman army."

Exsuperius nodded, slowly and with a great dignity utterly at odds with his ditchdigger's appearance. Without
another word he turned and walked sedately past Julian's
fidgety guards and disappeared into the bowels of the vast
Roman camp.

It was once believed that the Romans were aided in their
struggle against the Lucanians in the Pyrrhic War by Ares
himself, though far be it from me to understand why such
a god, even if he did exist, would compromise his majesty
by consorting with mortals in such a way. The story was
that in the very heat of battle an armed soldier of tremendous stature was seen carrying a huge scaling ladder and
leading an impossible charge up the city walls to ultimate
victory. The next day, during review, no such soldier could
be found, though rewards and honor would have been his

to receive—hence the belief that he must have been a god.

No such problem confronted Julian, however, for Exsuperius lived up to all the Emperor's expectations of him, and happily received a laurel crown for his efforts. Long into the night, after the enemy's still-enthusiastic catcalls and jeering had finally subsided, the little miner led fifteen hundred picked troops slithering on their bellies through a tight, sandy tunnel a hundred yards long that had been hastily braced with bridging timbers carried by the river fleet. Shortly before they were expected to arrive at the end of the tunnel, trumpets sounded the attack and the entire army rushed to arms, throwing up simultaneous assaults on three sides of the city and raising a terrifying clamor to distract the wary inhabitants from the clinking of metal tools beneath their feet.

The ruse was successful. As the Persian garrison leaped to the walls to repel the night attack, the mine was opened, and Exsuperius and his band sprang out to find themselves in the bedroom of an elderly woman so fragile, or so weary, that she failed even to wake up at the sound of her floor bursting open and three cohorts of armed Romans storming through. They made their way into the streets, which were empty, as every able-bodied inhabitant of the city was fighting at the walls or cowering in their houses. After finding their bearings, the invaders raced to the main gate, slew the sentries from behind without difficulty, and threw open the doors.

The Persians stood shocked on their battlements, forgetting even to fling their missiles, as the Romans rushed into the city in a frenzy. Julian himself was in the front ranks, shouting his demands for the enemy to surrender, but his words were drowned by the screaming of women and children and the clamor raised by his troops as they destroyed everything and killed everyone in their path without regard to age or sex. He sat his horse in the middle of the tumult the remainder of the night, coldly surveying the destruction, watching expressionless as Persian soldiers on the high battlements drew their daggers and slew themselves, stabbing their own throats or hurling themselves to the ground.

Nabdates, the governor of the city, was brought in the morning with eighty of the King's soldiers, all of them badly mauled and beaten by their captors, some with eyes already put out or ears lopped off. They had been found cowering in a hidden cellar, hoping to survive the carnage above them until the Romans departed, when they would be able to emerge in safety. Julian put his face up close to Nabdates, who averted his swollen and blackened eyes, and then he turned back to Sallustius, his lip curled in a disdainful sneer.

"Turn them loose," he said.

Sallustius stared. "My lord?"

"You heard me. Turn them loose. Give them horses and a day's rations and let them go. They will bring to Ctesiphon news of the Emperor's strength and the fury of the Roman gods. And their very survival will be a permanent testimony to their cowardice."

At this Nabdates himself spoke up.

"No, mighty Augustus," he pleaded in courtly Greek. "Kill me now."

"Nonsense. Do it yourself. You are free to use the cliffs or ropes as you wish."

"Augustus, I cannot face the Great King, or my people . . ."

But Julian had already turned away dismissively, making his way slowly down the street through the throngs of guffawing, drunken soldiers who slapped his back and reached for his hand. He picked his way carefully through the rubble of what had once been an elegant main thoroughfare, now completely demolished, roofs thrown down into the street, pots and furniture broken and hurled through the crumbled window frames. Everywhere were the dead— bodies cut and smashed, men's faces destroyed by bricks and stones, women lying naked, their pale bodies bloody and askew, violated and then fatally discarded through fourth-story windows. The Emperor kept his gaze straight as he shouldered through the mob of cheering and rampaging soldiers, showing no emotion at either the dreadful carnage or the evidence of his astounding victory, until he finally arrived at a small forum where a Persian-speaking Roman tribune was directing the collection of captives and plunder from all quarters of the city.

Even a town preparing for war, ostensibly hiding its valuables and sending its nobles to safe havens, contains booty sufficient as to make most soldiers' eyes glaze over, and doomed Maozamalcha was no exception. The pile was already large, and growing every moment as legionaries entered from every side street. Their arms were laden with gold and silver plate from the palaces and houses of the rich, rings and bracelets dripping with blood from the dead limbs from which they had been hacked, golden and marble statuary from the temples, and all manner of costly fabrics, silks, and linens, some unused and wrapped on their original bolts, others in the form of beautiful gowns and vestments still warm from the bodies of their final wearers. Girls and women huddled wretchedly around the heap of riches, keening and wailing in their misery, many swollen and bleeding if they had presented any resistance to their attackers, most of them still undamaged. The value of their beauty had been recognized by even the most brutal of their captors, whose craving for slave gold exceeded even the ache in their loins. A few young children had also been included in the group, having followed their female relatives and been spared by their own resourcefulness or the soldiers' mercy.

When Julian was recognized, the tribune and soldiers backed tactfully away from the plunder, and even the desolate females quieted their wailing to a slightly more respectful sob. It is known by all, of course, that the Emperor has first pick of the spoils, half of which belong to him, and after his lot has been separated the remainder is to be split among the rest of the army in accordance with rank and deed.

He walked solemnly around the gleaming pile, picking

up a trinket here and there and, tossing it back onto the heap, reaching down to touch the chin of a weeping young girl and force her face up so he could inspect her more closely. An unusual vase caught his eye, and after holding it to the sunlight for a moment for a better view, he carefully set it upright in a more sheltered location. One ragged young boy and his older sister sat slightly apart from the others. The boy alone seemed to be untroubled, his large, limpid eyes fixed not on the Emperor, as were those of every other prisoner and bystander, but on the lips of the girl as she rocked back and forth, crooning softly in Greek an ancient Christian children's hymn.

> *The Mother of Christ,*
> *Al-le-lu-ia*
> *Her most precious child,*
> *Al-le-lu-ia*
> *The Father in Heaven,*
> *Alleluia, Al-le-lu-ia.*

The girl became silent as Julian stopped directly in front of them, yet the boy remained staring expectantly at his sister's lips, ignoring the presence of the Roman Emperor, the man whose troops had destroyed his city and killed his family. The boy did not move, even as the girl shrank back in fear at Julian's approach. Julian stared, wondering at the boy's audacity, or whether he was simply an imbecile. He called the Persian-speaking tribune over to him.

"Ask the boy who he is, why he alone is not afraid."

The tribune looked down at the lad skeptically, and barked out a harsh command. The boy peered at him quizzically.

"That's not how you talk to a child," Julian reprimanded him. "Soften your voice, tribune, and question him. I am curious."

The tribune stood stiffly for a moment, collecting his wits, and then in a voice only slightly less jarring continued his guttural interrogation. Julian sighed.

"My lord," the girl mumbled fearfully, and as she looked up I could see why her voice had been so small, so tuneless, for her face was frightfully battered, her upper lip split to her nose from a blow. I reflected that with her beauty gone, she had little chance of surviving the distribution of spoils, and perhaps that was all for the better. "My lord," she said again in Persian that the tribune could barely hear, "the boy is deaf and mute."

"Ah," said Julian as he looked more closely at the lad.

Suddenly, however, the child seemed to perk up, for looking straight at the tribune, whose lips he had read, he carefully and silently pantomimed his life—his father was a presbyter in the small Christian church—I reflected that he had most likely traveled abroad in his studies, hence the Greek rhyme—his mother was a weaver, he had a small sister, or perhaps a brother. . . .

Julian watched, fascinated, as the boy's hands slowly and eloquently spun the story, many of the motions and concepts unrecognizable though all of them extraordinarily structured and deliberate. His eyes were still large and expressionless, but his lips silently formed the precise Persian words of his tale, imitating the mouthings of those around him who in the past had sought to communicate with him through his veil of silence.

"How old is he, tribune? Ask him. He looks about the same age my own son would have been."

The officer barked out the question in a loud voice such as is used by ignorant folk who believe that speaking in such a way will allow them to be better understood by old people and foreigners. The boy carefully studied his lips, and before the tribune had even finished, the child held up six fingers, turning solemnly to Julian. He then began rapidly making other counting motions with his hands, which I took to mean his indication of the precise number of months and days since he had turned that age. The lad was clever.

The tribune glared, as if at a street mime in Rome mocking passersby at the taverns. Finally, weary and uncomprehending of the boy's gestures, the officer turned.

"Perhaps, Augustus, if you would care to point out which articles are of particular interest to you, I could set them aside. Some jewelry, or a fine virgin?"

Julian snorted with disdain. "I have no need of virgins. Nor did Alexander or Scipio Africanus. It is enough to be victorious in war without staining some poor girl with my lust. My wants are few."

Bending down to a small cedar box he opened it to find it laden with coins, gold *darics,* and silver *sigloi,* a veritable fortune, along with several precious stones and a number of loose pearls—the entire inventory of a jewelry merchant, perhaps, or the carelessly hidden life savings of a wealthy nobleman. He squatted down and absentmindedly picked through the hoard with his forefinger, occasionally lifting an item to his eyes for closer inspection and then placing it back in the box. He finally stood up, holding in his hand three coins, the smallest, oldest, and most worn of the lot. He turned to the tribune.

"I shall take these," he said, "for they come from the time of Alexander and the fact that they have not been melted down for new coinage is a sign from the gods that they have been preserved for me."

The tribune stared at the tiny coins, and then glanced helplessly at the growing pile of plunder. "And what else, my lord?"

Julian smiled. "Just this," he said, placing his hand on the young deaf-mute's head, and leading him away, "for he speaks most eloquently in a language known only to the gods."

As we marched out the next day, the army was shadowed and harassed by a ragged and half-crazed band of Persians. They were unarmed, and so had passed through our outlying scouts and sentries without challenge, playing the part of desert traders or merchants, but as soon as they approached within earshot of the Roman column they began setting up the familiar hooting and catcalls that had so annoyed us outside Maozamalcha.

"What in the gods' name is that?" wondered Julian aloud, and a Gallic guard rode over to the unlikely mob of tormenters to gain a better look at them.

He galloped back with a wry smile.

"Nabdates and his men, my lord. They say they aim to accompany us to Ctesiphon."

"Tell them they are forbidden to follow us. Tell them to go away."

The sentry rode back to the Persians. A moment later the jeering rose up even louder, and the Gaul returned, shrugging helplessly.

The entire day the Persians followed our every move, loudly insulting our fighting ability, our strength, and our grandmothers. Julian had them run off, but they returned. Two of them he ordered blinded, in the hopes that would frighten off the rest, but Nabdates calmly blinded two more of his own men in return, and they continued to laugh and jeer as they doubled up on the horses of their comrades, blood streaming from their empty sockets. Finally, as we prepared to make camp that evening, Julian sighed.

"I refuse to allow them to torture me all night with their infernal wailing," he said resignedly.

Sallustius looked at him guardedly. "What do you suggest?"

"Give them what they want."

Sallustius ordered Nabdates to be ostentatiously thrashed and then burned alive, to which the poor man submitted with cries of thanks and praise to his gods. After a few hours of grief-stricken howling, the rest of his men were driven to the hills by Victor's cavalry, where they scattered and did not return.

Now nothing separated us from the great city of Ctesiphon.

V

I misspoke. There was nothing separating us from Ctesiphon except the Euphrates and Tigris, two of the largest rivers known to man. At this point of their flow, the enormous courses come within a mere several miles of each other, forming in their midst a rich region dedicated solely to the King's defense and pleasure, a fertile river island of smiling vineyards, bountiful orchards, and shade groves, dotted here and there with royal hunting lodges and reserves teeming with stocked game from all corners of the earth. Yet how to cross these two rivers and mount the steep heights of the left bank of the Tigris to the strategic location of Ctesiphon? And how to convey our valuable fleet across the land between the two flows? This, I confess, Brother, had kept me deeply worried ever since Julian had decided upon this route down the right bank of the Euphrates—in fact, I was not alone, for the Emperor's generals had been whispering their own fears concerning this very matter for weeks now. Only Julian and Sallustius appeared unconcerned about the approach to Ctesiphon; and so it should be, for only they had read their history.

Two centuries and a half before this time, when the Emperor Trajan had himself followed this precise path in attacking King Sapor's ancestor, he had had the foresight to bring with him a remarkable detachment of engineers, led by a hydrographic genius whose name has been lost to us, but whose works remain more enduring than those of Trajan himself. This man had seen from his study of the elevations and the lay of the land that a canal could be cut between the two rivers, diverting water from the Euphrates to convey ships to the Tigris. Indeed, Trajan had performed this very task, and though the great work had later been filled in by the Persians, a century later Severus reexcavated it in a similar effort. Again the Persians filled it in, this time blocking the water head with enormous boulders and disguising the actual course of the canal so that future generations would be unable to find it. They had not counted on Julian's persistence, however. After quickly assembling a pontoon bridge across the Euphrates, over which his entire army crossed, he captured and interrogated numerous peasants and farmers in the area. By doing so, he was able to ascertain the precise path where the soil was looser and more fertile than that of the surrounding river plains, and setting his own engineers to the task, they discovered the traces of the ancient canal and the boulders that had been rolled into place to block the flow.

It was an easy matter to dig it out again, once forty thousand men were put to work on it. A matter of a week of solid mudslinging, to which even Julian contributed his share, stripping naked and standing shoulder-deep in the enormous ditch like the lowliest slave, exhorting his men to haul the rubble and dirt of the generations for the glory of Rome. With a rush and a surge when the last boulder was removed, the mighty Euphrates immediately dropped two feet in depth downstream of the canal entrance and the enormous fleet sailed merrily upon a tide of muddy water to its junction with the Tigris, where it anchored scarcely two miles upstream and across from the city of Ctesiphon itself.

When he arrived at the Tigris in the lead vessel, festooned with the banners and standards of all his legions and lined with a ceremonial guard of burly legionaries, Julian was hardly able to concentrate on the task at hand. He gave scarcely a glimpse toward the massive walls of the city now visible just downriver, but rather focused an unrelenting gaze on the horizon to the northwest, anxiously anticipating the arrival of Sapor at the head of his hordes at any time. He prayed aloud that Sapor might have been delayed, or even defeated, by the forces of Armenia in alliance with his general Procopius, from whom he had not heard a word since the split of the armies weeks before.

"It's suicide," Victor exclaimed, glancing at the other generals gathered in the tent to ascertain their support. "Utter suicide!"

Outside, we could hear the cheers of the troops gathered on the near bank of the Tigris in the waning light of the early evening as the horse races continued. Julian had ordered a spontaneous series of games to celebrate our imminent arrival at Ctesiphon, hastily laying out a hippodrome-sized horse track, sandpits for the wrestling and boxing events, and a long, straight course along the shore for the footraces. He had gone so far as to delineate precisely where the spectators—the bulk of the footsore army—were to stand for the betting and lusty cheering of their comrades, carefully arranging it so that the blare of the trumpets and the roar of the excited troops would carry over the water to the left bank of the river, even to the city itself. He had also taken the precaution of posting military guards at discrete intervals along the water's edge to prevent spectators from gathering on that side to watch the events. He wanted the Persian garrison on the other side of the river to have an unimpeded view of the activity, and in this he was rewarded, for like low-caste Romans able to afford only the cheap seats at the games, the entire Ctesiphon garrison, some twenty or thirty thousand men, had gathered in ranks a quarter mile across the water, watching the proceedings with huge interest. They hauled stools and blankets to the water's edge and passed wine flasks among themselves, cheering on their favorites and audibly moaning when they lost, and in general behaving precisely as if they were guests—which they were, by personal invitation of the Roman Emperor. He observed it all with amused satisfaction.

Another deep roar drowned out Victor's comments in the tent. When it had subsided, Julian glared at the other generals, pointedly ignoring Victor's pessimism.

"Delaying," he said dismissively, "will not make the river any narrower, nor the opposite bank any lower. Time will only make the enemy's position stronger, their numbers greater. Our success cannot be achieved by waiting— we must act now. The enemy is relaxed, thinking our men will spend tonight in revelry. There is no better opportunity. Rome cannot wait." He then turned away.

Sallustius stood up and made to leave. "Unload the largest vessels," he ordered the others, "and form them into three squadrons. Keep the men reveling—the more noise, the better. It will keep the garrison off its guard. At midnight we move. Victor, you lead with five vessels. Directly across and a mile downstream. Take the beachhead silently to divide the garrison from the city. The rest of the fleet, carrying the army, will then join you, squadron by squadron. Now, move."

The generals filed silently out into the evening's dusty heat, leaving Julian and me alone in the tent. He bent silently over his work for a time while I reviewed some notes, occasionally pausing to look up as some particularly raucous cheering wafted in through the door from outside. After a while he sat back against the frame post and stretched, rubbing his eyes wearily. Suddenly he stopped and gazed at me, as if having just noticed my presence.

"Caesarius," he said, almost apologetically. "Still the only man in the entire camp who will stay awake with me. Still the truest friend I have." He grinned at me, and shook his head slowly.

I smiled back, but said nothing, and he noticed the air of hesitancy about me, my unwillingness to fully accept his olive branch, to repair the friendship that had been so deeply cracked at the palace the previous year. A shadow passed over his face, and his eyes grew troubled.

"And yet there is still that distance between us," he said. "That barrier, which I created, which I am unable to tear down. You still begrudge me my rudeness at that wretched banquet—Caesarius, if I haven't told you before, I will do so now: I am truly sorry for my behavior that night."

I shook my head. "It's not that—that is long past. But you're right, the barrier is there. I can't help but regret your hostility toward your past, to all things Christian, to—"

He interrupted my words with an exasperated sigh, standing up suddenly and walking to the side of his table, where he commenced pacing.

"Does it always come down to that, Caesarius? You still refuse to compromise, to even meet me halfway? I have outlawed no religion, I have thrown no man to the lions or the gladiators—is it not enough that I allow all sects to peacefully coexist within the Empire? Why must I kiss the feet of the Pope before you will be satisfied?"

"Because God does not coexist with other gods," I said simply.

"No?" He whirled on me, his face flushed and excited. "Caesarius, we have marched through the desert and conquered the lands of the most powerful king Persia has known in generations. We have destroyed every stronghold we have encountered along the way—all to the steady beat of our paeans to Ares, and with our hands washed in the blood of the sacrificial oxen. Surely, if your God were so jealous of other gods, he would not have allowed me such success in battle? Caesarius, Caesarius—be rational! By insisting that I worship as you do, that I enslave myself to your God, you mock me! You mock everything I have accomplished thus far!"

I remained seated where I was, gazing at him calmly as he resumed his agitated pacing against the short side of the tent wall. Then, as now, eloquent words did not come to my lips, and I resolved to take your advice, Brother, to speak simply and to utter only the truth.

"And for my part," I said evenly, "I see nothing but

God's benevolence in allowing you such success. And yet you demand that I shift the credit for your glory to some long-discredited Greek deity. If I were to change gods like the shifting of the winds, that would say very little for my character in your eyes, would it not? Would you have me convert to your gods at your merest word and whim? How would that reflect on me, or on your choice in comrades?"

He stopped his pacing again and stared at me a long moment, then relaxed and gave a low chuckle.

"For someone who has always claimed ignorance of the art of rhetoric, that was very well put," he said grudgingly. "So meanwhile, I am made to look the fool if you remain the token Christian in my court, yet I am damned for allowing a moral weakling if I insist that you convert. Either way it is I who loses. You strike me with an arrow fletched with a feather from my own wing."

"I had no such intent. I have made no insistence on your beliefs. Why concern yourself with mine?"

"Ah, but you *have* made insistence, Caesarius," he said, his eyes narrowing. "Not in so many words, but in your expression. You accuse me every time you look at me. You speak to me, if at all, with the barest minimum of words. You walk away and hide during my sacrifices, refusing the place of honor set for you with my other advisers, leaving an unsightly vacant chair. Everything you do is insistence upon me."

I stood up. "Perhaps it is best, then, that I not attend you any further. I will provide my services among the camp surgeons."

Julian reflected on this briefly, and then his face softened somewhat. "No, I won't have you relegated to working with those sawbones. The problem is mine, Caesarius, and mine alone, if my own peace of mind is so disturbed by a single man of stubbornness in my midst. Your services are needed here."

He resumed his seat, and the openness and yearning I had seen flicker briefly across his face were immediately removed, like the snuffing of a candle, to be replaced by a neutral, determined expression. I stood silently for a moment, waiting for him to say something more. He did not look up further from his work. His own silence, however, I took as a sign that my presence was no longer needed, and I slipped out the door.

The five vessels slipped quietly from their moorings, each carrying eighty picked men, their weapons and shields carefully wrapped to prevent clanking, their oars muffled with rags to reduce splashing. The troops remaining in the camp had been warned of what was to come, yet even as they sharpened their weapons and assembled in ranks on their own vessels, they continued to feed the hundreds of camp-fires lining the shore, and kept up the hoots and laughter of revelry, automatically and absentmindedly, shouting bets and curses to each other and singing bawdy songs that coursed their way across the silent, black river.

The five darkened ships pointed their prows straight into the river for fifty or a hundred feet until they were clear of the sandbanks along the edge, then eased downstream, aiming to land at a point reconnoitered stealthily just before dark, where the banks seemed to rise more gradually. No moon lit their way, for the night had been carefully chosen. Three scouts had swum the distance to the landing beach at dusk, each bearing a sealed jar containing a smoldering coal, and an oilskin packet containing dry kindling smeared with pitch. If any of the swimmers still survived after hiding submerged in the reeds for several hours, they would stealthily light a signal fire to guide the landing boats into place.

Julian stood among the fleet assembled at the shore, surrounded by his generals, staring intently into the darkness. The forced shouts and singing around us were intolerable, clashing and dissonant, for the tense moment cried out only for silence, for concentration. Across the river, at the Persian camp, all remained as before, fires burning gently down to coals, the occasional cries of the pickets calling the watchwords to one another in the darkness. I struggled to block out the harsh, irritating cacophony around me, focusing on other sounds and sensations, but my eyes could see only blackness as I peered down the river in the direction the ships had disappeared. My overly sensitized ears were tormented not merely by the revelry, but by the insignificant sounds of mere being and existence—the slow lapping of the water against the sandy bank, the soft squelching of the sandals of the man next to me as he rocked irritatingly back and forth on the balls of his feet.

Suddenly Julian stepped forward into the water.

"Look!" he said in a hoarse whisper. "Is that the signal fire?"

Faintly, like nothing more than a spark thrown up from one of our own bonfires, I could see a tiny orange speck far across the water. It flickered for a moment, seemed to disappear, then suddenly grew larger as it made contact with the tinder and kindling, and its maker frantically blew it and added the pitchy wood he had painstakingly carried on his back. Within a moment it was visible to all, reflecting its twin in the rippling blackness of the water below it.

"The swimmers made it!" Julian shouted in relief, and all around us men clapped one another on the shoulders, for the five advance vessels would be landing in moments to secure the beach. We began climbing onto our own ships, preparing to cast off, when suddenly the eastern sky lit up with a thousand balls of fire, arching through the air in streaking, yellow trails. The men around us erupted in panic.

"Fire arrows! The Persians have attacked them with fire arrows!" someone shouted. More fiery trails streaked through the sky and a bluish conflagration spread to reveal the hellish roaring of a ship destroyed. Running figures began to be visible in front of the flames, and faint shouts were carried to us on the wind.

"No!" Julian cried, leaping out of the water and clambering over the gunwales of the nearest ship. "That's the signal! They've secured the beach! They're signing for us to come, that the heights are ours for the taking!"

Sallustius stared at him, agape. "Lord Augustus! That's not—"

"Release the fleet!" Julian bellowed, shouting him down. "That's the signal! All hands to the oars! Ctesiphon is ours!"

With a roar the men leaped at the ships, pushing those already loaded out into the swift-moving current, surging onto those still awaiting their loads. In a moment the fleet was in the river, the men no longer concerned with stealth, but lighting lanterns, chanting the count of the oars as the vessels raced with the current to the designated landing spot. Across the Tigris the Persian camp was in an uproar, men and horses scurrying madly in all directions in front of the fires, a confused shouting and clamor rising up and drifting across the water to fill the gaps between our men's chants.

By the time we arrived Victor's ships were only fiery hulks, destroyed by the pots of naphtha and flaming arrows hurled at them by the large detachment of Persians cunningly posted to patrol this portion of the river in case such an invasion was to occur. Victor's men, however, had managed to leap out into the reeds and attack and kill many of the enemy, who had run splashing gleefully into the water to plunder the Roman vessels before they burned to the waterline. These survivors bought time for the rest of the fleet to safely land, as Julian had predicted with his fortuitous lie. They took the heights of the bank before the bulk of the Persian garrison could race back down the road to intercept us. By the time the garrison arrived, it was too late for them: thirty thousand Roman troops had already landed and leaped ashore, and more were arriving every moment on the vessels that were left, on barges and livestock rafts, some men even paddling across on their curved, wooden shields, towed by ropes dangling off the backs of the vessels if there was no room for them on board.

The night was long, but the beachhead held. As the first rays of the morning sun peered over the massive walls of

Ctesiphon, a mere half mile distant, the entire Roman army was drawn up in battle array at the top of the high river-bank, the Tigris below them filled across its width by half a thousand bobbing transport craft. Despite Victor's initial hesitation, he had performed magnificently, clearing the ground of defenders and bringing the incoming troops to order. Artillery weapons and heavy equipment were being assembled by the engineers, some even before being removed from their landing craft. Even livestock were now beginning to be ferried across, a deliberate indication to the Persians of our intent to remain on the Tigris' left bank.

The Ctesiphon garrison, for its part, had recovered from the turmoil of the night before, and to the Persians' credit, the size of the forces opposing us had grown considerably from what we had estimated the previous day, to a level close to or even larger than that of our own army. Either a large body of troops had been held in reserve inside the city walls, or the local governor had quickly summoned garrisons from neighboring towns and villages to augment his own forces. As the Romans stood calmly in formation, awaiting the command to attack, we watched with considerable trepidation as the Persians made their own preparations. The advantage of the field was theirs, situated as they were at the top of a long, upward slope that rose to the very gates of the city, and supported by a series of bulwarks and ditches that had been dug over the past several days as they anticipated the Roman approach. A half mile uphill is an eternity to run in full armor while facing withering Persian arrow fire, and the defenders intended to make us sweat blood for every step of ground. Thousands of onlookers from the city, even women in finery, had set up positions on top of the walls, shaded under awnings and umbrellas, to watch the affair.

Opposing us the Persians had set up thick ranks of archers, their tight-fitting, fish-scale armor polished to such a brilliance that it hurt our eyes. They were supported by glaring detachments of infantry, bearing the foot-to-shoulder curved shields of the King's guard, sturdy though lightweight contraptions of wicker hung with hardened, polished rawhide for strength. The officers' white stallions were protected by the same wrought leather, and the officers themselves wore helmets and armor gilded and bejeweled with stones of such size that we could make out their colors from where we stood. Most terrifying of all, however, were the squads of elephants looming skittish and impatient behind the serried ranks of troops, looking for all the world like moving hills with their huge, gray bodies. Our troops eyed them nervously, for we had heard that such beasts were used by King Sapor, though we had hoped that they had been taken with him on his march to meet us up the Tigris.

Despite the chaos and turmoil of our crossing only hours before, Julian had left no detail forgotten in preparing his own battle lines. He had taken care to identify his weakest forces, the Asian troops who had joined us in Antioch, and to place them not in the rear, where they could panic and retreat with no one to stop them, nor in the van, where they might stumble in their fear and lead the entire army into rout; but rather disbursed in small groups amongst all his other companies, between the beefy Gauls who had stood with him steadfast ever since Strasbourg and on whom he could count to remain loyal even in the face of a charging bull elephant. Julian himself, shadowed by a squadron of light-armed auxiliaries and his council, ranged widely from one end of the lines to the other, bullying a laggard squadron into formation here, shouting encouragement to a cavalry officer there. His relentless energy drove the waiting troops into a fever of anticipation.

Suddenly he stopped in front of his lines, the eyes of all the troops upon him. Sallustius and Victor rode up and flanked him on either side with their skittish mounts. They also stopped, facing the troops. Silence fell over the field as Julian slowly surveyed the lines of sunburned, dusty men, men who had marched with him five hundred miles from Antioch, across burning sands and leech-infested marshes, some of whom had traveled with him even thrice that distance more, from the farthest western reaches of the Empire. All stood silent, watching, as a smile slowly spread across his face, a gash of white teeth gleaming through the brown beard that had grown thick and unruly on the march. Wordlessly he grinned at them, this trained orator and rhetorician, a man who had never in his life been at a loss for words and had never failed to take the opportunity to lecture to his men, to encourage them in battle, to admonish them, even to give them a history lesson. His broad smile demonstrated, however, more than any words of praise, his love and pride for them and for all they had accomplished, and wordlessly they grinned back. As they responded, he raised his right arm to the men in the Roman salute, a gesture reserved only for the men themselves to give to their own conquering general. After a moment of stunned silence, with an almost audible intake of breath from the vast forces, they burst forth in a roar capable of shaking the thick walls of Ctesiphon itself, a bellow that made Julian's mount rear in startlement, though his broad grin and outstretched arm did not falter. After a moment, however, his smile disappeared back into his beard, and lifting his fist straight up in the air, above his head, he brought it down to his hip in a slashing motion, the field signal for attack.

Immediately the ox-hide drums sounded their deep, anapestic rhythm, the ominous, repetitive, three-beat tattoo that marks the Pyrrhic march step. Developed by the Spartans, it is dancelike in its movement, hypnotic in its relentless, deadly rhythm. Three steps forward, pause for a beat. Such concentration on the rhythm, each man keeping in step with his comrades, gives a soldier substance to occupy his mind, distraction from the approach of painful death. Three steps, pause. Gleaming shields swinging deliberately from left to right in strict unison. Sixty thousand men marching thus in utter precision, the strange, trance-inducing beat and vast walls of swaying shields striking terror into the watching enemy. Three steps, pause. Thud, thud, thud, silence. The low chanting of the hymn to Ares served as an undercurrent to the beat, growled rather than

bellowed, felt as a vibration in the gut rather than heard.
The vast, swaying monster of metal and death advanced
slowly and implacably toward the lines of astonished defenders.

The Persians didn't stand a chance.

The first volley of arrows, a thousand whistling missiles,
struck our front ranks full on. From this distance they did
slight damage, sticking harmlessly in the troops' heavy
shields or skittering off to the ground. A few men fell,
though the mesmerizing rhythm of the drums did the work
for which it was designed, and there was no faltering in the
steps. The ranks behind simply stepped over the fallen, and
moved up to take their place. The Persians paused for a
moment in their shooting, dumbstruck at the display.

Another hundred yards the men marched, shields swaying in perfect unison. Thump, thump, thump, pause. The
Persians fired another volley, this time from a more lethal
range. More men stumbled and fell. Victor, I saw, who was
as heedless as the Emperor in riding at the front of his
forces and engaging the enemy directly, caught an arrow
in the right shoulder and lurched back on his horse in pain.
Julian saw it too and whipped his horse toward the front to
investigate, but Victor recovered and waved him off, sitting
bolt upright on his mount now, the arrow emerging straight
out in front of him. Julian stared a long moment to be sure
he was able to ride, then raised his sword high in the air
toward Victor, the long-awaited signal to charge.

Victor did not hesitate. Spurring his horse forward he
raced to the front of the Roman lines, transferring his sword
to his left hand as his right arm dangled useless and bloodied at his side. Raising the weapon high in the air, he
opened his mouth wide to bellow the command to charge,
though before the words reached my ears it was drowned
by the shrill howl of the Gauls' battle cry, which the entire
army had taken up as its own.

Breaking their three-step rhythm, the men burst into a
mad dash, shields held high, straight into the midst of the
enemy arrows, which now rained down on them in a thick

hail, a cloudburst of whizzing death. Long had we known that the Persians' greatest strength lies in the skill of their archers, and the most effective though painful method of defeating them is to charge into their very teeth, straight into the bows, and simply bowl the devils over, for the archers have little defense besides light wicker shields, which they prop up before them on the ground, braced with one foot. Such a charge is terrifying—into the very maws of death, hiding your face in the concave shelter of your shield, running blindly forward and struggling to align yourself with your comrades on either side, peering occasionally over the rim to gauge your distance. The steady pelting of the missiles on your shield and armor intensifies and thickens, and sometimes arrowheads emerge through to pierce your cheek or your eye if you huddle too closely behind the deceptive wall of ox hide and bronze you are carrying.

With the sudden clash of the lines a huge cloud of dust arose on the plain and I lost track of the battle, concentrating instead on keeping Julian in sight, should my services be required. He ranged back and forth across the field, straining to peer into the roiling haze, shouting furious oaths in his frustration at being unable to see. At one point he leaped into the thick of it on his horse, and I despaired of seeing him emerge alive, but emerge he did, several moments later, hacking viciously at a pair of Persian cavalry riders who were flanking him and attempting to trip up his horse with their lances. They were quickly dispatched by his guard, who had been as disconcerted as I when he had disappeared into the dust and as relieved when he rode out again, though to their horror he quickly dove back into the fray and emerged once again many moments later, his sword and greaves covered in gore.

The fighting that day was horrendous, hand-to-hand under the broiling sun and that fatal dust cloud. When the filth rose occasionally, lifted by the faint wafting of a breeze, one could see mountains of corpses and writhing horses in the ditches and at the bulwarks where they fell, so covered by layers of blood and filth that I was unable to make out to whose side they belonged. In the end, the dust cloud began slowly moving back, yielding toward the thick-stoned walls of Ctesiphon, as the Persians retreated. The cloud moved gradually at first, then faster, until with a final clash and a weary shout the Persian lines finally broke, and from the rear of the haze thousands of enemy raced panic-stricken toward their city, and I saw the enormous gates begin to swing ponderously open to receive them.

"The gates!" Julian cried, rushing toward the battle line, which was quickly moving away from him as the men raced to the walls to head off the Persians. "Victor—seize the gates!"

It would have been impossible to hear him above the mad fray, but Victor was still there with his men, now slumped painfully over his horse's neck, supported by a guard who rode alongside him. The wounded general, weak from loss of blood, struggled to shout out his orders. The rout swirled around him as the Romans followed hard on the terrified enemies' heels, hacking at their backs and calves, hamstringing hundreds and tripping them up, then quickly slashing them to immobilize them and leave them to die in their own spilled juices. The Persians ran headlong toward the city and began pouring through the gates as the townsfolk on the walls above wept and tore their hair, raining rubble and bricks down on the Romans who were as yet too far down the slope to be hit.

"The gates!" Julian called as he thundered forward on his mount, his voice hoarse from his exertions but his eyes glinting in triumph at having thus achieved his goal. "Look, Caesarius! The city is ours!"

Victor, in a supreme effort, pushed himself up from his horse's neck and rode directly in front of his line of men, between them and the fleeing Persians, the now broken arrow shaft still protruding forlornly from his injured shoulder. Stopping his mount and facing his troops, he raised his left arm, holding the sword sideways. It was the signal to halt. The exhausted Romans did so immediately, some almost collapsing in their weariness, falling to their knees, and then to their sides in fatigue, mingling indiscriminately with the thousands of cadavers already occupying the height.

Victor sat swaying on his horse, triumphantly surveying the terrible carnage before him, as the last of the Persians scrambled up the hill toward the walls. As they limped and scurried inside, the huge gates again swung heavily shut; Julian stopped and sat thunderstruck, watching the scene before him, and a single, enraged, sobbing bellow filled the air, echoing over the field.

"Victor, you fool . . . *you fucking fool!* The gates!"

Two and a half thousand Persians had been killed, to our seventy Romans. The ground was covered with enemy cadavers, and wealth greater than that of all the cities we had taken on our march thus far was stripped from the bodies of the officers alone. Still, Julian was desolate, for Ctesiphon remained unconquered, its vast walls impregnable, its defenses intact. Victor was delirious from loss of blood and the pain of his wound, but in a lucid moment he justified his halt of the attack because he felt the exhausted men would have been endangered had they continued their mad rush into the circuit of the walls and been overwhelmed in the streets of the strange city. The argument had merit, but Julian was inconsolable.

After raging in his tent for an hour, talking and muttering to himself while the generals cowered outside in the doorway, Sallustius entered.

"My lord—the men have fought hard . . . fearfully hard. They will require some words from you, perhaps a sacri—"

"And so they shall have one," interrupted Julian, "so they shall have one. Tonight let them sleep the sleep of the dead, for this they deserve even more than the dead themselves. At first light we shall have a sacrifice such as has not been seen this entire march!"

The next morning as Dawn, the saffron-robed child of morning, spread her rosy fingers across the purple sky, the men were rousted from their sleep and gathered haggardly at the enormous altar that had been set up almost within an arrow's distance of the very gates of Ctesiphon. They limped and groaned into formation, stretching their protesting muscles, some of them bearing armor still slathered with the gore of their efforts the day before, but their quiet chatter was content as they looked forward to the sacrifice and the distribution of plunder that would follow soon afterwards. I stayed to watch, Brother; for one of those rare occasions I willingly stayed to watch Julian's sacrifice, for in truth, in that vast, empty plain, occupied only by our army and the enormous walls of the huge city, there was nowhere else for me to go. I stood among the ranks of a body of archers, rather than take one of the places of honor he always reserved for his inner court, Maximus, Sallustius, Oribasius. In any case, he was so accustomed to my absence from these bloody ceremonies that I suspect he would have been startled to know that this time I was watching the entire proceeding.

At the very moment the sun's rays shot over the horizon, Julian slowly climbed the steps that led to the makeshift wooden platform on which the sacrifice to the war god Ares was to take place. He was dressed in the spotless white linen of a high priest, the only concession to his political standing being the broad purple border embroidered to the hem and sleeves of his robe. The men broke out in a lusty, enthusiastic cheer that swept over the plain and reverberated off the hard stone walls of the city, causing the heads of Persian guards and spectators to pop up over the edge of the ramparts to view the commotion, and drowning out the women's eerie keening and wailing that wafted over the walls, and which had been a constant background din ever since the end of the battle the evening before. Ctesiphon, I wagered, had never before experienced the death of so many of her native sons all at one time, and the city was in a paroxysm of mourning and fear for what was to come.

As the men's cheering died, Julian gave a nod to Maximus, who stood waiting with the Etruscan haruspices on the ground just before the steps to the platform, and one by one they solemnly filed up, their flowing robes and conical hoods lending a funereal pallor to the clear brightness of the early morning rays. Each was accompanied by a herd boy leading by the halter a pure-white ox, ten in all, carefully chosen for the sacrifice from King Sapor's massive herds of cattle that had been grazing in the green pasturelands between the rivers. From these herds, our army had taken sufficient head for our immediate needs and scattered the rest. And on this day, as the ten bulls were led carefully up to the platform, a most extraordinary thing happened.

The first bull balked at climbing the four steps, not an unusual occurrence, for cattle are unaccustomed to such structures. This one did not do so out of stubbornness, however, but out of sheer lassitude—it was physically exhausted. As it began slowly walking up, it collapsed on one foreleg, and it was only with great difficulty that the herd boy and two of the Etruscans were able to force it back to its feet, jerking at its halter and whipping it from behind, until it made its shaking but docile way to the edge of the altar.

Had it been overdrugged? Poisoned? I wondered. It is well-known that such large beasts, who spend most of their time grazing in the wild, must often be fed drugged fodder to sedate them sufficiently to stand quietly at the altar until they can be clubbed and their throats cut—still, the seers were generally more skillful with their dosages. Perhaps Persian cattle were less tolerant of the poppy extract than were our hardy Cappadocian animals? In any event, the poor beast made its trembling way to the edge of the altar and promptly collapsed. Julian stood agog, and the entire camp went silent at this spectacle.

Nor did it end there. All the rest of the oxen did precisely the same thing, stumbling and collapsing in various postures on the platform, draped over the steps, on the ground at the base, where they stood waiting to climb the riser. Their tongues lolled lazily out of their mouths and their flanks heaved as if from a great exertion, while their great moist eyes simply stared straight ahead, dumbly, unlike the fearful rolling one would expect to see in an animal being led before sixty thousand men. All the beasts, that is, but the tenth, which, after being urged to step over its prostrate and flagging comrades, suddenly perked and rebelled, emitting a bellow and kicking its rear legs into the air like a newly captured colt brought in to be broken. It shook its great head in terror and flung a spray of foamy spittle and mucus over the nearest soldiers, who recoiled in fear of being trampled. A dozen burly guards leaped onto the maddened animal, wrestled it to the ground, and held it immobile as the poor beast continued to bellow frantically, calling perhaps for its companions under Helios to come to its rescue, but the only response was from Julian himself.

The Emperor, his face red with fury and the veins in his neck standing out in his tension, vaulted off the stage, ignoring the sickened and prostrate animals surrounding him, and without a word strode directly to the trembling, struggling bull lying on the ground. A priest brought the iron hammer crashing down onto its forehead to stun it, and with a swift knife stroke to the throat, the animal was dispatched and fell silent. Julian, without even waiting for the assistance of Maximus, as was his custom, bent down, sliced open the lower belly, and thrust his hands blindly into the steaming stew in search of the critical organ.

What he found left him stunned, and the Gallic guards around him sucking in their breath. The liver was cancerous, riddled with dry spots and scar tissue, swollen to twice its normal size. The crowd of soldiers surged forward for a better look, until driven back by the swatting swords of the bodyguards. In the end Julian rushed back onto the platform to hand the organ to Maximus, who, after a quick examination of it, turned his back to the troops and left the stage without a word. Julian turned back to the men and raised his hand still bearing the bloody knife, to call their attention.

"By the king of gods, Zeus!" he cried, his voice unnaturally high-pitched and shaking, and the troops fell silent. "By the holy god Mithras and by all the inhabitants of Olympus, I swear: never, by the gods, *never* shall I make sacrifice to Ares again! For a more fickle and treacherous god than he has never before cursed the race of man!"

The men stood silent a long moment, frozen in their shock at his cursing of the god of war. Julian leaped off the platform, his gaze avoiding the panting and twitching bulls littering the ground around him, and swept past his court to his tent without a word. Shaking their heads ruefully, the men slowly scattered to their quarters while I stood gazing at the ruins of the ceremony. It was not the first pagan sacrifice I had ever witnessed, but it was undoubtedly the foulest ever undertaken, and I confess the question crossed my mind as to whether the cursed results had been due to my presence.

Julian kept his oath, to the letter.

VI

"Burn the fleet." Maximus' head shot up, his red-rimmed eyes wide in a kind of malignant amazement. Even staid Sallustius recoiled.

"Sire?" he inquired after a moment, setting to one side the maps he had been examining in Julian's tent.

"You heard me. Burn it. Every vessel. We'd have to occupy half the army dragging the damn ships up the Tigris, and they would be a temptation for us to flee. Burn the fleet, or it will prevent us from meeting Sapor with all our strength and wits."

Already the decision had been made not to lay siege to Ctesiphon. The city was simply too strong, its surviving garrison too numerous, its supplies, according to information we had received from defectors, too copious. Moreover, our position at the foot of the walls was untenable, if only for a hazard we had not counted on: the enormous clouds of biting flies and mosquitoes that swarmed in from the nearby river and canals, in such quantities that they dimmed the sun by day and obscured the stars by night, driving the men and animals to near madness. Thus God's tiniest creatures summon the attention of His largest. Sapor's prime minister within the city had sent Julian a cautious embassy, offering to cede back to him all the Roman cities the Persians had taken in the last decade, but this proposal was scornfully rejected.

"Returning that which is already rightfully ours is no concession!" Julian stormed, flinging the calligraphed document back in the face of the startled ambassador. "Let the cowardly Persians emerge from their walls and fight on the plains like men!"

But this the Ctesiphon garrison would not do. They shouted taunts and fired arrows at us desultorily, challenging the Emperor to demonstrate his bravery by seeking out the Great King himself and engaging his army rather than a besieged city garrison. Julian took the insult to heart. But to attack King Sapor without being pincered by the garrison on the other side would require leaving Ctesiphon and marching north along the Tigris—upstream. It would be impossible to bring the enormous fleet.

"Burn it," he repeated stubbornly.

"Augustus," Sallustius interjected cautiously, as if addressing an overexcited child, "at least keep it here where it is, as a . . . as a . . ." he faltered uncharacteristically for a moment as Julian glared at him stonily ". . . as a fallback. Post a guard on it to defend against attacks by the Ctesiphon garrison. If worse comes to worst, our men can burn it then, to prevent it from being captured. Otherwise, if Sapor forces us to . . . retreat, we would still be able to sail down the Tigris to the Gulf and make our way safely from there to Egypt."

These were more words than Sallustius was accustomed to speak at any one time—clearly the issue was important to him. Julian would have none of it, however.

"Retreat is not an option, Sallustius," he snapped, "and I will suspect your loyalty, as I already do your wisdom, if you raise the issue again. Nor do we return the way we came. We have already laid waste to that country and there would be no provisions for us. Tomorrow we march up the Tigris to meet with Procopius, and Sapor, sooner or later, will meet us and fall. Burn the fleet."

As he looked around the tent, all his old comrades, Oribasius, Sallustius, myself, all of us who had served him so faithfully in Gaul, whose advice he had solicited and followed in the past, all fell silent. Even Maximus remained motionless, refraining from his customary whispering in Julian's ear.

Julian surveyed our sullen faces with what seemed a look of satisfaction.

"Is that clear?"

As we left, Sallustius pulled me aside. It was the first time, I believe, he had ever sought me out directly.

"Physician," he said gruffly, as if embarrassed, though staring at me intently, "you have served him for years. Has he gone mad?"

"Yes," I said, without hesitation. "Years ago, when he first made sacrifice to Mithras."

Sallustius snorted. "Then we are all of us mad, are we not? Except you. Are you the one voice of sanity in the Emperor's circle?"

"Perhaps. I cannot speak for the rest of you."

At this, Sallustius' face became uncharacteristically tense.

"If he is mad, why did you follow him to this hellhole, rather than staying in your precious Nazianzus?"

I paused, slightly stunned at this one time I had ever seen Sallustius drop his perpetual mask of calm and self-composure. Sallustius apparently thought I had not heard, for his face contorted even more. "I said, physician, if he is mad—"

I snapped out of my reverie and interrupted him.

"You are asking the wrong person, General," I said. "I go where healing is required. It is *because* he is mad that I followed him to this hellhole. You would do better to ask that question of yourself."

The next morning the greasy, black smoke from the sacrifice was uncustomarily thick. For twenty miles around the city, every field, every mill, every orchard, house, and vineyard had been torched. The pall mingled dolorously over the river with the thin wisps still wafting up from the smoldering remains of a thousand ships—the largest destruction of a Roman fleet since Actium four centuries before. Within an hour we had broken camp.

The inhabitants of Ctesiphon lined the city ramparts to watch our departure, shaking their heads in relief and wonder.

For a week we marched north, our goal the Roman province of Corduene, some three hundred miles distant. We lived only on the provisions we carried with us, for all about us, for miles on every side, the country had been laid to waste, first by our own troops in the vicinity of Ctesiphon, and thereafter by the Persians themselves. A large body from the Ctesiphon garrison followed us at a respectful distance. Not large enough, Brother, to engage us in pitched battle, for the Persians had found that their forces were no match for us in direct combat. Nevertheless, they continually harassed and raided our flanks, making off with precious supply wagons, diverting troops that could otherwise have been used to assist with the provisions, and burning the country far ahead of us, leaving us to march in ashes. At one point we were unable even to move for two days, surrounded by flaming grasses and choking smoke on all sides.

Finally, Julian could take no more of the men's muttering and fears, for even the Gallic veterans were beginning to openly express their doubts as to our prospects. He resorted to an old tactic of the Spartan king Agesilaus, and calling a hurried assembly, he stood before them with Arintheus, a burly Thracian commander. Exhausted in both body and mind, Julian could scarcely bring himself to talk, much less compose a rousing speech of the kind he had habitually used in the past to encourage his men.

"Tribunes, centurions, and soldiers of the Roman army!" he shouted hoarsely. His voice barely carried beyond the front rows. "Word has come to my ears of the fright you are taking from the enemy's harassment. Their armor, you say, is impenetrable. Their archers are unerring. Their cavalry too fleet of foot for our heavy Roman ponies to catch."

He paused, and disgruntled muttering was heard from all around.

"Look you!" he shouted. "Look here at your fears!" And as Arintheus nodded, three Persian prisoners were brought forward, clad in the magnificent, gleaming mail of the King's infantry, the articulations of the joints so skillfully worked as to conform precisely to the wearers' muscles and limbs, and with representations of human faces so closely fitted to their heads that the men seemed to be clothed in metal scales. The only openings where a weapon could possibly lodge were small holes for the nostrils and eyes. The overall effect was terrifying. The impact was muted, however, for the hands of the three soldiers were tied behind their backs and they shuffled and cowered shamefully, as if afraid of being beaten by their captors. Indeed, they undoubtedly already had been, for as they stood before us one of them was dribbling blood into the ashes at his feet.

The men were silent as they gazed at the three prisoners. Arintheus nodded again, and three heavily muscled guards stepped forward, one to each prisoner, and rudely began stripping them, tearing their helmets off with a roughness that bruised the Persians' faces, hastily cutting through the straps and clasps in the back that cinched the armor. The men were pushed before us, naked but for their loincloths, and were made to stand thus before the Roman army, a thing supremely shameful to the modest Persians. At the prisoners' clear signs of embarrassment, their hands clenching uncertainly in front of their groins, some of the Roman troops began laughing uncomfortably.

"See here your fears!" Julian shouted, his eyes bulging and his face flushing in rage as he stared at the bewildered prisoners. Truly it is a condition peculiar to man alone to hate his own victims. "See here the flower of the Persian army! Filthy little wretches who throw down their arms and flee like she-goats whenever battle is joined."

Indeed the scene was ludicrous, for as they stood next to the huge, tanned Thracians Julian had handpicked for the demonstration, the Persians looked like wretched beggars, their chests and limbs scrawny, their emaciated bodies white. They shrank away from the enormous legionaries, who glared at them in contempt.

This time he himself nodded, and each Thracian quickly put his arm around the neck of his assigned prisoner and without further instruction cracked it to the side. The three captives crumpled to the floor without a word, their dead eyes staring upward in surprise. The Roman army fell silent.

"Thus the fate of King Sapor when he dares to confront our forces!" Julian screamed, his voice rising to an almost hysterical pitch. He was rewarded with scattered, desultory cheers, and he stalked away, back to his quarters, muttering angrily to himself and gesturing broadly.

The men shuffled off to their duties, and I ducked into my tent in shame at this appalling demonstration. Julian was cracking. For years I had suspected it, for months I had been convinced, but now even the troops could have no doubt in their minds. I pored through my medical texts in increasing despair at finding any remedy that would stabilize his looming paranoia, his overweening desire for glory even at the expense of his very survival. It was a disease that, I feared, was not organic, it was not of the body, for if it had been, it would have long been cured by the geniuses of medicine in recent centuries. No, it was one of mind, and not just of any mind, but the mind of the powerful and ambitious. Indeed, with few exceptions, it had afflicted to a greater or lesser extent every Roman emperor since time immemorial. And even philosophy was not an antidote for him—if it ever truly had been.

Soon after departing the next morning we spied on the horizon an enormous cloud of smoke or swirling dust, a dark mass rising suddenly above the plain, far beyond the distance our scouts dared to range. Rumor spread at first that it was a huge herd of onagers, the wild asses that abound in these regions, traveling in a dense pack to protect themselves against attack from the equally numerous lions. This thought then gave way to the rumor that it was the

army of Procopius, arriving with the Armenian hordes of
King Arsaces to give us sufficient strength to resume our
attack on Ctesiphon and to capture the city once and for
all. The fear then surfaced that it was the mighty forces of
King Sapor, finally returning from his misguided attempt
to intercept us in the north. Julian listened to all these reports impassively, eyeing the cloud like every other man as
it rose brown and soiled-looking into the sky, but he, too,
was unable to divine what it might mean.

To avoid making a fatal mistake in an uncertain situation, he ordered the trumpets sounded and the men to make
camp where they were, on the banks of a small stream,
though it was scarcely past the noon hour. He ordered it to
be fortified by a palisade of shields stacked in serried se-
quence and braced in the earth like a wall. The dust from
the enormous cloud moved toward us, blowing far ahead
of the vast numbers of moving bodies that were at its
source, and it soon enveloped us, blocking out the meager
light of the setting sun and reflecting an odd, glowing red
on the men's faces and skin. We went to bed that night in
considerable alarm, still unable to make out what was approaching in the silent cloud to the north.

We woke at dawn to find ourselves surrounded by a Persian
army. They were silent, mysteriously subdued. They did
not attack, nor bluster, nor even send envoys—they merely
observed us from a safe distance. We struck camp and continued our march north, the barbarians parting before us
from afar as we moved, accompanying us cautiously from
the sides and behind. We soon found that their passivity
was due not to fear, but rather to the fact that they were
waiting—for this was merely the van of the King's army.
Another huge body arrived the next day, an enormous troop
of a hundred thousand infantrymen, archers, and elephants
commanded by the King's senior general, Meranes, and
assisted by two of the King's sons. Nor was this all. Heaven
help us, a third detachment, of equal size to that of Mera-

nes, yet advancing somewhat more slowly because of its heavy equipment and additional elephants, arrived soon afterwards. The third army was commanded by King Sapor himself.

Still the Persians refused to join battle with us, and wisely so, for time was on their side. The full force of the summer was now dead upon us and the heavy-set veterans of Gaul and Germany were wilting under the suffocating layers of dust and the incessant heat. Their heads and bodies baked if they wore armor, yet they were wary of removing it, for the constant flank attacks and alarms by the Persian archers and cavalry forced them to be constantly vigilant. The men's faces and necks, especially those of the palest races, were reddened and blistered from the constant beating of the sun, and raw from the bites of the blackflies that hovered everywhere. Stinging insects landed and lingered on any place where moisture was to be had: a sweaty armpit, a corner of a mouth, a draining sun blister on a neck or shoulder. The men were in constant torment, and still the Persians harassed us only from a distance, burning every living plant around us, forcing us to march through miles of smoking desert waste which only hours before had been grassy plains and fields of ripening grain.

At a dry, desolate valley known in the local dialect as Maranga, the king finally showed himself, commanding a cavalry charge against our troops in an action almost worthy of being termed a battle, though still nothing on the scale we were desperate to provoke. Nevertheless, the clash was marked by a considerable loss of Persian satraps and cavalry, and not a few infantrymen on our side as well. The conditions were most favorable to the training and skills of the Persian cavalry, able as they were to dart their javelins and shoot arrows at full speed from any direction on their swift horses, and then flee in a cloud of dust before any Roman defenses could be brought to bear.

On the evening of this action, the twenty-fifth of June, with Julian still unsure as to which side had taken the greater losses, a truce of three days was arranged for the two sides to clean the field and tend to the wounded. Our men worked in the darkness by torchlight to collect the Roman dead, for it was Julian's intent to take advantage of the truce to depart the next morning and put space between us and the King, or to at least find favorable ground on which to draw up lines and provoke a full-scale battle. Our strategizing session that night extended so late, and Julian's advisers were so weary, that most of us simply dozed off fitfully where we were, on benches and the floor in Julian's crowded and paper-strewn field tent.

And thus we come full circle in my narrative, Brother, for this was the night of which I have already written, the darkest night of my life, when I dreamed that the strange woman of unearthly beauty had entered the tent and silently approached Julian, bearing the mysterious burden in her arms.

After I awoke in alarm from the vision, Julian ordered us all to return to our own quarters. I trailed out the tent behind Sallustius and Maximus, while Julian attempted to laugh off my bewilderment, which was apparently still evident by the paleness of my face.

"A dream!" he pronounced. "Our physician has had a dream! Perhaps it is the gods finally coming to communicate with him after all!"

I winced. When we emerged from the tent, however, an enormous meteor streaked across the sky from the house of Ares, just as it had in the mountains of Thrace, trailing flame in its wake until it vanished into the dark horizon as suddenly as it had appeared, startling Julian into silence. Without his saying so, I knew he was thinking it a response from the gods to his oath at Ctesiphon, when he swore he would not sacrifice again to the god of war. I could see from the perspiration suddenly standing out on his brow that he regretted those hasty words.

"Maximus and the haruspices will say that we must abstain from action until a more favorable sign is revealed to us," he said, as if unaware as to where my own sympathies lay in this wizards' game.

"If you believe in omens, Julian, there is no reason to think that a comet is not a favorable sign for you," I said.

He paused long, still staring into the dark sky.

"Caesarius, I have lost my confidence. My dream appeared to me again tonight, the Genius of Rome."

"I know, Julian."

He looked at me, surprised. "But it was different from before. She held out the cornucopia to me, but this time it was—empty."

"It was only a dream," I said cautiously.

He considered this for a moment. "The ancients say there are two gates of Sleep: the first is of common horn, through which all spirits easily pass. The second is of flawless, gleaming ivory, pure white—yet through this gate false dreams are sent by wicked shades, to torment us in the upper world. Through which gate did my dream come to me?"

I waited for him to say more, but he fell silent, and when I turned to look at him he appeared exhausted and small, his shoulders slumped, his face discouraged.

"Tomorrow," I said firmly, "you will do what you must to protect the safety of the army." He sighed wearily, and looked at me in resignation.

"Caesarius, pardon me for mocking you in the tent a few minutes ago," he said after a moment. "You know I consider no man braver than you, either on or off the battlefield. Stay close beside me tomorrow."

May the Lord forgive me for obeying his order. To Julian's great loss, I stayed with him to the end.

VII

The next day witnessed Sapor's treacherous elephant attack, which I have already recounted for you, Brother. As the furious Gauls clambered over the dead and dying animals and raced after the Persians in retaliation, I bent to my task, feverishly extracting the long iron spear tip from where it had embedded itself in Julian's rib, breaking the bone in the process. Hesitating, I held the point of the weapon up before my face, viewing its symmetrical, deadly outline against the pale sky. For a long moment I stared at the tip, at its beautifully cast smoothness and blackness, the carefully balanced barbs, the razor sharpness of its point and edge undulled by its recent impact with hard bone, its effectiveness unimpeded, its deadly potential yet unfulfilled.

Christ on the desert mountaintop was offered the opportunity to change the entire course of history by committing one small, degrading act. The motive for such an act was unworthy and carnal, and He Himself was divine, and He refused. By contrast, my own motive was divine, but it was I who was carnal. I accepted the trade, though at the time no such complicated considerations, such weighing and balancing, passed through my head. Looking down at the unconscious Julian, I saw that he bore the same drawn, anguished expression as he had when I had first found him dreaming of devils and Christians in his tent, and I simply obeyed the Spirit that impelled me to do what had first come to my mind that night. I bent back down, and I fulfilled the bloody potential that had been hammered and filed into that carefully cast spear tip by an anonymous blacksmith who would never know the feat his work had accomplished.

As I stood up, I summoned the squad of horse guards to rush Julian to the cluster of hospital tents that had been set up by the quartermaster. No one had suspected that the fallen would include the Emperor himself. After they left, I groped around in the weeds and ashes of the battlefield, picking up the medical bags and instruments I had dropped when treating him, and then climbed stiffly onto my own horse and galloped behind.

When I arrived a few moments later, filthy and caked with dirt-streaked sweat from the day's riding and fighting. I found that he had already been lifted from the horse and carried inside the tent. Outside, the guards exclaimed loudly in rapid, Gallic-inflected camp Latin that I could barely understand. I shooed away the clamoring knot of men that was beginning to form around the tent door, stooped, and entered. Julian had been laid in a clean camp cot and was being gingerly undressed and washed.

Oribasius looked up briefly as I approached. "Thank the gods you were with him when he fell, Caesarius," he said. "Wash quickly, and come assist me. The spear point has penetrated his liver."

"I was afraid of that," I muttered, and stepped away to find a skin of water.

"Were you indeed?" asked a cold voice.

I stopped and turned back. I had not noticed him when I entered, but now he moved forward out of the shadows and advanced to Julian's side, though his eyes did not leave mine.

"Good day, Maximus," I said evenly. "I hadn't seen you here."

He ignored my greeting, and spoke to me in his high-pitched, condescending voice.

"The guards who brought him in said the javelin had

been stopped by his ribs. Yet here we find it in his liver."

I scoffed. "The guards know nothing of medicine."

"Ah, but you do. And yet you did not attempt to pull it out?"

I paused. Maximus had still not looked down at Julian, though he was standing next to him. Oribasius was bent over the wound, holding a poultice of dittany, but had stopped his probing, listening to the conversation.

"When I saw that the point had penetrated past the barbs, I felt it would be better to bring him into camp to remove it," I said cautiously.

"I see," Maximus replied, and looked down thoughtfully, glancing at Julian's wound for the first time. Only the thin iron shank emerged from his side; the spearhead was completely buried in the flesh, which prevented one from even seeing whether or not it had barbs. I realized my mistake in stating that it did. "I'm not familiar with this type of spear," Maximus continued slowly, "but apparently you are. It's remarkable that you already knew that this spearhead, so deeply embedded in his liver, was barbed rather than smooth-cast."

I held his gaze steadily and forced myself to remain calm, to speak simply. "It's a standard-issue infantry javelin, used by both sides. I've seen many such injuries among the men during the march."

A flicker of disappointment passed across Maximus' face. Still, he was undeterred from his sly questioning. "And these cuts on his hands—the guard said he had grasped the point so tightly that it sliced his fingers. Yet despite his Herculean efforts, he was unable to extract it, even though it is merely embedded in the soft tissue."

No matter what Maximus says, even when he is silent, my jaw clenches in anger and the sweat begins trickling down my sides.

"The Emperor must have cut his hands on his own blade when he fell off his horse," I answered, "and was too weak from the fall to pull out this shaft himself. As you can see, he is still unconscious."

Maximus glared, his eyes smoldering, and I stalked out of the tent.

That night Julian distributed his worldly possessions among his friends, pointedly refused to assign a successor to command, and in his last moments sought to engage Maximus and grief-stricken Oribasius in a discussion on the nature of the soul, to pass the time and distract his mind. He talked a great deal, and much rumor has been spread about the wisdom and depth of his dying speech, his alleged acknowledgment of the victory of Christ, his reflections on the curious nature of death and the calmness with which Socrates and Seneca and other heroes of philosophy accepted their own fates. All of those speculations are false, for in truth the man was raving and incoherent, as would be anyone pierced in the liver and surrounded by a hostile army.

Just before dawn, with a tremor and a groan of pain, Julian died. Oribasius was in attendance, Sallustius and Maximus watching silently at the foot of the bed, the deaf-mute boy sitting wide-eyed and silent in the corner. I sat vigil at his side, staring at his drawn face, tormented at both his suffering and the sheer enormity of the act I had committed, until the very moment he was finally taken. It was only a little over three months since the army had departed Antioch on its conquering march.

The five of us gazed at the body in silence. It was a moment of calm before word of his death spread throughout the camp, generating fear and lamentation among the men. Maximus bent his scaly face down to Julian's, his long, wiry beard brushing the motionless chest, his eyes peering deep into the unblinking, stony depths of the dead man's orbs, glassy as beads. We all held our breath, watching, and then with a sigh, Maximus slowly leaned back again.

"His soul has gone to the Underworld," he pronounced, turning away and beginning to leave the tent. "It is gone."

There was silence, and Oribasius looked curiously at me. I hesitated, then said a prayer over the body, commended him to God, and made the sign of the cross. Maximus stood in the door of the tent watching, his lip curling contemptuously. I finished my prayer and shouldered wearily past him to return to my own quarters, but he departed the tent behind me, quickened his step, and sidled up to me.

"I said, his soul is *gone,*" he muttered to me.

I stopped and looked at him, surprised that he would even bother to address me. "I believe," I said, "that if he repented before he died, he will rise again. His soul will be in Paradise. For this I prayed."

Maximus shook his head scornfully as we walked together in the pale gray light of early morning. "Everything has its opposite, physician, as day has night, as heat has cold. The opposite of life is death, the opposite of existence is nothingness. If he is no longer living, he is dead. His soul will be born again, in another time, in another entity—but Julian himself is dead."

I stared past him and picked up my pace. Maximus, however, would not be ignored. His short legs churned as he matched my speed, two steps for each one of mine, as if unaccountably hungry for my company. Again he spoke, an insistent and compelling tone to his voice.

"So too has every man his opposite," he continued. "As Caesar had Brutus, as Jesus Christ has Lucifer." I shuddered to hear Our Lord's name spoken by these blasphemous lips, but nevertheless I hesitated, intrigued by the little man's words, at his vision of the world as so black and white, every object with its opposite, every man his Manichean double.

"As Julian had, perhaps, Constantius?" I ventured cautiously, though still attempting to draw away.

"Perhaps."

I paused, and he still continued to peer at me, an inscrutable expression on his face.

"And who would my opposite be?" I asked.

Maximus grinned, exposing the rotten stumps of his teeth. "You are a healer, physician," he said simply. He glanced over at the camp altar, to which even now one of the Etruscans was leading an ox in preparation for Maximus' imminent morning sacrifice. "That would make your opposite—me."

He chuckled as he drew his long blade, turned, and walked over to the sleepy-eyed animal. All was uncommonly silent in the exhausted camp, except for the moaning of the wounded and the faint sound of high-pitched singing nearby, which I did not at first acknowledge as being as peculiar as it truly was. I stood for a long while, lost in thought, staring at the strange little man, the antihealer, my self-proclaimed converse, my negation, my antidote.

And I knew, in this, that Maximus was wrong.

I turned and began walking slowly toward my own quarters, yet the odd singing slowly broke in on my thoughts, and I realized that it seemed to be following me. At this revelation I stopped and stood motionless, listening carefully to the tuneless crooning, and then with dawning astonishment I turned around. Standing in the middle of the dirt track between the rows of tents, staring at me yet not daring to approach, was the deaf Persian boy, who had also followed me out of Julian's tent when I left. The nearly unintelligible lyrics of the ancient Christian hymn he intoned were, I believe, the first words that had ever passed his lips, but the repetitive chanting of the simple phrase will forever be burned into my brain.

> *Father in Heaven . . .*
> *Alleluia . . .*
> *Father in Heaven . . .*
> *Alleluia . . .*

Tears glistened as they coursed in tracks down his dirt-caked cheeks. His little song was so humble—a croak, a slur, a mere four words chanted in a tune that could barely be discerned, an earthy paean that was simplicity itself— yet to my ears it was as triumphant and as heartfelt as the grandest chorus in the Great Church of Constantinople. He stood barefoot and ragged in the dust and looked at me, and his face shone radiant in a broad smile.

Simple words. A wise man once told me that one cannot possibly express more joy in Creation, more optimism in the perfection of the Kingdom to come, than through simple words.

And the sun rose on another day.

AUTHOR'S POSTSCRIPT

The Emperor Julian died at Maranga from a spear thrown by an unknown hand in the year 363. Upon his death, the Empire was offered to Sallustius, who refused it on the grounds of old age. The crown passed instead to Jovian, one of Julian's generals, who was forced to surrender enormous tracts of Roman territory to the Persians and escaped out of the desert only with great loss of life among his men. He died six months later from the poisonous smoke of a charcoal brazier in his room. Like Julian, he was buried at Tarsus, the home of Paul the Apostle.

Maximus fell out of favor with the Emperor Valens and after various changes of fortune was beheaded in Ephesus in the year 371 on charges of conspiracy.

Saint Gregory of Nazianzus, Caesarius' brother, was appointed Bishop of Constantinople and became known as one of the greatest of the early Church Fathers.

Caesarius was appointed provincial treasurer of Bithynia by the Emperor Valentinian, and miraculously survived a terrible earthquake that devastated Nicaea. This experience led him to return home to Nazianzus to live a life of prayer and solitude, but in the year 369, at age thirty-eight, he suddenly died in mysterious circumstances. He was later canonized, for reasons now lost to the mists of history. Saint Caesarius' feast day is celebrated February twenty-fifth.

Ut digni efficiamur . . .

ACKNOWLEDGMENTS

Julian's life is one of the most fully documented of all the Roman emperors, a fact that is both benefit and bane to the historical novelist. Julian himself was a prolific, indeed even an obsessive writer, and his extant works fill three complete volumes of the Loeb Classical series. From them one can glean quite an interesting impression of his personality, his intellectual concerns, his fears and religious beliefs, and even his daily life. Wherever possible, I made a point of including his own words in the dialogue of this novel.

Of equal value from a military-historical perspective is the history of the later Roman Empire written by Ammianus Marcellinus, a soldier who accompanied Julian and his predecessors on many of their campaigns. Ammianus offers a fascinating "man-in-the-trenches" view of these events, one that is often so vivid and heartstopping as to be impossible to improve upon in mere fiction. His works cover many years before and after the events chronicled in this book, and make fascinating reading for anyone interested in pursuing the subject further.

Many of Saint Gregory of Nazianzus' epistles survive as well, yielding a documentary picture of the Christian opposition to Julian during his later years, though Gregory's objectivity is somewhat marred by his unmitigated hatred for the Emperor. His seventh Oration also provides us what little information we have on the life and career of his brother Caesarius, the imperial physician to both Constantius and Julian.

Reliable secondary sources include both the classics, such as Gibbon's indispensable *Decline and Fall,* and lesser known but equally valuable works, such as the wonderful biographies of Julian by Giuseppe Ricciotti, Gary Warren Bowerstock, and Polymnia Athanassiadi; general histories such as Carcopino's *Daily Life in Ancient Rome*; specialized works such as *Pagans and Christians* by Robin Lane Fox and *The Elephant in the Greek and Roman World* by H. H. Scullard; and ancient technical manuals such as Xenophon's *On Horsemanship,* and the *Epitoma Rei Militaris* of Vegetius. Extrapolations of ancient lifestyles and ways of thought were also gleaned from works that were almost, but not quite contemporary with Julian: *The Secret History* of Procopius, the *Meditations* of Marcus Aurelius, and the *Confessions* of Saint Augustine are perhaps the best known among many that fall into this category, and on which I relied.

Those interested in classical literature will find many references in this book if they read closely, particularly to Virgil's *Aeneid.* And like any writer dealing with classical times, my well-thumbed editions of Homer were never far from my side.

I will be the first to admit that I could not have accomplished a work such as this alone, and though space limitations prevent me from acknowledging everyone who assisted me, I would surely be remiss in failing to mention some of the most important. Most obvious, of course, is my editor, Pete Wolverton. His generous commentary and frank opinions were always appreciated and carefully applied, and they improved the book immeasurably. My friend and Latin instructor, M. D. Usher, provided valuable technical and historical advice, for which I am grateful. Richard Ruud, Commissioner for Clallam County (Washington) Fire Protection District No. 2, taught me everything I needed to know about organic combustion. And my agents, Bob Solinger and Mir Bahmanyar, were always present to give me a prod or a lesson in reality when I most needed one.

The greatest appreciation of all, of course, is owed to my family, for their never-ending patience and support in the face of the pressures and difficulties that go with a writer's work. Thank you, Eamon, for the morning coffee and the invitations to play. Thank you, Isa, for the humming accompaniment and the great bedtime hugs. Thank you, Marie, for the dreams and anticipation. Most of all, thank you, Cris, for your encouragement and consolation, and for making everything complete. Life just doesn't get any better.

M. C. F.

The hawk circled silently and broodingly over the desert sands, so high he was a mere speck against the cloudless blue sky, peering down at the scene below.

The Persian army marched in stately procession, just as it had for a hundred leagues or more, raising a dust cloud that could be seen by Alexandria's garrison from a distance of two days' march. The fierce, leathery Arabs of the camel corps, robes billowing behind them, were followed in close order by the lumbering beasts of the elephant brigade, each bearing a platform carrying five armored lancers. Five thousand elite Parthian archers rode next, mounted on identical white stallions and bearing saddle quivers containing a hundred barbed reed missiles fashioned by the most skilled weapons makers of the Mesopotamian armories; they were succeeded by another five thousand Armenian horse troops, whose skills with the bow, less developed than those of the Parthians, were supplemented by heavier, ashwood shafts and poison-tipped barbs.

Fifty thousand regular infantry marched implacably behind in the dust and filth of the enormous bestiary. These men were resigned to the wretched road over which they traveled, inured to the suffocating heat and dust by seven years of campaigning, from the Persian Gulf to the Aegean Sea, from the frigid Caucasus to the Syrian desert. Fresh from a monumental victory at Pydna, the men were laden with plunder and cocksure in their strength. Their general was no mere tribal headman of roaming Bedouins, nor even a royal satrap of ancient noble family. Leading the massive invasion force was none other than Antiochus IV Epiphanes, King of Kings and Brother of the Planets, descendant of Darius the Great, heir to the vast Seleucid Empire and monarch of Lesser and Greater Armenia. Only forty-seven years of age, he was in the prime of life, ruler of a domain that extended to the distant birthplace of the rising sun and the frigid shadows of the Scythian north. And Antiochus was leading his men to the greatest prize of all, the opulent city of Alexandria, the seat of Egypt's boy-king Ptolemy, whose agents had for days been accosting the Great King on the march, pleading for mercy. Each soldier's share of the plunder from this one city alone would allow him to retire with incalculable wealth, households filled with slaves, and the silks and artworks of generations.

Antiochus encountered no opposing army as his forces entered the fertile Nile delta. Even at several hours' distance from his objective he could see that the entire population of the floodplain had retreated behind Alexandria's walls, its portals sealed tight, even the forward trenches and defensive works abandoned. *A pity to besiege it,* the King thought to himself. *With elephants and engines the gates will fall within hours. Siege merely increases the men's thirst for plunder, limits their restraint once the walls finally crumble. The boy Ptolemy deserves his fate, for employing such incompetent advisors.*

In the final miles before arriving at the city, the men's excitement grew visibly, and the army's lumbering pace picked up. Even the King felt the glow of anticipation at the thought of this additional jewel in his crown. Brushing off the chattering and importuning of his captains and advisors, who were already pressing him with plans for the coming siege, he galloped forward to be alone with his thoughts, to savor a few moments of calm. Peering far ahead, he spied three mounted figures just visible down the deserted road. Although they were too distant to be recognizable, Antiochus could still guess who they were, and he sighed in exasperation at the thought of being forced once again to listen to the disgraceful begging and fawning of Ptolemy's ambassadors. He glanced back at his corps of camel drivers, their eyes glittering fiercely behind the swaths of wrappings masking their faces. The restless Bedouins had been uncharacteristically patient on the long, uneventful march. He would give them a chance to stretch their legs.

Spurring his horse forward into a sprint, he loosed the shrill war cry of the Arabs. Instantly the lead camel drivers began furiously whipping their mounts, sending them into ungainly runs, all knobby knees and flailing heads, and then the entire corps followed suit. The furious sprint of the thousand beasts straining to catch the King's lead set up a deafening thunder as they approached the trio of figures. Smiling to himself, the King spurred his horse again and pounded even more furiously, the hot wind in his face raising water in his eyes, making it difficult to distinguish the three riders he was rapidly approaching. *Not to worry,* he thought. *After I catch them I shall permit the Arabs to chase them down with their lances. Let them play a round of that barbarous game with which they amuse themselves in camp—that foul sport with the headless carcass and the goalposts . . .*

Looking up, the King spied the hawk circling lazily overhead—an opportunistic creature, waiting for a sign of weakness or exposure among small life, for death to occur on which he might feed. The King smiled. *Best reserve your place in line at Alexandria, evil bird,* he thought. *The pickings there will be much more to your liking than a mere three skinny diplomats, even if there is anything left after the Arabs have their sport.* He pushed away thoughts of the hawk and focused on the trio ahead. Something was amiss—he was approaching them far too quickly. The King knew his horse was the fastest steed in the army, yet it would be impossible to catch up with mounted quarry this quickly. Still sprinting, he wiped his eyes with his sleeve and peered again at the men. Oddly, they were not fleeing. They stood as still as mileposts, facing him calmly. The lead man was not even armed and wore only a white ceremonial robe, although the two flanking him were handsomely equipped with newly polished bronze cavalry shields and bore beautifully cast breastplates and helmets, with lances butted into the leather holsters in the vertical rest position. One of the men had a pennant draped dispiritedly from the point of his lance. The king squinted at the dusty fabric of the banner as it hung limply in the oppressive air, and he swore under his breath. An eagle.

A Roman eagle.

The exasperated King skidded to a stop only steps from the motionless riders, and the camel corps behind him did the same, though not as smoothly. The evil-tempered beasts reared and bellowed, angry at being made to run in the first place, even angrier at being forced to stop. The King's horse skittered and danced, eyes rolling nervously at the snorting and spitting animals towering over its rear, and the King struggled to control his mount. The three smaller Roman ponies facing him stood as motionless as their riders, staring in seeming disdain at the undisciplined display before them.

With not a little trouble the King forced his horse to stand, and he glared for a moment at the trio of silent Romans, considering what to make of this incongruous welcome. Resolving to force the encounter, he held up his right hand in the universal gesture of welcome and boldly announced himself.

"Greetings, Romans!" he intoned in measured Greek, the common language of the civilized lands of the eastern Mediterranean. "Behold the conquering army of Antiochus IV Epiphanes, King of Kings and ruler of these lands. Welcome to all men of good intent. State your business."

For a long moment the lead Roman, the one in robes, remained staring in silence. He was tanned and somewhat tired-looking, or perhaps merely world-weary, just approaching the paunchiness of prosperous middle age, but with the steely gaze and erect bearing of a military man. He neglected even to remove his own hand from the reins—a grave insult to the King, who had offered his peace first. Without a word, the Roman slowly dismounted and strode imperiously forward to a spot precisely between his own pony and Antiochus' white charger, where he stopped, looked into the King's eyes, and pulled out a papyrus scroll he had been carrying under his arm.

The enormous army had by this time caught up to their position and rumbled to a puzzled halt, and the cloud of dust wafted stiflingly over the King and the three Romans. The Persian generals eyed the Romans contemptuously, and the camels continued to bray fiercely, spoiling to continue with the march to the city they could see and smell in the distance. Still the three Romans did not budge, and the King realized that in order to continue, he would have either to read the scroll or physically remove these men from his path. The sound of swords sliding from leather holsters behind him told him the opinion of his officers. Incredibly, the two Roman soldiers drew their own short cavalry swords from their holsters in response. *By the gods!* the King thought. *Do they intend to take on my whole army?* Still, a voice inside him warned him to be prudent.

The man identified himself. "Gains Popilius Laenas," he declared in brazen, monotone Latin, which, although the King spoke it well, he received as a second insult, as a failure to recognize his status by speaking to him in the common language of these parts. "My rank is senator of Rome. I bear a senatorial decree, which I request you read. Your response thereto will determine how I, and the Roman Senate, will reciprocate your greeting, and whether we are to consider you friend or foe." With that, he pursed his lips, held out the scroll, and fell silent.

A murmur of outrage could be heard behind the King. He glanced behind at his captains, affixing a confident smile on his face and lifting his chin, as if to tell them to humor him in this jest. They glared, but the King nodded amiably and they retreated several paces on their mounts. Then swinging his leg over his horse's haunches, he dropped athletically to the ground, strode to where Popilius stood waiting for him, and seized the scroll, feigning an amused expression. Upon reading it, however, he was unable to disguise his astonishment and outrage.

"How dare you present me with this, insolent jackals!" he sputtered, his face reddening. " 'Forgo the attack on Alexandria and depart Egypt?' By what right do you order this, by what authority—!"

"Your response, if you please, Majesty," Popilius interrupted him, his expression cold, his gray eyes burning into the King's. "Alexandria is under the protection of Rome. The Senate awaits your response."

Antiochus stared at his adversary for a moment and then burst out laughing. 'The Senate awaits my response? Your Senate is three weeks' sail across the Mediterranean! It sends a junior senator and two tribunes here to insult my army and demand my response? I haven't time for this nonsense, but I am not so ill-bred as to insult your illustrious Senate with the same rudeness as you have shown me. My counselors will draft something appropriate—"

But Popilius interrupted Antiochus by calmly turning his back, and the King's speech faded into astonished silence. The Senator strode to the lead tribune, seized the lance bearing the pennant, and returned, holding it vertically before him. The restless Arabs tensed and edged forward, but the King nodded them off. Popilius planted the butt-end of the lance in the dirt, the eagle fluttering lightly over his head, and then calmly, deliberately, paced one revolution around the King, tracing a circle in the dirt that enclosed the monarch. He then stepped back outside the circle, handed the lance back to the tribune, and crossed his arms.

"No," Popilius said simply. "Your counselors will do nothing of the sort. You yourself will give me your response before you step out of the ring."

Antiochus caught his breath. He stared at the determined Roman, then down at the line in the sand, and back up at the Roman. The entire army of beasts and men, sixty thousand strong, stood at his back. A defenseless city, bursting with wealth, stood within his very sight. The King was an intelligent man and know how to weigh his gains against his risks.

And he knew he had been beaten.

"I shall accede to the Senate's request," he said quietly.

With that, the Roman stepped into the ring and gravely shook the King's hand. He then turned and mounted his horse, and without a single look back, the three riders trotted calmly back to the city walls.

Antiochus returned with his enormous army to Syria and, to the end of his life, never overcame the disgrace of this display of cowardice. Indeed his shame and his resulting hatred for Rome were passed on, like a disease or a curse, to his own daughter Laodice, who herself swore she would never be put in a position to be so humiliated. And so she wasn't, though her methods of avoiding such compromise were ineffectual and controversial at best. In reality, it was left to her own eldest son, King Mithridates, to regain the family honor for the scandalous treatment received at Rome's hands. But that is a matter not to be discussed quickly, nor dismissed lightly.

All this detail, for an event that occurred over a century ago. How would I know such things? Because I have studied Polybius' history of Rome to understand my enemy; I have paced the deserted battlefields like a conscientious commander; I have analyzed Roman speeches and Roman foreign policy like a competent administrator. But more important: Because I am Pharnaces, son of King Mithridates the Great of Pontus, who was the grandson of that disgraced monarch Antiochus. Because my father was Rome's most fearsome enemy, scourge of its greatest generals and destroyer of countless legions, a dagger in Rome's side for forty years, a terror who was beaten in battle but never defeated in spirit.

And because like his grandfather, Mithridates was also driven by a desire to conquer and unify, to create a magnificent empire of all the Hellenistic lands; and like his mother, Laodice, Mithridates was cursed by a fatal fear and a hatred for Rome. It was a hatred that would confine him and encompass him, much like that circle drawn in the sand years before, a hatred that would shape his very destiny—and mine, as well.